Tales of the Barf Table

Book One: From the Gridiron to the Fire

Tales of the Barf Table

Book One:

From the Gridiron to the Fire

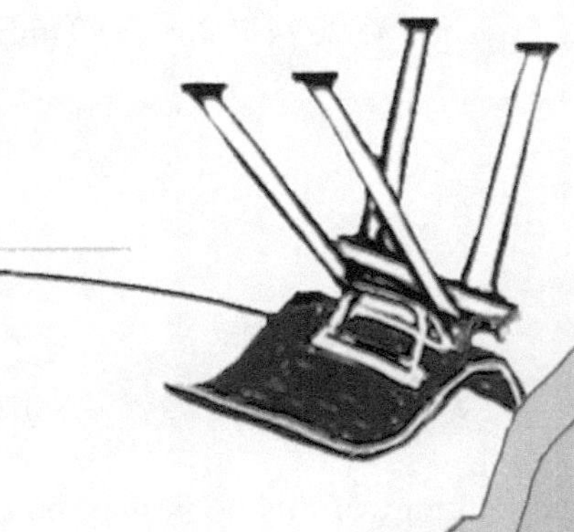

RAHN & TIMBERLEY ADAMS

Gaillardia Press

Written by Rahn and Timberley Adams

Illustrations by Timberley Adams

Published by Gaillardia Press

Copyright © 2024 Rahn and Timberley Adams

All characters in this book are fictitious. Any resemblance to actual persons, living or dead, is purely coincidental.

ISBN 979-8-9869431-1-4

First Edition, January 2024

"Confidence is contagious. So is lack of confidence."

— Vince Lombardi

CHAPTER 1 – All the More Raisins

"I'VE BEEN LOOKING FORWARD to this all summer," said the 10th grader with bleached-white streaks in his short, dark hair. "I'm gonna ask for *two* cups of raisins. I even brought a straw."

His companion in the lunch line—a tanned teenager with shaggy blond locks—laughed. "Knock yourself out, man," the boy said. "The newbs can use extra servings of fruit. Remember last year? I had raisins all in my hair, even in one ear. I should've worn my hoodie."

"That ratty old drug rug of yours?"

"Whatever," said the shaggy boy. "It keeps me warm on the beach."

The one with streaked hair held up a soda straw still in its white paper wrapper. "Snagged this baby at the surf shop yesterday—in your dad's grill. These are the best for shooting spitballs and raisins and stuff, you know. Let's try 'er out. Keep your eye on Fatso over there."

He tore the top of the wrapper and unsheathed the straw like a sword. Wadding the paper into a ball, he popped it into his mouth for a few seconds and pursed his lips around it. The long line that the two boys stood in crept forward toward a double stack of lunch trays at the door to the serving counter and kitchen.

From experience, the boy knew he could fire his spitball and duck into the food service area out of sight while his victim scanned the line for a shooter. The only real complication was getting off the shot past a nearby table of teachers without hitting one or being spotted with the straw at his mouth. But, as usual, the teachers weren't paying attention.

In slow motion—if this had been a touchdown pass or field goal kick on the Game of the Week—the spitball exploded from the barrel of the straw in a burst of moisture, and flew far and straight before hitting its broad target, the back of a heavyset boy sitting at a round table.

The big teenager sat across from a skinny girl, the two sitting alone at the table but not together. If he felt the shot, the boy didn't show it. He continued to talk to the girl.

* * *

To freshmen at Arbor High School, the only thing scarier than the first day of classes was their very first lunch period in the school cafeteria. Gender didn't matter, as the same fear struck the hearts of freshman boys and freshman girls alike at this small charter school in quiet Monk's Landing. No 9th grader at Arbor High, home of the Bruins, wanted negative attention from *any* upperclassmen, but they feared 10th graders the most.

The new sophomores had endured being picked on the previous school year and now looked for someone to pick on themselves. Hazing in one form or another was a burden that most brand-new Bruins bore, at least during their first weeks or maybe even months. Exactly how long and how hard individual freshmen were hazed depended on their reactions to the punishment they received.

Perhaps the most dreaded part of that first lunch period was getting stuck at the last table with open seats in the cafeteria—a small, isolated table down front near the tray-return window and garbage bins. That table almost always had open space because *no one* wanted to sit there so close to the mess and smelliness. This table was round with eight ordinary chairs that could be pushed aside or moved away, if necessary.

The rest of the cafeteria—divided into a higher and a lower level so that upper- and lowerclassmen could sit separately—had long, rectangular tables with attached stools. In each grade level, cliques of kids would send lunchtime scouts to *reserve* stretches of seats while their friends waited to fill their trays and pay the cashier in the single, long, service line. These scouts, or human placemats, rarely let anyone they didn't know or like sit in one of their grade-level gang's seats. The lowly freshmen were the worst at this, because they *really* didn't want to sit at that round table near the stinky trash cans—for good reason.

Another circular, free-standing table stood on the opposite side of the lunchroom for teachers to use. This faculty table was only steps from the end of the serving line and cashier's stand, presumably because teachers had less time at lunch than students did. Both of the round tables—the one for teachers and the one for students—were the only places in the lunchroom where wheelchair-bound students could easily sit and eat.

However, not even handicapped kids attempted to sit with the teachers during lunch. That just wasn't cool under any circumstances. Also, most handicapped upperclassmen found room at the far ends of their class's long tables, even if friends had to carry the wheelchairs up the steps and through tight spaces. It was better to park at the end of a rectangular table far from one's friends than to sit at the round student table next to hopeless geeks, nerds and loners.

So the round table down front near the garbage bins—the one for students—was the place to find Arbor High School's most unpopular or unfortunate 9th graders. Sitting at that table was a guarantee to be teased worse than any other freshmen at Arbor High, not just for the opening days and maybe weeks of school, but for as long as one sat there.

Some of the stunts that 9th graders sitting at that table had to endure were legendary, some even recorded for posterity in the school newspaper and yearbook. Some pranks were traditional, having been passed down from year to year, usually from sibling to sibling, since the small charter school wasn't old enough for their parents to have attended. But all the food-related misbehavior was messy, if not downright stomach-turning.

That's why this round table with eight ordinary chairs—this desert island in a sea of noisy teenagers, this dredge spoil of midday mischief, this dumping ground of high school dining—became known as the Barf Table, a legend in itself.

CHAPTER 2 – Welcome to the Barf Table

TWELFTH GRADER ARTIE BAUER was extraordinary in every way. At six-foot-four and 300 pounds, he was bigger and stronger than everyone else at Arbor High—except, of course, for Coach "Jug" Johnson, whose nickname alluded to the shape of his 350-pound body. Jug was a head shorter, though, than Artie, his star offensive lineman. Not only did Artie excel at football, he was the wrestling team's first-string heavyweight and had been the baseball team's starting catcher ever since his sophomore year.

That was when Jug—who coached football in the fall, wrestling in the winter, and baseball in the spring—saw Artie's potential behind the plate (other than with a knife and fork) and by season's end had given the pudgy farm boy the nickname "Yogi," after the legendary New York Yankees catcher Yogi Berra. Having rooted for the Yanks since childhood—and against the Red Sox—Jug never, ever would have called his best pitch-caller "Pudge," even though that was another popular nickname for catchers.

Artie didn't especially like being called Yogi, but it was better than what the previous year's 10th graders had called him while he sat all year long at the Barf Table with the other 9th-grade outcasts. The sophomores had called him Fatso, Porky, Lard Butt and worse names—that is, until Artie's growth spurt before his 10th-grade year added a full six inches to his height, and his farm work at home turned what had been flab into solid muscle.

But through it all, Artie "Yogi" Bauer decided that he liked sitting at the Barf Table, and he stayed there in his 10th-, 11th-, and now 12th-grade years, even though he could have sat anywhere else he wanted. Like his namesake, he had a way with words—without sounding like an oxymoron—and he shared his wisdom with the 9th graders who got stuck at the table.

On this last "first day" of his high school career, Artie headed toward the Barf Table with his lunch tray and saw that someone was already sitting there alone. This surprised him, because seniors were always served first, then juniors, then sophomores in the long lunch line. Freshmen, whose classrooms weren't released to the lunchroom until last, brought up the rear.

This person who had beaten Artie to the Barf Table appeared to be a slight, 9th-grade girl who had skipped the lunch line entirely. Reading a paperback book, she had no food in front of her, not even a bag lunch from home or chips and a soda from the snack machines in the lobby. Her dark hair was pulled back into a tight ponytail, and she stared at the cheap crime novel resting in her hands on the smooth green tabletop.

"Hi," said Artie, as he laid his tray on the table across from the girl. "My name's Artie Bauer. I'm a senior." He pulled out his chair, sat and scooted up to the table. When the girl didn't look up from her book, he added, "Uh, I always sit here. So, what's your name?"

When she still didn't respond, Artie wondered if maybe she was deaf and couldn't hear him speak. So he extended one large hand and tapped on the table to draw her attention. At that, she looked up and said simply, "What?" She spat out the word and glared at him.

"I'm sorry," Artie said. "I didn't mean to bother you. I just asked your name. You look familiar. Have we ever met before?"

She smirked, though he hadn't meant the line as a come-on. "Kind of," she said. "You came to my house once—with the football team."

"Really?" Then he stopped and slowly nodded. He remembered, and he understood who this girl was and why she wanted to be left alone. She looked different now—paler, thinner, older than the year gone by should have aged her.

"You're Leah, right? Reuben's sister? I'm sorry. I'll just sit here and be quiet. You won't be bothered—not until some other 9th graders join us. They're at the back of the line."

She frowned. "I don't plan to sit here that long. But thanks." She went back to her book and left Artie to start on his lunch.

* * *

By school rule, all upperclassmen had to stay in the cafeteria for at least thirty minutes during 3rd period—a true lunch *hour*. A bell would ring at twelve forty-five, which was the halfway mark. Most of the teachers who ate lunch in the cafeteria were long gone by then. With a written excuse to go visit a teacher or coach, underclassmen could leave at that early-release bell, too; otherwise, 9th and 10th graders had to stay in the lunchroom the entire sixty minutes. Fourth period, the last class period of the day, was when all freshmen took required physical education courses that often extended beyond the three o'clock bell into extracurricular activities after school for all four grade levels.

For the sporting crowd, there were either interscholastic teams in season or intramurals that mirrored the regular school squads. For the more cultured and less athletic kids, there were band, chorus, art and drama groups, among an assortment of specialized clubs and organizations. The chess and personal computer clubs were popular with nerds. The School Spirit Squad and Bible Searchers gave peppy and positive teens something to do. There were also special groups for kids who were interested in auto repair, carpentry, cooking and cosmetology. All Arbor High students had to do *something* to stay busy after school, whether they had talent or not. The Barf Table's misfits were no exception to that rule.

* * *

Bruins couldn't be slackers, even though Leah Russo appeared to be headed down that worrisome road. Artie wondered if she wanted to sneak off as soon as she could to smoke or do drugs. But he remembered, this *was* Wednesday, the day each week when the lunchroom ladies always put a small paper cup of raisins on every student's tray whether they wanted it or not. A dose of raisins would help clear up the kids' acne, the cafeteria manager claimed. Maybe Leah had heard from her older brother Reuben about lunchroom antics at Arbor High.

"I guess that's a good idea—not to hang around," said Artie to his quiet tablemate in between bites of meatloaf and mashed potatoes. "It *is* 'Waisin Wednesday,' you know."

Behind him in the 9th-grade section, a small commotion drew Artie's attention. He assumed the raisin-throwing had started early and didn't even turn around to look. "It gets old, but at least the principal banned straws on Wednesdays, you know?"

Leah nodded and raised the hood of the oversized Arbor Bruins sweat jacket she wore. This time she smiled just a bit. "Thanks, Artie," the thin girl said. "I almost forgot. Reuben told me about the 'Waisin Wednesday' thing."

Artie chuckled and took another bite of lunch. He had looked up to Leah's older brother, Reuben Russo, the Bruins' star quarterback in previous years. For two seasons, Artie had been a starting offensive lineman. It had been his job to protect Reuben on offense. At center, Artie had been even more important to Leah's brother, especially during Reuben's senior season when he had gotten so much attention from college scouts. The two teammates—one a senior, the other a junior—had practiced long and hard to start each play right and to direct the line's blocking well. Their dedication had paid off, as Reuben had received scholarship offers from top colleges. That was something Artie hoped to repeat for himself this year—the athletic success, that is, not what happened to Reuben before he could accept one of those scholarships.

Just then, a diminutive 9th grader, who was wearing old dungarees, a faded T-shirt, and a good part of the food from his lunch tray, walked up next to Artie. Holding the empty tray by his side, he said nothing but waited for Artie to notice him. The boy nodded at the section of table between Artie and Leah, and looked back at the senior for permission to sit. "Have a seat," said Artie. "Welcome to the Barf Table. I'm Artie, and that's Leah."

The embarrassed youth pulled out the chair closer to Artie and sat, carefully placing his dirty tray on the table in front of himself. "Thank you," he said. "My name is Ricky."

Sizing up the situation, Artie tried to ease Ricky's mind. "Don't worry about your T-shirt, buddy," Artie said. "They keep clean ones in the office. They'll give you one."

Ricky shrugged. "No money," he said. "I'm okay."

"No," said Artie. "They'll *give* you one. They save them for this kind of thing. It happens all the time. Of course, the T-shirt might be a funny color and say something square like 'Arbor High Spirit Guy,' and it might be a little too big for you, but you won't have to *pay* for it—well, not with money, anyway. Know what I mean?"

Ricky nodded but just sat there looking at his empty tray. "Oh," Artie added, "and you can go tell the cashier over there what happened, and he'll let you get another lunch, no charge. Frankie's a good guy. He looks scary, but he's all right. Trust me."

Ricky looked up for the first time since sitting at the Barf Table and glanced across the lunchroom at Frankie, the mean-looking cashier, who was still checking out the last of the lowly 9th graders at his register. Artie was right about Frankie. He was a good person, even though he looked like a pro-wrestling villain and always wore black clothes from head to toe. His favorite T-shirts bore bloody images of his favorite punk rock bands. He regularly attended death-metal concerts up in Iron Harbor near the naval base or down in Mimosa Beach. Nothing like that ever happened in quiet Monk's Landing or in neighboring Port Oleander, an even sleepier town.

"Okay," said Ricky, doubting Artie's assurances but too hungry to argue. Ricky picked up his tray, took it to the drop-off window, and then walked across the room to Frankie's cash register.

Artie looked over at Leah again and saw that she was still reading her book. But she also had one eye on the lunchroom clock mounted on the far wall, squinting up at it every half-minute or so. She couldn't seem to wait for the release bell to ring, hopefully before Ricky or any other unfortunate freshmen joined her and Artie at the round table. It was fate that kept the pale girl's escape plan from succeeding.

As the thin second hand on the cafeteria clock swept past 12 to begin that last long minute before the release bell, two 9th-grade boys—one in a wheelchair, the other carrying two lunch trays—parked themselves on the side of the table where Ricky had sat a couple of minutes earlier. The able-bodied youth laid one tray before his wheelchair-bound companion in the spaces at the table next to Leah, and sat himself down near Artie. Both boys looked lost, but in different ways.

"Hi, guys," Artie said. "You might want to cover your trays with a napkin or something before the bell rings in a few seconds." He turned to Leah again. "And you might want to hold your horses just a minute or two longer," he told her. "Trust me."

Her smile didn't reappear, and she glared at Artie once more. "No," she said, shaking her head. "I'm getting out of here. I have a note."

Artie shrugged his shoulders a bit and gave her an "okay, you'll see" kind of look before turning back to the two boys. "One other thing . . . ," he began, just as the release bell rang and all heck broke loose around them.

A hailstorm of raisins rained down on 9th graders' tables from on high—that is, from the raised section of the cafeteria where the upperclassmen sat. As a group, the 11th and 12th graders had stood to leave and, as one, had slung their tiny paper cups of raisins at any table on the lower level where freshmen sat.

Most of the 9th graders had just gotten through the long serving line and had settled down to eat when the first shower of raisins fell upon them, often in sticky clumps like brown toads in a biblical plague. Only the last sophomores to be served were still eating at that point, but even they knew to stop and cover their trays at the bell. The 10th graders who had gotten through the lunch line quickly and had finished eating could more easily shield themselves from getting hit in the fusillade of raisins aimed at the freshman tables.

But sophomores all knew that collateral damage always occurred in these food fights, and the wise ones planned their attire accordingly. Bruin hoodies like the one Leah wore or "drug rugs" like the ones surfers wore were popular with 10th graders. Baseball caps couldn't be worn indoors at Arbor High, whether with bills to the front or to the back. Teachers were more serious about enforcing the cap rule than other school policies.

Only the most aerodynamic raisins—or the heaviest clumps—reached the Barf Table, which sat beyond the regular lowerclassmen section. However, all the upperclassmen, on their way to empty and return their trays, had to pass the round table where Artie, Leah and the two boys now sat. Last in the serving line, Ricky had remained at the cash register when the barrage of raisins began, and had taken Frankie's advice and stood there a few minutes longer to let the 11th and 12th graders exit the cafeteria.

Frankie had cleaned up after more Waisin Wednesdays than he cared to recount. It was small consolation that his own son, as a toddler years earlier, had accompanied Frankie to school one Wednesday and had given the tradition its name by screaming, "Daddy, wook at all the waisins!" as the small gobs of dried fruit sailed through the air and stuck to tables and walls with sickening splats.

Leah did leave the table as soon as she could, even as upperclassmen approached. But surprisingly they left her alone, mistaking her for a sophomore because of the gray Bruin hoodie she wore. They didn't bother Artie, as he was a senior and one of the best athletes at Arbor High to boot. Ricky hadn't returned yet. So that left only two targets at the Barf Table—the two boys who had just sat down. The upperclassmen—mostly the boys, not many girls—didn't care that one of their victims was disabled.

As they passed, the 11th and 12th graders balled up their empty raisin cups and deposited them onto the two 9th graders' napkin-covered trays. The piles of paper balls rose and spilled onto the tabletop, but otherwise left the two dismayed boys unscathed. The upperclassmen dumped the last of their uneaten food in the nearby garbage bins and tossed their hard-plastic trays through the return window with a clatter.

In passing, the last two students in the throng—both of them seniors—reached over and grabbed the two 9th graders' milk cartons, and stopped long enough to open the containers and pour their contents onto the younger boys' untouched food. The napkins and piles of paper cups covering the trays were of little help.

"Don't say a word," Artie advised. "If you do, they'll—"

"Hey!" said the boy in the wheelchair, when the senior standing next to him dropped the empty milk carton into the soupy mess and splashed him. "I'm sitting here! Seriously?!"

With that, the senior grinned, shrugged and flipped the boy's entire tray—food, milk, trash and all—into his lap. The other tray was left untouched because its owner had kept quiet.

"I told you not to say anything," Artie said, once the boys' tormentors had left. "Go get yourselves new trays—like our buddy Ricky over there did. You've already paid for them—for real. I'll help Frankie clean up this mess. I'm Artie, by the way."

Artie stuck out his hand to the boy standing near him, the able one who would actually be going for the food. The other freshman was busy muttering and wiping meatloaf, mashed potatoes and gravy, green beans, a half-pint of milk, balled-up paper cups, and a cupful of raisins from his lap and wheelchair seat.

"Thanks, Artie," said the boy who was standing. "I'm Tommy. And he's Bennie—Bennie Pressler. He'll be okay."

Artie nodded to Tommy as the boy turned to walk back to the serving line. *Pressler* was a name that Artie knew well, because there was only one Pressler family in Oleander County, from Iron Harbor in the north to Mimosa Beach in the south, then from Port Oleander near the shore to Ebenezerville thirty miles inland near the county line. The Presslers were the wealthiest family not only in Oleander County, but also in the whole state, maybe even in the entire region. They owned the Pressler's Department Store chain, with nearly a hundred stores in five states.

Monk's Landing didn't have a Pressler's store, but larger Iron Harbor, Mimosa Beach, Port Oleander and Ebenezerville did. That was where Artie shopped for clothes, because they had the best selection of everything Big & Tall. Also, they carried a line of workwear for the farmers and fishermen of Oleander County. Pressler's left no one out.

"Can I go get you some paper towels, Bennie?" said Artie. "Or I can push you over to the water fountain so you can get that spot out?"

Bennie Pressler scowled as he tried to clean a gravy stain from his pants. "No," he said, "I don't need anybody's help. What do you think I am? A cripple? Yeah, I sit in this wheelchair for all the laughs I get—because I'm a standup comic. You know? I'm into computers, too—just so I can do an impression of Stephen Hawking."

"Really?" Artie didn't know if he should laugh or not. "Well, you can get a new T-shirt in the office—like Ricky, the guy coming over here to sit—but they don't give out clean pants, not that I know of."

Bennie eyed Ricky as he took a seat at the clean section of table across from him. "So they got you, too?" Bennie said in greeting, but Ricky kept his head down and just nodded. "Us freshmen don't get *no* respect," added Bennie.

"*We* freshmen," corrected Artie, having come from his senior English class last period.

"See?" Bennie said. "What'd I just say? We don't get no respect—no respect at all." He looked up at Artie. "Aren't you kinda big for a 9th grader? Jeez, how many grades did *you* get held back?"

Artie did laugh at that crack. "I'm a senior," he said. "I just like sitting here."

"Glutton for punishment, huh?" said Bennie. "So what was that chick's problem who was sitting here a minute ago? It looked like she was mad about something."

"That was Leah," said Artie, to both boys still sitting at the table. He paused as Tommy rejoined them with two new lunches for Bennie and himself. "I don't know if Leah—her name is Leah Russo—if she'll keep sitting here," Artie continued. "She doesn't have to."

"Russo?" said Bennie. "Like Reuben Russo? The football star? The guy who got killed in that big car crash out on the bypass last winter? Jeez."

"Yeah," Artie said quietly. "So go easy on her, okay? I mean, if she *does* sit here again."

Ricky and Tommy looked up from their food and nodded. Bennie held up his spork like a cigar and tapped it with his ring finger. "You bet your life she will," Bennie said, "and I'm just the fellow to cheer her up. *Everybody* loves Bennie

Pressler—well, sooner or later they do."

Artie smiled. "Even upperclassmen? You sure?"

"*Soitenly*," Bennie said, like the Three Stooges.

"Well," Artie said, "just be glad this wasn't Krakatoa Tuesday."

Bennie stuck his spork into the white mound of mashed potatoes on his tray, and dug out a mouth-sized lump. "Yeah?" he said, before taking the bite. "Why's that, big guy?"

Artie nodded toward the mountain of balled-up raisin cups on the table. "If today were Krakatoa Tuesday," he said, "that would be a volcano—complete with brown lava. And you, Bennie, would be the freshman those seniors sacrificed to the gravy gods." Artie didn't point out that something had already overflowed into Bennie's lap, even on Waisin Wednesday.

With a thoughtful look, Bennie tasted his sporkful of spuds, then asked, "So what are we in for tomorrow, Artie? We got Krakatoa Tuesday and Waisin Wednesday. What's tomorrow?"

"Thirsty Thursday," Artie said, predictably. "Just be sure to buy an extra bottle or can of something to drink from the vending machines—or, Bennie, you can bring an extra box of Juicy Juice from home. Just make sure you keep it out of sight until after the release bell tomorrow."

"Juicy Juice?" said Bennie. "I'll have you know, big guy, that I'm a Yoo-hoo man. All of us computer hackers are." He added, "Or should I have said, 'all of *we* computer hackers'? See? I'm not stupid. I know stuff. I learn quick."

Artie smiled again. "You were right the first time. But, okay, we'll see how quickly you learn, Bennie."

Artie Bauer remembered how long it had taken three years earlier for the upperclassmen at Arbor High to let him eat in peace. He hoped that Bennie—and Tommy, Ricky and especially poor little Leah, too—didn't have to wait nearly that long to enjoy their lunches as Bruins. On the first day of school each year at Arbor High, always the first Wednesday after Labor Day, the nine months that lay ahead seemed like they might last forever until the next summer break.

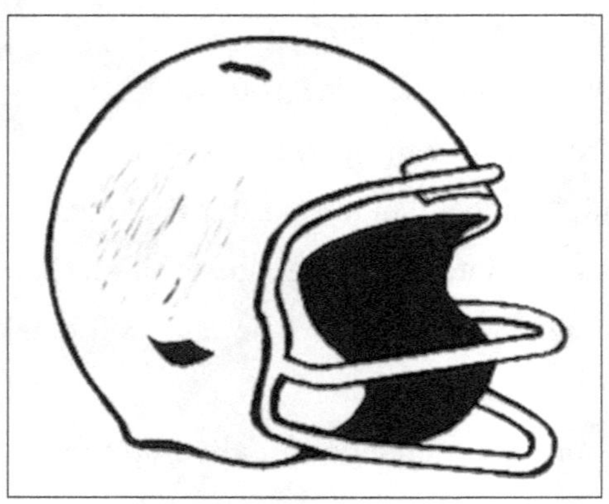

CHAPTER 3 – Where the Fun Never Ends

AS A CHARTER SCHOOL, Arbor High's athletic facilities were smaller and not nearly as fancy as the stadiums and gymnasiums at the larger public schools in Oleander County. In fact, Arbor had started as a private, religious academy for boys decades earlier before becoming an official charter school in recent years. That meant that Arbor High now received state educational funds but didn't have to follow the same rules that regular public schools in the county followed. The Arbor High School Board of Trustees was able to institute longer school days, a shorter school year and a more innovative curriculum than other schools could. Also, the Arbor trustees could hire a more progressive principal, and more unorthodox teachers and staff members (like Frankie the Death-Metal Cashier) than other schools would employ or even interview.

But Arbor High was still playing catch-up when it came to renovating its athletic facilities. The soon-to-be rededicated Reuben Russo Memorial Stadium had been little more than a cow pasture surrounded by bleachers until that summer. A new grandstand with a big press box on top and wide concession window in back had been built on the home side of the field. The visiting bleachers sat on what was the skinned infield for the baseball team each spring.

To pay for all those improvements, the Arbor High football Bruins needed to do something special on the gridiron—other than lose their star quarterback in a horrible auto accident. Until the football stadium was to be rededicated at homecoming that season, it officially kept its plain old name, Arbor Field. The grass was real and grew so fast that Coach Jug Johnson had threatened to buy a herd of goats to save him from all the mowing he did.

But Artie "Yogi" Bauer felt right at home in a pasture, because he had lived all his life on his grandparents' farm between Monk's Landing and Ebenezerville, and he knew a thing or two about horses, cattle, chickens and pigs. Artie's grandpa still did things the old-fashioned way, still plowing with his workhorses, but he trusted that Artie would learn new methods to grow crops and make money on the farm. He wanted Artie to go to Iron Harbor A&M, to study agriculture and maybe even business, and to apply that knowledge to running the Bauer family farm for at least one more generation.

Artie's mother, who had been too young to raise him herself, had left him with Grandma and Grandpa Bauer when Artie was just six months old. She had simply disappeared, never to return home nor to contact her parents again. Artie also didn't know who his father was. But none of that mattered to him all that much. Even though they were strict, Pearl and Harry Bauer were the best parents that Artie could have ever had.

* * *

"Ready to go, Yogi?" said the coach. "Let's get this party started."

At four o'clock sharp, Jug Johnson blew his whistle and motioned for Artie to get the other football players lined up for calisthenics. Jug wasn't a fan of all the fancy stretching and karaoke running drills that the county's other football teams did before practice. He believed in good, old-fashioned jumping jacks, pushups and squat thrusts to get his boys ready to bust heads on the field. And after practice they always finished up with what he called "suicides," until only the best-conditioned player was left standing.

Artie nodded and whistled for his teammates to assemble in rows five yards apart from midfield back. Standing at the fifty-yard line atop the block A spray-painted in green and gold, Artie waited for the players to settle down before he shouted, "Jumping jacks! Twenty of 'em! Count off!"

As he led the team, Artie checked to make sure that everyone was participating; then he looked through the stadium's chain-link fence at the 9th-grade flag footballers on the adjacent field. They had divided into six-man teams and were already playing games. He noticed both Ricky and Tommy, his Barf Table buddies, playing together on one team, and he saw Bennie Pressler in his wheelchair, watching them from the sideline. Artie smiled, knowing that Barf Table roots grew deep, whether one wanted them to or not.

As Artie and the players continued their warm-up exercises, Coach Johnson walked over to the fence and talked to the young P.E. teacher supervising the flag footballers. Artie figured Jug was telling the teacher to keep an eye peeled for 9th graders with particular skills that the varsity could use—like punting, passing and kicking—if not this season, then next fall when they were 10th graders.

This season's star sophomore was last year's flashiest *little flaggot*, which was what a few varsity players called the freshmen on the other side of the fence. Artie and his best friend, Tyrone Green, who had been Reuben Russo's backup last year at quarterback, didn't approve of name-calling, especially not abusive names like that. As co-captains this year, Artie and Ty wanted to keep their teammates from harassing the flag footballers, but—like in the cafeteria—the 10th-grade players, in particular, seemed determined to pick on the younger kids.

The sophomore with the biggest mouth that day was last year's freshman flash, Joshua Stark, who had beaten out Ty for the starting QB job and was also first-string punter and kicker. Josh was a true triple-threat player on the gridiron—and he wasn't going to let anyone forget it, especially Ty, who had worked hard for two varsity seasons and had waited his turn to start as a senior. Now, on offense, Ty had to be satisfied with playing tight end and with being Josh's holder on placekicks. That was usually the first-string quarterback's duty, as Reuben Russo had done the past two seasons as the Bruins' starting QB.

Not even all-star Reuben Russo had started as a sophomore, though he had certainly been good enough. Back then, Jug had stuck with the senior who had waited for the starting spot. The old coach had told Reuben that "paying your dues" was part of being a good team member. But for some unexplained reason, this season was different as far as rookie quarterbacks went. Jug didn't hesitate to start the sophomore ahead of the senior. Josh was a good player, but he wasn't *that* good. He was no Reuben Russo—except in his own mind.

* * *

Arbor High's first football game of the new season was that Friday night against the private Solid Rock Christian Academy in Ebenezerville. The Bruins opened their football season each year—either at home or on the road—against the Solid Rock Harvesters, so named because of the town's Harvest Home Bakery and Harvest Home Weavers. Formed by members of Solid Rock Christian Church in the 1890s, the bakery and textile mill had started as ways to employ the community's hard-working residents.

Despite being surrounded by the Great Oleander Swamp, the two companies thrived and the town got its name as the place where the people had "raised their Ebenezer," a Bible word for "stone of help." Much of the swampland was drained through the years, and was replaced by agricultural fields. Ebenezerville remained a good place to live and work. The church and later its Christian academy were, in fact, the "solid rock" upon which the town sat, on the highest ground or island in the swamp.

That was the reason why developer Joel Stark decided years earlier to move his young family to Oleander County, where he bought oceanfront property near Monk's Landing to live on and swampland around E-ville to drain and develop as residential subdivisions, later as golf courses. As the popularity of Oleander County beaches grew, so did the influence of Stark Realty. Sole owner Joel Stark's only son was the big-mouthed spitballer of Arbor High, Josh Stark. And that explains why young Josh was the Bruins' first sophomore starting quarterback.

CHAPTER 4 – The Double Reverse Flea Flickerooski

AT FIVE O'CLOCK that Waisin Wednesday afternoon, the varsity took a water break at the same time that the flag footballers were dismissed for the day. All the athletes from both levels of the sport—11-man, smash-mouth tackle and six-man, freshman flag—mingled at the green water hoses near the chain-link fence that had divided them. As team captains, Artie Bauer and Ty Green hung back to let their teammates get water first, though the varsity had to wait until the last of the 9th graders finished drinking. Artie's Barf Table brothers Ricky Duran, Tommy White and Bennie Pressler, seated in his wheelchair, were last in the two freshman lines. Josh Stark and his shaggy-headed sidekick—halfback Brett Woods, also a sophomore—stood at the front of the two varsity lines. Josh wanted water to slick back his own white-streaked hair.

"Hi, guys," Artie said to his three tablemates as they waited. "How'd practice go?"

Josh Stark, standing only feet away, overheard Artie's question and laughed out loud. "Practice?" Josh said. "Ha! These little flaggots don't need to practice grabbing flags. They're already pros at playing grab-ass. Right, Pressler?"

"I was just watching," said Bennie, not taking the bait. "I haven't decided what I want to do after school yet."

Artie started to intervene but hesitated when Bennie didn't bite Josh's head off. As it turned out, Artie should have followed his instincts, because Brett

Woods—yet another mouthy rich kid and one whose family had a history with the Presslers—decided to speak up. "I know what you can do, Pressler," said Brett. "You can be our waterboy so we don't have to drink out of these nasty hoses. You can roll around on the sideline with a water cooler in your lap."

"Yeah," Josh Stark said. "Like all the food that got dumped in your lap at lunch today. You're a big joke—a little flaggot, even though you'd suck at that, too."

Artie stepped forward. "Hey, that's enough, guys," he said. "We don't call our teammates names—or anyone else, for that matter. Besides, isn't that what you two got called last year until Coach put a stop to the name-calling?"

"They aren't *our* teammates," said Josh. "Right, Brett?" The quarterback glanced over at his backfield buddy, expecting him to agree.

But Brett Woods had good reason not to press the issue with Bennie, now that Artie had stood up for the freshman boy. "I don't care," said Brett. "I'm too thirsty to give a crap."

"Oh, come on," Josh said, looking from Brett to Artie. "They're stupid freshmen. We're *supposed* to dump on 'em. It's part of the game."

"Not *this* game," said Artie. "All you need to think about now is how to handle yourself between the lines on the field over there. That's football. And that's the only game we're playing right now. Okay?"

Josh smirked. "Yeah, whatever," he said, then with a muddy cleat kicked one wheel on Bennie's chair. "Hurry up, cri—I mean, *Pressler*. Jeez, don't you want to get back to the beach and watch the surfers until dark—I mean, now that you can't surf anymore yourself?"

That remark pushed Bennie over the edge. He spun the chair around and smacked Josh in the shins with the metal footrests sticking out in front. "Hey, sorry, man," said Bennie. "Back off, and I'll let you jump ahead of me—if you're *that* thirsty. Or I'll give you the bottle of Yoo-hoo in my backpack. You can suck on *that* for a while."

Not even Josh Stark was low enough to fight a boy in a wheelchair. But he wasn't above running his mouth. "Yeah, well, you can just—" Josh started, but was cut off by the fist that grabbed the front of his practice jersey and jerked him to the side.

"Shut up, Josh," said Ty Green. "I'm not nice like Artie. And if you got anything to say to *me*, just go ahead and say it, and we'll settle things once and for all. I'm not scared of you *or* your dad's money." Ty released his grip on Josh's uniform and shoved him backwards a step, waiting for the boy's response.

Artie again stepped in. "Come on, Ty," he said. "Give him a chance. He'll straighten up once he figures out how being on a team *really* works."

"I don't need you guys," Josh continued. "Anybody can *hike* a ball, and anybody can *hold* a ball. Besides, we're gonna kick Solid Rock's butt Friday night. We would beat 'em even if ol' Ty here was running the offense. They're the worst team in the conference."

Artie watched as his new friends Ricky and Tommy finished getting their water. They started to leave with Bennie. "Come on, buddy," Artie said to Ty. "Let's go see what Coach wants us to do during the second half of practice. It's gonna take that long for everybody to get water—and to cool off."

Ty nodded and followed his friend and co-captain over to the bench, where Coach Jug Johnson and the young phys-ed teacher who had been coaching the freshmen compared notes. As Artie and Ty waited to speak to Jug, they saw Arbor High's principal exit the school building and cross the bus parking lot with Leah Russo by his side. Leah carried a big clipboard under one arm and a blue-plastic grocery bag in her other hand. Even at that distance, the paleness of the frail girl's face and hands still stood out against the oversized Bruins hoodie she wore. Also, she had let her ink-black hair down since lunch, and it darkly framed her white face.

Principal Jerry Church, a tall man whose nickname was "Lurch," towered over the girl beside him. He wore dark suit trousers without a jacket, and a white, long-sleeved shirt with rolled-up sleeves. The shirt was unbuttoned at the neck behind a loosely-knotted tie. His attire gave the impression of an administrator who worked hard and did more than sit behind a desk. That he was escorting Leah to the football field—despite his chronic back problems—showed that he was determined to do his job right, even though he did lumber a bit and stand stiffly like the Addams Family butler when the pair reached the bench where Jug sat.

"Coach Johnson?" said the principal, waiting a second for Jug to look up from the list of flag-footballers that the phys-ed teacher had shared. Patient to a fault, Principal Church nodded to Artie and Ty, then continued, "Coach, I have a young lady here who wants to help support the football team this season."

Still seated, Jug glanced at Leah, then looked up at the principal. "Now, Jerry," said Jug, "you know I don't have nothing to do with the cheerleaders. Little Miss Russo here needs to go talk to Thelma. I think they're still practicing in the gym."

Leah's eyes flashed. "I'm *not* a cheerleader," she told the old coach. "Not anymore. I'm on the newspaper staff, and they assigned me to cover the football team. I just figured you might want me to keep statistics, too—you know, to kill two birds with one stone? I already know all the players' names and numbers—the ones who played last year, anyway."

Jug nodded. "Well, that's a *fine* idea. We ain't had a good stat man in a couple years—I mean, stat *person*. Okay, you're hired. Well, then, I'll see you on the sidelines Friday in E-ville. You can ride the activity bus with the team, or you can get there on your own—with your folks. How're they doing?"

"They're fine, I guess," Leah said. "But they won't be coming to the games. Dad said he needs to start getting away on the weekends—you know, do stuff outdoors. Mom found a cabin for them to rent up at the lake this fall. She's looking forward to seeing the leaves change."

At that revelation, Principal Church frowned. "They're not leaving you home alone every weekend, are they?" he asked. "Aren't you going off with them?"

"No," she said. "Mom said I should stay with one of our neighbors. I *want* to go to the games. It wouldn't be right not to—not for me."

Everyone was quiet for a few seconds. Jug nodded sadly and spoke. "Okay, then," he said. "I'll look for you when we're loading up the bus. Yogi? Green? Don't let me forget, little Miss Russo here will be riding with us. And you two help me look out for her, okay?"

"Gotcha, Coach," said Ty Green, and he winked at Leah for good measure.

She glared at the senior co-captain for an instant, but eased up when he smiled and added, "I was Reuben's backup for two years, so I guess that makes me Leah's backup big brother, too. It's meant to be."

"From your lips to God's ears," said Jug, with a nod.

Artie winced, hoping that Leah didn't haul off and smack either his friend or the coach, but she wasn't too bothered by their sentiments. "I appreciate the concern," she said, "but I can take care of myself, guys." She added, "And, Coach, I'd like to keep stats for you every day at practice, too—if you don't mind me hanging around. I'll stay up in the stands out of the way."

Jug was confused about why anyone would keep practice stats, but he didn't want to get Leah upset again. "Why, sure," he said. "You come talk to me tomorrow at lunch—after you eat, I mean—and we'll figure out how to work that out. Do I need to give you a note?"

"No," she said, then looked up at the principal. "My pass from the newspaper staff will work just fine—won't it, Mr. Church? We met today right after school, and they went ahead and printed passes for everybody."

The principal nodded. "Okay, well, I need to get back to my office. I'm expecting a call. You boys—and Leah—you all have a good rest of the day. Don't practice too hard. It still feels like summer out here in the sun."

Jug laughed at that. "Now, Jerry, you know I take good care of my boys. Ain't none of them gonna pass out from the heat. Besides, we ain't gonna be scrimmaging. We're gonna show the boys a couple of special plays this afternoon. Don't think we're gonna have to use either one this week against Solid Rock, so this is a good time to learn them."

"You're not going to try the old fumblerooski again this year, are you?" the principal said with a grin. "That play has *never* worked with our boys. Or are you dusting off the old Statue of Liberty to use this season?"

"*Heh-heh,*" said Jug. "You never can tell. I got all kinds of trick plays up my sleeve this season. Learned a new one during a poker ga—I mean, in a *workshop*—in a workshop at the coaches conference last summer at State College." He cleared his throat.

The tall principal threw up his hand as he moved away. "I hear you," he said. "Things haven't changed much since back when I attended those summer coaching clinics. Of course, I went to the, uh, to the—what was it, *workshops?*—for basketball coaches. See you tomorrow."

* * *

The second half of practice was uneventful, even enjoyable, as Jug and the older players showed the rookies how to run the old fumblerooski. He also taught the whole team the new trick play that he had learned the previous summer. It didn't have a real name yet, at least not a good one like *fumblerooski* or *Statue of Liberty* or *double reverse* or *flea flicker*. Jug just called it "the new trick play," even though Artie reminded him that he'd need to come up with a memorable name before they faced Solid Rock on Friday night.

Jug had devised the play to be run by a quarterback with at least the athletic ability of Reuben Russo, who had been a great passer but also a solid runner with a good head on his shoulders. This new play basically combined all four trick plays that Jug *did* have names for, but the *Double Statue of Reverse Flea Flickerooski* was too much of a mouthful for any quarterback to remember and call in the huddle.

Leah sat in the bleachers and watched with amusement as the offense ran through the new trick play—which, like the team's game experience with the fumblerooski, never seemed to work the way it was supposed to. Quarterback Josh Stark, standing alone in the backfield, would take a long snap—a "shotgun" snap—from Artie, then drop back three more steps, cocking his right arm as if to throw. With the football plainly visible at his ear, Josh would look left for a receiver, as all but two offensive players would be headed in that direction. The exceptions would be center Artie, pulling to the right, and tight end Ty, who as backup QB could throw the ball as well as Josh. Just as Ty passed behind Josh, the quarterback would drop the ball behind his back into the tight end's hands, then bring his right arm forward in a fake throw downfield. Ty could either run with the ball around the right end, using Artie as his only blocker; throw downfield to any receiver who was open; or—and this was Jug's preference—immediately flip the ball back to Josh, who would either pass to a receiver on the left side of the field or run to the left side himself.

But the new trick play never worked, mainly because it was a bit too tricky, even for all the offensive players who knew what was supposed to happen. After the fourth run-through that failed, Leah spoke up. "Hey, Coach," she called from the bleachers, waving her clipboard to get Jug's attention. "I can tell you how to fix that play."

Jug lifted the whistle that hung on a lanyard around his neck and blew three short blasts. "Take a knee, boys," he yelled. "Coaches, huddle up." He waved his two assistant coaches—both of them players' fathers who were volunteering for their first years—over to the bench area just below where Leah Russo sat in the bleachers.

The old coach took a seat and wiped his brow with a stray towel before looking up at the girl. "Okay, missy," he said. "What did you see us doing wrong?"

"For starters," Leah said, "you should line Ty up on the *right* and put him in motion to the left before the snap. That'll clear out the defensive back on the right, if he follows Ty to the other side of the field. Putting Ty in motion makes the defensive back think on his own. He has to decide whether to stay put or follow the play. Isn't that why you have 'trips' left? Those three receivers overload the left side, and the defensive backs have to set up on that side, too."

Grudgingly, Jug shrugged and nodded. "Well, yeah," he admitted, "but we still got that weak-side linebacker over there on the right. He ain't going nowhere."

Leah looked down at her clipboard, then up again at Jug. "That's Artie's block," she said. "He has to wait and see how the play develops, anyway, but if Ty ends up running the ball, Artie can head downfield and block. Otherwise, he can't go past the line of scrimmage."

"Why not?" asked the assistant coach who handled the offense.

"Ineligible receiver," said Leah. "Right, Coach Johnson?"

Jug cleared his throat again. "Uh, yeah," he said. "I was just getting ready to point that out. So is that *all* we need to fix?"

"No," said Leah, shaking her head. "The trips need to run different pass routes—down ten yards, then fly, post and corner routes, from left to right. That has the two slotbacks crossing, and maybe they can pick for each other."

"Dang," said the defensive assistant, "she knows more than the guys do."

"*Most* of the guys," Jug corrected, then turned back to Leah. "Did you learn all that from Reuben—or your dad?"

Leah frowned. "Dad played soccer in college," she said. "Reuben taught me everything I know about football. He said even if I couldn't play, it would help me be a good sportswriter—or a good *coach*. He didn't like me being a cheerleader. That's why I quit."

The offensive assistant pointed at Leah. "Hey," he said, "aren't you the girl who almost won the county Punt, Pass & Kick last year? That hotshot from Solid Rock only won because he had a rifle for an arm. I heard he's starting this year— as a 9th grader. You were *good*."

Leah nodded shyly, as Jug harrumphed. "Heck, that boy's been shaving since the 5th grade," Jug said. "PP&K needs to start checking birth certificates." Now he looked at Leah in a different light. "So you're pretty good, huh?" he said. "And you want to be a sportscaster? Like Phyllis George?"

"Sports-*writer*," Leah said. "Or a coach. I'm better at baseball. You coach baseball, too, don't you, Coach Johnson? Reuben also taught me how to pitch."

"Well, one season at a time, little miss," said Jug. "Now, let's get back out there, boys, and see if these changes work. And I think we got a name for this play now."

"What's that, Coach?" asked the offensive assistant.

Jug nodded up at Leah again. "Little lady," he began, "if you don't mind, I'd like to call this play the *Reuben*. That all right? I mean, since you fixed it and he taught you everything?"

The two assistants nodded in agreement as they waited for Leah's reaction. "Yeah, okay," she said finally, "because if it *doesn't* work, whoever ends up with the ball is gonna be the meat in a big linebacker sandwich."

The three men laughed and returned to the field, where they explained the changes to the team and ran the Reuben play flawlessly three times before ending practice with sprints. As usual, Josh Stark won the "suicides" competition by outrunning everyone in the first sprint that counted and then being the first player to be allowed to head to the locker room. Halfback Brett Woods was excused second. Ty Green ran fast enough to stop after the third suicide, leaving his co-captain Artie at the goal line with the rest of their teammates, the slowest and weariest ones. Artie was still standing, but like the rest he was bent over and breathing hard.

This time, only the last-place man would have to run again. When Coach Johnson blew his whistle, the remaining players took off down the field, touched the 10-yard line, and back-pedaled to the goal line. From there, they sprinted to the 20 and back-pedaled to the goal again. The last leg was a sprint—if one could call it that—to the 30, before a backwards run to the suicide's finish line at the goal.

Big Artie could have finished ahead of at least his fellow linemen, whether starters or benchwarmers, but he eased up just enough over the last 30 yards to come in dead last. After catching his breath and giving Jug a little wave, he dutifully ran a final suicide by himself, cheered on by the other boys from the previous heat. Ty Green, who hadn't left for the locker room when he could have, patted his tired buddy on the shoulder and walked back to the school building with him. As friends, they always stuck together—except in the lunchroom, that is, because Ty didn't want to relive his freshman year as a member of the Barf Table.

* * *

Grandpa was sitting in his rocker on the enclosed back porch of the white farmhouse, reading the latest copy of *The Solid Rock*, Ebenezerville's little weekly newspaper, when Artie came in the back door from practice. Without a spare vehicle—just the old red Chevrolet pickup that Grandpa had driven for thirty years—Artie had to catch rides home from Monk's Landing every school day. He rode the big yellow bus to school each morning.

Ty Green was a country boy, too, so he could usually give Artie a ride home in the old hooptie that his father had given him on his sixteenth birthday almost two years earlier. Ty loved that old white Ford LTD. It wasn't a cool car like some of the vehicles that wealthier teammates drove, but it carried him everywhere he and Artie needed to go. Ty called it the "White Whale," a reference to its length and to *Moby-Dick*, required reading in English class his sophomore year when he had gotten the car.

Artie, who preferred Chevys, often said a better name for the car would be "Likely To Die." So far, the white LTD had broken down on them five times, always on their way home from practice, never on Ty's way to school in the morning or on a late-night date with any of the girls chasing him. Ty was a love 'em and leave 'em kind of guy, at least until that first week of his senior year, but he would never pretend that the car had a problem just to go parking with a girl. It was a matter of pride.

Looking up from his newspaper, Grandpa greeted his only grandson with a grunt and a reminder to get old Bessie and Bossy milked before dark. "I will, Grandpa," said Artie. "Any good news in the paper this week?"

"*Heh*, good news my stinking foot," snorted Grandpa. "That durn real estate company in Monk's Landing is trying to buy up more land between us and E-ville—all around us, as a matter of fact. Far as that goes, that fast-talking Joel Stark—he said his son plays ball with you?—he came by here this morning and tried to buy *this* farm. He had the nerve to say me and him needed to 'play ball' together—like you and his boy on that football team of yours."

Grandpa reached over to the little end table beside him and picked up a folded sheet of paper. Holding it out to his grandson, he said, "This was his offer. What do you think about it?"

Artie took the paper and looked at the letter typed there, and at the six-figure number that Joel Stark had written in pen and initialed. Artie gave a low whistle. "Gee, Gramps," he said. "That's an awful lot of money. What did you tell him?"

"What do you *think* I told him?" said Grandpa. "I told Joel Stark he could stick that paper where the sun don't shine, but he just laughed at me and said, 'You'll come around.' Is his boy as much of a jerk as he is?"

Artie smiled. "Yeah, pretty much," he said. "That trait must run in the family."

"Yeah," said Grandpa, "like being an egg-sucking dog. Speaking of which, you need to stop by the chicken coop on your way back from the barn and pick up a half-dozen eggs for our breakfast in the morning. Your grandma didn't feel good this afternoon and didn't go out and gather up the eggs like she usually does."

"Is she okay?" Artie asked.

"She's resting on the bed. I've been checking on her every so often, and I think she'll be all right. Could be her allergies. But that's why I ain't got much done myself today, staying close to Mama all afternoon." He took the real estate company's letter back from Artie and tossed it on the table again.

"You sure she's not just upset about that offer?" said Artie.

Grandpa shook his head. "Nah, that ain't it. We do need money, but we ain't gonna make money *that* way—not by selling out your future. You're gonna go off to college and learn how to run this old place right. We got confidence in you, son—and faith, too. Don't you worry. Your mama ran off. We don't even know where she is now. So she don't have nothing to do with this farm anymore, and we're not gonna let her just show up and sell it, soon as we're too old to take care of it. That ain't gonna happen, not if I can help it. This farm will be yours."

Artie nodded and walked past Grandpa to the kitchen door. "I'll go wash up a bit before I do the milking," he said, "and I'll look in on Grandma for you. I hate that she's feeling so bad—for whatever reason."

"Yeah," Grandpa said. "I don't have to tell you, she's been feeling poorly off and on ever since we went to that Fourth of July picnic over at Solid Rock Church. They were trying to get us to start coming back on Sundays, but all they did was drive us further away."

"Why's that, Grandpa?" asked Artie.

Grandpa shook his head and replied, "I think one of the women there said something to Mama that got her upset, but she won't tell me. I think the woman made fun of Mama's dress and my overhauls—not in so many words, but you know how people do. She also said the smell of pigs and cows turned her stomach. Well, making fun of this farm is like making fun of me and Mama and *you*, too. Don't you forget that, Arthur. This is *our* farm, this is *part* of us—smell and all—and it's nothing to be ashamed of. But if we lost this farm or sold it, we'd never get it back. Same's true with a man's reputation, son. And a good part of *that* is the company a man keeps."

Artie eyed his grandfather uneasily. "Are you talking about Ty, Grandpa? You know he's a good guy. We've been friends since primary school. He's eaten more meals here than anybody who isn't a member of the family."

"Oh, heck, no," said Grandpa. "I like Ty Green, always have. I'm talking about people like that uppity church lady and that money-grubbing Joel Stark— two people cut from the same cloth. If that Stark boy is on your football team, you better make sure you don't pick up any of his bad habits. We still got a willow tree out there in the yard, and I can grab me a switch any time I need to. You ain't so big that you can't still get a switching."

Grandpa laughed out loud. "Now, wouldn't *that* be funny," he said. "You're a big boy and about the *best* boy in the whole wide world, and here I am threatening to whup you for something you ain't done yet. Ain't that something?"

"That's why I love you, Grandpa," said Artie. "You keep me straight. Always have." He paused for a moment, then added, "And I hope you always will."

CHAPTER 5 – It's Thirsty Thursday

DONICIA EVANS WAS CALLED 'NICIE,' but there was nothing "nice" about what got her transferred to Arbor High on the second day of school in Oleander County. The first syllable of her nickname sounded like "Neese," not "Nice," so no one who knew her by name at Mimosa Beach High School expected to see any better behavior than what they got from the tall, strong, angry girl on the first day of her 12th-grade year. She mouthed off to every teacher she met—in particular, to the ones who mispronounced her name—and she got into three fights that day: one before school with a girl on her bus, one at lunch with a boy who made a pass at her, and the last one after school when the MBHS assistant principal for girls said that Nicie would either transfer out immediately or face a long-term suspension. Even worse than being suspended, she wouldn't be allowed to play volleyball that fall for the Lady Waveriders.

Arbor High had no girls volleyball team—or, rather, no volleyball team that played other schools. But Arbor did have an intramural, co-ed, *beach* volley-ball program that played all of its games during the required "5th Period" after school. Nicie Evans had been playing semi-pro ball on the beach for a couple of summers, taking money under the table from Mimosa Beach hotel and restaurant owners who put on tournaments and wanted their team to win. Nicie figured that getting a college scholarship was out of the question, anyway, but she hadn't liked hearing the principal say she *couldn't* play volleyball that fall. Nobody told Nicie

Evans that she couldn't do something she really wanted to do, not without a fight.

Intramural beach volleyball at Arbor High would be good practice, Nicie figured, and in the winter she could play interscholastic basketball for the Bruinettes. Again, she didn't expect to get a free ride to college as a basketball player, but she liked being the star of a team and leading it into battle against other squads of skilled athletes. She could have made most boys' teams, if hardwood talent had been the only requirement. But whupping up on girls and reading about those whippings in the newspaper made her happy enough.

* * *

It was two minutes before the lunch release bell when Arbor High principal Jerry Church escorted Nicie Evans across the cafeteria to her new seat at the Barf Table. He explained to her in front of the others seated there that she would *not* be allowed to leave the cafeteria with the other seniors that quarter, which would end at Thanksgiving. "Then, Miss Evans, if you behave," Mr. Church said, "we'll talk about restoring your senior privileges. Okay?"

"Yeah," Nicie said flatly, not looking up at the principal as she took the empty seat at the table beside Bennie in his wheelchair. She didn't bother pointing out to Mr. Church that she had never had any senior privileges at Arbor High, being a new student there.

Artie had heard of Nicie Evans from previous basketball and volleyball seasons, and he had even seen her play against Arbor High a few times. But the two had never met and had never exchanged so much as a greeting despite living in the same county all their young lives. "Nicie?" he said. "I'm Artie—Artie Bauer. I've seen you play basketball. You're good. Let me introduce you to the rest of—"

"Don't bother," Nicie Evans said. "I can do that myself." She looked at the others seated around her and let her gaze rest on Leah first. "Girl," said Nicie, "you're too skinny. Are you sick or something?"

"No," said Leah. "Just sad. That okay with you?"

Nicie's reply was lost in the fracas that followed. The release bell rang, and a horde of upperclassmen descended from their section of the lunchroom down through the 9th and 10th graders toward the Barf Table, garbage bins and tray-return window.

Artie watched Leah rise and melt into the oncoming rush. Like the day before at the release bell, she headed toward the door to leave. Artie remembered to warn the boys still seated with him. "Hey, guys," Artie said. "Quick. Grab your Yoo-hoos." Nicie hadn't gotten a lunch tray yet and had brought nothing from home to eat or drink.

Ricky and Tommy followed Artie's instruction and snatched up their drink cartons. Always the comedian, Bennie quipped, "Grab my Yoo-hoo? That sounds like a personal problem, Artie." Bennie started to laugh—until a senior boy reached down and grabbed the drink box on Bennie's tray and squeezed out its chocolaty contents onto the boy's lunch. In the process, stray streams of the brown liquid splashed Bennie and, seated next to him, Nicie, too.

She shot out of her chair. "I *know* you didn't just do that," she said to the senior. "Picking on a crippled boy, are you? Well, why don't you pick on some-body who can fight back?"

With a look that turned from satisfaction to fright, the senior boy dropped the carton and held up his hands in surrender. "Hey, I'm sorry," he said to Nicie. "Just having some fun. It's Thirsty Thursday, you know."

"You get away from us," said Nicie, "or I'll have some fun rearranging your face. Got it, boy?" She looked down at Bennie. "You okay, kid?"

"Yeah, I'm all right," said Bennie. He added, "Nicie, I'm Bennie Pressler. I think you and I are gonna be really good friends this year—but I'm not a cripple. I'm just in this thing for another month or two, hopefully. If there's anything I can do for you, just say the word."

Nicie's eyes widened as she took her seat again. "Pressler, huh? Your folks run that store in Mimosa Beach?"

Bennie nodded. "Yeah, that's us," he said. "Do you shop there?"

"No," she said, "but I wouldn't mind *working* there—maybe after gradua-tion?"

"You just let me know," Bennie said, "and I'll put in a good word for you. I bet you'd be great at the Customer Service counter, especially handling complaints." When her brown eyes narrowed, he quickly added, "I'm just teasing. It's what I do. Right, Artie?"

Artie smiled. "Yeah," he said. "Bennie likes to live dangerously. And let me introduce Tommy—Tommy White—and Ricky Duran. That was Leah Russo who just left."

"Russo?" said Nicie. "As in Reuben Russo, the quarterback? That's his little sister?"

"Yes," Artie said. "So now you know what she's sad about."

Nicie nodded, then nudged Bennie. "You won't mind, then, if me and Leah are good friends, too, will you?" she said. "She's sad, and I'm mad. You boys might want to find other places to sit at lunch."

"Nope," said Bennie. "We're all stuck here at the Barf Table for the duration—well, all of us except Artie. By the way, big guy, what's the lunch theme tomorrow? Freaky Friday? Farting Friday? What?"

Artie laughed. "No, but you're close," he said. "It's *Fishy* Friday. And you'd better hope they serve fish sticks instead of tuna salad. The fish sticks bounce off. The tuna leaves a stain."

"What kind of messed-up place *is* this?" Nicie asked. "I thought coming to Arbor High would be boring, but who knew? Can we fight back?"

She looked at Ricky. "Well," she added, "maybe not you, little guy. But me and Leah and Pressler, here, and Tommy—that your name?—and *Mr. Artie Bauer*—yeah, I know who you are, buddy—we don't have to take nothing off nobody. Right?"

Artie shrugged. "The Barf Table has never fought back before, not while I've been sitting here," he said. "But there's a first time for everything, I guess."

Actually, no one like Nicie Evans had ever sat with Artie and the other unfortunate kids at the Barf Table, and so he wondered how the new girl's presence would change the balance of power in the Arbor High lunchroom, if at all.

CHAPTER 6 – Thursday Afternoon Shade

ARTIE'S NEW BARF TABLE BUDDY, Nicie Evans, was the main topic of discussion Thursday afternoon in the football locker room. Artie himself had nothing to say about her. Of course, he never said anything bad about anyone, not in a locker-room setting. It was the team's two hotshot sophomores—QB Josh Stark and halfback Brett Woods—who insisted on ribbing their junior and senior teammates who had backed off at lunch when Nicie had defended Bennie Pressler.

As usual, Josh was the more outspoken of the two. "Hey, Waters," said Josh, as he sat at his locker and laced his cleats. "Why didn't you speak up when that big girl threatened to punch Anderson's lights out? Were you scared of her, too?"

Waters, a senior lineman like Artie, just shrugged before dropping his shoulder pads and practice jersey down over his head.

But Josh wouldn't drop the subject. Turning to his backfield buddy at the next locker, he asked, "What do you think, Brett? Should Waters have spoken up and told that big girl where to go? Would you have stood up for *me* if she had threatened to rearrange *my* face?"

"You know it, Josh," said Brett. "All for one, and one for all. I'm not scared of any girl, not even a big, mean-looking one like Nicie Evans." He paused for a second. "But, you know, I did hear from a buddy of mine down at Mimosa Beach that she beat the crap out of the school's best wrestler. They got into it one day at lunch."

Josh took the information in and replied, "Well, he probably didn't want to fight a girl. If she ever touches me, I'll make her regret it."

"What?" said Waters. "You gonna bleed on her shirt or something?"

"Oh, shut up, fat boy," Josh shot back. "She'd knock *you* out cold, right on your big butt. You wouldn't get a chance to even *bleed* on her."

Having heard the exchange from the restroom, Artie returned to the lockers and walked over to Josh and Brett's bench. "That's enough," Artie said. "You two need to be nicer to your offensive linemen." He glanced over at Waters. "Right, Phil?" said Artie, before turning back to face the two 10th graders. "We're the only real protection that you boys in the backfield have."

Josh sneered. "Yeah?" he said. "Well, tomorrow night you boys won't even have to block against Solid Rock's sorry defensive line. They suck. Me and Brett can outrun those boys if they get past our O-line."

"Think so?" asked Artie. "You might be surprised how good Solid Rock's defense is this year. I hear they got a new head coach who likes to blitz. And their outside linebacker—Jimmy Gore—he was second-string All-State last season." Artie pointed at Brett. "You're gonna have to block Jimmy tomorrow night if they run a red-dog blitz. Otherwise, your good buddy here might get more than his face rearranged. Jimmy was good last season, even though the rest of the team wasn't."

In full practice uniform, Ty Green walked up and slapped Artie on the back. "Better get dressed, Artie," said Ty. "Coach is on the warpath today for some reason. Besides, these two rookies are just gonna have to learn the hard way, right?"

Artie nodded, then headed toward his own locker across the room. "Yeah, I guess," he agreed. "So let's get out there and have a good practice today. Coach is probably worried about Jimmy, too—and how we're gonna handle that new coach's red dogs."

"Red dog, *shmed* dog," said Josh. "We can take care of Jimmy Gore. Right, Brett? ... Brett?" But Brett Woods had slipped off to the restroom, leaving Josh Stark to fend for himself. "Oh, whatever," said Josh. "Coach will know what to do about Gore."

As it turned out, Coach Jug Johnson was upset about a number of things—including the numbers on his players' jerseys. Josh Stark, as first-string quarterback, had asked for No. 13, because that was the number of Miami Dolphins QB Dan Marino, Josh's hero in the professional ranks. But Jug didn't want his own quarterback to wear what he thought was an unlucky number, and so he had turned that request down flat.

Then Josh asked for the No. 3 jersey, which the late Reuben Russo had worn all three of his varsity seasons, the last two as a starter. Jug didn't go for that, either, as he knew that Reuben's uniform and the No. 3 would both be retired at homecoming later that season when the stadium was to be rededicated. So that left Josh's third favorite number—1—which Josh said was okay since he was as the team's "number one player." Jug didn't especially agree with Josh's reasoning but also didn't argue with him when he handed out the white, visiting-team jerseys at that Thursday practice.

Artie had always worn No. 55, and no one—not even Brett Woods—had the nerve to ask for it. Besides, Brett wanted Ty Green's old jersey, which was No. 19. Ordinarily, Ty would have had first pick as a senior, but Brett was insistent and did everything short of holding his breath and stamping his feet to get his way. No. 19 had been his father's number at Mimosa Beach High back in the early 1970s, and Brett—both on the football field and as a surfer—was following in his dad's footsteps.

Brett's family owned and operated Woody's Surf Shop & Grill, with three locations in Oleander County—at Mimosa Beach, in downtown Iron Harbor near the A&M campus, and at the local Sandpiper Beach near Monk's Landing. Unlike his son, Woody Woods was a nice guy whom everyone liked. He looked and dressed like an old surfer but with short hair. He was generous to a fault and rarely refused the requests of Arbor High coaches, who often took their teams to Woody's grill at Sandpiper Beach for pregame meals and postseason banquets.

So Jug said "yes" to Brett's uniform choice. Ty was handed the No. 17 jersey, which he could wear either at tight end or quarterback. As a team player, he didn't complain. But as it happened, 17 was the number of Ty Green's favorite NFL quarterback and Super Bowl MVP from his childhood, Washington's Doug Williams. That coincidence satisfied Ty Green.

Football jerseys weren't Coach Johnson's only concern that Thursday. He had been told about the dust-up at lunch involving Nicie Evans, and he knew that several players—not just Phil Waters—had been standing nearby when Bennie Pressler's drink was poured over his food and when Nicie objected to being splashed.

"You know, boys," Jug began, "if you get into trouble for doing something stupid in the lunchroom, you might have to sit out a game or two—and that's even if you *don't* get suspended from school. And that includes in-school suspension. Anybody who gets written up ain't gonna practice that day and ain't gonna play on Friday night."

"Come on now, Coach," said Josh. "You mean we can't play even if we get in trouble on a Monday and only miss one practice?"

Jug eyed his quarterback suspiciously. "Sounds like you got plans to misbehave," said the coach. "You'd better cancel those plans. We need everybody pulling together on this team, even tomorrow night against Solid Rock. They got a boy—a linebacker—who will clean your clock if you ain't careful."

Jug continued, "That's what we're gonna do today—run through some blocking schemes to teach you boys how to pick up the red-dog blitz. We don't have to hit to do that. And I want us to run through our new trick play again, too. What did we decide to call it?"

"The Reuben," shouted Leah from her seat in the bleachers. She had been busy recording each player's number on the official team roster for Jug to give to the officials at Friday's game in E-ville. She had also heard his advice about hazing and pulling together, and she knew it was only a matter of time before certain team members forgot their coach's warnings.

With the shorter, lighter practice the day before their game, the Bruins finished up around the same time that the flag-footballers called it quits. As a result, both sets of players ended up at the water hoses at the same time before heading to their respective locker rooms. Again, Artie and Ty hung back to let their team-mates and the 9th graders drink first.

As usual, Josh and Brett pushed to the fronts of the two lines to make every-one else wait for water, even Bennie Pressler, who was all set to take his first, long-awaited sip. Just as he lifted the green hose to his lips, the water stopped abruptly. But when Bennie turned up the hose to inspect the nozzle end, a geyser spewed out into his face. He threw down the hose and reached to wipe his eyes with his shirttail.

"What a dork," Josh Stark said with a laugh, his foot poised above the hose that Bennie had tried to use. "Go ahead, Pressler. Take another drink—if you can. I'll wait."

Artie stepped forward. "That's enough, Josh. Leave him alone—and go to the back of the line." This time Artie wasn't smiling.

Josh held his ground. "Yeah? Says who?"

"Says me," replied Artie. "You can either go to the back of the line, or we can take this up with Coach Johnson. He just got through telling us to quit picking on people and to act like we're all on the same team."

Josh snorted. "Pressler isn't a football player," he said. "He can't even stand up. *Can* you, Pressler?"

For a few seconds, Bennie tried to rise from the wheelchair but didn't have the strength to do more than struggle with the armrests. "I may be physically dis-abled now," Bennie began, "but at least my problem isn't mental—and it's only temporary. When I'm up and walking, you're still gonna be a jerk."

"Yeah, well, we'll see about that, crip," said Josh, bending down to pick up the bubbling hose that Bennie had dropped. But when he lifted it, the water stopped again.

This time it was Artie who stood on the hose. "Unless you're ready to fight," began Artie to Josh, "you need to go to the back of the line, like I said. So what's it gonna be? We can have it out, and then both of us sit out tomorrow night; or we can play ball. You know what that means, don't you? That's what your dad told my grandpa yesterday—that we 'play ball' together."

Artie wasn't sure how much Josh knew about his family's real estate business, but Stark Realty's offer the previous day had weighed heavily on Artie's young mind ever since Grandpa told him about Joel Stark's quip about buying their farm. It turned out that Josh knew more about his father's dealings than Artie expected.

"Dad offered way too much for that dump you call a farm," Josh said with a sneer as he moved away. "Your old granddaddy had better take the offer, if he knows what's good for all you hicks out there in the sticks. Besides, there's nothing but rundown sharecroppers' shacks and useless swampland out there. You can either sell it, or we'll take it."

With that, Artie started for Josh. But Ty Green got to him—to Josh Stark—first. Ty spun Josh around and grabbed him up by the front of his jersey. "No, Artie," Ty said, still glaring at Josh. "You need to play tomorrow night, but I don't. All of us sharecroppers who live out in the county—like me and Phil and Smitty—we already have our forty acres and a mule to make our livings, or our daddies do, anyway. We don't need to play football—or work so hard *blocking* for young Josh here. Right, boys?"

Like Artie, seniors Phil Waters and Johnny Smith were starting offensive linemen who had protected Reuben Russo for two years. And this year at tight end, Ty Green would also do his share of blocking to protect Josh Stark or whoever held the football in the backfield. Phil and Smitty just stared at Josh without answering, but he got the message—for the moment—and took off walking toward the locker room without running his mouth further.

Later, on their way home in Ty's LTD, Artie thanked his friend for sticking up for him. "Yeah, I *do* need to play every Friday night," Artie said, "if I'm gonna get a scholarship offer in football. But you do, too, Ty. I mean, you're a good basketball player, and you're a *great* pitcher, but around here the football team gets the most attention. You're good enough to play next year with me at A&M, at tight end *or* at quarterback, if that's where we go."

"Dang it!" Ty said, popping the steering wheel with the flat of his hand. "This was *my* year to start. Darn that rich little jerk—*and* his daddy. He stopped at *our* house last week and made my mama and daddy an offer, too. And they *might* just take it. Mama doesn't want to sell, even though she wouldn't have to keep working at the hospital in E-ville. But Daddy's tired of having to drive into Iron Harbor for work every day."

"Was it a good offer?" asked Artie. "I mean, will you guys be okay if your folks sell to them? Do you have somewhere else to live?"

"Yeah," said Ty, "we'll be moving into the Four Seasons soon. I think the first one's called *winter*."

"No, really," Artie said. "Where would you stay? Am I gonna need to find another way to get home from practice every day?"

Ty glanced at his passenger, then back to the road ahead. "Is *that* all I am—a ride home?" he said, but smiled. "No, don't worry, bud. We ain't going nowhere, not unless my daddy learns how to squeeze blood out of a turnip, anyway. I heard him say Stark is gonna have to come up with a lot more money than he offered us before *we* sell. Daddy found out what he offered some white neighbors for *their* farms, and it was considerably more than what he offered us.

"So," Ty continued, "tell me about this new girl who sat at your lunch table today—Nicie Evans, I mean, from Mimosa Beach High. I heard she's *fine*, but feisty—and a good ballplayer, too. Course, that's how I like my women—fine and feisty."

"You already have a girlfriend," Artie said, laughing, "and Felisha's pretty fine, too."

"Oh," said Ty, "that's why they call me Mr. Love 'Em and Leave 'Em." He signaled to turn off the highway onto the dirt lane to the Bauer farm, and waved as they passed Grandpa Bauer on his tractor cutting hay in a nearby field. "Your granddaddy is a good fellow," Ty said. "I bet he was a love 'em and leave 'em kinda guy, too."

Artie laughed again. "Well, if you mess around and leave *this* girl," he said, "she's liable to break something other than just your heart. She's one tough girl. I mean, she's already talking about organizing a Barf Table revolt, and this was her first day."

"No offense, Artie, but the Barf Table is already revolting," said Ty, reaching across to punch Artie's shoulder. "Get it?"

"I got it," said Artie. "Now, watch where you're driving, buddy, and keep both hands on the wheel, or you might run us into the ditch. Grandpa had a man come out here the other day with a backhoe and clean them all out. The shoulder isn't quite packed down yet."

"I'm being careful," Ty said. "I wouldn't do *anything* to damage this beautiful car of mine. Forget all those women. The White Whale is my true love." He was quiet for a moment. "But just to be on the safe side," he added, "I might come sit with you folks at the Barf Table tomorrow, and introduce myself to this fine-looking new friend of yours—give her a proper welcome to Arbor High. I just need to have a little talk with Felisha first. I'm *not* a cheater."

Ty pulled up in front of the farmhouse and watched as Artie rolled out of the car. "Okay, well, I'll see you tomorrow, Romeo," said Artie, as he got out. "Thanks for the ride. Be careful how you break up with Felisha tonight. Isn't she in the Health Occupations Club? I mean, if you go out with Nicie Evans and screw up too bad, you might need a good nurse." Ty winced.

With a wink, Artie pushed the car door shut, threw up his hand and walked along the flower-lined path through the backyard to the screened-in porch where Grandpa liked to sit and rest when he wasn't working. Today Grandma was sitting there instead, breaking green beans to be canned the next day. Her hair, like Grandpa's, was gray, but it had the faintest tinge of blue dye from her monthly visits to the hairdresser in Ebenezerville.

Grandpa's hair—thick for his age but cut short every two weeks by his old E-ville barber—was mostly gray but had light patches and dark guard hairs, like the coat of a police dog. He kept his head covered by a railroad cap when he was working in the sun. He'd always had a nice head of hair. In their youth, it was what had attracted Grandma to him, she always told Artie.

"Artie, did you see your grandpa out there when you boys were driving in?" Grandma asked. She was always concerned about her husband of almost fifty years, even more so than she was about herself. "Was he okay? He's been out there a long time."

"Yes, Grandma," said Artie. "He was cutting hay in the field near the high-way. You want me to take him some water—or some lemonade, maybe? I could use some, too."

"No," she said, "I want you to take the truck back out there and tell him it's quitting time. He doesn't need to work from sunup to sundown. Besides, it's almost suppertime."

Artie studied her for a second as she laid aside her pot of broken beans and struggled a bit to rise from her chair. "What about you, Grandma?" he asked. "How are you feeling today?"

"I'm just fine," she said stubbornly. "You and your grandpa would make me stay in bed all the live-long day, if it were up to you two. If I take my pill every morning, I feel fine. I just forgot to take it yesterday, and my blood pressure shot up on me. That was all."

Artie nodded. He knew there was no point in arguing with his grandmother, either about her health or about him calling Grandpa in from the hayfield. Artie followed Grandma from the porch into the big farmhouse kitchen and took the pickup truck key from the hook over the sink near the door—not the kitchen sink, but the small lavatory that Grandpa, Artie and farmhands used when they came in from the fields. The twin-bowl kitchen sink was Grandma's singular domain. No one else dared smudge the sparkling-white, porcelain basins or their gleaming silver fixtures. They did so at their own risks, because in her youth Grandma had been a fine and feisty gal herself and still was on her better days.

"What we having for supper tonight, Grandma?" asked Artie, not recognizing the steamy aromas rising from covered pots on the stove.

"You'll see in a few minutes," she said. "Now you drive out to the hayfield and tell Harry to come in. And if you don't find him out there, look across the road at the old homeplace. Harry spends too much time over there. I'm afraid he's gonna get hit crossing the highway one of these days, or he might fall into the old well in the yard. His eyesight isn't what it used to be."

Artie nodded again. "I know, Grandma," he said. "The shape that old house is in, it's hard to believe anybody ever lived there. It doesn't even have running water or a bathroom."

"Oh," said Grandma, "it's got a *bathroom*, all right—a slop jar in every bedroom and an outhouse out the back door, or used to be out back, anyway. I don't want Harry to fall into *that*, either. At least, I don't want to have to help clean him up."

She continued, "That's where we spent our wedding night, you know. We lived there with his folks until this house was built. The barn and the chicken house was already here. Boy, were they ever glad to see us move out, and I was glad, too, to be honest. Two women in one kitchen ain't gonna work, not one bit. And his mama was particular about how she wanted things done in her kitchen. Well, I'm particular, too. Now, you get on out there, Arthur, and bring your grandpa in for supper. Anything he ain't finished can be put off until tomorrow."

She added, "The only other thing on Harry's schedule tomorrow is to take me to that ball game of yours in E-ville. We want to see you play every Friday night since it's your last year at Arbor. Now, get a move on."

"Yes, ma'am," said Artie. He was glad that his grandparents were planning to attend his football games that fall, because neither one of them had seen him in uniform on the field since his freshman year. Coach Johnson had moved him up to varsity from the intramural flag football team for the last game of the season—the big game with rival Solid Rock Academy—but then had used him for only one play, the *last* play of the game when all Artie had to do was snap the ball to Reuben Russo, who took a knee. Neither Arbor nor Solid Rock went to the playoffs that year, so that game and Artie's forty seconds on the field were meaningless.

Jug had thought he was doing Artie a favor by giving the 9th grader *any* playing time, but Grandpa had taken it as a slight and had never forgiven Jug for not playing Artie earlier in the game. Grandpa had also not appreciated having his own time wasted and had sworn not to attend another game until Jug was no longer the coach. Artie was happy and a bit surprised that Grandpa had changed his mind.

When Artie drove out to the highway, he saw that Grandpa had, in fact, stopped cutting hay. Grandpa had left the tractor in the field and had walked across the two-lane highway to the old homeplace. It sat back in the trees with a cornfield on one side and an apple orchard on the other. Looking both ways, Artie pulled across the main road into the dirt driveway on the other side. He drove the truck up the thirty yards of the sandy lane and parked next to the spooky-looking, unpainted house covered in vines and broken branches from the old oaks that shaded it from the late-summer sun.

Rolling down the passenger-side window, Artie called out for his grandfather and waited. Just as he got set to yell again, Harry Bauer appeared from around back. Buckling the shoulder straps of his overalls, Grandpa waved and headed toward the truck.

"I had to see a man about a dog," Grandpa said. "Well, not a dog, really. More like a big racehorse than a dog. That durn highway is getting so busy that a man can't relieve himself in his own field anymore, you know?"

Artie chuckled. "I know, Grandpa. Come on and get in, and I'll give you a ride back to the tractor. Grandma has supper on the table by now, and she's ready to eat, I think."

"Well, that's a good thing," said Grandpa. "She has her appetite back. I'm glad about that, and I'm hungry myself. Let's go. I'll finish cutting the hayfield tomorrow."

There was still an hour of sunlight left that day, but the Bauers spent it enjoying the pork roast and vegetables and especially the apple pie that Grandma had fixed for her men. And then, while she washed the dishes and pots and pans, Artie and his grandpa retired to the porch, where they talked about farming and football, and watched the sun set on the western horizon.

CHAPTER 7 – Fishy Football Friday

AS SOON AS THE RELEASE BELL RANG, crunchy ends of fish sticks rained down upon freshmen tables in the cafeteria like a biblical plague. Most upperclassmen would have thrown whole fish sticks if the crusty, four-inch-long treats hadn't been a favorite lunch entree dipped in ketchup. Many seniors, though, saved one stick to use in playing Fish Jenga as they passed the Barf Table on their way to the garbage bins and tray return. The stack of fish sticks rose and rose in front of Bennie Pressler until it toppled and spilled into his lap with help from the last senior in line, as had happened the two previous days.

Newcomer Nicie Evans, who the day before had promised to be a Barf Table activist, had left before the fishy shower began. As predicted, Ty Green had joined Artie at the table in order to be introduced to Nicie, and the pair had become fast friends, slipping out together even before the release bell rang. Old Mr. Carson, whose classroom door was closest down the hall to the cafeteria, was supposed to spend his lunch hour making sure that no one left early; however, he liked smoking next to the windows at the back of his room and, therefore, missed many kids who left right before the release bell. That day, as it happened, Principal Church himself had noticed Ty and Nicie leaving together, but had elected not to intervene, knowing that her absence for Fish Jenga at the Barf Table would be a good thing. In his job, looking the other way was sometimes better than enforcing school rules to the letter—or so it seemed most days.

Leah, too, had already left before the excitement began. She and Nicie had gotten along well enough, though they hadn't interacted much. Like most everyone in Oleander County, Nicie remembered Reuben Russo and felt bad that Leah had lost her big brother. Principal Church used to put it another way—that Reuben's death had "created a vacuum of leadership within the Arbor family" the previous winter and spring. But a new year had arrived with a new senior class, and its leaders wanted to have a good time again at lunch, just not at Leah Russo's expense.

On the other hand, Bennie once again bore the brunt of the upperclassmen's worst hazing and now found little to joke about. "You don't have to keep putting up with this," said Bennie's friend and helper, Tommy White, as the disabled boy brushed fish sticks from his lap. "Your dad could make one phone call and put a stop to it if you'd just tell him what's happening. The other day you said it was about respect. Well, Mr. Church would respect what *your* father has to say."

Tommy turned to the Barf Table's senior member. "Isn't that right, Artie?"

"I guess so," said Artie, "but it would mean more to the older kids if Bennie stood up for himself and didn't get his father to do his fighting."

"*Ba-dump BUMP!*" blurted Bennie, imitating a snare-drum rimshot. "You're too funny, big guy. Me, stand up?"

Artie shook his head. "You know I didn't mean it that way," he apologized. "Besides, you said yourself that your chair is temporary—that you're working on walking again. Right?"

"Yeah, Bennie," said Tommy. "But we don't even have to sit here *now*. We could sit at a different table that isn't Ground Zero for those jerks." This time he turned to Ricky Duran, who was always quiet. "Ricky, what do you do when people keep picking on you?"

The small boy looked up from his food. "I don't do anything," he said softly. "I *can't* do anything. It would hurt my family."

Artie's eyebrows rose. "How?" he asked. "Would you get deported?"

"No," said Ricky. "I'm an American—because my father is an American. He met my mother in Guatemala. We lived there until he lost his job. Then we moved here—when my father found a new job. He grows trees for the paper company."

"So, it's your mother who could get deported," said Artie. "Does she have a green card? Is that what it's called?"

"Yes," said Ricky. "She wants to be an American—like Father and me—but it's hard."

"Does she work?" asked Artie.

"She cleans houses, at the beach," Ricky said, without elaboration. "She likes to cook, too, but her English isn't good—not yet."

Bennie Pressler could have gotten his father—or his mother—to call Jerry Church and make him punish the older students for hazing. That's how influential the Pressler family was in Oleander County. But, more than anything, Bennie wanted to be liked at school, respected even, and he agreed with Artie that he'd have to fight his own battles. If nothing else, he would learn who his real friends were and who merely liked him for his family's wealth.

The disabled boy thought for a few seconds before announcing, "I'm with Nicie Evans." He looked from one face to the next, but got no response, not even from Artie. "I'm talking about her saying we should fight back," Bennie explained. "Maybe I can't do it by myself, but we're a team now, right? And teamwork wins every time, right?"

Artie smiled at Bennie's spunk, but Ricky and even Tommy appeared concerned. "I can understand why you need to be careful, Ricky," said Artie, "but, Tommy, what's going on with you? Would you get in trouble with your folks at home?"

Bennie spoke up. "His parents aren't *at* home. Right, Tommy?" When Tommy remained silent, Bennie continued, "He's staying with us—for a while, anyway."

"Really?" asked Artie. "For how long?"

Tommy still didn't want to answer. But a mischievous look appeared in his eyes. "Oh, I don't know," Tommy said. "Ten to twenty years, according to the judge—maybe sooner, with good behavior."

"*Ba-dump BUMP!*" blurted Bennie again. "Hey! What're you trying to do, buddy—cut in on my routine?" He patted his friend and helper on the shoulder.

"You're an *honorary* Pressler," he added, "even if you are taller and blonder and don't like lox and bagels on Sunday morning."

Ricky still seemed confused about how serious his tablemates were. Artie turned back to him. "Get used to all the big talk, little buddy," Artie said, shaking his head and chuckling a bit. "I think the Barf Table is in for a long year."

"One day at a time," said Bennie. "Let's see now. We got Krakatoa Tuesday, Waisin Wednesday, Thirsty Thursday and Fishy Friday. So what's Monday gonna be, Artie? I'm afraid to guess. Tommy? Ricky? Do you guys know?"

Ricky nodded and shrugged. "I heard we have soup on Monday," he said, "and some kind of sandwich—maybe a cheese sandwich?"

"Yeah," Tommy said, "I heard that the seniors do something weird with sandwiches on Mondays. And somebody said that the cafeteria doesn't serve meat on Mondays—that they're trying to turn us all into vegetarians or something."

This time it was Artie's turn to remain silent. He listened with amusement, as he knew what lay ahead. At least no one would get wet for a change. It wasn't the soup that Bennie and the others would have to worry so much about. He knew, though, that if he told them what to expect, then Bennie, at least, would hatch a plan to retaliate that might make the situation worse.

"Don't worry about it now, guys," Artie said finally. "I know what we can do to protect you three, because nobody's gonna mess with Nicie or Leah or me—not Ty, either, if he's still sitting here." That seemed to placate Bennie.

"Besides," added Artie, "we have a game to worry about tonight. You guys coming?" He looked around the table.

"We wouldn't miss it," said Bennie. "Dad is driving Tommy and me to Solid Rock." He looked at Ricky. "Hey, buddy," Bennie said. "Are you going? Do you need a ride? You can come with us, if your folks will let you."

Ricky shook his head sadly. "No," he said. "I have to do something tonight." His eyes turned toward Artie. "But I will listen to the game on the radio, and I will root for you to be the hero of the game, my friend."

Artie smiled and patted Ricky on the arm. "Thanks, little guy," he said. "Maybe you'll be able to come to our home games. And I appreciate the good thoughts. But I'm never the big hero on the football field. I'm just an offensive lineman."

Bennie leaned forward. "Oh," he said, "now don't be so hard on yourself, big fella. You aren't *that* offensive." He struggled to keep a straight face.

"*Ba-domp bomp* … right?" said Ricky, with a shy grin. "Artie *is* the hero—of *this* team."

The bell rang ending lunch. Artie just smiled again and waved goodbye to his friends, as all but Bennie rose to go to fourth period.

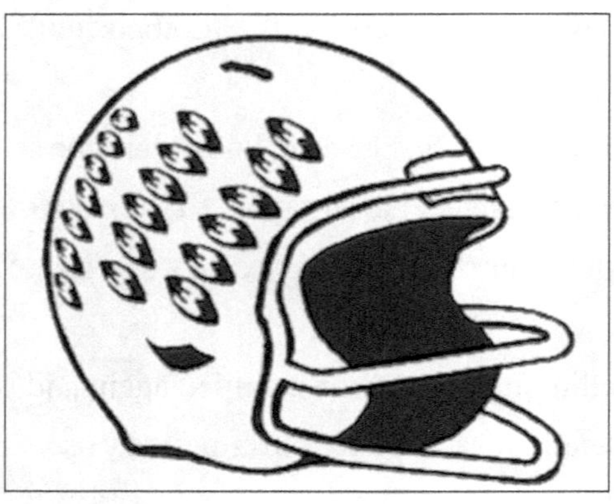

CHAPTER 8 – Game Day Afternoon

AFTER 4TH PERIOD THAT FRIDAY, students had fifteen minutes to go to their lockers, then hurry to the gym for the first pep rally of the season. The Bruin marching band—actually, more of a standing-around pep band in matching AHS T-shirts—was already there, playing the Arbor High Fight Song over and over at one end of the bleachers. The School Spirit Squad assembled at the opposite end of the gym and sang along with the band. They chanted, "Go, Bruins, go! Go, Bruins, go! Beat Solid Rock! Go! Fight! Win!" while the rest of the student body took seats in the stands by grade level. As it was Friday—the end of the week— some students wanted to slip out early, but several teachers and both assistant principals watched the exits.

Facing the crowd, the jersey-clad football players stood on the basketball court behind five chairs that sat across the center jump circle. Three seats were already occupied by Principal Jerry Church, Coach Jug Johnson, and AHS Spirit Squad advisor and cheerleading coach Thelma Hopper. Team co-captains Artie Bauer and Ty Green mingled with their teammates and did not sit down in the two empty chairs at center court until Mr. Church ambled over to the microphone that stood at the edge of the jump circle nearest the students.

"Quiet!" shouted Mr. Church, while fiddling with the mic. "Quiet, please! If I can have your attention for a few seconds, we'll get started." Though the din in the stands subsided only a bit, he continued, "Here's someone who needs no introduction—our great football coach, a local legend on the gridiron, wrestling mat and baseball diamond, Coach Jug Johnson! Let's all give him a big hand as he steps up here for a few words!"

Jug rose to shake the principal's hand as they passed one another. He tapped on the microphone to make sure it was "on," cleared his throat twice, and finally leaned in to speak, his lips almost touching the mic. "Howdy, folks," Jug said in his gravelliest voice. The kids shouted "howdy" back at him before he went on.

"I sure do hope all of you can come see us play tonight," Jug croaked. "All these boys behind me have been working hard in the hot sun for the past month to do Arbor High proud on the football field this season. We got some really big doings coming up later on—you know, at homecoming and all—but we want to start things off right tonight in E-ville against Solid Rock."

He paused for a few seconds as the students cheered again. "As you all know," he continued, "we lost a great player last year. Reuben Russo—God rest his soul—did a lot to put us on the right path, and so we're dedicating this season to him. We even got a special play worked up to remember him by. Now, the boys don't know this yet, but Miss Thelma Hopper here and the Booster Club parents has found a way for us to recognize Reuben and to reward our boys for setting an example of what made Reuben such a fine young man both on and off the field." Jug led the students in clapping respectfully.

He reached into his back pocket and pulled out a folded sheet bearing rows of small green-and-gold stickers shaped like footballs and bearing Reuben Russo's No. 3. "Starting tonight and after every game," Jug said, "the coaches and I will award stickers to players who have done Reuben Russo's memory proud on the field or in the classroom or in this fine community of Monk's Landing and Oleander County. After tonight's ballgame, you'll see more and more of these stickers on the boys' helmets right on to the last game of the season against Solid Rock … WHEN WE WIN … THE SUNCOAST CONFERENCE … COUNTY CHAMPIONSHIP!"

At that, the kids were back on their feet, with their fists in the air and their voices shaking the walls of the small gym. The band broke into the fight song again, as Jug waved Artie and Ty up to the microphone. "Get up here, boys," Jug said and turned back to the crowd. "Folks, these two young men are our captains this year. You all know Artie Bauer and Ty Green. They have a few words about tonight's game, and then they can introduce the seniors on our team. Give 'em a big Bruins welcome."

The band played the fight song one more time. The cheerleaders and spirit squad waved their pom poms and cheered. The students roared as their football co-captains waited for a break in the wall of sound. "How's it going, guys?" Ty Green managed first, sending the crowd into another tizzy. He stepped back and let Artie greet their schoolmates.

Artie leaned toward the mic. "Hi, I'm Artie Bauer," he said, pausing as some seniors hooted at his shyness. Despite his humility, Artie had been one of the most popular boys at school since his sophomore year when Coach Johnson had helped bring out the big farm boy's all-around athletic prowess, first on the football field that fall, then on the baseball diamond that spring. Success in wrestling came later. But in his mind, Artie was still the flabby freshman who had been forced to sit at the Barf Table with other unpopular kids his 9th-grade year. And now he felt deep down inside that the only thing between him being the big man on campus and being the fat boy who got no respect again was continued success on the field. Everybody loved a winner, even if it was just one player who reaped individual glory, not the team as a whole.

Artie used that situation as motivation to do his best every time he took the field or went to the mat in his sports, but he also believed that peak performance for him—especially as the center on the Arbor High football team and as the catcher on the Bruins baseball team—meant helping his teammates succeed. He knew he was responsible for helping more players than just the quarterback in football and the pitchers in baseball. In both of those sports, play on the field started with him, whether it was snapping the football or calling the right pitch.

Coach Johnson had pounded that philosophy into Artie's head—team before self—but the boy had already learned the necessity of teamwork from working on the farm with his grandfather. Grandpa, too, was a team player, especially when he left his tractor in the toolshed and walked behind the old plow pulled by his team of workhorses, Tom and Dick. Old Harry Bauer was a standout in every field, except when the corn was tall.

After Artie and Ty introduced the other seniors and pledged that every Bruin would "give 110 percent" on the football field that night in Ebenezerville, the band played the fight song yet again and the cheerleaders danced and cheered some more to pick a class to keep the Spirit Stick until the next week's pep rally. As usual, the senior class won, with the juniors and sophomores coming in a close second and third, respectively. The lowly freshmen cheered the loudest but still finished dead last. The pep rally ended at four o'clock when Jug Johnson got the team on the activity bus and hauled them over to Woody's for their pregame meal.

CHAPTER 9 – On the Road to E-ville

THE TEAM BUS RIDE to Sandpiper Beach was short and uneventful. No one but players and coaches—not even managers—were allowed to join in the pre-game meal or ride the long, green-and-gold activity bus to and from Woody's Surf Shop & Grill on the oceanfront. To Jug, this was a sacred time, and not just because Woody served up the tastiest barbecue ribs and pulled pork in Oleander County. This was when Coach Johnson wanted his boys to get their minds straight and form a bond with their teammates that would be unbreakable for the rest of the night. Jug would give his official pep talk after the meal, even if a particular week's game was farther away than E-ville and Woody had to pack boxes of pulled-pork sandwiches and sports drinks for them to consume on the bus.

Only Jug Johnson and the other coaches were allowed to talk from the time the bus pulled out of the Arbor High lot until it parked outside that night's field of battle, whether home or away. Then and only then were the players allowed to start talking, but only about the game that they were preparing to play—no talking about next week's game and looking past that night's opponent. The quickest way to get pulled from the lineup was for a starter to let a coach hear him say some-thing about any team other than the one they were playing that night.

"Now listen here, boys," Jug said to open his pep talk. "Solid Rock ain't gonna roll over for us tonight, not by a long shot. They may have been the weak-est team in the league last year, but that don't mean a thing now. Both them and us is looking to be 1-0 after tonight. We're both starting out fresh—them more so than us because they got a brand new coach."

Jug was standing at the head of one long row of tables in Woody's private dining room, where the Monk's Landing Chamber of Commerce met for breakfast each Wednesday morning. The assistant coaches remained seated around Jug but kept their eyes peeled for players who might not be paying attention. As co-captains, Artie and Ty sat facing each other at the end of the other long row of tables that had been pushed together. They, too, wanted to encourage the others to listen to the coach's speech, but the pair had heard all of Jug's pep talks at least twice, and so it was hard for them to look too inspired by his words.

"They're gonna be red-dogging us every chance they get," Jug continued, "and we need to protect our quarterback like he's got the key to Fort Knox in his back pocket. But we can do it. Yessir, we can. Ain't that right, boys?" When no one spoke—as they'd been told not to—the old coach looked over at Artie and Ty, and repeated, "Ain't that right?"

"Yes, sir," said the co-captains in unison.

"Now," Jug said, "we're gonna have to watch that Gore boy tonight, because he's one of the best linebackers in the state. He sacked Reuben twice last year and tackled our other backs for losses *three times*. You heard me, boys—*three times*. That's six plays he kept us from doing what we—"

"That's *five* plays, Coach," interrupted Josh Stark. The sophomore quarterback and his buddy Brett Woods were sitting side by side, their backs to Jug, halfway down Artie's row of tables. Josh leaned to one side and whispered to Brett. They both snickered.

The coach's eyes narrowed as he focused on his brash young signal caller. "Mr. Bauer, Mr. Green," Jug said, turning to address his captains. "Before we get back on the bus, please take Mr. Stark and Mr. Woods aside, and impress upon them the importance of *not* contradicting the coach, especially during the pregame pep talk."

"Yes, sir," Artie and Ty said in unison. Artie, sitting on the outside across from the two 10th graders, cut his eyes toward Josh. Artie saw him smirk, nudge Brett's elbow and laugh again. Hearing a soft tapping on the table in front of him, Artie looked back to see Ty shake his head softly as if to say, *Not now, Artie. Just let it slide.*

"As I was saying," Jug resumed, "we need to keep Jimmy Gore out of our backfield so we can establish our running game. Once we do that, it'll give us time to connect on some longer pass pl—"

"You mean, give *me* a chance to complete some passes," interrupted Josh once more, elbowing Brett and grinning again. "Isn't that what you mean, Coach?"

From the shade of red that Jug's face turned, Artie thought the angry coach's head might explode. But it didn't—not right then, anyway. Jug eyeballed Josh and frowned at Brett. Then he glanced up and saw Woody Woods, Brett's father, slide into the private dining room from the grill's main seating area outside. Woody waved affably at Jug.

"Yes, Mr. Stark," said Jug finally, "that's what I meant to say. But please don't interrupt me again. We don't want you to get strike three, if you know what I mean, not before your first game as a starter."

Josh Stark looked like he wanted to respond, but didn't. He kept quiet for a change. But the same annoying smirk stayed on his lips as he picked at the food left on his plate. With Woody in the room, Brett Woods knew better than to keep misbehaving, because the Arbor High Booster Club paid Woody a hefty sum for those pregame meals. Brett also didn't want to get into trouble with his father by embarrassing him in front of the whole team. Josh, however, was shameless.

Jug ended his pep talk by assuring the boys that if they lost that night's game to Solid Rock—or if they didn't win by at least two touchdowns—practice on Monday would be "pure H-E-double hockey sticks." The coach was known to let an actual cuss word slip on the sideline or in the locker room, but he was careful not to curse around administrators or parents.

Woody, who had earlier greeted the players and coaches by saying the blessing before their meal, stepped forward again and led the team in reciting the pledge of allegiance. In his younger days, Woody had answered an ad in the back of *Surfer* magazine, paid a few bucks, and was ordained as an official beach preacher. Later that night he would kneel on the sidelines with the team and lead them in the Lord's Prayer before they would stand for the Solid Rock marching band to play the National Anthem at the end of its pregame show. The Arbor High School Board of Trustees didn't mind mixing in a little bit of *church* with the large chunk of state funding for the charter school, as long as it wasn't an employee who led the prayers and devotions. A zealous parent was quite okay, especially one as rich as Woody Woods.

On their way out of the building, Artie and Ty buttonholed Josh and Brett in the surf shop and warned them again not to keep testing Coach Johnson's patience. "He'll bench you—yeah, even you," Ty told Josh. "Coach benched Reuben Russo—that's right, Reuben Russo—against Solid Rock two years ago, when Reuben was a junior. Well, he didn't start him, anyway. I ran the first series for us, and then Reuben took over for the rest of the game. But he didn't start."

Josh snorted. "I saw that game. My folks took me." He fiddled with the display of surfboard leashes on the aisle where the four boys stood. "You fumbled the snap on first down," Josh said, "you muffed the handoff on second down and got sacked, and then you came close to throwing a pick-six on third and long. Coach had no choice but to play Reuben that night. You stunk up the place then, and you'll do the same thing tonight if I don't play. Coach isn't gonna bench me, not for just having a little fun with him."

Artie stepped forward. "You don't know Coach like I do, Josh. He'll take a lot of guff off a good player—like he did off Reuben at first—but there's a limit to what he'll stand. And if he decides that you're hurting the team more than you're helping it, he'll make an example of you, just to keep everybody else in line."

"That's bull," said Josh. "If I don't play, we don't win. Coach found that out when he benched Reuben Russo and started this guy." He jerked his thumb at Ty. "You guys need me."

"*You guys?*" Ty said. "You act like you aren't part of the team. Well, I've got news for you, buddy. You ain't no Dan Marino, and even *he* needs good blockers and good receivers. Besides, I was just a sophomore back then, like you are now."

"Yeah?" said Josh. "Well, I'm not a drop-back passer like Marino. I can run if

I have to. Matter of fact, I'll bet you that I have more rushing yards tonight than anybody else on the team. I'm a scrambler."

Artie laughed. "If you try to run too much tonight, you'll *get* scrambled. Jimmy Gore will scramble you good. Your best bet is to let me and the O-line do the blocking, and then you either hand the ball off or throw it to Ty and his boys. That's how we'll win."

"What do you know, fat boy?" said Josh Stark. He turned to Brett Woods, who until now had stayed out of the fuss. "Come on, Brett. Let's go get a good seat on the bus."

Still looking at the surfboard leashes, Brett shook his head and said, "Nah, you go on. I need to tell Dad something before we leave. Save me a seat."

Josh gave him a funny look, then shrugged. "Whatever," he said, not sure why his friend wasn't sticking with him. Josh turned and strode out of the shop.

Brett finally looked up at his co-captains. "Sorry, guys," he said. "Josh shoots off his mouth and gets himself in trouble. He gets *everybody* in trouble some-times—like these leashes here. You know about that mess?"

Artie shook his head. "No. I know Josh surfs. But what kind of trouble did Josh cause with a surfboard leash?"

"See this one right here?" said Brett, taking up one end of a six-foot-long leash. "Look at this cuff. It doesn't hold half the time, but Josh pushed us to carry it because he was trying to get the company that makes it to sponsor him—you know, at surfing events."

Ty took the cuff from Brett to inspect it. "I think I know where you're going with this," Ty said. "Didn't a kid get hurt—hurt pretty bad—in a surfing contest that you guys held a while back? My mom—you know, she's a nurse at the hos-pital—she told me about it."

Brett nodded. "Yeah," he said, "and do you know who that kid was who got hurt?" He gave Ty a chance to shake his head before looking at Artie. "*You* know, don't you?"

"Just tell us," said Artie. "It must be someone we know. So who is it?"

Brett stood there in silence for several seconds, then shook his head. "I'm not allowed to say. The kid's family is suing us because of that leash, and Dad won't let us talk about it until the trial's over—if there *is* a trial. The leash company's lawyer is trying to work it all out. We're just kind of along for the ride."

"But you're still selling the bad leashes," Artie said. "Shouldn't you quit selling them?"

"I didn't say they're *bad leashes*," said Brett, "and if you tell anybody I said they are, I'll deny it." He frowned. "I've said too much as it is. Now, I need to go see Dad."

As Brett turned toward the counter where his father stood talking to Coach Johnson, Artie told Brett, "Don't worry, man. We're a team. We got you covered. That's how it is."

Brett Woods nodded without looking back.

* * *

Everyone was quiet, even the coaches, on the bus ride back to the school building. Solid Rock Academy's new head coach was an unknown quantity as far as his game plan for that night went. It was yet to be seen if Solid Rock, led by all-state linebacker Jimmy Gore, had figured out how to stop the Bruins' option plays. Also unproven was sophomore quarterback Josh Stark's ability to recognize the right option to take—to hand the ball off, to pass, or to run himself. As the intramural team's best signal caller the previous year, Josh had learned Jug's option offense and had handled it well. But funny things happen to players on Friday nights under the stadium lights, with the stands filled with fans. How brash young Josh Stark would react to Jimmy Gore patrolling the defensive line and blitzing when he had a chance was also unknown this early in the season. That's why the whole Bruin offensive unit—the O-line, the receivers, the backs—had to work together.

The activity bus pulled up to the front of the school where the team managers and new statistician were waiting. There were three managers, all boys, all wearing tan cargo shorts and gray Bruins Football T-shirts, and statistician Leah Russo, the only girl who would be on the bus. Her hair was pulled back into a tight ponytail pulled through the back of a white tennis cap. She wore jeans and her brother's No. 3 jersey that he had donned for road games. The jersey, oversized for such a slender girl, was satiny white with black numbers and green-and-gold piping and trim. In block letters, BRUINS adorned the front above the number, RUSSO the back. The four students waited for the bus door to open, mounted the steps and stood for a moment at the top, looking for open seats.

Artie and Ty occupied two separate seats, one in front of the other, about half-way back. Josh and Brett had commandeered the two back seats. Those spots—the otherwise unoccupied halves of the four bench seats—were the only places for Leah and the three managers to sit. Artie waved for Leah to join him. The senior manager—there was one from each grade level—sat with Ty, and the other managers trudged to the back of the bus, where they knew they would be easy targets for Josh and Brett's abuse. Ty rose and let the manager have the window seat. He wanted to sit next to Leah across the aisle so he could consult with her about Nicie, who needed as many friends as she could get. Ty was already thinking of Nicie as his girlfriend, even though they had just met that week. Talking still wasn't allowed on the bus, but Ty and Leah could pass notes.

The two-lane highway from Arbor High on the outskirts of Monk's Landing to Solid Rock Christian Academy in Ebenezerville passed through ten miles of farmland, five miles of swampland, over an estuarine tributary of the Oleander River, then through ten more miles of agricultural fields and scattered residential subdivisions, like the ones being developed by Stark Realty. The farms that Artie's and Ty's families owned sat off Ebenezerville Road in that general area but outside the Solid Rock attendance zone.

The bus ride to E-ville usually took about thirty minutes, but this afternoon the gods of Bruins football were not smiling on the team. Before the bus reached the swampland halfway to Solid Rock, Josh's obnoxious behavior became unbearable toward the two managers in the back seats with him and Brett. When Josh began berating the manager next to him, Jug rose from his front seat and turned to see what the commotion was about. Holding onto the chrome pole at the top of the bus stepwell, the coach spotted the source of the fussing and ordered Josh to the front.

"Stark!" Jug shouted over the bus engine's roar. "Get up here! Now!"

Josh stood but made no move toward the aisle. "What's that, Coach?" he said, cupping one hand at his ear. "You wanna review that stupid trick play with me again?" He cackled, even glancing at Leah, who, like everyone else, was turned around and watching Josh put on his show. He snickered for her benefit, adding, "What a stupid name—the Reuben."

Jug Johnson's face turned bright red again. "Boy," the coach bellowed, "if I have to come back there, you're gonna *wish* that's all we talked about. Now get your narrow butt up here so we can have a word of prayer."

"I can't," Josh called above the road noise. "It's against state law. Can't do that with the bus still moving."

"What?" said Jug. "Pray? Or walk up here?"

Everybody on the bus laughed, even though the coach hadn't meant his questions to be funny. That made Jug even angrier. "Stop the bus," he ordered the driver. "Pull over at the next farm road." Steaming, Jug sat back down and waited for the bus to cross the estuarine creek and pass through the remaining swampland. By the time they reached a farm road five miles up the highway, Jug's complexion was closer to its normal shade of pink.

Once the bus stopped, Jug rose again, pointed at Josh, and beckoned for him to come up the aisle and follow him out the door so that they could talk outside. But the obnoxious 10th grader had other ideas. Instead of following his coach out the front door, Josh popped open the emergency exit and tumbled out the back of the bus onto the sand, crushed shells and loose gravel of the farm road. Josh was picking himself up when Jug collared him and slammed the emergency door shut. Faces from the bus pressed up against every inch of the back windows to watch the confrontation.

"What's the matter with you, boy?" Jug shouted. The coach looked up and saw their audience. Taking Josh by the arm, Jug pulled the boy toward a shade tree at the corner across the lane where a battered mailbox stood. There was no farmhouse in sight, just one corn or soybean field after another for as far as the eye could see.

No one on the bus could hear what Jug was telling Josh, as the coach had managed to lower his voice. But Jug's gestures—like a tent preacher during altar call—let the team know that this was anything but an ordinary word of prayer. This was what Jug later called Josh's "come to Jesus" moment, which made what happened next even harder for everyone to believe.

Admonished—or so it seemed—Josh left Jug standing next to the mailbox and walked back toward the bus. His teammates rushed to the side windows and pushed their heads outside to whisper to Josh, some to ask if he was still playing that night, others to rib him quietly about getting in trouble. Artie, Ty and Leah did neither. They kept their seats and waited for Josh to reenter the bus and walk down the aisle past them. When he reached their seats, Josh stopped, stood there for a moment and checked to see where Coach Johnson was, then looked down at Leah, at the No. 3 jersey she wore, and scowled.

"If I can't wear that number," Josh said, "then a spoiled brat like you shouldn't either."

"What?" she said.

Josh shook his head in disgust. "What gives *you* the right? You aren't an athlete. You aren't even a cheerleader. You're just an anorexic little loser. You look stupid."

Leah didn't know how to respond. Artie was starting to rise, but Leah sat between him and Josh, the true brat. Ty, however, did not hesitate. He reached up and grabbed Josh by one shoulder and jerked him around so that they were face to face for the few moments that the senior needed to correct the brash sophomore.

"If I *ever*," Ty Green growled, "if I *ever* hear you say that again to her, I'll—"

"You'll what?" asked Coach Johnson, stepping up from the front door. "Sit down, Green. Leave him alone."

Ty turned to look at Jug, "But, Coach, he j—"

"I don't care what he did," Jug said. "Sit down. We got a game to play tonight."

"But, Coach…," said Ty again, taking his seat. He released Josh, who looked down and laughed again, this time at Ty.

The sophomore QB started to return to his back seat. That would have been the end of the matter, except that Leah finally decided on her own course of action. On Josh's first step down the aisle, Leah stuck out her lower leg and tripped him, sending him sprawling face-first onto the soiled walkway between the rows of seats. Coach Johnson jumped to the conclusion that Ty had thrown Josh down, and no one, not even the embarrassed sophomore himself, tried to correct the misconception. The players didn't want to get Leah into trouble for tripping the jerk, and Josh didn't want to admit that he'd been knocked down by a skinny girl. That wouldn't look good for him, not in the head coach's eyes, at least.

Jug shook his head at his starting tight end. "You just had to do that, didn't you, Green? Now you're gonna have to sit out tonight's game."

"But Coach," Ty said again. "He had it coming."

"I don't care," said Jug. "If it had been him, I'd be sitting *him* down tonight. As it is, he's still got two strikes. So he's gonna behave himself. Right, Stark?"

"Yessir, Coach," said Josh as he dusted himself off and started back toward his seat. No one but the players he passed could see his smug look, and they weren't about to tell on him. Josh Stark was used to getting his own way and never getting punished for misbehavior. That's how his parents had raised him, and they didn't care that he was a young man who would soon be responsible for his own words and deeds. No one on the bus figured that Josh's comeuppance was waiting for him that night in E-ville.

CHAPTER 10 – Friday Night Lights

ONCE IT WAS CLEAR that Jug Johnson wasn't going to relent on Ty Green's punishment for knocking down Josh Stark on the bus—or for *appearing* to do so against the coach's orders—the team's spirits sank. Ty was just one player, but he was a senior co-captain, the starting tight end on offense and strong-side linebacker on defense, and he was the team's backup QB for the third straight season, ready to fill in if anything happened to Josh during the game.

Every man and boy in the Arbor High bus knew that Solid Rock linebacker Jimmy Gore was the smartest, fastest and hardest-hitting defender in the Suncoast Conference, and that rookie Josh Stark—or whoever took the Bruins' snaps that night—was only one misstep from getting the most vicious lick of his career from Gore. Leah Russo knew that, as she had watched her brother take one hit after another from the Solid Rock all-stater last season. Rather than argue with the head coach on the bus, Artie decided to wait until they got to E-ville so that he could speak to Jug in private.

As it turned out, Artie never got the chance to plead Ty's case. No one thought too much about the ambulance—its red lights flashing and siren shrieking—that whooshed past the bus on the highway to E-ville. But when the bus parked outside Academy Field and Ty Green's mother was standing there waiting for them, they soon learned who had been in the ambulance and why it was rushing them to the nearest hospital.

At first, when Mrs. Green knocked on the bus door and asked to speak with Coach Johnson in private, Artie—and Jug, too—wondered how she could have learned so quickly about her son's one-game suspension.

"I didn't know you had a cell phone," Artie said to Ty, as Jug and Mrs. Green spoke quietly outside. In those days, cellular telephones—the early models that could handle talking and texting, certainly not digital smartphones that do everything—had become small enough and affordable enough for some students to carry. Even though cell phones weren't allowed in school, rich kids like Josh Stark and Brett Woods had their own phones; ordinary kids like Artie and Ty didn't and wouldn't have them, not even cheap ones, for a few more years.

"I don't have a phone," Ty said, leaning forward to talk around Leah. "I don't know *what* Mom's talking to Coach about—not about what just happened with Josh, I hope."

"Maybe Josh texted his folks," said Artie, "even though you didn't do anything. Maybe *they* called your mom." He looked at Leah. "You didn't call anybody, did you? Do *you* have a phone?"

"Well, yeah," she said, "but it wasn't me. Mom gave me her cell phone so I can call the neighbor I'm staying with to come pick me up when we get back to the school tonight. Mom said not to waste her minutes, so I haven't even turned it on yet." She shrugged. "Maybe Coach told somebody to call your mother, Ty— one of the other coaches, maybe."

But that wasn't it, either. Artie watched as Mrs. Green spoke calmly to Coach Johnson but with a worried look on her face. Now and then she glanced up toward the bus windows near where Ty, Leah and Artie sat. A minute later Jug gave her a serious nod, returned to the bus door and waited for the driver to open it for him. He mounted the steps and when he got to the top squinted halfway back toward his co-captains. "Yogi?" he said, having softened up enough to use Artie's nickname again. "You and Ty come up here. Bring whatever you have with you."

Ty led the way, with Artie having to wriggle past Leah to reach the aisle. "What's up, Coach?" Ty asked when he got to the front.

Jug held up his hand to silence Ty until Artie caught up. "You boys need to go with Mrs. Green. We'll get your equipment bags back to the school tonight. It would take too long to get them out from under the bus right now." He leaned back against the dash to let the boys pass.

But Ty stayed put, with Artie looking over his shoulder. "I don't understand, Coach," Ty said. "Why's my mom here? And what does Artie have to do with this? Did that little rat tell his parents that Artie and I *both* tripped him?" Ty's eyes blazed. He turned and would have gone for Josh then and there if Artie hadn't been standing in the way.

"No, hold on, Ty," the coach said. "This isn't about you—well, not really. Just get off the bus and you two go with your mama, and she'll explain everything." He hesitated, adding in a softer tone, "This is about Artie. Your mama's here to help out, Ty. And she and I need your help right now, too."

If the boys hadn't known their coach better, they might have sworn they saw gruff old Jug start to tear up. But he waved them past him and on down the steps, where Mrs. Green hurried the pair to her car. "Get in, guys," she said, opening the driver's door. "I'll explain on the way to the hospital. We need to hurry."

Ty sat up front with his mother; Artie sat alone in back, but he noticed how Rachel Green would glance up at him every few seconds in the rearview mirror. "Mrs. Green, is my grandma sick?" Artie asked before they were out of the stadium parking lot.

"No, Artie," she said, as she braked the car to a rolling stop at the highway and looked both ways before pulling out. She glanced up at her mirror again. "It's your grandfather."

Now Artie felt his own eyes suddenly well up and his throat tighten. "What's wrong with Grandpa?" he said. "Did he have a heart attack? Or a stroke?"

The woman shook her head, but Artie could see from the concern in her brown eyes that whatever had befallen his grandpa, 67-year-old Harry Bauer, was just as serious, if not more so. "First of all," she told Artie, "your grandpa is alive. He didn't have a heart attack or stroke."

She looked up at Artie again. "He had an accident on his tractor—broken bones, some burns and other injuries they're looking at. The EMTs brought him into the emergency room just as I was punching out. I waited to see how he was before I left. I knew then I couldn't go on home."

She paused for a second, then said, "You need to be there for your grandmother, Artie. She rode in the ambulance with Mr. Bauer, and she's scared. Ty and I will be there for you—for you both, actually, for you and your grandmother."

For all the thoughts in Artie's head, he couldn't put any of them into words. He didn't know what he'd do without his grandfather. And Artie knew that Grandma had to be even more frightened at the idea of losing this good man with whom she had shared her life for almost fifty years.

All Artie could say was, "Thank you, Ms. Rachel," using her given name but wanting to show her the respect she deserved. "And you, too, buddy," Artie added, leaning forward to put his hand on Ty's shoulder.

Ty patted Artie's hand and looked back at him. Artie saw no tears but fear in his buddy's eyes—fear for Grandpa Bauer, whom Ty had always admired; fear for best friend Artie, whose future hinged on this night in more ways than one; and, selfishly, for Ty himself, whose football career, at the very least, was now in serious jeopardy.

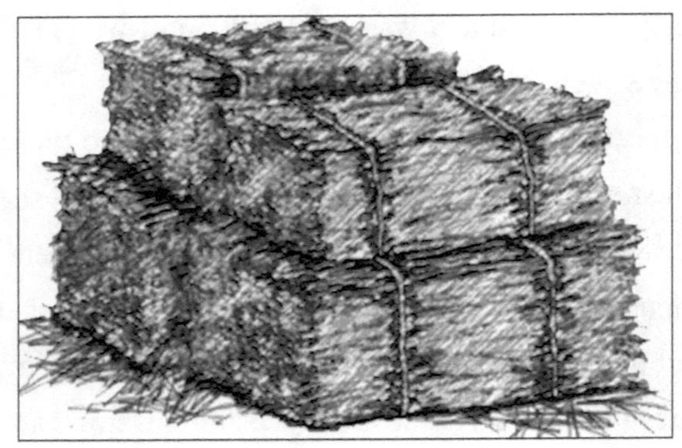

CHAPTER 11 – In a Different Light

MRS. GREEN PARKED across from the emergency room entrance. She bypassed the waiting room by leading the boys through the sliding doors that EMTs used to wheel patients inside from their ambulances. Being a nurse herself, she seemed to know exactly where Grandpa Bauer lay, but he had already been rushed into surgery. The brightly lit cubicle where he had received initial treatment was empty except for a tangled sheet and wads of bloody gauze on the padded bed and tiled floor.

"Stay right here," she told the boys and hurried off to find the ER supervisor. When she returned minutes later, she directed Artie and Ty to the surgical wing down the hall and around the corner, where Pearl Bauer sat in a special waiting room. Pausing outside the room to look in through the door's safety-glass window, they saw that Grandma waited there alone, seated in one of six thinly padded chairs along the side wall. A soda machine and a counter bearing a sink and coffeemaker stood on the opposite side of the room.

Rachel Green tapped three times on the glass before opening the door. "Mrs. Bauer?" she said softly. "I'm back with Artie. Ty's here, too."

Grandma's eyes looked more tired and worried than usual, Artie thought. He brushed past Mrs. Green and took a seat next to his grandmother, leaning closer to give her a hug. "Grandpa's tough," Artie said. "He'll be okay, Grandma."

The old woman tried to smile. "Poor Harry didn't look tough in the ambulance," she said. "He looked so, so scared, worser than I've ever seen him."

She turned to address Rachel Green, who had taken the chair on her other side. "Rachel, have they told you anything yet?" she asked. "The nurses come in here every so often, but all they say is that he's still in surgery."

"The surgical nurses here are good," said Rachel. "They'll give you some details as soon as they can, Miss Pearl, and they won't tell me anything they won't tell you. We just need to be patient. Let me make us a fresh pot of coffee." She rose and walked over to the counter, where she took the old pot and poured it out, and refilled the machine with new grounds and fresh water from the sink tap.

Ty had already wandered over to the drink machine and was checking out the selections, as if he wanted a soda. On game days, both Ty and Artie tried to drink plenty of water and sports drinks before kickoff so that they didn't cramp in the late summer heat under the stadium lights. Artie, in fact, had felt his thirst growing on the bus ride, but forgot about it completely after learning about Grandpa's predicament. Wanting a soda or anything else to drink—or to eat—was the last thing on Artie's mind.

"What happened, Grandma?" he asked.

Pearl Bauer looked up at her grandson and shook her head sadly. "I shouldn't have let him stay out so long," she said, "but you know how he is, Arthur. He wanted to finish cutting that hayfield this afternoon. He said he'd be back at the house in time to wash up and eat a quick supper before we rode over here to see you play." She put her face in her hands.

"It's not your fault, Grandma," said Artie, resting his hand on her shoulder. "But what *happened*? What happened with the tractor?"

"As best as I can figure," she said, "he finished cutting hay and then ran the tractor off into the ditch where he'd had that man work on the shoulder of the road the other day. I was sitting out on the porch, waiting for Harry to come home when I saw the neighbor boy—you know, the little one that's still at home—I saw him come running up the lane to the house, just screaming and yelling at the top of his lungs for me to call 9-1-1."

She paused again. "Well, I called the EMS," she continued, "and then I ran as fast as I could to where Harry was trapped under that tractor. I must've been a sight. It took me so long to get to Harry that the ambulance got there about the same time I did. The neighbor man and his boy had driven by and happened to see the tractor turned over. If they hadn't come by when they did, we wouldn't be here now." She started to cry again.

Artie knew exactly what she was implying—that Grandpa wouldn't be alive if he hadn't gotten immediate help and medical attention—but Artie didn't want to worry about what *might* have happened. He wanted to focus on what was happening right then and there.

* * *

The next three hours were excruciating for the small group of friends. At Rachel Green's suggestion, pairs of them took turns going to the hospital canteen for sandwiches and drinks from the vending machines there. Grandma didn't want to leave, but Rachel convinced her that they'd be gone only a few minutes, and that Artie and Ty would stay in the waiting room in case a nurse or doctor brought word from the operating room. Artie promised that if anyone came with news, he'd immediately go get Grandma.

Those assurances eased Pearl Bauer's mind enough to let her accompany Rachel to the vending area in the hospital basement, where the younger woman got them packaged sandwiches and canned drinks. Pearl had no money of her own, as she had hurried down the farm lane and into the ambulance with her injured husband without so much as a sweater, much less the huge handbag that she always held close when away from home.

Every thirty minutes or so, a nurse from the operating suite had entered the waiting room and had told Mrs. Bauer that the operation was progressing on schedule and that the surgeon was optimistic about Mr. Bauer's recovery. The nurse's last visit came just as Grandma was returning with Rachel from their second visit to the canteen. Her news was that Harry's surgery had ended and that he had been moved to the recovery room, where they would keep close watch on him for an hour or so while he came out of anesthesia. He would be moved to the intensive care unit, and, if conditions allowed, Pearl could go in to see him for a few minutes.

"He's doing fine, Mrs. Bauer," the nurse said again. "Maybe now is a good time for you to fill out some paperwork for us." The nurse turned to Rachel standing next to them and asked if she might accompany Grandma to the business office. "Or, Rachel, maybe you and Ty need to go on home and get some rest," the nurse added, knowing that her co-worker's own shift had ended six hours earlier and that she was scheduled to be back on duty in another six hours.

"No, no," Rachel said. "I'm just glad we're here to help Mrs. Bauer. I'll take her down to the office. All that paperwork can be confusing, and she doesn't even have her purse." As an afterthought, she asked, "Can you bring us Mr. Bauer's clothes? Maybe his billfold is in his pants, and we can get his insurance information from it. Can you do that for us while we're still here? Surely the hospital isn't in *that* big of a hurry to get paid."

The nurse smiled. "Well, not the hospital," she said, "but all the doctors have young new wives, you know." She winked, turned and left. A minute later she returned with a large white bag containing Grandpa's oil- and blood-stained overalls and work shirt, both of which had been cut off him by the EMTs and ER doctor, and a manilla envelope containing Grandpa's personal effects—his billfold, wristwatch, pocketknife and wedding band.

"We'll dispose of Mr. Bauer's undergarments," the nurse told Grandma, taking a paper and pen from the front pocket of her white nursing smock. "Now, Mrs. Bauer, if you'll please sign this form saying I'm giving you Mr. Bauer's things."

Grandma took the pen and signed the form in a shaky hand, then gave both back to the nurse before taking the clothes and envelope from her. The overalls, in particular, reeked of oil that had leaked from the overturned tractor's engine. "Is Harry burned bad?" Grandma asked the nurse. "That oil must have been scalding hot. He cusses every time he has to change the oil on that old tractor, 'cause he always burns hisself."

"Yes, ma'am," the nurse said. "The surgery was to fix the broken bones and other internal injuries. But, yes, Mr. Bauer did suffer some severe burns, too. The surgeon will come talk to you about that before you leave."

"I'm not going *anywhere*," Grandma said. "I'm gonna stay right here in this hospital until I see my Harry and know that *he* knows he ain't alone." She started to tear up again, and Rachel took her arm to hold her steady. "He's probably scared half to death," said Grandma, "waking up in a strange place with all these bright lights shining on him."

Rachel patted her arm. "No, Mrs. Bauer, he isn't alone. He has someone sitting with him right now, I'm sure. And we keep the lights in the ICU turned down low so that the patients can rest as much as possible. He'll be fine. But I'm sure he'll rest easier knowing you and Artie are here. I imagine he's already been told that." She looked at her colleague. "Right, Sarah?"

"That's right," the nurse said. "That was the first thing we told him when he woke up a few minutes ago. And he nodded his head when the anesthesiologist asked if he understood."

"Did he say anything?" Grandma asked.

The nurse shook her head. "No. He's very tired, and he'll be groggy from the anesthesia for several more hours. That was a long surgery for someone his age. But he'll be fine, I'm sure, once his bones have a chance to mend and his burns can heal. I can tell from looking at him that he's a strong man. He'll be back working on your farm before you know it."

Grandma nodded but didn't look too enthusiastic about her husband getting back on that tractor again. When it came to plowing, though, Harry could always rely on his workhorses Tom and Dick to pull a plow or any other farm implement. In all his years as a farmer, Harry Bauer had been slow to convert from the old ways of farming to modern methods, and he had kept all the old farm equipment ready to use, if necessary. He had even shown Artie how to rig and maintain the plow, harrow, baler and spreader.

Harry wasn't Amish by any means, but he had never liked spending money on modern equipment when the old ways were tried and true. So Grandma didn't have to worry about Grandpa using the tractor—but she did, anyhow. She also knew how stubborn he could be and that he might want to prove to everyone that his accident hadn't made him too frightened to get back on the tractor seat to work his fields.

* * *

With Rachel Green at her elbow, Grandma Bauer left Artie and Ty in the waiting room and moved slowly down the hall toward the business office to fill out Grandpa's paperwork. The two boys hadn't been alone long enough to settle on a TV channel to watch, when another quiet knock came at the door glass. They looked up and saw a handsome man with a dark, pencil-thin mustache and lighter soul patch framing his smile. He wore a tasteful green sweater and a green ball cap with AHS embroidered in gold thread on the front panel. Pushing the door open just enough to stick his head in, the man asked quietly, "Artie? I'm Abe Pressler—Bennie's father? Can I come in?"

Artie tossed the TV remote to Ty and stood to greet the richest man in Oleander County. "Why sure, Mr. Pressler," said Artie. "Please do. How can I help you?"

"I'll stay for just a minute," Pressler said, entering the room but making no move to take a seat. He removed his cap and studied the floor for a moment before speaking again. His dark hair was well-groomed, though thinning enough in front to give him the start of a widow's peak.

Pressler lifted his head and turned his dark eyes on his son's friend. "Artie," he said, "I'm here—well, *we're* here—to help *you*. Bennie and his friends— Tommy and two girls—are down in the main waiting room, if you boys have a chance to go talk to them before we leave. And I wanted to check on you and your grandparents to make sure you're all okay. How's Mr. Bauer? That is, if you don't mind telling me."

Artie told Abe Pressler everything he knew about Grandpa's condition. Pressler nodded and asked, "And Mrs. Bauer? Is she holding up okay? I believe I saw her walking down the hall just now with a nurse."

Ty stood and extended his hand. "Hi, Mr. Pressler, sir. I'm Ty Green. That was my mom with Miss Pearl. Mom's a nurse, but she's off duty. We're neighbors— just helping out."

"And Ty's my best friend," added Artie. "Rachel—Mrs. Green—she came and got us at Solid Rock, and she's been here with Grandma all evening." Artie didn't really know what else to say. "Bennie and Tommy sit at my lunch table," Artie said, then glanced at his best friend and smiled. "And Ty, here, is gonna be joining us, too, from now on, I think. Right, Ty?"

Though he was a self-proclaimed ladies man, Ty's face turned a shade darker, and all he could do was look away with a sheepish grin. Pressler patted Ty's shoulder. "Yes, my Bennie has kept me posted on the goings-on at school this past week," said Pressler, not specifying if what Bennie had told him was good or bad. "I want to thank you, Artie—and you, too, Ty—for befriending my son. He has some growing up to do, but he's a good boy. He has some challenges to deal with, the wheelchair being just one of them."

"Yes, sir," Artie said. "We'll do what we can to help Bennie." Ty nodded in agreement.

"Yes, well," Pressler began, "that isn't the main reason I stopped by." Again he seemed hesitant to speak freely. "Artie," he continued, "I want you—and your grandparents—I want you all to know that you have our support if you need it. I'm aware of some things going on now in this county—things that make some people's lives more difficult—and I want you to come to me for help, if you ever need it." He looked Artie in the eye and added, "Talk to me *before* you do anything drastic about finances. Do you understand? I can—and I will—help you."

"Yes, sir," said Artie, though he didn't quite understand why Pressler was making such an offer to help. The man took Artie's hand and shook on this unspoken deal that they were making, the extent of which Artie also didn't entirely grasp as they stood there in the small waiting room.

Pressler withdrew his hand and started to move toward the door. He stopped as if he'd forgotten something. "Hey," he said, "how about if I sit here for a few minutes longer while you guys run down to the big waiting area—you know, the one off the main lobby—and say a quick 'hi' to your friends down there. I'll wait until you get back in case Mrs. Bauer and Mrs. Green return while you're away. I'll tell them where you two are so they don't worry."

"Yeah, I guess we better," Artie said. "Thanks, Mr. Pressler. We won't be long. I may not see Bennie and Tommy on Monday—I mean, if I'm still here at the hospital with Grandpa. I need to tell them about, well, about lunch on Mondays. And I want to thank them for coming to check on us."

"And the two girls," said Ty. "We need to thank them, too. Right, Artie? By the way, Mr. Pressler, sir—uh, do you happen to know the two girls' names?"

"No, I'm sorry, Ty," said the man. "I didn't catch their names. But they knew Bennie and Tommy." Pressler chuckled. "One of the girls even asked if I'd make the pink lady sitting at the front desk let them all come up here to see you with me. But the lady said they were too young and that they had to stay down there with her. My goodness. She was one tough cookie."

"The pink lady?" Ty asked.

"No, the big girl who told me to get them up here," said Pressler. He laughed again. "I hated to say 'no' to her—even though I was just repeating what I'd been told."

"What about the other girl?" asked Artie. "What did she look like?"

Pressler thought for a second. "You know," he said, "I don't really remember. She was smaller than the assertive girl, I think. And she didn't say anything that I heard."

"Was she Black or White?" asked Ty. "The smaller girl."

"White," said Pressler, "and the other young lady was Black."

"Oh, I figured that," Ty said, "and I already have a pretty g—"

Artie took Ty by the arm and pulled him toward the door that Pressler held open for them. "Thanks, Mr. Pressler," said Artie. "We'll run down and say 'hi' to Bennie and Tommy, and I'll be right back." He nodded toward Ty. "This guy might want to stay down there just a bit longer and make you wait while he talks to his girl, but I'll come back as quick as I can. Thank you so much—for everything."

The boys hurried down to the main lobby where, sure enough, Bennie Pressler, Tommy White, Leah Russo and Nicie Evans sat. As Artie and Ty approached, they saw that Bennie and Tommy were looking at the TV on the wall across the room—the Cubs and Braves finishing up an extra-inning affair—Leah was thumbing through a dog-eared magazine from the coffee table in front of her, and

Nicie was staring daggers at the blue-haired pink lady hiding behind the front desk. The boys had arrived in the nick of time.

Nicie was first to see them. Her face relaxed, first into a smile at her man Ty, then into a concerned look when she saw Artie and remembered why they were there so late. "How's your granddaddy, Artie?" she asked, rising from her chair. Tommy and Leah followed suit. Bennie wheeled himself over with them to meet the two boys at the head of the hallway.

"He's in recovery now," Artie said. "I need to get back up there. But I want to thank you guys for coming over to see me tonight. You didn't have to do that."

"Sure we did," said Bennie. "It's what friends do. And we're your friends. I've been telling Mom and Dad about you sitting with us at lunch, even though you're the best athlete at school—and a senior, even."

Ty feigned indignation. "Hey," he said. "I'm standing here! *I'm* a senior, too, *and* a pretty good athlete, if I do say so myself."

At that point, Nicie stepped up and popped Ty square in the chest with the back of her hand. "Oh, shut up, turkey," she said. "Artie sits at the loser table because he's a nice guy. You just came over to sit with me, lover boy."

Holding up his hands in mock surrender, Ty smiled. "Hey, now, baby" he said, his eyes wide. "I'm a lover, not a fighter."

She slapped him again. "Don't you 'baby' me, Ty Green. I heard what you did on the bus. Leah told me you took the bla—"

Artie had heard enough. He patted Ty on the shoulder as if to say, *You're on your own, buddy*, and waved to the others as he moved away. "Thanks again, guys," Artie said. "Oh, and Bennie? Tommy and Leah don't have to worry too much about Meatless Monday, but you need to ask Ty what to expect at the Barf Table in case I'm not there. Mondays can be pretty rough."

"Wait a darn second," said Bennie, looking confused. "I sit at something called the *Barf Table*? And it's for … *losers*?" He smiled. "I thought our table was for the *coolest* kids at school—like me." He looked up from the wheelchair and winked at Leah standing beside him.

She popped him in the chest. "Oh, shut up, turkey," Leah said to Bennie, then addressed Ty still standing with them. "Is Artie's granddad going to be okay?"

Even walking up the hall, Artie heard the girl's question but didn't stop to answer her himself. One reason was because he didn't know the answer, and he was afraid that anything he said might jinx Grandpa's chances in the recovery room or in ICU. Artie also didn't try to hear Ty's response to Leah, because he feared that Ty, being the son of a nurse, might have overheard or understood more than Artie had gleaned from the nurse's updates during Grandpa's surgery.

Artie wasn't prepared to even consider the possibility of Harry Bauer dying so soon. In Artie's seventeen years, Harry was the only grandfather—and father—that the infant, the boy, the adolescent and now the young man had ever known. Whatever Artie chose to do with the rest of his life, it would be thanks to his grandpa's unquestioning grace and selfless care. Harry Bauer also knew how to administer tough love when needed—for a fact. But now his grandson wanted nothing but the tenderest mercies for the man he loved most.

* * *

It was still Friday but just before midnight when Grandpa was finally settled enough in the intensive care unit for Grandma and Artie to see him for a couple of minutes at a time. Sure enough, as Rachel Green had promised, the lights in ICU were kept low so that the desperately ill patients could rest as easily as possible. Rachel and Ty themselves had gone home at least an hour earlier, both of them giving Grandma and Artie hugs and promises that they would return to check on them the next morning.

Ty had learned from Nicie and Leah—who had ridden together in Nicie's car—how Arbor's game at Solid Rock had gone earlier that night. Leah even showed him the official team statistics that she had kept and called in to the TV stations after the game. But when the girls went home and Ty finally rejoined his friend under the small waiting room's harsh fluorescent lighting, he knew that Artie cared nothing about what had happened under the even brighter Friday night lights across town.

The struggles that Artie's family and real friends had witnessed that evening in E-ville were neither an entertainment nor a mere game.

CHAPTER 12 – Meatless Monday?

MONDAY FINALLY ROLLED AROUND. The steady rain that began to fall mid-morning only underscored the dreariness on the Arbor High campus. *Underscored*, in fact, was a good word to describe not just the students' general feelings that morning but also certain athletes' actions the previous Friday night at Solid Rock Academy. All the buzz was about the Bruins' 54-6 loss to the Harvesters and about Solid Rock linebacker Jimmy Gore's state record eight, count 'em eight, quarterback sacks, all in the first three quarters before the new Solid Rock coach decided to give his second- and third-stringers playing time. Arbor scored its lone touchdown—a pick-six of the Harvesters' backup quarterback—in the fourth quarter. The point-after kick was blocked.

That Monday morning, sophomore QB and kicker Josh Stark stayed home until the start of third period in order to nurse an "ankle sprain or strain" and to lick his various other wounds. Artie made it to school that Monday during lunch after visiting his grandparents at the hospital in Ebenezerville and driving Grandpa's pickup truck back to Monk's Landing for a half day of school and football practice. Grandma had decided to rent a room in a boarding house near the hospital for as long as Harry Bauer needed intensive care. If Artie could keep up the farm chores, he could continue attending school and playing football, Grandma said, or else he'd have to make a choice between his home life and his school life. To her, it was that simple.

Grandpa had other ideas, though. When Principal Church stopped by the hospital to visit the Bauers on Sunday afternoon, Grandma had asked him if the school might possibly give Artie the rest of the year off—to delay his graduation—while he worked the farm in Grandpa's stead. "I've talked to Harry about this," Grandma had said, "and he disapproves, but I just don't see any way around it. Otherwise, the farm work won't get done."

"Well," Mr. Church had replied, "there *is* night school. But then Artie couldn't play sports for us. He'd be busy all day on the farm and all evening with classes. He'd be giving up his future—the athletic scholarships, all the benefits of a free education to study whatever he chooses, the chance to pursue whatever profession he desires, not just play professional sports. But as a football player or baseball player, he could be *that* good, Mrs. Bauer, after four years in a solid college athletic program. As a matter of fact, ma'am, I venture that Artie could even get a small-college scholarship as a wrestler."

Sitting in the waiting room with Grandma and the principal, Artie had listened to their conversation without interrupting. But after a few more minutes of discussion about the young man's future, Mr. Church had turned to Artie and asked, "Son, what do *you* think about all this?"

Artie had just shrugged, not knowing what to say with Grandma sitting right there with them. Anywhere else, outside of his grandmother's hearing, he might have been able to discuss the situation with the principal. But his mind had gone blank.

Church had continued, "Is there anything that I can do—or that the school can do—to help you through this difficulty? I hate to see you lose a chance at a scholarship, but I understand that a young man's family always comes first. Now, you don't have to answer me this minute. I want you to think about what kind of help you need and how we can help you get it. Talk to your grandmother here and, of course, to your grandfather when he's able to discuss these matters, and then you come to my office and we'll do the very best we can to handle whatever situation we're facing. I'm here for you, son. Okay?"

Enheartened, Artie had nodded and risen to shake Mr. Church's hand as the principal had bid them farewell. Grandma had immediately gone to see her husband again, this time staying longer than usual. Upon her return, she had said, "Arthur, your grandpa wants to talk to you—right now. He has something important to say while he's good and awake."

"What is it, Grandma?" Artie had asked.

The old woman had appeared to frown, though it might have been concern, not anger or sadness, that lowered the wrinkled corners of her mouth and made deeper furrows in her brow. "You just go into that room and let *him* tell you," she had said. "And remember, Arthur, we *do* love you very much. *Both* of us do."

Once again, Artie had stood at his chair and waited there for a moment to process the words that he had just heard. Whereas Principal Church's little speech had been supportive and hopeful, Grandma's instruction had been ominous, foretelling news that Artie wouldn't like. Or maybe it was a pronouncement from Grandpa that Grandma herself hadn't liked. That possibility had also occurred to Artie as he had left the waiting room and walked the dozen steps down the hall to the double doors of the ICU.

As he'd paused for a moment at the nurse's station inside the doors, Artie had been able to see across the unit into his grandfather's room, and he had noticed that Grandpa, too, wasn't smiling. But his steely blue eyes were open, already on his grandson.

* * *

Taking his usual chair at the Barf Table, Artie took a moment to look over the food on his tray before addressing his friends. Something had changed. There was no soup or sandwich. On this first Monday in September, the cafeteria's dietary requirement of a protein-rich entree, two vegetables and a starch translated into three hard meatballs in an icky tomato sauce, a floret of broccoli and two curds of cauliflower, all covered with yellow cheese, and a single slice of toast slathered with garlic butter. *Mmm-mm*, murmured Artie. He popped open his half-pint carton of milk and took a swig from the spout-like opening, not bothering with a straw.

"Thanks again for coming to the hospital, guys," Artie said, looking around the table at Bennie, Tommy, Ricky and, for the time being, Leah. "Did Ty fill you in on Meatless Monday before he and Nicie took off? The bell's gonna ring in a few minutes."

Bennie nodded. "Yeah, he said that since it's meatballs and not soup today, the jerks will probably use them as projectiles—well, he said 'throw them' at me."

Artie laughed as he cut into a meatball and soaked it in the red sauce. "Yeah, I didn't think Ty would say 'projectiles.' But that's a good guess." He took a bite and found the meatball to be tasty. "These aren't bad," he said. "Maybe they'll all get eaten up before the bell rings."

"No," said Tommy, his eyes looking past Artie toward the upper level of the lunchroom. "We've been watching the juniors and seniors up there. They're planning something. They keep going from table to table, and pointing at us down here.

"Well, whatever they do," said Artie, "just don't overreact … Bennie."

"Hey," Bennie said, "I'm sitting here. I'm sitting here."

"Yeah, yeah," said Artie, with a smile. He finished the meatball. "I know what," he said. "You could use a tray as a shield. Quick, Tommy, run over to the cash register and tell Frankie we need three more trays—just the trays, not food. I don't think Leah and I will need one."

As Tommy ran to get the trays, Leah flipped up her hoodie to cover the top of her head. "You got that right," she said. "I'm outta here as soon as that bell rings. We can talk later, Artie."

Artie nodded and looked over at little Ricky Duran, who had been silent so far. "I want to thank you, Ricky, for coming over to the hospital yesterday with your parents. Grandma and I enjoyed meeting your folks. They're really nice. And the cookies your mom made were great!"

Ricky smiled and nodded. "She's a real good cook—and a good *panadera*, too, I mean."

"A good baker?" said Artie. "Yes, she is. My grandma even said she might sneak one of your mom's *champurradas* into ICU for Grandpa to try. He loves a good cookie."

Ricky beamed. "Really? Your *abuela* said that? I will tell *mama*."

Tommy returned empty-handed. "No dice," he said, taking his seat. "Maybe if we clean our plates real quick? Then we wouldn't need extra trays."

Shaking his head, Artie said, "Not enough time. The bell's about to ring." He looked over toward the vacant serving line and saw black-clad Frankie walking toward the Barf Table. The big cashier was carrying six shiny, metal containers, the size of large soup cans, three in each of his big hands. That was one container more than the number of current Barf Tablers.

"Hey, man," Artie said to Frankie. "What's up? Are those cans for us?"

Frankie merely nodded and placed them in a flat triangle pattern on the table in front of Bennie. The release bell rang, and the noise level shot up with the shouting, laughing and scuffling of teenagers coming down from the upper section to empty their trays.

Artie reached out to get himself one of the six cans, but Frankie waved him off and shook his head. "No," Frankie said. "Leave 'em just like that." He winked, turned away and walked back toward his cash register before the first seniors arrived. Artie obeyed the big man's order.

Bennie's chin ratcheted up and down—his wide eyes going from the fast-approaching seniors, back to the six tall cans sitting in a triangle just inches in front of his chest. "Holy crap!" Bennie said, moving his chair away from the table with one pull backward on his wheels. "It's meat-*bowling*! And I'm the pin monkey!"

A boy in the first wave of seniors circled around behind Bennie and took the wheelchair by its handles. Laughing, he pushed Bennie back to his assigned space at the Barf Table and even made a couple of adjustments to park him directly behind the "meat-bowling pins." It was a new game that hadn't even had a name until the upperclassmen heard Bennie's exclamation. But now "Meat-bowling Monday" was on everyone's lips, ensuring that the day would live in Barf Table infamy, if not in a regular weekly observance. (On the rest of the Mondays that year, the cafeteria menu again featured a meatless soup and bland sandwich, with vegetarianism certainly not being the main reason for this return to tradition.)

At the heads of two lines, a pair of senior boys took positions beside Artie and directly across the table from Bennie. Each bowler hefted his meatball, dipped it in the remaining tomato sauce on his tray, then hefted the spheroid of ground beef again to test its weight and rollability, as it were. The two players nodded and shrugged as they negotiated who would go first, with the wheelchair bearer staying in place to make sure that Bennie didn't move away. When the first to roll was decided, the other bowler used a napkin to wipe clean the free hand of the one who was about to toss his icky meatball at the pins. But instead of rolling the wet meatball, the boy reached into his pants pocket, withdrew a shiny quarter and flipped it through the air at the standing metal containers. He took out a handful of coins and slid the whole bunch across the table for Bennie, Tommy and Ricky to deposit in the cans.

The slimy sphere of meat? The senior boy tossed it into the nearest garbage bin, like Michael Jordan sinking a three-point jumper for the Bulls. His partner did likewise, right down to the pocketful of change. They both patted Artie on the back and whispered in his ear, and walked away without terrorizing Bennie and the other freshmen further. Leah was so surprised that she had forgotten to leave. She was genuinely touched by the senior boys' gesture.

The two lines of players moved quickly from that point on, as all the seniors and most of the juniors gave up their silver coins in this love offering, this compassionate collection of quarters, dimes and nickels, for their classmate and hero whose grandfather had been hurt so badly. Tears were in Artie's eyes as he sat quietly and watched as the lines dwindled and the six soup cans filled one by one until money spilled onto the tabletop and surrounded the containers. There were many more pats on his back, whispered best wishes and even quick hugs from some of the girls.

Artie knew he couldn't quit school that year, with this show of support, his graduation in the spring and all the other benefits of having worked so hard as a student and athlete. He loved his grandparents, and he loved the farm he'd been raised on. But there had to be a good way to make everything work, even with Grandpa laid up and Grandma growing more fragile herself.

Everyone wanted to help Artie and the Bauers—or so it seemed. Ty and

Rachel Green had already done so much. Abe Pressler and Principal Jerry Church had offered their considerable help. So had Jug Johnson on Saturday morning when he and the other football coaches had come to the hospital to see Artie. It was the same with Ricky and his parents who had dropped in with Mrs. Duran's cookies on their way to church Sunday morning. Then there were the other Barf Table buddies, Bennie, Tommy, Nicie and Leah; and now so many other caring students at Arbor High. Artie resolved to do whatever it took *not* to sell the Bauer farm, or himself, short. He knew that Stark Realty's offer to buy the farm—a bid that Grandpa had flatly refused—would loom larger and more attractive the longer that Harry Bauer was out of commission. But there had to be some other solution, some respectable way to hold onto the farm until Grandpa got well.

* * *

Grandpa had said as much to Artie on Sunday afternoon in the ICU. "Don't let Pearl sell the farm," Grandpa had said in a low voice as soon as Artie had knelt at his bedside.

It had been hard for Artie to see his grandfather in such pain, covered in bandages and with tubes in all directions. "I won't, Grandpa." Artie had tried to focus on the old man's blue eyes. They were squinched and red with hurt, but there were no tears. And they were familiar to Artie, who had looked into those eyes seeking approval and comfort, understanding and mirth, ever since he was a babe in gruff old Harry Bauer's arms, a child on his grandpa's knee.

"She's afraid," Grandpa had said. "I am, too. But don't sell it. It's all we have."

"I won't let her sell it," Artie said again, finishing the thought he hadn't completed. "And I won't sell it, either."

Grandpa's eyes had relaxed, as if he had suddenly grown more tired. "Good," he had said. "And you stay in school, boy. I want to see you play ball."

Artie had smiled weakly. "You'll be up and around by baseball season, Grandpa. You'll get to see me catch Ty Green. He's a great pitcher, you know."

Slowly shaking his head, Grandpa had grunted, "Huh-uh."

"What?" Artie had said, afraid that Grandpa might drift off before he could say what he had meant. "You know how good Ty is. You'll enjoy seeing us play."

"Not baseball," Grandpa murmured, in fact succumbing to sleep. His eyes closed, and his breathing deepened after one last word—"football"—left his parched lips.

CHAPTER 13 – Rainy Days and Mondays

DURING ANNOUNCEMENTS at the start of 4th Period after lunch, Principal Church passed along Coach Johnson's decision to move football practice into the gym that afternoon because of the rain. That meant the players would have to find something to do while the extracurricular teams and clubs that normally met in the gym after school played for at least sixty minutes. The older football players—the ones with vehicles, anyway—went off campus instead of hanging around the gym. Ty Green took the opportunity to give Nicie Evans a ride to Sandpiper Beach in the White Whale, even though she had to leave her car in the school parking lot. Her beach volleyball club didn't mind getting wet in the summer rain, because they usually ended up in the surf before 5th Period was over, anyway. The school surfing club, on the other hand, decided to hold an impromptu shindig on the covered patio outside Woody's Surf Shop, complete with a bonfire and hotdogs after club sponsor Woody Woods determined that the surf was too choppy and the undertow was too strong for surfing. Even the volleyballers joined in.

One section of stands had been pulled out in the gym as a place for the remaining football players to sit and talk or study while they waited for their own practice to begin. Under ordinary circumstances, they might have been relegated to the weight room, but it was occupied by the school weight-lifting club and the flag footballers who had hopes of someday being called up to the regular football team. Tommy White and even Bennie Pressler, in his wheelchair, took turns in the weight room that afternoon to work on their upper-body strength. Little Ricky Duran, who was on the intramural flag football team, had decided to run up and down the gym floor with the girls varsity soccer team that had also been moved inside that rainy day.

"Wow," Artie said to Leah sitting near him in the stands. "Ricky sure is quick. And, boy, can he kick the ball."

Leah looked up from the book she was reading, watched Ricky for a few seconds and nodded. "Yeah, he's pretty good," she said. "Too bad we don't have a varsity soccer team for him to play on. How do you think he'd look in a wig?"

Artie laughed. "Well, you know," he said, "there's no reason the soccer team couldn't be co-ed. The wrestling team is. Matter of fact, the only other heavy-weight—the wrestler I have to practice with—*she's* a girl."

"*She*?" said Leah. "She *is*? A girl? What else would *she* be?"

"No, Wilma's a good wrestler." Artie scooted down the bleacher to be closer to Leah. "I wish more boys—and girls—would come out for wrestling," he said. "We could use wrestlers on both ends of the scale—the lower weight divisions *and* the heavier ones. You know, I bet little Ricky there would make a good wrestler. Tommy White probably would, too. You think Bennie can wrestle—I mean, once he gets out of that chair?"

Leah shook her head. "Nah, Bennie isn't into contact sports. He's a surfer. And you know he likes playing with computers and other gadgets. As a matter of fact, Principal Church asked Bennie to be the public address announcer at our home games this year, starting with the game this Friday night."

"How do you know that?" asked Artie.

"Because Bennie asked me to sit up in the press box with him," she said. "He wants me to spot for him and feed him some stats—like how many interceptions Josh has thrown, how many times he's been sacked, stuff like that."

Artie smiled, even though he noticed that Josh Stark, sitting a couple of rows below them on the bleachers, had turned his head at the sound of his name. "Yeah, I heard it got pretty bad Friday night at Solid Rock," said Artie. "But you know it might not have been like that if Ty and I had played. I kinda felt sorry for Josh."

Again, Josh turned to see who was talking about him, and this time he narrowed his focus on Artie and Leah. Rising with a frown, Josh twisted to face them. "Hey!" Josh said. "Why don't you two just shut up about Friday night?" He glared at Leah and added, "Besides, it was all *your* fault, you anorexic little witch."

Artie stood. "Whoa," he said. "Hold up there, buddy. No name-calling, okay?"

"I'm not your buddy, Bauer," said Josh. Then the sophomore jeered, "Artie Bauer, the poor boy who needs a handout so bad that he takes everybody's lunch money. You wouldn't need a handout if that ol' granddaddy of yours would take my dad's offer. Just so you know, we're gonna get that farm, and the longer you hicks wait to sell it, the lower the price will be."

Artie was already moving toward Josh when Coach Johnson's voice cut through the noise of the gym. "Bauer! Stark! Stop right there!" To be such a heavy man, Jug shot across the gym to the spot on the floor just below the two boys. "The next one of you that moves a muscle is off the team," said Jug. "I ain't having any fighting among teammates. Save it for Friday night."

Josh turned to look down at the coach but remained standing. "They started it," Josh said. "I was minding my own business, and I heard them making fun of me."

"No," said Leah, addressing Jug before Artie could respond, "that was *me* making fun of him, Coach. All Artie said was he felt sorry for Josh."

Even that remark infuriated the young quarterback. "Yeah, well, nobody has to feel sorry for me," Josh said. "My dad could buy and sell this Podunk school, and the only reason I'm here is because you needed a quarterback this season."

Artie started to argue that Ty Green had been in line to fill that position and would have played well if Josh's arguable football skills and the Stark family's money hadn't given the brash sophomore an advantage on the field. But Artie remained silent, because Jug jumped in with his own response.

"Tell you what," said Jug. "I'll go right now and give your daddy a phone call, and invite him over here for a short conference after practice today. I think the three of us need to come to a little understanding about the right way to treat teammates—with respect."

Josh snorted. "I don't have to respect them, and they don't have to respect me. If Artie Bauer had cared anything about the team or about me, he would've played the other night. His granddad didn't die or anything. And I'm tired of living in Reuben Russo's shadow. His sister here is just a brat who thinks she can trip me on the bus and get away with it because nobody will let *her* get in any trouble."

Jug held up his hand for Josh to hush. "I shouldn't have to tell you, boy, that remarks about *family* is off limits. Besides, we're *all* family here." Jug shook his head sadly. "Now, I'm gonna go call your daddy. You get down here and come with me, Josh. What happened the other night wasn't all your fault, not by a long shot. We need to get practice started and work out what *did* go wrong. Come on."

The aggravated boy hesitated but finally pushed through the kids sitting below him and walked with Jug across the floor and out of the gym toward the coach's office. Artie looked over at Leah, surprised to see her nose already in the book again. "Aren't you worried?" he asked.

"About what?"

"Josh just ratted on you," said Artie. "You know, about tripping him on the bus the other night. Coach'll have to do something now."

She sighed. "He already did," she said. "I got kicked off the activity bus—for the time being, anyway. He said I have to find my own ride to the next away game."

Artie was confused. "But … he just now found out, right? Who told him?"

"I did," said Leah. "Friday night after the game. I felt bad about it. But I'd rather ride with Nicie Evans, anyway. She doesn't take anything off anybody."

"Yeah," Artie said, "I'd rather ride with Nicie, too—and so would Ty, for sure. But that isn't gonna happen. Josh is the *real* brat who always gets his way. You just wait and see. His dad will come over here and throw his weight around—"

"And his money."

"Yeah, and that, too," Artie continued, "and Coach will be nominating Josh for Player of the Week before it's all over."

Leah grinned. "Well, he *did* set a record the other night."

"Yeah," said Artie. "For being sacked." They both laughed and went back to waiting for 5th Period to end so that football practice could begin.

* * *

Joel Stark walked into the gym halfway through practice. As he'd said he would, Coach Johnson had called the busy real estate developer about a meeting to discuss his son Josh's bad attitude and behavior, but the coach hadn't counted on Stark dropping by early. This meant that Stark would be able to sit and observe Jug's own attitude and behavior as the aging coach of a young squad that had just been trounced by a team they should have beaten. Stark, wearing a poplin overcoat on the rainy afternoon, stood in the doorway closest to the bleachers for fifteen minutes, removed his rain jacket and took a seat in a metal folding chair that had been left next to the door. He watched with a bemused smile, as if he already knew what Jug was going to say about Josh and how the meeting would go.

For his own part, Jug showed more patience with the boys than he might have under less pressurized circumstances. Since a full-out scrimmage on the gym floor was out of the question, Jug opted first to walk the Bruin defense's linebackers and secondary through various coverages that they had blown Friday night against Solid Rock's passing attack. He reviewed rushing and blitzing assignments with the entire defensive unit. Jug pointed out that no football team can give up 54 points and expect to win, no matter how good its own offense is.

Then Jug Johnson focused on the Bruins' offensive woes. "Okay now, boys," he said, "I don't have to tell you that we ain't gonna have *that* happen to us again this season, not if I'm still the coach here."

Jug proceeded to line up the starting offense in its regular formation, but without Artie and Ty, in order to replicate and correct the mistakes that they'd made against Solid Rock. After running through all the plays that the Arbor High offense had muffed on Friday night, he inserted the two co-captains into the lineup and ran through all the plays again, right this time. What they learned was that the biggest problem had been Josh's failure to trust his blockers, and that the inexperienced quarterback had left the protective pocket of linemen too soon, thinking he could outrun the entire defense, including star linebacker Jimmy Gore.

"Now, Josh," said Coach Johnson at one point, "you gotta stay in the pocket long enough to let your receivers get free downfield. We've talked about you getting into a routine of taking a five-step drop, then hitting one of the boys on a slant or cros—"

"That isn't right, Coach," shouted Joel Stark from his chair at the door. "I've taught Josh the *three*-step drop. Then if nobody's open, he can run."

Eyebrows raised, Jug turned and studied the seated man for a few seconds. "Excuse me, Mr. Stark," said Jug, "but this is a closed practice. I'd appreciate you waiting outside until we're done for the day."

Stark pointed toward the single set of bleachers where Leah Russo sat. "Closed practice?" the man said. "What about her?"

Jug looked at Leah and back at Stark. "Miss Russo is our statistician," said the coach. "She belongs here. All due respects, sir, you don't. So again, Mr. Stark, I'll thank you to wait out in the lobby. I'll be with you directly."

The real estate mogul wasn't used to taking orders from anyone, particularly not from one of his son's coaches. Stark glanced over at Leah again, then across the floor at Artie for a second, and finally at Jug before rising and walking out the open door. He shook his head and kicked away the rubber wedge that was holding the door open. Standing outside, he peered through the safety glass of the closed door's small window.

Jug turned back to the team. "As I was saying, boys," he began, "here at Arbor High our quarterback does the *five*-step drop on pass plays. That gives all you receivers enough time to get open and run the routes you've been practicing all week. Now, last Friday night, we di—"

"Three-step drop is better, Coach," blurted Josh.

"Is that why we can't scrub Jimmy Gore's number off your jersey from the other night," Jug shot back. "You need to be quiet for a change."

Artie could have sworn he heard Leah giggle in the stands, and he knew then that the coach's quip would come back to haunt them all. Like most bullies, neither Josh nor his powerful father could tolerate being laughed at, not without making the person pay for poking fun at them, not even if the ridicule were deserved. But Josh said nothing more during practice. He knew that he and his father would have Jug outnumbered in their private meeting, and that Joel Stark would not be cowed by an old coach who needed to retire.

But Jug also wanted to retire on his own terms as a winner, and until Friday night's debacle he had thought Artie and Ty's senior season would be his last, best chance to win a county championship. Now, with Josh Stark leading the team, that goal was in doubt—in the minds of everyone except Josh and his dad.

* * *

What happened in the private meeting between Jug Johnson and the Starks didn't leave the coach's office that week. The skies cleared and late summer weather returned, allowing the team to practice each afternoon on the field to prepare for Friday night's first home game. Their opponent would be Mimosa Beach High, whose Waverunners had beaten Port Oleander handily the previous week in the season opener for both teams.

Mimosa Beach didn't have any defensive "mansters" like Jimmy Gore, but their secondary was quick and experienced. As a result, Arbor's quarterback would have to stay in the pocket longer than usual to complete his passes. Artie was afraid that Josh would do as he pleased in the game on Friday despite having been drilled in practice on the five-step drop and on being patient in the pocket. In school that week, expectations were that the Solid Rock loss had been a fluke and that the Bruins would beat the Waverunners with Artie and Ty back in the lineup.

Artie himself wasn't so sure, because he was more tired that week than he'd ever been in his life. Each day he rose before sunup to milk the cows and do other farm chores, and he would call both the hospital to check on his grandfather and the boarding house to awaken Grandma and assure her that everything was okay on the farm. After that, Artie would hop into Grandpa's old pickup and drive to Monk's Landing for school and football practice, then back across the county to Ebenezerville to visit his grandparents and to let Grandma eat supper in the cafeteria. Artie would sit and talk to Grandpa, who was getting stronger every day but was still in pain as his broken bones mended and his burns healed.

On Wednesday that week Grandpa moved from ICU into a regular room, which made visiting him easier for Artie and for Grandma, though she decided to keep her room at the boarding house for the time being. Artie was keeping up his end of their bargain; he would leave the hospital with enough daylight left to finish all the farm chores before dark and do all his homework at the kitchen table, falling asleep there on his books and papers Tuesday and Wednesday nights. Artie was one tuckered-out Bruin.

Besides Harry Bauer's improved prognosis, the best news that week came thanks to little Ricky Duran. The Duran family had just started attending Solid Rock Christian Church, one of the churches that the Bauers had attended but quit. Still, after Ricky requested prayer in church for his friend's grandfather, for Harry Bauer, farmers from the congregation showed up that Thursday at the Bauer farm and baled all of the hay that Grandpa had cut the previous week. Ricky's father organized the effort.

The helpful harvesters might have come earlier in the week if not for Monday's rain that had wet the cut hay on the ground. They were forced to let the hay dry in the sun before they gathered it into two big truckloads of tight, square bales, enough to feed the farm livestock all winter. Little Ricky himself stayed out of school that day and, according to his father, worked as hard as any of the men.

When Artie finally got home that evening and saw what had been done, he called Ricky's father and tried to give him some of the money that the Arbor High community had given to him on Meatball Monday and other days that week. Contributions to the Bauer family had continued at school on Krakatoa Tuesday and Waisin Wednesday, with the faculty and staff giving Artie a big check to help put gas in Grandpa's truck and to cover Grandma's room and board in E-ville.

On Wednesday, Principal Church announced that the school's half of the 50-50 raffle on Friday would benefit the Bauers. Raffle tickets started selling early, and it looked like the family's share of the take might be in four figures. As usual, the drawing would be held between the third and fourth quarters on Friday night. Artie couldn't believe Mr. Church's announcement at first. The young man had been worried that he wouldn't be able to pay all the new medical bills that Medicare wouldn't cover, along with all the Bauers' regular bills. But this help went a long way toward easing Artie's worries about the future.

Arbor High's juniors and seniors, for tradition's sake, still managed to observe Krakatoa Tuesday and Waisin Wednesday the old-fashioned ways. On Tuesday, they stepped on Tommy White's toes as they passed the Barf Table on their route to the garbage bins. They didn't bother Bennie Pressler once they saw that his shoes sat in the footrests of his wheelchair and couldn't be stomped on the hard floor. On Wednesday, the upperclassmen half-heartedly rained down raisins on the freshmen tables and seemed to forget about punishing the Barf Table bunch.

By lunchtime on Thirsty Thursday, the entire student body was abuzz about the football game with Mimosa Beach, and no one was interested in tipping over anyone else's drinks. Instead, a number of juniors and seniors sacrificed their own sports drinks and left them for Artie and Ty to consume over the next couple of days. The upperclassmen wanted to make sure that the football team's co-captains were well hydrated for their battle with the Waverunners on Friday night, they said. Or, Nicie offered, it might be fun to see Artie and Ty chug the sports drinks. Leah promised to hang around for that.

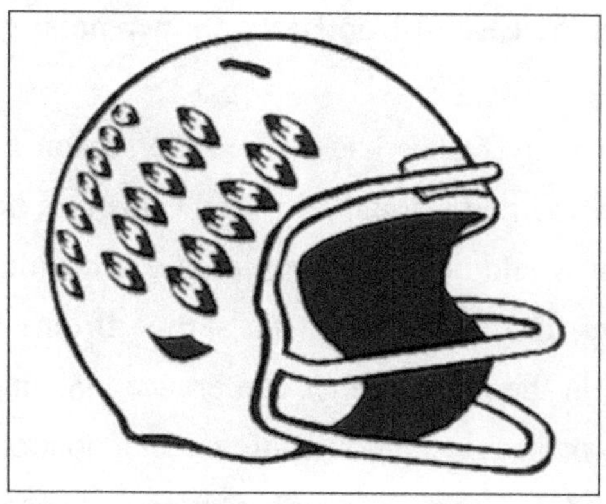

CHAPTER 14 – No Place Like Home

AS COACH JOHNSON HAD REQUESTED, no pep rally was held on Friday afternoon before the Mimosa Beach game. Jug wanted his boys to be laser-focused on that night's opponent, not be distracted by reminders of the team's failures the previous week in E-ville. Also, he knew that they wouldn't profit from being told, again, how good they were and how badly they should beat the opposing team. They'd been there, and they'd done that—to no one's benefit. Jug felt it was better to leave his young men alone and let them motivate each other to play their best. The fact that Artie needed to drive home right after school on Friday, make a call to the hospital, and take care of chores had also been on Jug's mind earlier in the week when he had nixed plans for a pep rally. It was the Bruins' home opener—Jug had told the principal, the young cheerleading coach and finally the band director—and that situation alone should have generated enough excitement for players and fans alike, he hoped.

The Suncoast Conference was unusual in that it contained only the five high schools of coastal Oleander County, from small secondary schools like charter Arbor High and public Port Oleander High, to medium-sized public Mimosa Beach and private Solid Rock Academy, to the large, inner-city Iron Harbor High, which also served the naval base there. Every Friday night in late summer and fall, the football teams of those five schools would play two games within the conference and one outside the conference against usually larger and tougher opponents, except in the case of Iron Harbor, a perennial gridiron power in the state.

The Iron Harbor Gray Dukes had opened the season a week earlier with a road win against the vaunted Capital City Red Caps in a non-conference affair, and this Friday night would open their conference schedule at home against the improved Solid Rock Harvesters. With the Arbor Bruins hosting the Mimosa Beach Waverunners in the night's other conference matchup, the Port Oleander Pilots would hit the road against a non-conference opponent inland.

All five Suncoast Conference football teams played each other twice during the regular season and rounded out their schedules with two non-conference games apiece before the Iron Harbor Gray Dukes, more often than not, won the conference championship outright and entered the state postseason playoffs. The so-called "county championship" went to the team that came in second, usually with the two guaranteed losses to Iron Harbor and no more than two losses to the other three league foes combined. That team also earned a state playoff spot.

The boys from Monk's Landing had started their fall campaign in a definite hole with the season-opening loss to Solid Rock, but now, with the Harvesters taking on the invincible Gray Dukes that night in Iron Harbor, the Arbor Bruins had a chance to pull dead even in the early-season standings with a home win over the favored Mimosa Beach Waverunners. Jug Johnson had prepared his boys for the challenge by drilling them all week on their best plays and on what they could expect from the Waverunners. But now it was up to the Bruins themselves to execute their old coach's game plan.

* * *

Sophomore Brett Woods took the opening kickoff on the 8-yard line and streaked up the right sideline across midfield to the Mimosa Beach 37 before being pushed out of bounds by the Waverunner kicker. Veering into his team-mates' arms on the home sideline, Brett accepted their slaps on his shoulder pads and backside as he turned and jogged back onto the field with the rest of the offensive unit led by sophomore QB Josh Stark.

With the game starting at seven-thirty, daylight would muddle with darkness for another half hour, so the stadium lights were already on, adding a glare to the sticky coastal heat of late summer at Arbor Field, which would be renamed Reuben Russo Memorial Stadium later that season at homecoming. Fans in the packed bleachers didn't seem to mind that renovations were still underway to the stands on both sides of the gridiron, and to the home-side press box. The Marching Bruins in their green-and-gold uniforms played the school fight song from their section at the far end of the grandstand. Spread along the foot of the home bleachers from 20-yard line to 20-yard line behind the team, the Bruins cheerleaders pranced, kicked and jumped as the music blared and the crowd cheered.

Steam rose in the dusky evening air from the bare heads of the Bruins subs, as they stood with helmets tucked under one arm and waited for their chances to play. Arbor's starters played both ways—on both offense and defense—except for Artie, who this season accepted his coach's suggestion to play defense only if needed in a pinch. Jug wanted Artie to focus on playing center in order to maximize his odds of getting a college athletic scholarship. Jug also didn't want his best heavyweight wrestler and all-conference baseball catcher to get hurt on the gridiron at the start of the school year. Principal Jerry Church doubled as Arbor High's athletic director, a post that gave him final say in every situation involving his school's sports teams and coaches. So far he had agreed with Jug's handling of the various situations facing the football squad.

Jug Johnson had called the Bruins' first play from scrimmage before the offensive unit took the field for their opening series. And so, as the offense's "signal caller," all Josh Stark had to do in the huddle was repeat the play code and the snap count—in other words, which "hut" to hike the football on to start the play—and say nothing else to the ten helmeted boys who, hands on knee pads, peered down at the kneeling quarterback before this first play. But this was Josh, who only seven days earlier had been sacked a dozen times by Solid Rock rushers, eight of those times by all-everything Jimmy Gore. Getting tackled behind the line of scrimmage, Josh had lost close to 100 yards—the length of a football field—all by himself. So he had something to prove this week against Mimosa Beach, to the home crowd and also to his own coach and teammates.

"Awright, guys," said Josh, looking up from left to right into ten pairs of eyes. "Let's put last week behind us and kick these wimpy Waverunners' butts. These chumps aren't gonna know what hit them until they get back home and see the headlines in the paper. We're gon—"

"Call the play," Ty said, knowing that the play clock was running and that the offense had less than 25 seconds before a delay-of-game penalty would be called.

Josh shifted knees. "Shut up, Green. We've got plenty of time. Forty sec—"

This time a blast from the white-hatted referee's whistle interrupted Josh. The ten players turned to see the zebra-striped official pull the yellow flag from his back pants pocket and toss it into the air, the flag's weighted ball and gathered tail looking like an injured canary falling to the green turf. The boys moved their huddle back five yards to make room for the referee to walk off the penalty.

So, now, instead of first down and 10 yards to go on the Mimosa Beach 37-yard line, it was first-and-15 on the MB 42. With a shorter whistle blast and vertical arm pump, the referee reset the play clock to 25 seconds and waited for the teams to meet at the line of scrimmage.

The Bruins huddled up again, with all eyes once more on the young QB. "Option right, on two," Josh said flatly, holding his hands apart to clap. All eleven boys clapped as one to break the huddle, with Artie hurrying to the line and bending down to adjust the tacky leather football in his callused right hand.

Lining up directly behind the crouching center, Josh placed the back of one hand against the underside of Artie's rear, and his other hand slightly lower within the arc of the center's legs. "Green 43," shouted Josh, head up to check the defensive alignment. "Green 43, hut, hut." The ball slammed into the young QB's hands as Artie and the other linemen rose to block oncoming defenders. At halfback, Brett Woods waited upright a second; then—arms ready to take the ball against his torso—he rushed forward and expected to feel the ball impact his belly.

But as Brett brushed past the quarterback toward a gaping hole that Artie and the right guard had opened in the Waverunners line, Josh pulled the ball away and turned back to the left side, away from where he had encountered so much trouble the previous week. What Josh didn't consider under fire on this Friday night was that Artie, not the backup center, was protecting him on the right side of the line, if he had decided either to run in that direction himself or throw downfield. His protection, what little there was on the left, collapsed, and he was tackled for no gain. It was second-and-15.

From the huddle, Josh looked for Coach Johnson's signal, then knelt and passed along the play call and cadence. "Option right, on three this time," Josh said, peeved that the coach would call the same play even though it had just failed to gain any yards. But it was an option play, and Josh could hand the ball off this time, carry the ball himself again—presumably through the hole that Artie and the right guard would open—or hit a receiver on one of the short patterns that they were trained to run on option plays.

From his crouch over the ball, Artie heard Josh once again call, "Green 43," meaning that there were still four "down linemen" rushing on defense and three linebackers patrolling the area just behind the line of scrimmage. Artie paid attention and snapped the ball on three, even though what Josh actually shouted was, "Hut, hut, HIKE!" and took no one on defense by surprise.

Artie and the linemen rose again to block, but this time he immediately felt a hand in his back, as if he were being pushed aside to make way for the rusher. "Move!" Artie heard Josh yell, before the boy lowered his shoulder and crashed into the small of Artie's back, causing him to twist and fall into the legs of the right guard. Both linemen ended up on the turf underneath their quarterback, who managed to hold onto the ball in the tsunami of defenders that toppled him for a gain of just one yard. Now it was third-and-14 on the Waverunners 41.

Coach Johnson called timeout and waved for the offense to meet him halfway between the ball and the sideline. At that early point in the game, Jug shooed the waterboys back to the bench and beckoned for his young quarterback to come closer. Jabbing a big index finger into the front of Josh's green jersey—right between BRUINS in yellow block letters and the big numeral 1 in white—Jug was ready to explode after only two plays.

"You're doing it AGAIN, boy," the coach shouted, over noise from the band blaring in the stands. "Will you *please* just HAND THE BALL OFF?" Jug shook his head. "You're a good player, Stark. But you CAN'T DO IT ALL YOURSELF. Okay?" When Josh kept looking at his shoes and didn't respond, Jug shouted louder, "OKAY?!"

This time Josh nodded weakly and turned away without waiting to hear the next play. Jug grabbed Artie and said, "We're gonna have to teach that boy a lesson, Yogi-boy. They're gonna be expecting a pass, but we need some yards. So it's 'Screen right,' okay? Let 'em through, and he'll either throw the screen pass or they'll cream him in the backfield. Oh, and *you're* looking at me for the plays from now on. Got it?"

Artie nodded and ran to the huddle, where he passed along the play call and said for Josh to use the same cadence—"Green 43" for the usual defensive *front four* and "Green 34" for only three down linemen—and for everyone to expect the ball snap on the count of three until further notice.

At the line of scrimmage, Artie looked right, then left at the defense, and he wondered if Josh would run the play correctly or pay the painful price for doing his own thing again. Another big sack would turn the home crowd against the young quarterback and might even keep him on the bench on offense for the rest of the evening. Then Ty Green would have to take over behind center, where he belonged.

Except with their new trick play, the Bruins rarely used the shotgun formation, which had the quarterback line up two strides behind the center and take the longer snap to start the play. The shotgun was popular with college and professional teams. Even high school offenses had started using the shotgun, almost always on 3rd-down passing plays so that the quarterback could take a shorter three-step drop and get off his throw before the secondary could cover all the receivers. Some teams used the shotgun on every play from scrimmage.

Jug didn't like the shotgun formation because his option offense relied on trickery—the quarterback taking the snap under center, handing off to the halfback or faking the handoff, and either running or throwing, depending on how the defense reacted to the quarterback's decisions. In the shotgun, the QB usually lined up alone in the backfield, thus almost ensuring that he would be passing and guaranteeing that the defensive linemen would rush the passer, not look to defend the run. Another problem—for high school quarterbacks, at least—was that the shotgun snap was harder to handle than a direct snap from center.

Waiting to hear the snap cadence, Artie noticed that Josh was taking longer than usual to begin and that he hadn't taken his normal starting position behind Artie yet. Still waiting, the big center dropped his head and looked for the quarterback's familiar black cleats on the ground behind him, but the grass turf was empty as far back as Artie could see.

Artie heard Josh call, "Green 34 … Green 34 … hut … hut … hut …." The slight change in cadence—from Josh's previous "HIKE!" to a simple "hut" on three—was enough to throw Artie off, not to mention the fact that Josh had lined up in the shotgun without letting his center, or any other teammate, know what he was doing.

On the sideline, Jug was screaming, "NO!" But Artie hiked the ball, though an instant late, and stood to put up just enough resistance to delay the rush and set up Josh's planned screen pass to Brett Woods.

Even though they, too, might have been confused, the rest of the Bruins line did likewise and let the three defensive linemen and two blitzing linebackers storm into the backfield past Brett toward Josh, who had stooped to pick up the weak snap that he had dropped. Instead of crashing into him, the wave of defenders washed over the ducking quarterback, giving him just enough time to secure the ball and, with a desperation block from Brett, find a hole into the empty Waverunners secondary.

A Mimosa Beach safety recovered and knocked Josh off his feet just beyond the first-down marker. So the drive continued, and—to the cheering crowd, anyway—Josh Stark had come through for the home team. It was first-and-10 on the MB 30.

Jug called his second timeout, leaving him only one more to use for the rest of the game. The old coach didn't wait for the team to come to him; he met Josh at the huddle, fast-walking in his odd, stiff-legged gait from the sideline. His face was red, not from the summer heat, humidity or physical exertion, but from the steam that had collected under his white ball cap when he saw Josh line up in the shotgun.

"You better be glad you got that first down, Stark!" Jug hollered. "We haven't practiced that formation, not when we're running the option!"

With the cheers from the stands still echoing in his head, Josh just glared at the coach and said nothing. Jug screamed at the boy, "Who do you think you are? And that ain't no oratorical question, dadgummit."

Still, Josh was silent, but now he glanced up into the stands where his parents sat. "This is your last chance, Stark," said Jug. "You run the plays that I call and that we practiced, or I'll play someone who will. Simple as that."

Artie knew it really wasn't—simple, that is. He had watched Jug Johnson coach football, wrestling and baseball for the past three years, and Artie had long ago recognized all of the many factors that went into high school coaching decisions, even those made by someone as successful as his mentor, if not his friend. Even then, most high school coaches were only one losing season or one disgruntled athletic booster away from being shown the exit.

To his credit or blame, Josh Stark stuck to the playbook for the remainder of that series. The Bruins ground out another first down the old-fashioned way, with Brett Woods rushing for three yards off tackle, four yards on a draw play up the middle, and finally four more around the right end. But at first-and-10 on the MB 19, the Waverunners defense stiffened and shut down Arbor's one-man running attack.

Josh could have helped out his buddy by keeping the ball on the third-down option play, but the chastened quarterback had decided to find other ways to make his value to the team apparent. Josh now wanted to punish Coach Johnson for dressing him down on the field in front of his fans. And he now didn't really care if the Bruins won or lost the game, if only he could separate himself from the team's outcome. As long as he was quarterback and kicker on offense, the team's performance would be a reflection on him. That he also played safety on the Bruins defense was of little concern to him, as defensive backs got little recognition anyway.

It was fourth-and-6 at the MB 15, and Jug called for the field-goal unit to take the field. That meant little more than a reshuffling of the players already out there, with Ty Green moving from tight end to placekick holder—as Reuben Russo and most previous Bruins quarterbacks had always done—and with Brett Woods coming off the field for a bigger lineman and better blocker. Artie remained at center in order to snap the ball back to Ty, who would place it point-down and spin the laces out of the way for Josh's soccer-style kick.

Over the past month, the three boys had practiced hundreds of kicks from various yardages, and all three knew from experience that Josh could split the uprights from 30 yards out but no farther. Just inside the "red zone" at the MB 15, the field goal unit was close to its outer limit, with the tall, white goalposts sitting at the back of the end zone. Technically, that extra 10 yards beyond the goal line and the 7 yards behind the line of scrimmage where Ty would place the ball pushed Josh just outside his comfort range, but Jug Johnson didn't want to risk a failed fourth-down run or pass and come away with no points on this opening possession. Jug Johnson wanted his team to make a statement, and so they did.

Ty called for the ball, and Artie snapped it straight to the spot they had practiced so many times. On one knee, Ty spun the ball so that Josh, stepping diagonally from the left, could swing his right leg and catch bare leather, not white laces, with what would have been a special kicking shoe—if he had bothered to change into it in the huddle. But for whatever reason, he hadn't done so, and the odd feel of his regular right cleat striking the ball threw off the kick just enough to send it sailing like a dying goose toward the uprights.

The knuckling spheroid barely cleared the outstretched hands of the defenders on the line, rising just enough to clang into the goalpost's crossbar, then up and over it with only inches to spare. The crowd cheered, but they also laughed and slapped each other on the back as if their team had stolen something that it hadn't deserved. Listening to the laughter, Josh Stark felt the same way. He had succeeded in putting the Bruins ahead 3-0, but he was still a laughingstock.

On the ensuing kickoff, Josh decided to shut everyone up. Instead of kicking away and sending the ball to the far end of the field for it to be returned, he kicked the pigskin into the turf mere yards in front of himself, causing the football to bounce high into the air where the closest Waverunners players would have to handle it.

As an onside kick, the ball had to travel at least ten yards before a Bruins player could recover it and give Arbor possession. This was usually done as a last-ditch effort at the end of a game when a team was trailing or, maybe, when a bold coach wanted to surprise the opposing team at the start of a game or half. An onside kick should never be attempted when neither the coach on the sideline nor the rest of the kicking unit on the field has been forewarned. That was Josh's situation. And his bright idea backfired.

A Mimosa Beach player snatched the ball out of the air before it had even traveled ten yards, and barreled down the field through the surprised Bruins defenders into the end zone. He spiked the ball into the turf in celebration while being joined there by his jubilant buddies, who jostled and tugged him back to the visiting sideline. The home crowd wasn't laughing now.

Neither was Jug Johnson. Josh tried to avoid him by staying on the field after the MB kicker added the extra point giving the Waverunners a 7-3 lead. But Jug called his kick-return unit into a huddle near the sideline and beckoned for Josh to come join them. The look on Jug's face could not be mistaken for anything but bottled-up rage. When Josh finally reached the huddle, Jug addressed him alone in just five words: "No … more … surprises.… Got it?" It wasn't an oratorical question, not even by Jug's definition. He expected an answer.

When Josh didn't respond, Jug asked, "Am I being clear?"

"Crystal," said Josh, doing his best impression of a bratty subordinate.

Brett Woods returned the Waverunners kickoff to the Arbor 23. From there, Josh ran the plays that Coach Johnson relayed to the offense through Artie, but the young QB's heart wasn't in his execution of the coach's calls, especially when Josh couldn't be the center of attention. If he was expected to hand off to Brett or Ty, who sometimes lined up in the backfield, Josh's timing would be off just enough to delay the running back an instant or cause him to pay more attention to the handoff than necessary to keep from fumbling. If Josh was expected to pass, his throws would be either too hard to handle or just out of the receiver's reach.

It turned out that the only plays highlighting Josh were the punts that ended every Bruins possession until the final play of the half, when, on third-and-long with only seconds left on the clock, Josh threw an interception that was returned for a touchdown, a pick six that made the score 21-3 in the Waverunners' favor.

The other Mimosa Beach touchdown had come at the end of a long, second-quarter drive that had started on the MB 2-yard line. Josh's booming punt into "coffin corner"—his best play of the half—had pinned the Waverunners offense deep in their own territory, but they had mixed runs and short passes to grind out first downs on their march up the field. As far as the visitors had been concerned, the only bad part of the drive had come at the end when the Waverunners kicker had missed the point-after attempt. But that lost point was put back on the scoreboard at the end of the half with a successful two-point conversion after Mimosa Beach's interception and touchdown.

The Waverunner QB, kneeling to hold for the kicker, had snatched the ball away at the last instant, as Lucy always did Charlie Brown in the funny pages, and had run the ball around end across the goal line untouched. The closest defensive back on the two-point run had been Josh Stark, who hadn't even bothered to follow the play, never even considering that a *Peanuts*-like fake might happen. Once again, Josh had been wrong.

Minutes after the halftime horn had sounded and the two teams had jogged down the hill to their separate locker rooms near the gym, Josh learned that his half-hearted play on both offense and defense had not gone unnoticed. He hadn't refused to run the coach's plays but had simply done little to make them work, whether on the ground or through the air. That was just on offense and didn't take his equally lackluster defensive play tinto consideration. In the locker room, Josh Stark came face to face with the consequences of his wrongheadedness.

CHAPTER 15 – Finding His Heart's Desire

JUG JOHNSON AND HIS ASSISTANT COACHES gave the boys time to visit the restroom, then called them together to sit on the long benches in front of their lockers. Artie and Ty noticed that while the players found seats, Jug had taken Josh Stark aside and was speaking to his quarterback in a low voice but with a stern look. Josh studied his own cleats on the polished concrete floor, a hand on one hip, his helmet dangling by its white chinstrap from that fist.

Ty nudged Artie and nodded toward the locker-room door, where Josh's father, Joel Stark, stood to one side. Squinting, the man was focused on his son and Jug across the room.

"Uh-oh," said Ty, just loud enough for Artie to hear. "It's gonna hit the fan."

Artie nodded. "Yep. Coach doesn't let parents in here—ever."

Motioning for the frowning QB to join his teammates, Jug glanced over at Joel Stark but said nothing for a few seconds until Josh was settled on the bench near his locker. "Awright now, boys," the coach began, "we ain't gonna dwell on what we did wrong in the first half."

Jug took a long moment to look around the room, his gaze ending on Joel Stark still standing just inside the door. "Everybody in here knows good and well what just happened," Jug said, flipping a nub of white chalk in his hand, "so I'm not gonna fuss about it no more, because I *know* it ain't gonna happen again—not tonight, anyway." He turned to the blackboard at his back and wrote the word

"T-E-A-M" in large block letters.

That was when Josh raised his hand. "Can I be excused?" asked Josh. The gleam in his eyes showed that he knew exactly what he was doing—that he was goading the coach into saying something sharp to him in front of his father.

Sidetracked by the ill-timed request, Jug stared at the boy for a few seconds and gathered his thoughts before responding. "Why certainly, young man," said Jug. "I thought you'd already visited the toilet before I stopped you a few minutes ago, but I apologize if I kept you from doing your business. You go right on."

Josh stood. "That's not it," he said, staying where he was. "I need to talk to my dad."

Again, Jug studied the boy, then looked across the room at the father without so much as a nod to him. "Whatever you need to tell your daddy can wait, son," said Jug. "Like I told him the other day, Mr. Stark can step outside and wait until we all talk—"

"He isn't your son," Joel Stark said, straightening up but making no move to leave. "He's *my* son, and I don't like the way you're coaching him—Jug."

The seated players stole glances at one another, figuring that their old coach would surely explode now. And they were right, though Jug's fuse was longer than they thought possible.

"Mr. Stark?" said Jug. "I'm gonna ask you one more time, politely, to please step outside so I can tell the boys about a couple lineup changes we're making this half. I *am* the coach, sir."

Stark stared at him for a second, then looked over at his son before focusing again on the coach. "Well, *Jug,* if my boy doesn't start the second half," said Stark, "this will be the last game you coach at Arbor High."

That remark made Jug Johnson's red-hot temper rise like mercury in an old-fashioned thermometer on a hot summer day, shooting up from his neck into his jowls and high on his flushed cheeks. "That's right, Mr. Stark," said Jug. "I may very well get myself fired tonight—for taking you by the scruff of the neck and throwing you out of my locker room. Now get outta here before I kick you where the sun don't shine."

Stark glared at Jug, then looked again at his son. "Sit down, Josh," the father said. "We'll talk after the game." He gave Jug a sidelong glance and added, "You need to show this old man what you can do."

Jug nodded to the two assistant coaches standing along the side wall and started moving with them toward Stark. When the real estate developer saw the three burly men approaching, he decided to give ground and delay his attack until he could rally his own supporters—and Josh's fans—in the stands. Stark was out the door before the coaches got halfway across the room.

Shaking his head, Jug turned and went back to his spot at the blackboard. "T-E-A-M," he spelled out, underlining the word and slamming the chalk in the tray. "Nosiree, there ain't no 'I' in *team*, is there, boys?" He looked at Artie and Ty sitting together. "Arthur Bauer and Tyrone Green? You two boys are our co-captains this season. Either of you got anything to say about the way we're playing tonight?"

Artie just shook his head. Ty spoke up with, "No, sir, Coach Johnson," but made the mistake of looking over at Josh Stark.

"What?" Josh said. "Are you saying this is all *my* fault?" He stood to challenge Ty, even though most of the team sat between them.

Ty remained seated. "I didn't say that," said Ty. "I'm just sitting here."

"I saw the look you gave me," Josh began, still on his feet. He pointed at both co-captains. "And I don't have to put up with that kind of crap, not from either one of you. Some captains you guys are."

Ty rose. But he drew no closer to Josh. Artie smiled to himself and quietly shook his head again, this time with less emphasis than a minute earlier.

Deciding to intervene before Ty and Josh came to blows, Jug shouted, "Awright, none of that, boys! Both of you, sit your butts down!" He nodded at Ty first, then turned to Josh. "Now, don't get your panties in a wad, Stark. Like I told you a few minutes ago, you're just having an off night. Everybody has them now and then." He waited for Ty and Josh to sit back down, and for Josh to look up again.

"So here's what we're gonna do," Jug continued. "We're gonna see how Ty

Green does running the offense this half. Ty's our co-captain, he's a senior, and he backed up Reuben Russo the last two seasons, so I'm giving him a chance to get the offense moving tonight. We don't just need a spark. We need—"

"You don't need a *Stark*?" said Josh, standing again. "Well, I don't need this abuse. I'm getting out of here." He looked over at his best friend, Brett Woods. "Come on, Brett. We don't need this crap. They'll turn on *you* next."

Brett had no intention of following Josh out the door, but he wasn't ready yet to tell his buddy to leave him out of this mess. Brett shrugged, shook his head and looked back at the coach for help. Josh threw up his hands in exasperation but didn't leave.

"Young man," Jug said, "I didn't say that, and you know it. I'm telling you one last time to sit down and to *stay* down—and to keep your mouth shut, too—or you won't even be playing the rest of *this* game, not on defense and not kicking, neither. You're *still* important to our team, but, hey, you can leave if you want to. It's up to you. If you do walk out, though, you won't be welcome back on this football team, not this season, anyway. So you better stop for one second and think, boy. Don't go off half-cocked."

Josh looked around the room one last time to gauge his support among the players. When he saw there was none, not even with Brett and a few other friends, he slung his helmet into the lockers, ripped off his jersey and shoulder pads, and stormed out of the locker room.

Jug watched the boy leave, then turned to the team. "Oh, he'll be back," said the coach. "Those football pants are ours. And his street clothes are there in his locker, right?" Though his face was still flushed, there was a gleam in Jug's eye. "The lesson here, boys," he continued, "is that if you want to make a dramatic exit, make sure you take your duds and car keys with you."

Even Brett laughed at that advice, mainly because he hadn't let Josh lead him down the same pot-holed road. "His cell phone is in there, too," Brett said. "I can swap out the clothes and other stuff with him after the game. I'm not afraid of him—or his dad."

"No," said Jug, shaking his head, "I'll take care of it. Thank you, but what we need to be talking about is the fight we're in out on that field. We got half a game to play yet, and I fully intend for us to beat these boys. Matter of fact, I got my heart set on it. They ain't that good, you know? Like I said, we've got off to a bad start—a *real* bad start, if you count last week, too—but we're doing what we got to do, and that's make some adjustments."

He turned once more to Artie and Ty. "Yogi," said Jug, "you can let Green make the calls in the huddle. And, Tyrone, I expect you'll run the plays I call from the sideline, right?"

"Yes, sir, Coach," said Ty.

Artie nodded, but raised his hand. "Coach Johnson?" he said. "What are we gonna do about a punter and kicker?"

"Way ahead of you," said Jug, with a wink. "We're down by three touchdowns, right? So I don't see us punting or kicking field goals on fourth down. Matter of fact, I better not even *see* any fourth downs this half—except when those dang Waverunners have the ball. And after we do score, we won't be kicking PATs, not tonight. We're going for two points each time—after all *three* touchdowns. Course, that also means we ain't giving up any more points to Mimosa Beach. That's the new game plan. Okay? Any questions?"

Artie hated to follow up his earlier inquiry, but he knew that Josh's absence would be felt immediately on the field. "Coach?" he asked. "Who's gonna kick off? I mean, *we* are, to start the half and after all those touchdowns we're gonna score. But who's gonna do the kicking?"

Wincing at Artie's question, Jug scratched his head for a moment, looked over at his equally stumped assistants, then addressed the players with another obvious query: "Anybody in here ever kick a ball? In a game, I mean. Ninth-grade flag, Pee Wee, Mighty Mite?"

This time it was Brett Woods who lifted his hand. "Does soccer count?"

Jug laughed. "Well, not normally," he said, "but we're kinda in a bind here. So I tell you what. You handle the kicking chores tonight, and I'll say some extra good things about you in the newspaper writeup. That little gal of ours is writing it, ain't she?"

Not having talked to Leah Russo since lunchtime, Artie remembered noticing her during the first half up in the press box with Bennie Pressler. Leah was keeping team stats there where she could see the entire field. Bennie was in the press box to help the public-address announcer, who was getting used to the stadium's new PA system and scoreboard that Bennie's family had donated.

"Coach, how are we gonna explain Josh being gone?" asked Artie. "It might help if we tell Leah and Bennie what just happened."

"No," said Jug. "All you boys just keep quiet and let me handle it. Now, we're going back out to the field. We need to get good and loosened up. Then you boys head on over to the bench and wait for me to give you one last word, all right?"

Jug waved his offensive assistant over. "Joe," he said, "I'm gonna call up to the press box and tell little Leah about our lineup changes. How about if you hang around here for maybe ten minutes, in case ol' Stark comes looking for his boy's things? If you don't see him right off—or if the boy don't come himself—make sure the door's locked good and tight before you head out, okay? We'll be on defense first, but I'll cover for you, if necessary."

The assistant coach nodded and walked over to the door as the players left for the field. His own son would be replacing Ty Green on offense at tight end. So as long as substitute kicker Brett Woods didn't surprise everyone with another onside kick—whether intentional or not—the coach had time to stand watch at the locker room and join the team in the stadium before his boy got into his first game. He just hoped that his son had paid attention during practice all those times the starters had run through the Reuben. But maybe the trick play wouldn't be needed.

CHAPTER 16 – The Point of No Return

BRETT WOODS'S FIRST-EVER KICKOFF wouldn't make any highlight reels on the Iron Harbor and Mimosa Beach TV stations' weekend sportscasts, but it wouldn't appear in any blooper segments, either. The kick was low and wobbly, not even as good as Leah's effort in the previous year's Punt, Pass & Kick competition. But it got the job done, and the Waverunners started their first drive of the second half on their own 28-yard line.

From there, the Bruins defense held firm on three straight running plays and forced the Waverunners to punt the ball away. Now a punt returner, Brett caught the ball on his own 35 and ran it back along the sideline to the MB 22, where he was pushed out of bounds.

Two plays later, senior quarterback Tyrone Green took the snap from Artie Bauer, faded back five steps and hit a streaking Bruins wide receiver on the 5-yard line. The boy took the ball in stride and fell into the end zone for the touchdown. The two-point conversion failed, an end-around play that used Brett as a decoy and Ty's young substitute tight end as the ball carrier. His father, the assistant coach, greeted him on the sideline with a slap on the back and words of encouragement. Jug Johnson did likewise. The other boys met their teammate with similar support and tried to ease the sting of his failed run. Arbor now trailed 21-9.

For the rest of the third quarter, the Waverunners offense was stymied. The

Bruins held the MB rushers to no more than three yards at a clip, and allowed only two short passes to be completed. Mimosa Beach was unable even to gain a first down and had to punt two more times that quarter.

The Arbor offense wasted no time scoring on both of its subsequent third-quarter possessions—once on Ty's quarterback keeper from the MB 25 after he was forced from the pocket; and, with a half-minute left in the quarter, on a 43-yard screen pass from Ty to Brett. Neither two-point conversion succeeded—one a pass that was broken up in the corner of the end zone, the other an off-tackle run by Brett that was stuffed by the defensive line. So going into the fourth quarter, the score was knotted at 21-all.

On the sideline between quarters, Artie and Ty sat together on the bench long enough to catch their breath and drink some water. The referees had agreed to lengthen the quarter break so that the Arbor Booster Club could announce the winner of its 50-50 raffle and make yet another appeal for donations, most of which would go toward Harry Bauer's medical bills. Taking the mic during the regular announcer's restroom break, Bennie Pressler had the honor of announcing that booster Woody Woods, of all people, had won the record-breaking raffle and that he had agreed to donate his considerable winnings to Artie's family.

Artie knew that many eyes in the stadium were on him, and the thought of accepting the crowd's charity again embarrassed him a bit, as he knew it also would his grandparents when they learned about it. But he wanted more than anything not to worry about his family's welfare, not only Grandpa's recovery but also their ability to keep the farm and make it self-sufficient once he went off to college the next year. For as much as he wanted to attend Iron Harbor A&M close to home, he really didn't know where he would end up, especially if he got scholarship offers from big athletic programs both in and out of state. For a great offensive lineman and hard worker like Artie, the sky was the limit. His desire was to make his grandparents proud and to thank them for raising him as their own.

Josh Stark had everything that Artie Bauer did not—a wealthy family including a mom and dad who adored him, good looks, nice clothes, a great car and a hot girlfriend. But above all, Josh had the self-assurance of never regretting any mistakes or feeling guilty about any missteps. He was always right, at least in his own eyes and those of his doting parents. And all who stood in his way—as Jug Johnson and Ty Green had earlier that night—soon learned that regret and guilt could be suffered even when one had done what was right. Josh's father called it "Stark reality" and never smiled when he used the phrase, always on purpose.

After being told that neither Stark had shown up in the locker room by the start of the second half, Coach Johnson had spent part of the third quarter scanning the stands in search of the disgruntled father and son. He didn't know—but could guess—how Mrs. Stark had taken Josh's decision to quit the team, but she wasn't the one whom Jug feared most. She didn't have the reputation of being vindictive, of getting her way at any cost, by hook or by crook. The male Starks were known for those particular qualities. It made Jug wish that he *had* kicked Joel Stark out of the locker room, literally. But with the fourth quarter left to play in a tie game, Jug Johnson turned his thoughts back to his team and their aspirations to erase last week's failure by scoring their first win of the young season.

* * *

The fourth quarter began with Mimosa Beach coming alive and marching the ball down the field into Bruins territory. Whatever the Waverunners head coach had said to his team during the long quarter break had been a slap in their collective faces, reviving the running game that had been able to grind out yardage in the first half. Their passing attack was still limited to short throws, but they were gaining one first down after another, and had used more than half of the fourth-quarter clock on that one drive when Josh Stark's absence at defensive safety finally hurt the Bruins.

Josh's sub had been playing his heart out that half, covering the MB receivers like a tent and batting down passes that came his way. But on third-and-9 at the Arbor 19, the backup safety didn't know—as Josh did know—that when his receiver got past him, it would have been better to be called for pass interference than to have given up a touchdown reception. An interference penalty would have put the ball on the 4-yard line, where it would have been first-and-goal for

Mimosa Beach. Instead, the Waverunners scored and took a 28-21 lead with five minutes to play.

"Okay, boys," said Jug in the huddle on the sideline. "There's no rush. There's plenty of time on the clock. We got one timeout left, but we're gonna hang onto it for the time being. Just keep working the sidelines, Tyrone. That'll stop the clock, and they'll stop it to move the chains on first downs, too. So everybody keep your head in the game. We can do this. Come on, now. 'Team,' on three. One, two, three—"

"TEAM!" the boys shouted and broke the huddle.

Brett Woods took the kickoff on his own 12 and dashed up the sideline again, all the way to the Arbor 43. Ty completed two sideline passes for gains of 5 and 6 yards, with the receivers stepping out of bounds on both tosses. Ty's third throw was incomplete, but that too stopped the clock. The big, new scoreboard clock showed 3:27 in bright yellow numbers between the teams' scores in white. The Bruins were driving toward the scoreboard, which stood on high ground just behind the end zone.

It was second-and-10 on the MB 46. Artie snapped the ball and rose to block, careful not to leave the line of scrimmage too soon. Seconds later, he heard pads crash into pads behind him, and he turned to see Ty on the ground, the ball secured in his grasp and a Waverunners linebacker celebrating the sack for a 6-yard loss.

Going without a huddle, the Bruins hurried back to the line and got the next play off without having to call their last timeout. Ty flung the pigskin down the middle of the field, leading the young sub who had replaced him at tight end. The boy leapt high to pull in the throw and tucked it under one arm before he was undercut by a Waverunners safety. He hit the ground hard but held onto the ball. With that 16-yard gain, the Bruins were looking at first-and-10 on the MB 36 with under two minutes to play.

As soon as the officials moved the chains for the first down, the umpire wound one arm to restart the clock and moved away from the line of scrimmage. Ty took the snap and dropped back, surveying the Bruins receivers on their pass routes. No one was open, as the Waverunners linebackers had sagged downfield to help their cornerbacks and safeties. The only receiver who might be open in another step or two was, again, Ty's tight end, who had taken the hard hit on the previous play. Without thinking, Ty led the boy with the pass, this time keeping it low so that it would either be caught for a short gain or fall incomplete to stop the clock. An interception and change of possession would have ended the game for all intents and purposes.

And that's what appeared to happen. The boy bent down to make the difficult catch, but mishandled the ball. As he struggled to get it under control, he got hit and slung the ball into the air, making it fair game for anyone nearby to catch.

The defensive lineman that Artie had been blocking scrambled backwards toward the dying quail of a ball and extended both arms to take it in. Just as his arms closed around the pigskin, Artie's bone-crunching hit from behind knocked it from the defender's grasp and sent it to the ground. The pass was ruled incomplete, stopping the clock. It was now second-and-10 from the MB 36. More importantly, there was only 1:21 left to play, and Arbor still trailed by 7.

Ty's second- and third-down passes also were incomplete. That left :58 on the scoreboard clock that stared down at them from above the distant goalposts. It was fourth-and-10 now, and Artie knew this could be the Bruins' last chance to pull out a win if they didn't score or at least get a first down on this play. With a turnover on downs, Mimosa Beach could run out the clock without gaining a yard. Arbor could use its last timeout, but the Waverunners QB could win the game by simply taking a knee on three straight plays in what was called, for good reason, the Victory Formation.

Up in the press box, Leah and Bennie's optimism about the team's prospects of winning had subsided. Both knew enough about football to realize that the odds were against their Bruins and that even a 10-yard gain from the MB 36 might take too much time off the clock. The Mimosa Beach secondary had shut down the Bruins' passing attack, and few of the rushing plays that Arbor had run that night had gained more than 10 yards.

In the stands, the home crowd buzzed in anticipation of what could be their team's last play. Ty's mom, Rachel Green, reached out with one arm and hugged

Nicie Evans. "Come on, Ty!" Rachel shouted. "You can do it!"

Nicie clapped her hands in rhythm to the band's umpteenth playing of the Bruins fight song. She had lost count of how many times she'd heard the song that night, but she still couldn't remember the lyrics to any of the verses, just the "Fight! Fight! Fight!" of the chorus, words that the old Nicie could relate to. Down on the field, the boys were in the fight of their young football lives.

"Green 34," Ty shouted at the line. But then he called, "Reuben, Reuben," and took two steps back into the shotgun formation. Artie and Brett immediately recognized the call—for *The Reuben*, the new trick play that Leah had joked could make a "linebacker sandwich" out of the ball carrier if everyone didn't do what they were supposed to do. Brett joined the twin receivers on the left side of the line, leaving Ty in the backfield alone.

As Leah had outlined to Jug when devising the play at practice, the tight end—which until tonight had been Ty—was supposed to go into motion and take the outside linebacker to the left side of the field. But Ty's inexperienced sub was unsure of himself and didn't move from his initial slotback spot on the right side. When Jug saw what was developing on the field, he immediately called timeout, his last one.

Standing at the stadium gate with his son and the school principal, Joel Stark exclaimed, "What a fool. He called timeout, and the clock wasn't even running. He just lost us the game."

Principal Church looked at Stark and at the son, now wearing street clothes. "What do you mean *us*? Your son quit tonight, didn't he?"

Stark snorted. "There's more to it than that, Jerry. I told you what that doddering old fool said in the locker room. And he's not going to get away with it."

"Well," said the principal, "this is neither the time nor the place to have that discussion. I need to see about the gate receipts right now and the 50-50 money. You and I can talk bright and early on Monday morning, if that suits you, Mr. Stark."

"I'll be here," Stark said, "and I'll have my lawyer with me." That too would have made for a good exit, but the Stark men held their ground to watch the end of the game. Somehow Joel thought that Josh's brashness would be vindicated if the Bruins lost. Mrs. Stark had already gone to the couple's car.

Josh had driven himself to school, but wanted to watch his old teammates lose, just out of spite. He didn't care if his quitting were vindicated or not, and he thought that a loss might even prompt Jug Johnson to beg him to come back onto the team as starting quarterback.

In the huddle on the field, Jug and the offensive assistant ran through the key players' assignments with what little time they had before the referees started the play clock. Lining up again, Ty set up over center, moved back into the shotgun, waited for his tight end to pass behind him in motion, and then called for the ball.

When the ball touched his hands, the clock started counting down from :58. Ty drifted back three steps, cocked the ball at his ear as if to throw, but dropped it backwards into the waiting hands of the young tight end as he ran behind Ty. Holding the ball with both hands, the boy continued to move toward the right sideline. Artie held his ground at first, then began to move laterally along the line to his right and readied himself to block for the ball carrier.

But as the young sub reached the line of scrimmage, he turned and flipped the football back to Ty, who cocked his arm again and stepped into his throw, hitting Brett for a circus catch on the Mimosa Beach 5-yard line. The crowd roared.

But Brett had fallen to the ground in bounds. So as soon as the official holding the down marker for the chain crew took his spot at the 3—it was now first-and-goal—the referee wound the clock at :28 and the game's final seconds began ticking down. Ty spiked the ball to stop the clock at :25, giving the Bruins time for one last huddle.

Both Ty and Artie looked to Jug on the sideline and saw him signal the play that they were to use. From the 3-yard line, they would have to cover the same yardage that they had failed to gain in any of their three earlier two-point conversion attempts. This time, Jug called for a pass play, knowing that an incomplete pass would give them one, maybe two, more shots at a touchdown before time expired. The receivers lined up in *twins right* and *twins left*, with Ty alone again in the backfield. One pair of receivers—one on each side of the line—were to do crossing patterns; the other pair, corner routes.

That was the plan, but two defensive linemen broke through the Bruins line and sacked Ty at the 9-yard line. Lining up in a hurry, he had to spike the ball again, this time on third down to stop the clock at :06, just enough time to run one last play. It was fourth-and-goal from the 9. The Waverunners expected another pass play, with so much ground to cover for a touchdown. Ty and Artie looked again to Jug, who made what he figured would be his last call of the night.

Ty stood over center, then moved back into the shotgun. With the snap, he drifted back again and cocked the ball as the young tight end ran behind him once more. But this time, Ty flicked the ball forward and hit Brett squarely in the chest at the back of the end zone. No one was happier than Woody Woods, the Bruins' biggest and best booster. No one cursed louder than Joel Stark and his son, who had bet that the play's failure would be Josh's ticket back onto the team. But the import of the boy's absence from the offense was yet to be fully apparent.

With no kicker to tie the score and send the game into overtime, the Bruins ran another two-point conversion attempt. As had happened thrice before, the conversion failed, this time on the ground, with Brett—the night's erstwhile hero—coming up a half yard short of the goal line. It was as simple as that. The final score: Mimosa Beach 28, Arbor 27.

Their effort didn't feel like a moral victory, though the boys had overcome so much that night to come so close to winning the game. At 0-2 on the new season, the Arbor High Bruins were at the bottom of the Suncoast Conference standings. Still, Jug saw several positive results in his team's heartbreaking loss. They had found the true quarterback that they should have had from Day One. The substitutes at safety and even the boy at tight end—despite his initial timidity—had proven themselves worthy of starting on Friday nights to come.

And yet the Bruins needed a new kicker. Also, depending on what happened Monday morning in the principal's office, they might even need a new head coach by lunch that day, especially if Jug Johnson didn't like what he heard in his meeting with Joel Stark and Principal Church. It was going to be a long weekend, not just for the Barf Table mates, but for everyone at Arbor High.

CHAPTER 17 – With a Little Help from His Friends

THE NEXT MORNING ARTIE WAS BUSY milking Bessie and Bossy out in the barn when the sun peeked above the eastern horizon on the Bauer farm. Grandpa was doing better at the hospital in Ebenezerville, but Grandma still insisted on spending nights close to him. While her desire to be with her husband was understandable, Artie had begun to wish she would move back to the farm, so that she could at least help him by feeding the chickens and gathering eggs.

Artie didn't mind picking up the daily chores that Grandpa had always done—like slopping their two hogs, Frick and Frack—but with Grandma not there to do any actual cooking, there wasn't much "slop," or leftovers, to give the big boys, just expensive bagged feed that was running low. Not only that. Before long, it would be what was called "hog-killing time," just after the first frost of autumn, something that Grandpa had always handled himself. Artie did not have the heart to kill, or butcher, Frick and Frack. And like them, he missed Grandma's cooking.

As he finished up with Bossy, Artie heard a car pull up outside the barn. Still holding two of the bindle cow's teats, Artie straightened up on the milking stool to peer out the barn window. He saw the wide windshield and black vinyl top of the White Whale parked just outside, and he assumed that Ty would know he'd be milking at that hour and would look for him right away in the barn's milking parlor up front. But no one exited the big LTD immediately, not Ty Green, not any of the passengers whom Artie hadn't identified yet.

When Artie emerged from the barn with two full milk pails, a handle in each hand, he was surprised to see that his buddy wasn't sitting alone—that Nicie Evans sat up front with Ty. Behind them, Leah Russo and, of all people, Brett Woods shared the wide back seat, but with plenty of room between them. Seeing Brett confused Artie and even gave him a twinge of jealousy, just for an instant.

"Hi, guys," said Artie, as he passed Ty's open driver-side window. "Give me a minute to put this milk in the creamery. I'll be right back."

Careful not to spill any milk, he moved like a tightrope walker and toted the heavy, steel pails to the small, cinder-block building next to the barn. There, he poured the warm, white liquid into gallon jars, and deposited them in the old refrigerator standing against one wall. He'd have to return later and strain the milk into smaller containers for the folks who regularly stopped by the farm to replenish their supplies of raw milk and to return empty quart jars.

Selling milk was another daily chore that Grandma usually took care of, partly because she enjoyed chatting with neighbors and with customers from town who didn't like store-bought dairy products. She also made butter and skimmed cream for them, but Artie didn't have time to add those tasks to his new list of chores.

His four schoolmates were out of the car and waiting outside for Artie when he emerged from the creamery, locking the door behind himself. "Hey, big guy," said Ty Green. "We all thought you might need a little help today, from your friends. And we'll do more than just help with your chores. We'll be your farm family—you know, your *farmily*." They all laughed at the tall boy's play on words.

But Ty was the only one of the four who appeared to be dressed for work. He wore old blue jeans and a T-shirt, with a scuffed pair of work boots.

Artie eyed the other three teenagers. "Wearing *those* clothes?" he said to them. "Thanks, but did you guys bring something to change into?" He looked at their shoes and added, "Brett, those flip-flops just ain't gonna work, not on a farm."

Brett laughed. "Hey, dude, I'm a surfer, not a farmer," he said, "but I want to help, too. You got any more boots like the ones you're wearing?" He nodded at Artie's brown dairy boots.

"As a matter of fact, I do," said Artie. "They're on the back porch. They're

Grandpa's. I'll go get them—and some socks for you, too." He turned to the two girls. "Nicie? Leah? Do you guys have something else to wear?"

Nicie had on shorts, a tank top and what appeared to be brand-new running shoes. Leah wore baggy jeans and her usual gray Bruins hoodie. She stepped back to the White Whale and leaned inside an open rear window. She took out a brown plastic grocery bag that held a change of clothes and some old tennis shoes. "I know how to dress on a farm," Leah said. "I've been going to horse therapy all summer."

Nicie spoke up. "Is it working?" she asked, one eyebrow raised at her thin friend.

Leah's face turned red, but she smiled. "Well," she said, "I don't know. Sometimes I think it's helping. But then something happens, and I have to start all over again. It's hard." She held up the spare clothes and shoes. "But, yeah, I have something else to wear if I get dirty."

"I like that Arbor High duffel bag you're using," said Artie, referring to the grocery bag. "You might want to go ahead and change into those old sneaks." Then he pointed at Nicie's new running shoes. "And, Nicie, I'll bring Grandma's boots for you to wear. Okay? Grandma has big feet, too." He grinned.

Nicie knew he was kidding, but she couldn't let him off scot-free. "Hey, now," she said, trying not to smile. "I'll bet those boots are just the right size to kick your butt, buddy."

Artie waved her off and turned back toward the farmhouse. Ty followed him, leaving the other three to look around the barnyard. "Have you heard?" said Ty.

"About what?" Artie said. "I've been milking the cows since before dawn, and Grandpa doesn't want a radio or anything in the dairy parlor. He says the noise would make the girls' milk sour, like they were being fussed at."

Ty chuckled. "Yeah, I hear you," he said, "but it would probably taste more like gin and juice—or a white Russian. No, I mean news—or sports, actually."

Artie shook his head. "No, I haven't heard *anything* this morning. After last night's game, I'm ready to think about something other than football for a couple days. I've got too much to do here. And then I need to drive to E-ville to see

Grandpa and to take some stuff to Grandma."

"Well, you're gonna want to hear *this*." Ty paused. "Solid Rock's quarterback got hurt last night—out for the season, broken leg—and the rumor is that our boy Josh is gonna transfer there and take his place, starting Monday."

"Really? Josh is gonna transfer to Solid Rock?" Artie stopped in his tracks and turned to Ty, placing his hand on his friend's shoulder. "That's a *good* thing, right?" Artie said. "That means you're the quarterback now, and Josh and his father can't keep pulling the team apart. Where did you hear that—about Josh transferring?"

Ty shrugged. "It was on the radio while we were driving over here—well, the part about Solid Rock's QB breaking his leg, anyway. The sports guy said there was talk about a 'surprise' replacement, but he didn't come out and say it was Josh. The guy said it wasn't official yet."

"So how do you know Josh is transferring?" said Artie, raising his eyebrows.

"Brett said so," Ty replied. "He caught me last night after you left for home, and he said the three of us need to talk before Monday. That's why he's here this morning. Last night he said he had just heard something that we—that you and I—need to know about. I told him that the girls and I had decided to come out here to help you on the farm today, and he said he'd come along, even if it meant he had to do some actual work."

"Is that the only reason he's here?" asked Artie. "I mean, to talk? Or do you think there's something else? Maybe he likes Leah. I saw them sitting together in the back seat. Do you think he's trying to get close to her?"

Ty looked confused. "Well, maybe," he said, "but she's already zinged him a couple of times this morning." He laughed. "She doesn't cut him any slack, not even with him being the *almost* hero of the game. You know, if Brett hadn't played as well as he did, we would've looked awful bad."

"Yeah," said Artie, "he played one whale of a game last night. He came within a foot or two of winning the whole shooting match for us." The two friends were quiet for a moment, imagining that they might have won, if only Josh Stark hadn't walked out of the locker room and left them without a kicker. "I'm glad he might be leaving," Artie added. "Josh, that is."

"Oh, he's already gone," said Ty. "Brett told us that Josh's dad made some calls last night and even talked to the Solid Rock coach at the hospital while his quarterback was still in surgery. What kind of jerk does that?"

Artie just shook his head. "Enough about them," he said, opening the screen door to the back porch. "You grab those boots over there, Ty, and I'll run upstairs for two pairs of socks. We need to get busy. There's a lot to do."

Once everyone had proper footwear, Artie assigned chores so that the teenagers could get to work that morning. Nicie took on Grandma's duties by feeding the chickens and collecting the eggs in the hen house, and by straining and storing quarts of milk in the creamery. Leah brushed down the two workhorses, Tom and Dick, and the two milk cows, Bessie and Bossy, taking care to make sure that the girls' udders were clean.

Brett rode the big riding mower and cut the grass around the farmhouse. He tried his hand at slopping the two hogs, Frick and Frack, though all he had to do was wade across the muddy hog lot to their trough and fill it with dry feed. Artie and Ty had the heaviest work—wrangling the fifty-pound bales of old hay to the front of the barn loft to make room in back for the new hay that had been baled earlier in the week.

Eventually, all five teens ended up in the hayloft, with the two girls working together to carry individual bales. Brett was strong enough to carry hay by himself and seemed to enjoy showing off to Leah and Nicie. They all worked until around ten o'clock that morning and then stopped for a break.

Artie retrieved a gallon of ice-cold water and five cups from the creamery, and carried the refreshments to his tired friends seated on bales of hay in the barn loft. "I wish I had some snacks to give you," he said to the four teens. "Grandma usually has fresh-baked cookies or fried pies in the kitchen, but they're long gone."

"Couldn't control yourself, could you, big guy?" Nicie said. "I thought you were looking kinda fat and sassy lately." She smiled.

With a grin, Ty took a sip of cold water. "Artie's just getting ready for wrestling season," Ty said. "He doesn't want to be the scrawniest heavyweight in the conference. I'm glad I play basketball. I can eat whatever I want and not worry about my weight."

"You *better* worry about your weight," said Nicie. "I don't date no fat boys." Thinking better of her remark, she addressed Artie, "No offense, big guy."

"None taken," Artie said, tipping up his own water cup. He looked over at Brett, who had grabbed the gallon jug and was pouring its cold liquid directly into his upturned mouth. "Hey, now, Brett," said Artie, "you're gonna get a br—"

"Arrrggghhh!" Brett sputtered, scrunching up his face in pain. "Brain freeeeeeze!"

Leah shook her head and said, "You'd think some surfers wouldn't fit the stereotype."

"Huh?" said Brett, whose head still hurt from swallowing the cold water. "What do you mean by that? "

Leah shrugged. "Well, you gotta *have* a brain," she said, "before it can freeze." She added, "I'm just kidding, Brett. You're a lot smarter than some other surfers I know—like Josh Stark, for one."

At her mention of the boy's name, Brett waved his hand for them to hear him out once the throbbing in his head subsided. "In the first place," he began, "Josh is still my friend, in spite of this mess with the team. I've known him since kindergarten, and we used to be neighbors. So watch what you say about him in front of me. Okay?"

Nicie set down her cup. "Why aren't you neighbors now?" she asked. "You have a nice place at the beach, don't you? That big house on the waterway? The one with the big boat dock? Isn't that where all the rich folks live? At the beach?"

Brett looked at her without smiling. "The Starks' house was bigger than ours," he said. "They sold it and moved to their golf course development on the river last year. Now they're in a *bigger* house, with a *bigger* dock and a *bigger* boat. But they don't *own* any of it. Their company owns everything."

"Why's that?" asked Ty.

"For legal reasons," Brett said. "I mean, people are lawsuit crazy nowadays. Everybody is suing everybody else for everything under the sun. I mean, we could end up losing everything if that lawsuit I told you about the other day goes against us. I guess Joel Stark was afraid they'd get dragged into it, and he wasn't taking any chances."

"What lawsuit are you talking about?" said Nicie.

Leah interrupted. "The Presslers' lawsuit?" she asked. "Yeah, Bennie told me about that. The broken surfboard leash? That's the company that sponsors Josh in surfing competitions. It's going to trial soon."

"Yes, it is," said Brett, "and I'm supposed to keep my mouth shut about it. But you know what? In elementary school, Bennie and I were good friends, too. And we got to be even better buddies when he started surfing. He used to spend Friday nights at my house, and then we'd surf all day long on Saturdays. My mom and dad liked him a lot—Dad, in particular. Josh, though, *never* liked Bennie. I'm not sure why. Josh was always so mean to him and treated Bennie like he didn't belong—you know, like Bennie wasn't as good as us. Speaking of Dad, he'll be here in a little bit. He's bringing us some lunch—if that's okay with you, Artie."

"Lunch?" said Artie. "I'm *always* okay with lunch. Thanks, Brett. I wasn't sure what we were gonna do. And I love the food that your dad serves us at pregame meals."

Brett smiled and glanced sideways at Leah seated on the bale next to him. "Yeah, Dad's a real grill master," he said, first to Artie, then to Leah, "but do you eat meat?"

"What do you mean by that?" snapped Leah. Frowning, she shifted her thin frame on the hay bale and brushed stray bits of straw off her knees.

Brett raised his hands in self-defense. "Hey," he said, "I never see you eat, so I thought you might be a vegetarian."

"Why are you even watching me?" said Leah. "Am I *that* interesting?"

Not knowing what to say, Brett blushed and just shrugged. He turned back to Artie. "I'll call Dad and see what he's putting together for us," said Brett. "Do you know if anyone else is coming around lunchtime?"

"I didn't know *you* were coming today—any of you," Artie said, with a laugh. He looked over at Ty and Nicie, who were smiling and whispering to one another on the single hay bale that they shared. "Hey, Ty, Nicie. Did you guys ask anyone else to come over here today?"

"As a matter of fact, we did," said Ty. "I don't know if they'll actually come, but Bennie and Tommy said they'd stop by sometime today—I'm not sure when. And I think Mom called Solid Rock Church—you know, since they came out here the other day—and she asked if they had anybody who could build a wheelchair ramp for your granddad. You know, he'll need one when he comes home, just to get into the house."

"I hadn't thought of that," Artie said, "and we're gonna have to figure out where he's gonna sleep, because he won't be able to climb all those stairs up to his and Grandma's bedroom. I guess we could fix him a bed downstairs in that old room off the kitchen. There's nothing but junk in there now."

Nicie spoke up. "We can do that next," she said, nodding at Artie and looking down at her mucked-up footwear. "I'm ready to do anything that doesn't make me have to keep wearing these dirty old boots."

"I second that," said Brett, studying his own boots that had carried him through the hog lot and back. "Those pigs are nasty."

"*Hogs*," Artie said, "and their names are Frick and Frack."

Brett laughed. "Well, you better not let Dad see them this afternoon, or their names will be Sliced and Chopped."

Nicie and Ty laughed, too, but they were scolded by Leah. "That isn't funny," Leah said. "I'm not a vegetarian, but I don't like killing animals—not even farm animals. I don't like killing anything. I just don't."

"I don't, either," said Artie, "but that's why Grandpa's raising those hogs. He loves ham and sausage—and especially bacon. I'm the one who gave the big boys names. Grandpa doesn't name animals he's gonna slaughter—like hogs and chickens and even a steer now and then. And I *do* eat meat. Yeah, I do like pork barbecue and fried chicken—and hamburgers. Grandma even uses lard and fatback from the hogs when she cooks vegetables and other stuff."

Leah shook her head sadly. "Fatback," she said. "That sounds awful."

"Oh, heck no," Nicie said, rising to her feet and clapping her hands to an imaginary beat. "Fatback is *phat*. My folks took me to a Fatback concert when I was little. They're my daddy's favorite funk band. C'mon, Ty. Let's dance." She tugged Ty to his feet, and the pair bopped and clapped while Leah frowned.

"Still," Leah continued, leaning forward to talk around the dancers, "fatback—as a food, anyway—sounds icky. It's like that other yucky mystery meat I refuse to eat—scrapple or souse or livermush or whatever it's called. That stuff is nasty."

Brett stood, too, but didn't start dancing. "Well, Leah, what *do* you eat?" he asked. "I need to call Dad so he brings something that you'll like. Pizza? Do you eat pizza? He makes great veggie pizzas."

"With cheese or without?" said Leah.

"Any way you want it," Brett said, with a nod. He took a tiny cell phone from his back pocket and looked down at it as he moved away from the group.

Punching some buttons, then pressing the bar-shaped device to his ear, he said, "Dad? … Yeah, we're good. … No, not just yet. We're taking a water break. Listen, we got some more people coming out here to work. Can you bring more food and drinks? Plates and cups, too … I don't know—maybe a dozen more? … Yep, sounds like a real party, doesn't it? … Okay, that sounds good. I'll see y— oh! And a couple slices of veggie pizza. For Leah Russo. She doesn't eat meat. … Cheese? Hang on. I'll ask her."

Brett put one hand over the front of the phone to cover the mic and turned to Leah. "So do you eat cheese or not?" he asked.

Her eyes narrowed. "And if I say yes?"

He smiled and put the phone back to his ear. "Yeah, Dad, she's okay with cheese. See you around noon. Bye."

The crew of friends got back to work and finished their morning tasks before heading to the farmhouse. There they washed up and waited for Woody Woods to arrive with lunch as they surveyed the jobs that would keep them busy that afternoon. Though they also expected to see Bennie Pressler, Tommy White and the Solid Rock Church folks—maybe even little Ricky Duran and his parents—no one else arrived at the Bauer farm that morning.

It was a beautiful, late-summer day, not too hot and not too chilly. Puffy white clouds floated in the deep blue sky. The five friends finally sat down together around the big farm table in Grandma's kitchen and chatted about interests other than fatback, scrapple and cheese—and surfboard leashes. Their easy-going interaction at the Bauers' table that morning wasn't anything like the challenges they faced each school day at the Arbor High Barf Table. There was no fear, no shame and no pressure. Just good-hearted fun.

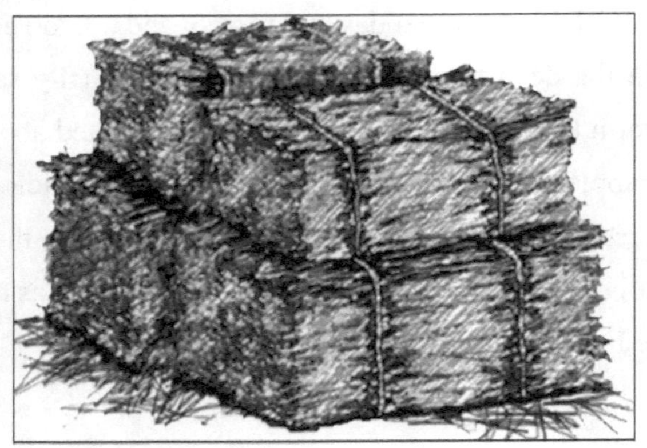

CHAPTER 18 – Ghosts of the Past Return

THE OLD WOOD-PANELED station wagon that Woody Woods used to make his grill's food deliveries pulled up to the farmhouse just before noon that Saturday. Brett, Artie and Ty went outside to help Woody carry bags of food and boxes of drinks into the kitchen, where Leah and Nicie finished clearing off the long farm table.

"It's been years since I was in this house," said Woody, looking around the kitchen and down the hall toward the stairwell to the upstairs. "My father—God rest his soul—was a friend of your granddaddy, Artie. He'd bring me out here to bird hunt in the fall, and I even learned to hunt with your mama. She was a good shot—for a girl."

"Hey!" said Nicie, careful not to insult this nice man bringing food and drinks to them. "I know how to shoot a gun better than most guys."

"I bet you can," Woody said. "That sounds like Artie's mom. She always got more birds than I did, *and* she knew how to clean them and cook them up. We had a blast back then!"

Leah frowned. "I'll bet the *birds* didn't have a blast," she muttered, shaking her head.

"Oh, come on, Leah," said Brett. "Birds aren't smart enough to know what's happening to them. That's where the term 'bird-brain' comes from."

Leah eyed Brett suspiciously. "Do *you* kill birds?" she asked, trying to decide whether she liked him or not.

"No, he doesn't," said Woody, before his son could reply. "I tried to take him hunting when he was about ten years old, but he refused to shoot any birds. He even cried when I shot a couple of doves and showed them to him. Right, buddy?"

Brett blushed again. "Come on, Dad," he said. "You're making me sound like a wienie." He glanced at Leah and looked back at Woody. "And, Dad, you were the one who said those birds didn't feel anything when you shot them."

Woody smiled and kept unpacking the bags of barbecue sandwiches, each one wrapped in red-checkered paper. "Oh, Brett. Everybody here knows you're no wienie. They all saw the game last night." He paused for a moment. "You're more of a … a *Reuben* sandwich."

No sooner than the words were out of his mouth, Woody himself glanced at Leah and got embarrassed. "I'm sorry," he said to her. "Brett told me what you said at practice that day when Coach Johnson needed a name for that trick play. We thought what you said was funny. But I'm awful sorry about what happened to your brother. I thought so much of him—not just as a player, but as a fine young man."

Leah nodded and looked away. Artie, who had said nothing at Woody's mention of his mother, finally found the words to ask about this woman whom he had never known and about whom he and his grandparents rarely spoke. "You really knew my mother?" Artie asked Woody.

"Yes, I did," said Woody. "Well, we knew each other in grade school, anyway. I even had a little crush on her—she was such a pretty girl. But once we got to high school, she and I went our separate ways and started dating other people. I hung out at the beach, and she started going over to Ebenezerville and spending time with all her new friends there."

"What did they do in E-ville?" Artie said. "Was it a party crowd?"

Woody thought for a moment. "They were just teenagers," said the man. "We *all* liked to party back then, and we all had our own little groups—cliques, I guess you could call them. Your mom hung out with the country kids. And like I said, I spent all my time—when I wasn't playing ball—at the beach, just like Brett. I loved the water, and I—"

The sound of a vehicle approaching on the farm lane caught Woody's attention. He looked out the kitchen window and saw a white van with "Pressler's Department Store" painted on the side pull up next to his station wagon. "Look, kids, I need to finish up here and get back to the grill," Woody said. "And, Brett, maybe you should come back to the beach with me. I sure could use some help with inventory in the surf shop."

Confused at first, Brett started to object, but looked outside and saw Abe Pressler and Tommy White exit the van. Bennie waited for them to open the sliding back door and lower the wheelchair ramp. "Oh, okay, Dad," said Brett. "I'll go grab my jacket out of the Whale—I mean, out of Ty's car."

Brett turned to Artie. "Thanks, uh, Yogi, for loaning me those rubber boots. I would have ruined my flip-flops—not to mention all ten of my little piggies—in that hog lot." He had put the flip-flops back on before walking to the house, but had left his jacket in the White Whale.

"No problem," said Artie. "That's what those old rubber boots are for—and why they're brown." Then he chuckled. "Grandpa calls them 'crap-kickers.'"

Brett laughed. "Yeah, I kicked some of that stuff this morning. Sure did, Yogi."

"You don't need to call me that—'Yogi,' I mean," Artie said. "That's Coach Johnson's nickname for me. Nobody else uses it. Right, Ty?"

"Right, Yogi," said Ty. "But, hey, now we can start calling ol' Brett here 'Boo Boo'—or 'Boo *Hoo*,' maybe." Ty turned and winked at their young teammate.

Brett's eyes narrowed, but he managed a weak smile. "I was *ten years old*," he said. "You guys aren't gonna let me forget that now, are you?"

Artie and Ty both shook their heads *no*. Ty slapped Brett on the back as the boy picked up an empty box and followed his father toward the door. "Oh, don't worry, Boo Hoo," said Ty, with a sly smile. "It'll be *our* little secret. See you Monday at practice."

"And thanks, uh, Brett, for working this morning," Artie said. "And thank you, too, Mr. Woods, very, very much for all this food, and for, uh, well, for what you said. You know?"

Woody nodded and smiled. "Say no more, young man. You come on out to the grill some day—whenever you're ready—and we'll have a long talk. Okay?" He nodded again and waved goodbye, opening the kitchen door for Brett and following him onto the back porch and out of the house onto the sidewalk.

Woody and Brett cut through the yard to their station wagon, leaving the narrow walkway open for Bennie sitting in his wheelchair, Tommy pushing it, and Abe Pressler walking behind them from their van. The two men gave one another quick looks and curt nods, but turned away without a single word.

With the Presslers' lawsuit going to trial before long, Woody knew better than to say or do anything that might be misinterpreted and affect the court proceedings. Dapper Abe, who always wore nice clothes from his stores, was harder to read. He was accustomed to handling legal matters and dealing with heavy hitters in his role as the head of a big company—much larger than Woody Woods's string of local surf shops.

Abe Pressler, with his pencil-thin mustache and soul patch, had seemed so down-to-earth in person, Artie had thought, especially when he had come to the hospital to show his support for the Bauer family. But Artie had heard stories that Pressler's corporate lawyers played hardball, even with employees, and that the CEO himself could be tough when he needed to be.

That Saturday afternoon, though, Abe was anything but hardnosed. In fact, he assured Artie again that he and Bennie would do anything they could to help out, and he even suggested a couple of ways that Artie could use the farm to earn some much-needed money that fall and on into the next year while Grandpa was laid up. An immediate venture could be to begin boarding horses in the barn and vacant pastureland, since the Bauers had no steers at present sharing stable space with their workhorses Tom and Dick. In fact, Abe said that he and his wife had decided to buy a gentle saddle horse for Bennie to begin riding the next spring as physical rehabilitation. They could have the horse delivered to the Bauer farm as easily as anywhere else, he added.

Abe Pressler's suggestion excited Leah Russo, in particular, because, as she had already told her Barf Table mates, she had personal experience with horse therapy, and she thought she might be able to talk her horse trainer into moving at least one mount to Artie's stable, too.

"I didn't know your family owns a horse," said Bennie to Leah. He was hanging around the kitchen because his dad's other big money-making suggestion involved him.

Leah shook her head. "We don't," she said. "The trainer—or her business, rather—owns four horses, and she boards them at Stark Stables on the other side of Mimosa Beach. It's a long drive down there. Who knows? She may want to bring all four of her horses here."

"Stark Stables?" Bennie said. "So, do you see Josh there very much?"

"No," said Leah, frowning. "He never came around when I was there. I only rode once a week. And I stopped once school started." She brightened. "But if my horse is stabled *here*, why, I can start riding again, maybe after school. That would be great."

Artie spoke up when he saw that Leah's comments about the horses and trainer at Stark Stables had even caught Abe's attention. "But I don't know if I can handle all that," Artie said. "I'm barely able to do all the chores now."

"I have that covered, too," said Abe. "That's where my other idea comes in—actually, it was Tommy's idea—but we'd need to get started with this next thing right away." He took out his cell phone and flipped it open, looking for a particular number. Before pressing the *Send* button, he continued, "If you don't mind, Artie, I can ask my personnel director if she's aware of anyone who has applied for employment lately with skills you could use out here."

"As a horse trainer?" asked Artie. He wondered why Pressler's Department Store would need someone to work with horses. Maybe to pull wagons during fall hayrides or parade floats during the holiday shopping season?

Abe smiled. "No, no," he said, lowering his phone for a minute. "I'm getting ahead of myself. When the three of us were driving over here a few minutes ago, Tommy saw the old house out on the highway—it's your family's old homeplace, isn't it?—and he said it would make a great haunted house for Halloween. And you know what? He's right. And we could set up a corn maze in that field beside it. That's your land, too, isn't it?"

"Sure," said Artie, "but the house is in really bad shape. It needs a lot of work. It doesn't have a bathroom or running water, even. And that's even *more* responsibility—two more horses to take care of, a haunted house and a corn maze to run, *and* everything I'm doing now. I would have to quit football. No question."

Abe blinked patiently and shook his head. "No, no, no," he said evenly. "Our company employs decorators and carpenters, plumbers and electricians, even architects and engineers all the time to work on projects in our stores—and to build new stores from the ground up. One of our crews could come out here and fix up that old house in no time."

The man seemed to read Artie's mind. "And the money is no problem whatsoever," Abe added. "I would look at it as a good investment in our community. Besides, Bennie here would get to install the electronics for the haunted house, and he needs something to keep himself busy on weekends this fall. Right, Bennie?"

The boy beamed. "Right, Dad. And, Artie, I brought some stuff to install today if you'll let me. It's an intercom system for you and your grandparents to use after they get home from the hospital. It won't be hard for Tommy and me to run some lines from your grandfather's room to other parts of the house, maybe even out to the barn, if I have enough wire left."

"Like a baby monitor?" said Artie.

"Yeah," Bennie said, "but with wires, like a computer network." With that thought, he added, "Hey, I'll bring out a couple of old computers later for your own local area network, one computer here in the kitchen and one out in the barn for starters."

"Why would I want a computer in the barn?" Artie asked. "I mainly just go out there to milk Bessie and Bossy. An intercom would be more than enough."

"Yeah, you do have your hands full, don't you?" said Bennie. "Well, maybe Bessie and Bossy would like to play Solitaire and Minecraft while you're milking them—or SimFarm. They could give you ideas on how to run the farm right. And, hey, I can even install a modem on your telephone line right here, and then Bessie and Bossy could have their own computer bulletin board system. They could call it—I don't know—maybe Ya-*moo*? You know, like Yahoo!"

Everyone laughed. Still overwhelmed, but now in a good way, Artie didn't know what to say for a moment.

Abe Pressler laid his hand on Artie's shoulder. "Young man," Abe said, "our community needs to do everything we can to support our young people, especially in their time of need, and our company is going to do its part. You're the future of Oleander County. All of you are—yeah, even Bennie, my little computer-hacking comedian."

Bennie faked indignation. "C'mon now, Dad, gimme a break. You know I'm gonna be the Jay Leno of the Information Superhighway, the Conan O'Brien of America Online."

"Is that right?" Abe said. "Well, I'd settle for the Johnny Carson of Com-puCow. He was from Iowa, you know. But Conan O'Brien? Isn't he the guy on the really, really late show? When we get back home, remind me to talk to your mother about getting you to bed earlier."

"Funny, Dad, funny." Bennie motioned for Tommy to help him maneuver the wheelchair back around the kitchen table so that they could start running the intercom wires wherever Artie wanted them to go.

Promising to return around five o'clock for Bennie and Tommy, Abe excused himself and went back to his van. He unloaded the equipment and supplies that Bennie needed for his project, and drove back toward Monk's Landing to take care of whatever business the owner of a big department store chain would have on a Saturday. Artie figured that Abe Pressler and, for that matter, Woody Woods were always busy with one thing or another. *That's probably the secret to their success*, Artie thought, feeling better now about how much he needed to do for his family.

Artie, Ty, Leah and Nicie had just started cleaning up the ground floor of the farmhouse when a different van pulled up outside, this one from Solid Rock Christian Church. Little Ricky Duran was the first person out of the passenger area, holding the sliding door open for his parents and for two ladies from the back seat. The driver and other front-seat passenger were both men, each wearing work pants and, like Mr. Duran, a white painter's hat.

Artie met the group outside and shook each person's hand as Ricky introduced them. The men had been among the church members who had baled the Bauers' hay earlier in the week.

"Thank you so much," Artie told them. "When I told my grandparents what you all had done for us, they both teared up—even my crusty old grandpa."

"We are happy to help our neighbors," said Ricky's father. "When our pastor and his wife get here with the wood and other supplies, we will begin building the ramps for your grandfather. We bought some white paint, too, as you can see." He pointed to the men's clean white hats, then smiled and added, "With such nice, new ramps leading into your fine house, we must make sure that the two porches look freshly painted and inviting, too."

Artie smiled. "Thank you again, Mr. Duran."

"Artie, you may call me Ricardo," the man said. "Gabrielle and I—and Little Ricky—we are honored to help your family, as are all of us here. Is that not right, Gabby? Everyone?"

The others standing around them agreed, some of them patting Artie on the back. They divided up, the women going inside to clean and cook, the men to stay outside to work on the ramps and porches. A pickup truck loaded with wood, paint, ladders, tools and full bags of groceries arrived a few minutes later. The church's pastor shook Artie's hand before joining the other workers outside; his wife gave Artie a hug before going inside to work with the women.

Late that afternoon when all the work was done, this gathering of old and new friends and loving neighbors—including Abe Pressler, who had returned early—stood together on the freshly mown, green grass of the back yard. Of the folks who had helped that day, only Brett and Woody Woods were absent. Used to shepherding his flock in E-ville, the pastor asked everyone to hold hands. They formed a circle to include everyone, even Bennie in his wheelchair.

"Thank you, heavenly father," the pastor said, "for this beautiful day. Thank you for this opportunity to show our neighbors how much we love them. Thank you, father, that we have the health and the strength to do this humble work. Bless this farm and this family, and help us never to forget that we are here to serve you by serving one another. And all the people say...."

"Amen," the church people said as one. Artie and the other teenagers were an instant late with their *amens*, but none of their neighbors from E-ville minded.

More than anything, Artie was grateful for the help that he had received since Grandpa's accident, but he was also embarrassed to be helped so much. Being the grandson of proud Harry Bauer, Artie wasn't used to accepting anything even resembling charity. Artie knew that a Bauer was supposed to be *stoic*—a word he had learned in English class, not one that Grandpa would have ever used, though it fit him like a glove.

In the gathering twilight, as the farm boy watched his friends, old and new, return to their vehicles and head back down the farm lane toward the highway, Artie knew that he was truly blessed to live near caring people who would sacrifice their time and resources to help someone in need.

Back in the kitchen, he called the hospital to tell Grandma and Grandpa about the work that had been done that day and to ask permission for all the work yet to come. Artie was sure they would be as grateful for their community's support as he was, because all three of them knew how fragile their futures had become.

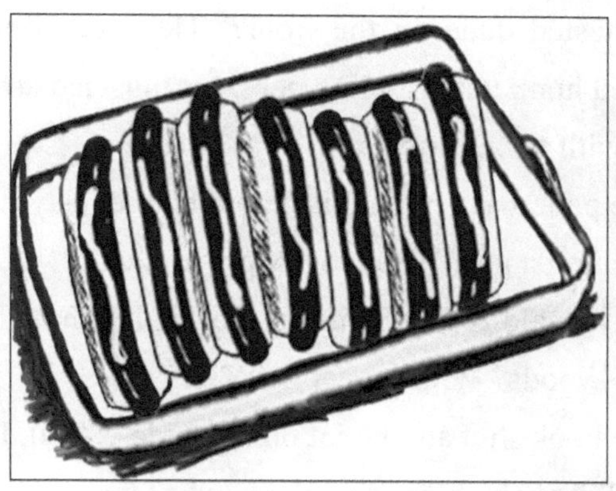

CHAPTER 19 – Monday Morning Coming Down

JOSH STARK'S SUDDEN TRANSFER to a new school had been the talk of Arbor High all Monday morning and only intensified during lunch hour in the cafeteria. He and his parents showed up at Principal Jerry Church's office at eleven o'clock sharp, just after the start of 2nd Period. After meeting behind a closed door with Mr. Church and Coach Jug Johnson for about an hour, Mr. and Mrs. Stark went to the guidance counselor's office to retrieve Josh's academic files.

Josh went to his locker in the main hall to gather his personal stuff, then to his football locker in the gym for anything he had left behind Friday night. Jug was afraid that Josh might do something stupid in the locker room, but the coach didn't want to be alone there with the boy for fear that he might falsely accuse the older man of verbal or physical abuse. Jug was no fool, even though he often looked or sounded foolish. Josh got his stuff and was leaving the gym as the bell rang to end 2nd Period at the start of lunch.

At the Barf Table, Leah sat quietly reading another paperback, this one a romance novel. Artie laid his tray of soup and a toasted-cheese sandwich on the tabletop, and slid out his chair. "Woh," he said, spying the steamy book cover as he sat. "How can you read that book?"

"What?" said Leah. "Are you saying I can't read romances?"

Artie arched his eyebrows. "But why did you pick *that* one?" he asked. "Did you see the bare-chested dude on the front?" He nodded at the cover, which showed a long-haired hunk with rippling pecs, his muscled arms wrapped around a beautiful woman with a torn bodice.

Leah flipped the paperback around and studied the lusty image. "What?" she said. "It's a guy hugging a girl. What's wrong with that?"

"Look at the guy," said Artie. "I mean, look at his face. Don't you think he looks just like Brett Woods? With longer hair?"

She snapped the book shut and laid it on the table. "Well, I do *now*," she said. "Thanks, Artie." Sulking, she flipped up the hood of her sweat jacket and crossed her arms.

Ty Green and Nicie Evans arrived and set their trays at their places. "Hey, girl," said Nicie. "Where's your lunch? I'll split my sandwich with you, if you want it."

Leah shook her head. "No, I'm fine," she said, before changing the subject. "So, now that Josh is officially gone, who are we gonna get to replace him?"

Ty bowed up. "Hey," he said. "I think *I* did a pretty good job at QB Friday night."

"No," said Leah. "Not at quarterback. At kicker. If we'd had a kicker the other night, we would've won the game. No offense, guys."

Artie and Ty exchanged a look. "None taken," Artie said. "I don't know, but we're gonna have to find somebody, and quick. Can you think of anybody, Ty?" Artie winked.

"Well, yeah," said Ty, "but *she* needs to put on a few pounds—eat some toasted-cheese sandwiches or something—to keep from getting snapped in two like a dry twig on kickoffs and punts, or if I should happen to fumble your snap when I'm holding for *her*."

Leah gave them a level stare. "*I* am not kicking—or punting," she said. "I'm a girl, and I am *not* gonna get in the middle of a mess like that." She turned and looked up as Bennie Pressler, Tommy White and Ricky Duran arrived at the table with their lunches. "But I *can* help the team in that area," she added. "I can *coach* our new kicker—and right here he is!"

Bennie set the brake on his wheelchair. "Hi, guys," he said, checking the clock on the far wall of the cafeteria. "What do we have—five minutes—before the bell rings? Do you wanna see me down this bowl of hot soup in five minutes?"

"Easy, pal," said Ty. "Nobody's gonna mess with your lunch today—not unless you mess with them first. Artie and I had a talk with some of the instigators this morning."

"Insti-*gators*?" Bennie said. "Are you trying to *drain the swamp* for us?"

Artie spoke up. "We just aren't in the mood for any foolishness today," he said. "Besides, everybody is bummed out about Josh Stark transferring to Solid Rock. We were just discussing who we can get to be our new punter and kicker." He looked back at Leah and asked, "So were you trying to be funny? Bennie couldn't kick the ball *before* he got hurt. Right, Bennie?"

"After my surgery," Bennie began, "I asked my surgeon, 'Doctor, doctor, will I be able to kick a football once I'm outta this wheelchair?' and he said, 'I don't see why not.' And I said, 'Well, that's funny, doc, bec—'"

"Yeah, yeah," Leah said, cutting him off. "No, not Bennie. And not Tommy, either. He's gonna help you on the line by the end of the season, Artie." She looked to the side of the table where Ricky Duran had taken his seat. "You guys can't watch the girls soccer team during football practice every afternoon," she told the group, "but I sit up in the stands to keep stats, and I've been keeping one eye on the soccer field for the past couple weeks. *Somebody*—who's supposed to be playing flag football—slips off and plays soccer with the girls." She nodded toward Ricky.

The boy looked up from his bowl of soup and saw that everyone was staring at him. "What did I do?" Ricky asked, not having heard the earlier discussion over the cafeteria noise. "I don't want trouble. I just want to eat my soup and sandwich before the bell rings."

"Like I told Bennie," said Ty, "cool your jets, little buddy. Leah just volunteered you for the football team. She says she can teach you how to punt and kick a *real* football—an *American* football. What do you say?"

Still unsure that he had more than a couple of minutes to eat his lunch, Ricky looked from friend to friend around the table, and smiled. "I can try," he said to Ty, then turned to Artie. "My father and mother have something important to ask you, Artie. Mr. Abe Pressler—yes, Bennie's father—came to visit us at our house on Sunday afternoon, and he said they should talk to you."

"About what?" said Artie. He glanced over at Bennie, who shrugged as if he didn't know what Ricky was referring to.

"About working for you," Ricky said. "My father is a good handyman, and my mother is a great cook and housekeeper. Mr. Abe Pressler said you need help on your farm so that you can stay in school and keep playing American football."

Artie was confused. "But I can't pay—I mean, we, my grandparents and I— we can't pay anybody to do any work. I mean, we're thankful for all the help lately, but we can't ask—"

Bennie chimed in. "Okay," he said, "so I do know what this is about. Dad's idea is for the Durans to move into the house out on the highway—the *haunted* house—and to help you, Artie. It's a win-win situation. You both benefit. And you *can* afford to pay them—with free rent and with some of the money you'll make from boarding horses, like ours and the one Leah's trainer owns. You'll make a bundle. That doesn't even count all the money you'll make with the haunted house and corn maze this fall. We don't mind helping."

"Yeah," Nicie said, cutting in. "My dad said he'd go pick up your grandpa's tractor one day this week and get it running again. If he does that, we can use it for hayrides, too—if you don't mind him doing that."

"Well, I'll have to talk to Grandpa first—and Grandma, too," said Artie. "I know we need the tractor fixed. But Grandma might not want another woman in her kitchen, you know? I'm not kidding, either. She's particular about things like that."

But that same idea—of asking the Durans to move into the old homeplace— had already occurred to Artie over the weekend, as he had spent a good part of Sunday working on the farm alone and driving to and from the hospital in E-ville to visit Grandpa. That Abe Pressler had come up with the same idea without discussing it with him made Artie feel more confident about himself, as if great minds do think alike. Pressler was undoubtedly a fine businessman.

For the first time, Artie began to seriously consider whether he should major in not just agriculture, but maybe agribusiness or agritourism in college, in order to help his family farm survive when so many others were failing. He had even broached the subject of needing to find new ways to support the farm when he had visited his grandparents on Sunday afternoon, but he couldn't go into detail because he wasn't sure how much more responsibility he could take on.

So now Artie decided to discuss these new opportunities with Grandma and Grandpa in his phone call right after school that day so that he could have an answer for the Durans when they called him that evening. He told Ricky to tell his parents to call after sundown so that his chores would be done and he could talk without being in a rush. He would still have homework to do, but that wasn't as pressing as milking the cows, currying the horses, feeding the chickens, or slopping the hogs.

* * *

In the locker room after school, the football team saw what mischief Josh Stark had done during his visit that morning to clean out his locker. Coach Johnson had found the mess earlier in the afternoon but had ordered it to be left alone, wanting his players to see it when they arrived to suit up for practice.

Josh had flung his game and practice jerseys, his pants, his helmet, and all of his various pads—shoulder pads, hip pads, thigh pads and knee pads—all over the place. On the big whiteboard at one end of the locker room, Josh had scrawled a message to them: "YOU'RE A BUNCH OF LOSERS!" The letters were in red marker, and the word "LOSERS" was underlined twice.

No one could say that Josh Stark was wrong about them, because they were still winless on the young season. They were 0-2. But they also knew that Josh had done more than enough by himself to cause both of their losses.

Once the players were in their practice gear, Jug Johnson sat them down and pointed at the message on the whiteboard. "Bunch o' losers," the coach said, holding each senior's gaze for an instant as he looked around the room. "I know we're 0-and-2. Don't nobody need to remind me of that. But I don't feel like a dang loser. Nosiree, I don't. Do you?" He paused and looked around the room again, daring anyone to agree with Josh's assessment of them as a team.

"Yogi? Ty?" said Jug. "You boys are our co-captains. Do you think we're all *a bunch of losers*?" Both boys shook their heads *no*. But Jug was hardly finished. "Brett Woods," Jug said. "Your friend just called you a *loser*. Is he right?"

"I'm not a loser," said Brett. "I came up short on the two-point conversions Friday night, but if we'd had a kicker—if Josh hadn't quit on us—we would've won. I heard people say so at lunch today." He had heard only Leah say that, but her opinion carried weight with him.

"That's right," Jug said. "We need a kicker—not so much a punter, 'cause we ain't gonna be punting on fourth down until we're in the win column. And we're starting that winning streak this Friday night against Port Oleander. Right now, our team's record—as far as I'm concerned, anyway—is 0-and-0, and we're gonna be trying for 1-and-0 *every dang week* for the rest of the season. We're gonna start fresh today and *every* Monday this fall."

Jug continued, "All we need is a kicker. And thanks to our co-captains and the little lady who keeps our stats, we got one—a kicker, that is. I already saw him kick some balls last period, and he can be a good one if you all let him be. As a matter o' fact, he's out on the field with little Miss Russo right now. Now, all you boys treat him right, even if he *is* a … a *soccer* player."

Jug almost shuddered when he said *soccer*, but the boys knew what he meant: Like him, they were afraid that soccer, the most popular sport in the world, might soon overtake football as the marquee, Friday-night game at American high schools.

Without Josh Stark's bad attitude on the field that day, practice went well. Leah Russo in jeans and her gray hoodie, and little Ricky Duran in soccer clothes and borrowed football cleats kept practicing by themselves on one end of the field, while the rest of the team ran through plays and formations on the other end. By the conclusion of the long, hot session, no player was thinking about Josh Stark's surly message on the whiteboard.

Instead, they all were feeling better about themselves as the winners they strived to be. To be on the safe side, though, Jug Johnson had wiped the white-board clean before leaving the locker room earlier. Knowing how easily high school players could be motivated or discouraged, Jug had used the insult to fire up his team. But he made sure that the whiteboard was spotless when his boys returned to the locker room after practice. Jug wanted no reminder, no hint, that Josh had been right about his old team.

Ricky met his new teammates in the locker room for the first time after prac-tice. He had been there before school let out and had even seen the mean words in red on the board while he had waited for Jug to find him some cleats. Before the players hit the showers at the end of the day, Jug introduced the new boy and gave him a chance to say *hi* to the whole team.

"Little man, I can't wait to see you kicking the extra points for all the touch-downs we're gonna be scoring beginning this Friday night," Jug said. "Are you ready to help us win some games?"

"I am," said Ricky, embarrassed at the attention, but adding, "because we are not losers anymore. We are a bunch of *weeners*." Everyone laughed as they headed for the showers.

"Weiners?" said Jug. "Oh, yeah, well, wieners it is, then." He spied Brett Woods heading toward the shower room with a towel around his waist. "Hey, Woods. Ask ol' Woody if we can have wieners for the pre-game meal this Friday. We *are* a bunch of wieners, aren't we?"

And that was how "We Are Winners!" became the team motto, though no player ever said it without smiling about that first true team practice of their brand-new season.

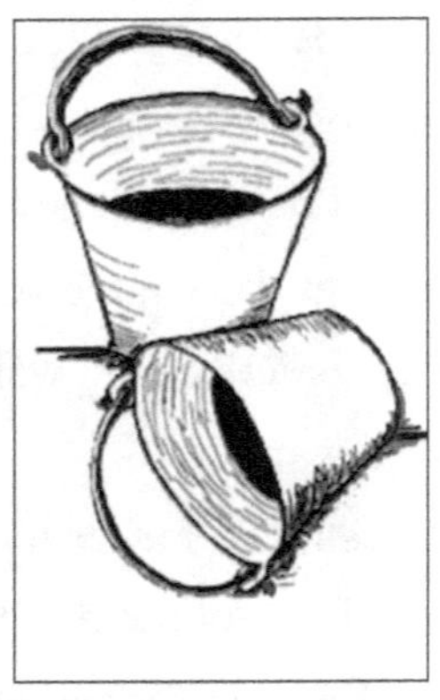

CHAPTER 20 – Ralph Learns How to Hoover

ARTIE HAD ALWAYS WANTED a little brother … or a big brother, or a little sister or a big sister—he didn't care. For as far back as he could remember, Artie had hated being an only child and had yearned to find a long-lost brother or sister, maybe even a cousin, who might move into the big farmhouse with Artie, Grandma and Grandpa, and to help with the farm chores. Not only that—not just to help with the work—but this brother would also teach Artie to play games of all sorts, or be taught, depending on whether this boy was older or younger than Artie. In fact—or, rather, in his fertile imagination—Artie had shared his childhood with *two* imaginary brothers, an older one named Eddie, after the outdoor clothing stores, and a younger one named Ralph, after, well, after a problem that Artie had often suffered as a child near the animal stalls and hog pen.

"Pearl!" Grandpa would shout as he pulled little Artie by the arm through the screen door onto the back porch. "This boy *ralphed* all over himself again out in the barn. Little *Ralph* here needs a clean shirt and overhauls so we can do the milking. I hosed off his boots."

"My goodness, Harry," Grandma would say. "Artie has the weakest stomach of anyone I know. He doesn't even have to *smell* the manure for it to turn his stomach; he just has to *think* about how bad it smells. And stop calling him *Ralph*. He's gonna think that's his real name."

Instead, young Artie named his imaginary little brother Ralph and took to blaming him whenever something bad happened on the farm, like when Artie threw up while mucking out the stables or slopping the hogs, or when he tripped, fell and cracked some eggs he was carrying from the hen house to Grandma in the kitchen.

"Ralphie did it again, Grandma," Artie would say, as he showed her his sodden clothes or the broken eggs in his little wicker basket. "He's a bad boy." But it helped Artie deal with his loneliness and with his fears over having been abandoned by his mother and father. He wasn't exactly an orphan, but he wondered if real orphans felt like he did on Mother's Day and Father's Day and all the other family-oriented holidays year round.

Eddie Bauer, Artie's imaginary big brother, got his name the first time Harry and Pearl Bauer took little Artie shopping for school clothes at the big outlet mall in Mimosa Beach. Even though he was starting kindergarten, Artie recognized his surname on the store sign and begged to buy his clothes there, but Grandma was afraid to spend so much money on the little shirts and jeans and shoes that Artie needed.

Grandpa hadn't wanted to go to the outlet mall, anyway, and had refused to get out of the truck in the huge parking lot. Pearl knew Harry would blow a gasket if she spent all their hard-earned money in one store, and so they left the mall without buying anything, drove back to their familiar Pressler's Department Store in Ebenezerville, and bought all of Artie's school clothes there. They even had enough cash left for Grandma to buy herself a new dress, though she tried to object over Grandpa's orders.

So, in Artie's active young mind, big brother Eddie Bauer came to represent all of the good things in life that were just out of his reach, at least until he grew up and could spend his own money.

Now, though, Artie could better understand why Grandpa had always been so thrifty with the family's finances. With Harry Bauer recuperating in the E-ville hospital, Artie was having to pay the bills and buy the food and supplies that were needed to keep him and the farm alive. So far Artie had gotten more than enough help from his friends and from community members like Abe Pressler, Woody

Woods, and the folks from Solid Rock Christian Church. Also, he felt good about the Durans—Big Ricardo, Gabby and Little Ricky—moving in that week to get everything ready for Grandpa's eventual return home and for all the other things that would be happening on the Bauer farm within a matter of weeks.

But Artie knew that Stark Realty's offer to buy the farm and developer Joel Stark's desire to win at all costs would loom larger and larger as time passed, depending on Grandpa's long-term recovery and on the success of Artie's agri-business exploits.

On the Wednesday after the Mimosa Beach game, the Duran family moved into two spare bedrooms upstairs in the Bauer farmhouse. Abe Pressler's construction and maintenance workers would arrive soon to begin renovation work on the old homeplace out on the highway, so Big Ricardo Duran went to work installing a new bathroom downstairs in the main house, while his wife Gabrielle finished setting up Grandpa's new digs in the old storage room off the kitchen.

Gabby retained her other housekeeping jobs to keep money coming in, but she rose early every day to have a big, farm breakfast ready for Artie when he finished milking the cows and before he and Little Ricky left for school on weekdays. Big Ricardo always made a point of sitting down with his wife and the two boys for not just breakfast, but also for supper around the farm table each evening. Ricardo always insisted on asking God to "bless this food and the hands that have prepared it" before the first morsel was placed on anyone's plate. Artie especially loved Gabby's omelets, her homemade biscuits, her spicy cornbread, and her baked desserts that he consumed like a human vacuum cleaner with tall glasses of cold, fresh milk.

Little Ricky was proud of his father's skill as a handyman and his mother's artistry as a baker, and the boy was even proud of himself for so quickly finding his place at Arbor High School. Artie loved having Ricky walk next to him as his real-life shadow. The pair quickly took to each other as friends and brothers. That was good for Artie, because Ty Green, though still his best friend, was falling deeper and deeper in love with Nicie Evans and was spending more and more time with her outside school.

That Friday—the day of the Port Oleander game—Abe Pressler hired a wrangler to haul Bennie's and Leah's horses to the Bauer farm in a double trailer. Mr. Pressler had worked things out with the trainer whom Leah knew, and had made arrangements for the trailer to arrive early, so that Artie and Ricky could help the wrangler and Big Ricardo before leaving for school. The two boys held workhorses Tom and Dick while the wrangler unloaded the two new horses and let them get used to the Bauers' corral. Ricardo unloaded the western saddles and other tack for the two horses from the bed of the wrangler's tandem-wheeled pickup truck. After exchanging brief instructions on feed and exercise, the wrangler hopped back into his pickup, gave a quick wave and roared back down the farm lane toward the highway in a cloud of diesel smoke.

As Artie and Little Ricky had held the workhorses, they had watched the wrangler work with Leah's and Bennie's mounts, both of which were beautiful animals, like racehorses the boys would expect to see in the Kentucky Derby.

"Are you nervous?" Artie asked Ricky.

"About the horses?" said Ricky. "No, I have ridden horses before."

Artie chuckled. "No," he said. "About tonight—about being our kicker. Port Oleander is like us. They haven't won a game yet, either, so there will be some pressure. But this is the first time *you've* ever kicked a football in a real game. Are you scared? I was, my first game."

"I have kicked *many* futbols in *many* games," said Ricky. "No, I am not so scared. I want to show Josh Stark that we are not losers. He is a bad person, and so is his father."

"Well, his mother is a good person, I think," Artie said. "She's pretty, any-way."

Walking past the boys and carrying a heavy saddle toward the barn, Big Ricardo heard Artie's remark. "That does not make a person *good*," said Ricardo. "My Gabby is beautiful *and* she is nice to everyone. And she would not allow Ricky or me to be mean to others. That is what makes a person *good*." He said all that without stopping and continued on to the tack room next to the stables.

Chastened, Artie felt for an instant as if Harry Bauer were home already.

"Your father sounds like my grandpa," said Artie. "I hope they'll get along—being so much alike."

Ricky nodded. "Yes," he said, "Father is very strict. He wants things done *his* way. But I have found that he is usually right, and I trust him. We would not be here now if I had *not* trusted him, you know?"

Artie studied the suddenly fearful glint in Ricky's almond-shaped eyes. "Do you mean, here in America?" asked Artie. "Or just here on the farm?"

"In America," Ricky said. "I was a small boy then—well, much smaller than I am now." That moment of self-awareness eased Ricky's mind, letting his face relax again.

"Yep, my grandpa's gonna see you and me standing side by side," said Artie, "and he's gonna laugh and call us 'Mutt and Jeff.' You wait and see. That means I'm tall and you're short."

"I look forward to meeting Mr. Harry Bauer," Ricky said. "When he returns home from the hospital, will he come to our games? I hope so, because I want your grandfather to be proud of me, as if he were my own *abuelo*." He smiled at that thought.

"I do, too," said Artie, "because he hasn't seen *me* play yet—well, not really. Neither has my grandma. Grandpa would always say he was too busy here on the farm to sit and watch a ballgame for two or three hours. That's what he'd claim, anyway. They were getting ready to drive over to our game against Solid Rock a couple weeks ago when Grandpa had his big accident. That was gonna be the first time they saw me actually play in a game. Now they may never see me play—not until baseball season, anyway."

Both boys were quiet, then Artie added, "I thought I was going to have to quit sports—and maybe school, too—until you and your mom and dad agreed to move in with us. You guys are like angels, you know?" Artie patted workhorse Tom's neck and smoothed his forelock.

Ricky didn't know what to say at first. "We are not angels," he said finally. "We are just people. Like our pastor says at church, we want to be good neighbors. You and your *abuelos* are our neighbors, and you, Artie, are my good friend. You made me feel welcome that first day of school when everyone else was laughing at me."

The diminutive boy was quiet for another moment before he grinned and shouted, "And we are *weeners*, not losers! You will see!"

* * *

Maybe rookie kicker Ricky Duran shouldn't have reminded himself that the Arbor Bruins were winless. Maybe he should have stopped by exclaiming, "We are winners!" Maybe whatever Ricky said to Bruins co-captain Artie Bauer that afternoon wouldn't have mattered one bit, since their opponents that night, the Port Oleander Pilots, were winless, too, and wanted to win just as badly as the home team did. But as it was, the victor of Friday's battle of losing teams at Arbor High was in doubt to the bitter end, as if neither squad wanted to cast off its mantle of defeat.

The lede sentence of cub sportswriter Leah Russo's article in the first issue of that year's school newspaper said it all: "After opening the season with two losses, the Arbor Bruins scored their first win last Friday night at Arbor Field by topping the winless Port Oleander Pilots on a controversial, last-second kick." Leah's second sentence gave the final score—Bruins 21, Pilots 18—and identified Ricky Duran as the game's hero on the record-setting, walk-off field goal that the AHS freshman and former Guatamalen soccer player kicked with no time left on the clock.

Leah buried the fact that the 35-yard field goal—a dropkick, like what soccer goalies do—was the tiny boy's only successful kick that night. He was 0-3 on point-after-touchdown attempts, and the game-ending field goal had not been designed as an old-fashioned dropkick. It was supposed to have been an ordinary placekick like the PATs, but Ty Green fumbled the snap and Ricky picked up the ball and ran with it—so to speak.

In the locker room after the game, Coach Johnson sat down with Artie, Ty and Ricky, and made sure that the three boys knew exactly why the three PAT attempts and, initially, the regular field-goal attempt had failed: poor timing from too little practice.

"Kicking a pigskin is like ballet dancing, but not in tight pants," Jug told them, as if he knew anything about ballet. "One … now, that's snapping the ball. Two … that's putting the ball down. And three … that's kicking the ball. Do it like that, and you'll have your extra point or field goal. We'll practice that next week."

Jug also made sure that all three boys—but especially little Ricky—knew that he wasn't blaming them for the kicking team's failures. After all, Ricky had been on the team and playing tackle football for only one week, not just touch football. Still, they needed to practice, practice, practice, Jug said, so that they could take advantage of having such a good and dependable kicker.

"Besides," Jug added, "I've got an idea of how we can put a new wrinkle in our Reuben play. Now we can run it off a field-goal try. We'll work on that, too. I'll have a talk with little Miss Russo about it, since she's our new kicking coach."

Before Artie and Ty left the locker room that night, Jug also talked to just the co-captains about bringing another flag-footballer up to the varsity. One of the offensive linemen had been hurt in the first quarter—another reason for the unsuccessful placekicks—and the boy who subbed in for the injured player needed a backup of his own. Artie suggested Tommy White. Ty agreed that Tommy was big and strong enough to be a good lineman with some coaching and experience.

"He can run, too," said Ty. "I saw him chase down Bennie Pressler's wheelchair in the parking lot before the game tonight. It was headed down the hill and would've hit something if Tommy hadn't been there."

"Where was Bennie?" asked Artie. "In the wheelchair?"

"Nah," said Ty, with a laugh. "He was up in the press box with Leah. I guess they couldn't get the chair up those stairs and had to park it outside. Somebody must've bumped into it."

Jug interrupted Ty's tall tale. "Well, boys, we got a big week coming up," said Jug, "and we all need to do a better job of getting ready for Oakmont Prep next week—me included. They ain't a weak sister like Port Oleander. We can't afford to make no mistakes against Oakmont at their place next Friday night. Those boys are always tough as nails."

With Bennie Pressler in tow, Tommy White came to varsity football practice that Monday and held his own on the line, though he hadn't played tackle football since middle school. But he was nervous and even vomited during the first water break, either from the heat or from the knot in his belly. Jug made Tommy run to the locker room and get a wet-and-dry vacuum to clean up his mess. Everyone but co-captain Artie laughed as Tommy threw up again while hoovering the former contents of his stomach.

For his part, Bennie rolled himself along the sideline and helped Leah by videotaping the scrimmage while she continued coaching Ricky on how to kick extra points and field goals. As Jug had suggested, Leah called out, "One … two … three," to train little Ricky to time his run-up and kick like ballet moves. Finally, the whole team ran through PATs and field goals of greater and greater distances for the last thirty minutes of practice. Jug wanted to test Ricky's leg, to see just how far he could kick with accuracy. Though most of the boy's attempts beyond 35 yards fell short or hooked left of the goalposts, Ricky did nail one 36-yarder that gave the team hope for game-ending situations to come. More importantly, he started hitting all of his PATs.

CHAPTER 21 – Krakatoa Tuesday at the Barf Table

EVEN THOUGH THE USUAL SUSPECTS had behaved themselves lately in the school cafeteria, Artie Bauer knew there would be trouble that Tuesday when the lunch menu called for mystery meat, green beans, mashed potatoes and gravy. Ironically, Bennie Pressler had started reading the daily announcements over the school intercom during morning break, and he, too, hesitated for a long second and gulped audibly before saying the phrase "mashed potatoes and gravy." He had just received a premonition of lunch hour at the Barf Table that day. His pregnant pause had also given birth to visions of a tall, volcanic peak of mashed potatoes spewing lava-like gravy. It was, after all, Krakatoa Tuesday at Arbor High.

The buzz about Josh Stark's defection to Solid Rock Academy had subsided by lunchtime on Tuesday; however, the students were now talking about the two newest Bruins—Ricky Duran, because he had been Friday night's hero, and Tommy White, because he was a raw rookie, as of the day before. That both Ricky and Tommy were members of the Barf Table, along with usual target Bennie, also made Artie uncomfortable as he moved through the lunch line. He paid Frankie at the cash register and carried his tray of meat, beans, mashed potatoes and gravy to his place at the round table near the trash bins and tray-disposal window.

As usual, Leah Russo was already at the table when Artie arrived. In her familiar hoodie, Leah sat reading another paperback, this one a dog-eared, science-fiction novel. She glanced up as Artie took his seat. Artie was busy unwrapping his plastic knife and spork when Ty Green and Nicie Evans arrived and slid out their chairs next to him. They had visited the vending machines in the lobby and had bought sodas and chips to go with the peanut-butter-and-jelly sandwiches that Nicie had packed for them both.

Ty looked from his sandwich in its plastic baggie to Artie's heaping plate of food. "I sure am glad I don't have *that* sitting in front of me," said Ty. "You know, it *is* Krakatoa Tuesday."

Artie looked down and eyed the amorphous mound of mashed potatoes and the brown slab of mystery meat covered with chunky, grayish sauce. "Yeah, I know," Artie said. "I have a feeling Bennie and Tommy might not eat lunch today—I mean, that they might get some peanut butter crackers or chips and stuff from the machines, too."

"They'll do that if they know what's good for them," agreed Ty. "What about Ricky? Do you think he's safe?"

"Not today," Artie said. "I heard some talk last period that 'the new boys'— that's what they called Ricky and Tommy—that they're gonna get *initiated* today at lunch. They clammed up when I gave them the stink eye."

With a laugh, Leah looked up from her book. "You, Artie?" she said. "You gave someone the stink eye? I don't think you can do it."

Nicie spoke up. "Yeah, Artie," said Nicie. "Let's see the look you gave them. Right now. Leah and I are pros at giving people the stink eye. Right, Leah?"

"That's right," Leah said and lifted one eyebrow at Artie. "Well? We're waiting."

Artie grinned and shook his head. "Yeah, yeah," he said, waving them off. "Look—over along the wall. *All three of them* are getting lunch today." Artie nodded toward the long line of students, where Ricky, Bennie and Tommy were waiting to pick up their trays and be served.

"Maybe they'll start throwing at them now," said Nicie, "you know, like a firing squad or something while they're standing up against the wall."

"No such luck," Ty told his girlfriend. "Too much collateral damage, maybe even splatter a teacher or two right now. Nah, they'll wait until the bell. So we'd better be long gone by then." He took a big bite out of his sandwich and almost got choked on the chunky peanut butter.

Leah shrugged, went back to reading her sci-fi novel, and left Artie alone to start working on his own tray of food. Artie knew he couldn't let the three freshmen boys face the firing squad by themselves, but he didn't want to have any more ammunition on hand than the instigators of the impending fusillade might bring with them. He knew from experience how messy Krakatoa Tuesdays could be, with gravy and mashed potatoes getting slung everywhere.

What Artie didn't know was just how closely the volcano worshipers might blend the ritual with their plan to haze Ricky and Tommy. Usually, only one 9th-grade boy was sacrificed to the Krakatoan gods on Tuesdays when mashed potatoes and gravy were served. In the annals of Arbor High, there had never been *three* offerings made on the same day. But three football games had been played so far, and the football gods might require three sacrifices, Artie feared.

Ty and Nicie gobbled their lunches and prepared to slip out of the cafeteria, as the three boys took seats at the Barf Table, chattering about something they'd heard in line. Leah ignored them, closing her book and watching the second hand of the clock on the far wall sweep toward 12. Artie had taken preemptive action by finishing his lunch and disposing of his trash and empty tray as the boys arrived. He took his seat again and braced for the onslaught that would begin within a matter of seconds.

The release bell rang. Bennie, Tommy and Ricky sat helplessly as the wave of upperclassmen rose, broke at the Barf Table and washed past them to the trash bins. The first grinning senior laid his empty tray on the table in front of the three freshmen. From both sides, each boy that followed slapped his remaining mashed potatoes on the tray, building a mountain of spuds that grew and grew until it resembled if not Krakatoa, then Mount St. Helens after its eruption. Once formed, the caldera of instant potato flakes and water awaited its own moment of glory, when it would spew its oozing, grayish, gooey lava all over the three victims.

The last three seniors in line made the volcano's eruption inevitable. One boy dumped two large cups of collected gravy into the crater that had been fashioned within the mountain's peak. The next senior jammed a small firecracker into the upslope facing the victims. Placed near the summit, the firecracker waited to be lit, giving Leah, Artie, Ty and Nicie time to jump up and scramble away.

The three freshmen boys were transfixed in their seats, partly by the spectacle before them, but mainly by the strong hands of the seniors kneeling behind them and holding them down by their shoulders. The last of the volcano gods' three senior acolytes finished the sacrifices by lighting the firecracker's fuse and ducking away.

The mound of spuds exploded, showering its cold magma and icky lava all over Bennie, Tommy and Ricky. But before they could wipe any of the potato residue from their faces, three juniors—these fellows bearing large cups of water, one in each hand—doused the freshmen after shouting, "Tsunami warning!" Another surge of water from three more juniors broke upon the helpless boys, this time from behind, soaking their clothes front to back.

Even Artie, who had started moving toward the seniors to make them release their victims, got caught in the tsunami's second wave, as he tried to free little Ricky from his captor's clutches. The back of Artie's shirt bore a dark, wet splotch from the water that had hit him.

Though a sophomore, Brett Woods had risen from his usual seat and wandered toward the Barf Table in all the excitement. When he had seen that Artie was about to be splashed, Brett had shouted, "Watch out! Get back!" His warning was too late because it was garbled in the cafeteria din. The senior boy restraining Ricky laughed. Even Artie turned and glared at Brett, as if he had just uttered something unacceptable.

Finally releasing Ricky, the senior tormentor cackled. "Did you hear what Woods said?" the boy yelled to no one in particular. "Woods called this kid a 'wetback'!"

"Huh?" said Brett. "No, I didn't. I said, '*Get* back.'"

Artie and Ty both looked confused, not knowing which teammate to defend—Brett, the accused, or Ricky, the victim. Both co-captains had heard Brett's shout but not clearly enough to distinguish between *get* and *wet*. With the accusation, the noise got even louder.

Nicie stepped into the fray. "Brett Woods, you should be ashamed of yourself," she said. "You know better than to call people names—or do you want to call *me* something?"

Now Brett looked confused. He held up his hands innocently, but Nicie's verbal attack wasn't done. "I dare you to," she said. "But if you do, you'll regret it. Right, Ty?"

"Huh?" said Ty. "Uh, yeah … I guess so." He turned to Artie. "What did *you* hear?"

Artie reran the preceding minute in his memory. "I don't know," Artie said. "That's what it *sounded* like. But I don't know. There was a lot of noise."

Across the lunchroom, Frankie, the mean-looking cashier, had called the principal's office to report the incident and summon help. Within minutes, Principal Jerry Church and Coach Jug Johnson showed up at the cafeteria door, flanked by three male teachers whose classrooms were nearby. They cleared the lunchroom of students and took the principle parties back to the school office. That included the three freshmen, to be cleaned up, dried off and reclothed, and the four other students involved in the verbal mess—Brett, Artie, Nicie and the big-mouthed senior who was responsible for the misunderstanding. Ty went along to support his best friend and his girl.

Mr. Church talked to the students one at a time. When it was Artie's turn, the principal asked him straight out, "Did Brett Woods call Ricky Duran a wetback? You're on your honor now to tell me the truth, Artie. What did Brett say?"

"Well, that's what it sounded like," said Artie, "but it doesn't make sense. I didn't think Brett was like that—I mean, not on his own, not without somebody else egging him on."

Mr. Church's eyebrows rose. "You're referring to Josh Stark, right?" he said. "Yes, I've seen a change lately in Brett, too, and I'm surprised by all this. I called his father, and Woody is on his way over here. This is a regrettable situation."

"What's gonna happen?" asked Artie. "You aren't gonna suspend Brett, are you?"

"I don't know," Mr. Church said. "But I *can* tell you that this Barf Table foolishness has got to end, right now. I'm glad that you sit with the young ones at that table, Artie, but you need to do more to *stop* all the harassment, not just teach those 9th graders how to survive it. Do you know what I'm saying?"

Artie nodded. "I think so, Mr. Church. I'll do what I can." Deep down, though, Artie felt that he was powerless to make anyone do anything. In his mind, he was still that tubby freshman, that loser, who had possessed no self-confidence and had survived just by living to eat lunch another day. If not for Jug Johnson discovering his athletic potential, Artie would have remained a fat and lonely farm boy for the rest of his high school years, he was sure.

Like former teammate and friend Josh Stark, Brett Woods was in an entirely different category of student from Artie Bauer, and everyone involved—including Principal Church and Coach Johnson—knew it. That Brett really hadn't called little Ricky that derogatory name now made no difference. The accusation had been enough to make everyone doubt that Brett Woods had shaken off Josh Stark's influence. Besides, kids believed what they wanted to believe about their peers, whether they were friends or foes in any school setting.

Brett wasn't suspended, neither from school nor from the team, not even for that Friday's game against Oakmont Prep—and rightly so, because he was blameless. But the aftershocks of that particular Krakatoa Tuesday lasted until that Thursday, when Coach Johnson announced that the team would not hold its usual pregame meal at Woody's Grill and that the team had "no place for name-calling amongst us," he said, before turning to his co-captains. "Ain't that right, Yogi? Green? You fellers want to add anything?"

At first, both boys shook their heads. Remembering the principal's admonition from Tuesday, Artie reconsidered and stood. Turning to face his teammates, he said, "I just want to say this one thing—well, *two* things, really. First of all, Brett and Ricky are our teammates. We're all Bruins, and we support each other through thick and thin. When the going gets tough, the tough start kicking butt, right?" Everyone nodded.

"And, second," Artie continued, "Brett swore he didn't say that word—that he didn't call Ricky that bad name—and so we *need* to believe him. Not trusting a teammate is wrong. It's for losers. And it isn't for us. Do you know why?"

The players looked at each other curiously, not sure whether they should say what was on their minds. Of all people, Ricky Duran hopped up and walked over to where Brett Woods sat with his shaggy head turned down.

"I know why," said Ricky, extending his hand to Brett. "It is because I am not a wetback—I am *not*—and it is because Brett and I are not losers. Is that not right, my friend?"

Knowing he was innocent, Brett took Ricky's hand as he stood, at his full height towering over the team's little kicker and his new buddy. "That's right, Ricky," said Brett, looking up and around the room with a sly smile, "because we … are … winners."

The team's pregame meal of barbecue beans and wieners was held in the school cafeteria that Friday afternoon, served up by the coaching staff, Principal Church and Woody Woods, who understood why making the change was necessary that week. In reality, what the players ate that day and where they ate it made little difference, as long as they were together. That evening, after a long, hot bus ride into the next county, the Bruins took the gridiron and then ran Oakmont Prep off the field, 35-12.

Oakmont had the best kicker in the state—the sportswriters all agreed on that—but the boy's four field goals in four attempts were all the scoring offense that his flustered team could muster on this night. On the Arbor High side, the scoring was balanced, with Brett scoring three touchdowns and Ty scoring two. Ricky wasn't called on for any field goal attempts, so he didn't have the chance to demonstrate his drop-kicking ability again. But with the timing and grace of a dancer, little Ricky Duran drilled all five of his PATs through the uprights.

And the Bruins (2-2, 1-2) showed once more that they were winners indeed.

CHAPTER 22 – Emotional Ups and Fourth Downs

THE NEXT TWO WEEKS were like a roller-coaster ride for Artie and his Barf Table buddies, as well as for the Arbor High Bruins. After beating Oakmont, the Arbor footballers were riding high. The non-conference win had evened their overall record at 2-2, but they were still 1-2 in Suncoast Conference play and in fourth place, ahead of only winless Port Oleander.

Undefeated Iron Harbor hosted Arbor the next Friday, and the joyride for Artie and his teammates ended, at least for that week. The Iron Harbor Gray Dukes lived up to their name and battered the Bruins with such mechanical precision that the contest was over before the end of the first quarter. The game ended for Artie late in the first half when a blitzing Gray Dukes linebacker crashed into Artie's legs and caused him to roll his ankle.

Coming to the rescue again, Ty Green's mother came down out of the stands and looked at Artie's swollen ankle on the sideline. Then Rachel Green drove Artie from the stadium to Iron Harbor Medical Center for X-rays in the emergency room. The results were negative—there was no break—but Artie was on crutches when the two of them got back to the stadium for the final minutes of Iron Harbor High's blowout win.

Even the Gray Dukes reserves dominated the Bruins first-stringers, though Artie's backup at center would have been rusty against anyone. His indecision threw Ty's and Brett's timing off and rendered them less effective than they might have been against the Gray Dukes' feared "Iron Curtain" defense. In turn, the new center, who had moved over from the guard slot, was replaced on the offensive line by rookie Tommy White, whose introduction to varsity football under the lights was harsher than both Artie and Coach Jug Johnson had envisioned for the big 9th grader.

In the visiting grandstand at Iron Harbor Stadium, Benny Pressler, Leah Russo and Nicie Evans winced with each vicious hit on Ty when his protection collapsed before he could throw the ball or hand it off to Brett. But Ty Green was tough, and he kept getting up to call the next play and try again to gain some yards.

On this night, the team didn't score or even get close enough for little Ricky Duran to try a placekick. But Ricky did get to practice punting the ball on fourth down. In fact, he set a conference record for the number of punts in a single game, as Coach Johnson had to admit that his Bruins were never in four-down territory all night, always in "fourth-and-long" situations.

The final score was Iron Harbor 66, Arbor 0. The loss was so demoralizing that even Jug Johnson was out of sorts after the game, and he decided to ignore his own team rule about players riding the activity bus home. He gathered the boys in the visiting locker room after they had showered and dressed. He told them that they could ride home with their parents if their folks had come to the game and hadn't left sometime in the fourth quarter.

Jug knew that this act set a precedent and worked against the solidarity he always sought for his teams. But the last thing he wanted that night was another argument or fight like what had happened with Josh Stark on the road trip to Ebenezerville to open the season. After this latest beating, the Bruins players—and the coaches, too—were frustrated, embarrassed and ready to fight anyone they could beat down, if for no other reason than to prove they weren't as weak as they had looked on the field. Even Jug would have ridden home with his wife if he could have.

Few team members rode home with Jug Johnson and the other coaches. If their own parents hadn't attended the game, many of those players got Jug's permission to hitch rides with friends. But even with his sprained ankle, Artie stayed on the bus, as did Ricky and Leah. Ty told Jug that he was riding home with his mother, but went with Nicie instead, as Rachel Green had given three other parents a ride to the game. Tommy rode home with Bennie and his parents; and Brett left with his own mother and father. It was good that the activity bus was far from crowded and everyone got a seat to themselves.

No one on the bus talked much at first. Leah broke the silence. "Hey, it was just a football game," she said. "Nobody died or anything."

Artie turned to look at her in the seat across the aisle. "Yeah," he began, pausing to find the right words, "but 66 to nothing?" He shook his head.

"Well?" said Leah. "At least Ricky set a new record for punts. *That* was a real bright spot, don't you think? We don't have to worry about his punting now. He got plenty of practice. And I'm being serious this time."

Ricky, sitting three seats back, heard Leah's remark. "Yes," Ricky said, "but I would like to practice without having those big boys from Iron Harbor trying to squash me like a bug."

That the Iron Curtain rushers blocked none of Ricky's punts that night was a miracle. A few times he had to scramble away from them before punting, but that strategy in itself added a new twist to the Arbor special-teams attack, Leah explained.

At that point, Coach Johnson twisted around in his seat behind the bus driver and peered back into the darkness. "Miss Russo," Jug said, "I do appreciate you pointing out the silver lining in tonight's disaster, but we ain't gonna beat many teams by out-punting them."

Leah nodded and fell silent again. Noting her uncharacteristic optimism, Artie felt bad about having discouraged her from exploring the bright side of that night's gloomy game. "Hey, Leah," he said, waiting for her to look up again. "Was there anything good in your stats about Ty or Brett? I missed most of the second half."

She glanced up toward Jug at the front of the bus. In a low voice, she said, "Ty tried hard, but he had too much trouble handling the snaps. They had to simplify the count, and that let Iron Harbor tee off on our O-line. Tommy couldn't hold his guy off." She smiled weakly. "That guy was big *and* mean. He was, like, 275 with a full beard. He even *looked* like Mean Joe Greene."

"Yeah, he's their heavyweight wrestler," said Artie. "I'll have to wrestle him this winter." The thought made him wince. "I guess Tommy looked like the kid in the commercial, huh—you know, the kid who gives Joe Greene his soda."

Ricky piped up, "But Tommy did not say, 'Thanks, Mean Joe,' at the end. Tommy was too tired and beat up." Ricky paused for a second before adding, "That boy scared me, too. That's why I ran away so fast when I punted."

Artie smiled at his little friend's confession. "So how did Brett do in the second half?" Artie asked Leah. "Did he do anything good at all?"

She shook her head. "No, not really," she whispered, as if she didn't want to be heard criticizing a teammate. "Actually, he and Ty both *lost* yards on the ground. To tell you the truth, I don't know how I'm gonna write this game up for the school paper—not that I mind giving Brett some bad publicity. He deserves to get knocked down a few pegs after the other day."

"You mean, the thing in the cafeteria on Tuesday?" asked Artie. "That whole mess is over and done with." He glanced back at Ricky, but couldn't tell if he was still listening.

"Not according to Nicie," said Leah. "She's still kinda ticked off about what Brett *might* have said. She knows how it feels to be called names. That's why she gets in so many fights. It's why she had to transfer to Arbor, remember?"

"Yeah," Artie said, "she's a tough girl—but I like her. And I'm glad that she and Ty are together. She keeps him straight. I think he asked her to represent him on the homecoming court next Friday. All of us senior players get to pick somebody, you know."

Leah nodded. "So, who did *you* ask?" she said. "Only seniors can be on the homecoming court—or be voted homecoming queen, anyway. Who's *your* representative?"

Glad that the bus's interior lights weren't on, Artie could feel his face turn red. "There are only two special girls—well, *three*—that I'd even consider asking," Artie said, "and the first two don't go to Arbor High, even though one *is* a senior—well, kind of."

"Oh?" said Leah. "Where do they go to school?"

Artie chuckled. "Ty's mom graduated twenty years ago," he said. "Besides, I don't think Ty's dad would let her go to the homecoming dance with me next Saturday night. The ER doctor said I'll probably still be on these crutches then, anyway. It's a pretty bad sprain."

Ricky, who *had* been listening, moved up two seats to join the conversation. "So, Artie," he said, "who are your other two special ladies? You could ask this 'senior' you mentioned to be your representative and let me ask the other girl for a date to the dance."

The diminutive kicker lifted himself a few inches on the back of the seat and spoke so that Jug could hear up front. "I am a good dancer," said Ricky, referring to the place-kicking routine that he had practiced. "Is that not right, Coach John-son?"

At the sound of his name, Jug turned around and stared at the boy for a sec-ond, but just shook his head and faced front again. Leah said, "Yes, Ricky, you can dance on the football field—you showed that tonight by dancing out of Mean Joe's reach twice—but can you boogie on the dance floor? That's the question. Can you shake your booty?"

"I can," said Ricky. "I am Latin, and I can dance."

"Well, isn't that a racial stereotype?" Leah asked. "Like what Brett said?"

Ricky's smile faded. "Brett is my teammate and my friend," said Ricky. "He did not say that bad word. But what hurt my feelings was when all the seniors said he did, and they laughed about it and used that word over and over again. I do not like that word."

Artie could think of nothing to add to the subject, so he changed it. "No, Ricky, I don't think my grandma can keep up with you on the dance floor," Artie said, with a grin. "She's my second special lady, and she *is* a senior … citizen. No, I'd hate for Grandma to fall and break her hip shaking her booty at the home-coming dance. Grandpa would never forgive us. He's supposed to come home this week, you know."

"Yes," said Ricky. "It is also *his* homecoming week. My mother and father look forward to welcoming him home from the hospital. I am sure you are glad, too, Artie." Ricky paused for a second, then added, "But that is only *two* girls. Who is the third one? Will you ask her?" Ricky sneaked a look at Leah.

Artie looked at Leah, too, and saw that she was now the one becoming embarrassed. He wondered how she might take being put on the spot right then—to be asked to represent him on the homecoming court and to go with him to the dance. Or maybe she didn't want to be asked at all. Maybe—since a freshman couldn't be voted homecoming queen, anyway—she wanted to be with someone closer to her own age.

Or maybe Leah didn't want to date anyone yet. Maybe it was too soon after her brother's death to enjoy or celebrate anything at Arbor High, especially on the same night when Arbor Field would be rededicated as Reuben Russo Memorial Stadium, and when the late, great quarterback's No. 3 home jersey would be retired. Maybe she didn't want to call any additional attention to herself that night, for whatever reason.

Or maybe a girl like her just doesn't want to go to the dance with a guy like me, Artie thought. And so he changed the subject again. "I don't know, Ricky," said Artie. "It's probably too late to ask her, anyway. Besides, this is going to be a really busy week. I have way too much work to do on the farm, and these crutches are gonna make it even harder to do."

"You worry too much, my friend," Ricky said. "That is why we are all there—my mother and my father and I—to help you on the farm. We are teammates there, too. I am sure that your *abuelos* would not want you to miss out on something so important as your senior homecoming. It is a great honor to have someone stand with you on the field."

That was Leah's opening. "If you don't want to ask the other girl, Artie, you can ask me," she said. "I'll be your representative. Ricky is right. It would be my honor—because you were so close to my brother." As if to herself, she added, "I miss him so much."

Even in the darkened bus, Artie could see her tearing up. He knew something about how she felt, because he had idolized Reuben for years and had lost him as a friend and teammate. Artie had lost one other person whom he must have dearly loved, though he did not remember her motherly gaze or tender touch. Perhaps he loved the mere *thought* that his mother had once loved him and that she still missed him all these years later.

Perhaps he wasn't ready to consider that the reason his mother had never returned for him or even tried to contact him was because she had never wanted him. Like his fear of asking Leah Russo out and being rejected by her, he had been afraid of finding his mother and learning that she really didn't love him or want his love. Perhaps that was how she had felt about his father, whomever and wherever he might be. But all that happened many years ago, and Artie knew that he might never know. Maybe Woody Woods could help him understand.

Shutting everything else out, Artie looked into Leah's eyes and whispered, "I know you miss him. I do, too. He was the best." She didn't look away. Artie took a deep breath and said, "I'd be honored to have you represent me, Leah, if you will."

Leah Russo smiled and nodded twice. Nothing else needed to be said. Artie Bauer would have the perfect homecoming representative the next Friday, and Ricky would have the chance to get her on the dance floor—along with every other eligible girl—at the homecoming dance in the school gym that Saturday night. That was appropriate, because Artie was a lover, and little Ricky truly was a dancer. Leah was glad that her two friends were so happy after such a difficult night.

CHAPTER 23 – Homecoming on the Farm and Field

HARRY BAUER'S RETURN HOME from the hospital the following Tuesday was a mixed blessing for everyone living on the farm—Grandpa, Grandma and Artie, and the Duran family. Grandpa understood why Ricardo was needed and welcomed his help. A week earlier Artie had explained to Grandpa how the Durans could be paid for their services. It was a plan that intrigued the old farmer and also relieved his worries about the family farm's sustainability.

If this arrangement that Abe Pressler had suggested worked, Joel Stark and his real estate company's bid to buy the farm could be turned down flat and forgotten. That in itself made Harry Bauer happy to welcome Ricardo, Gabby and Little Ricky Duran into his home with open arms.

Pearl Bauer, however, wasn't as happy about sharing her kitchen with Gabby Duran, as Artie had worried might be the case. Grandma also claimed not to like most of the Latino foods that Gabby cooked, though her main objection was that the bean dishes "smelled bad" and gave her gas.

Again, Abe Pressler had come to the rescue by having his construction crew renovate the spare room off the kitchen into a downstairs bedroom for Grandpa, with an adjoining bathroom that was wheelchair accessible. Once the Bauers were home in their new digs, Grandma used the new bathroom as much as Grandpa did. She still slept upstairs in the couple's old bedroom, but she grew to like the new toilet, sink and especially the walk-in shower. She told Artie and the Durans that the old upstairs bathroom with its pull-chain toilet and claw-foot tub was all theirs.

Ricardo and Gabby had their own bedroom upstairs. Ricky moved out of the other guest bedroom and into Artie's room. The small boy slept in the top bunk bed that had been used only to catch cast-off clothes and anything else that Artie hadn't wanted to put away. Having a roommate forced Artie to be as neat and organized in private as he seemed to be in public.

In the past, Grandma had always made sure that Artie was presentable before he left the house. Now, as she was preoccupied with caring for Grandpa—and with Ricky perched in the bunk above him—Artie had to grow up and clean up his own act, without relying so much on others to keep him on the straight and narrow path.

The new corn maze in the field next to the old homeplace out on the highway was anything but straight and narrow. Employing his son's computer savvy, Abe Pressler had hired workers to cut a simple but challenging maze designed by Bennie into the cornfield. With Tommy White's help, Bennie had installed an indoor-outdoor sound system that covered the property and would allow him to play growls, screams, boos, door slams and scary music throughout the old house and at various spots in the maze once the Halloween-week attraction opened.

After Halloween, the old homeplace could be converted easily into a rentable residence, presumably for the Duran family. Ricardo was helping with the renovation work at the house, as well as in the barn stables where the two new horses were being boarded. Grandpa called Ricardo a "jack of all trades"—in other words, a good farmer, Harry Bauer's highest praise.

* * *

At Arbor High School on this homecoming week, students were excited about each day's celebratory theme, which replaced their usual Barf Table shenanigans. It was called Spirit Week, with Marvel Monday for superhero costumes, Twin Tuesday for pairs of matching outfits, Wild West Wednesday for western clothes, and Tie-Dye Thursday for colorful T-shirts, caps and bandannas. Friday was Class Day. Members of each class dressed alike—9th graders in flannel pajamas,

10th graders in preppy clothes, 11th graders in all-black outfits, and 12th graders in tastefully tied togas with white T-shirts. Bruins football players had the option of wearing their game jerseys on Friday instead of whatever else their respective classes sported.

At the homecoming pep rally on Friday, Artie Bauer and Ricky Duran reprised their Twin Tuesday outfits, mugging for the student body as big Arnold Schwartzenegger and little Danny Devito from the movie poster for *Twins*. Ty Green wore thick-framed glasses and a Superman tee under a gray suit, tie and white shirt whose front he broke open every two minutes to reveal the *S* emblem. Tommy White modeled a new western shirt, stiff dungarees, shiny western boots, white cowboy hat and red bandanna that he'd bought at Pressler's Department Store with the company owner's help.

Brett was the only player who chose not to join in on the Spirit Week fun, wearing his usual T-shirts and jeans every day until Friday, when he put on his jersey but tried to fade into the background at the afternoon pep rally. Ever since Krakatoa Tuesday, Brett had tried to keep a lower profile than he would have liked. The previous Friday night's embarrassing game at Iron Harbor also had convinced Brett that being neither seen nor heard was the way for him to avoid more fallout in his personal life, especially considering who his date to the Saturday dance was.

* * *

"Brett Woods is going with who?" Nicie Evans had asked at the Barf Table earlier that day. "That's some way to treat your best friend. Did she ask *him* to be her escort, or did he ask *her*? And does Josh Stark know his girlfriend is going to the dance with Brett?"

Ty had shrugged. "I guess so," he'd said. "I can't imagine Brett escorting her and expecting Josh not to find out. I mean, she's a senior cheerleader, *and* she's on the homecoming court. Shoot, I asked her out when we were sophomores, and she didn't give me the time of day. She said she wouldn't be caught dead in my car."

Artie and Leah had been the only other Barf Tablers seated so far, as Bennie, Tommy and Ricky had been working their way through the lunch line. "And you know what?" Artie had said. "She'll probably be homecoming queen. I didn't vote for her, but I know a lot of kids who did. She's really popular—just like Josh and Brett. I never could understand why a senior like her would date a 10th grader—no matter what he drives."

Leah had looked up from her book and said, "I understand why. It's about the money. Bennie told me she chased after *him* at the beach until his accident. That was when Josh saw his opening and decided to ask her out himself. Well, she didn't even hesitate to say yes. Bennie calls her 'the digger,' short for gold—"

"He calls her what?!" Nicie had exclaimed, almost jumping to her feet.

"The *digger*—with a *d*," Leah had replied. "It's short for 'gold-digger.' What'd you think I said?"

Ty had immediately sensed the mix-up and moved to calm Nicie down, while Artie had gone on to comment, "You know what? That's *exactly* what happened last week with Brett and Ricky. Don't you think? One big misunderstanding. That's why name-calling is so bad. If people didn't use them in the first place, there'd be nothing to misunderstand."

"I don't know," Ty had said. "There's good names, and there's bad names— like Coach calling you Yogi because he likes you. Bad names have to do with stuff you can't help, stuff you can't change. That girl can help being a gold-digger. Calling her that is just calling a sp—"

Nicie had popped him before he could finish. "You say that word, Ty Green, and I'll wash your mouth out with soap. There's some words we aren't gonna say. But I guess 'Digger' is okay, since that's what she is—and she can help it."

Ty, Artie and Leah had agreed and had gone back to their usual banter and book reading. Then Bennie, Tommy and Ricky had arrived in their flannel PJs.

"Hi, guys," Bennie had said to the seniors. "Nice togas. Ain't it great that the school has a special day like this to make you guys change your bed sheets?"

All but Nicie had laughed. "I'll have you know, Bennie Pressler," she had said, feigning offense, "that last summer when I played beach volleyball, my sheets got changed every *day*—at the hotels where we played. Now if I can just get Mama to do that for me at home."

"I'm just kidding," Bennie had said, before addressing Leah alone. "Hey, girl, why didn't you wear your flannel jammies today like the rest of us lowly 9th graders? Tommy and Ricky get to change out of theirs before the pep rally, but I'm stuck in mine until I get home after school."

"And you went all out, too," Leah had said, after looking him over. "Gee, I didn't know Pressler's sold onesies for big boys. That one's even pink, like in that Christmas movie. But where's the hood and bunny ears? That's the funniest part of the costume."

"Hat rule, I guess," Bennie had explained. "Mr. Church met us at the front door this morning and told me the hood and rabbit ears violated the dress code, so I had to put it in my locker. Dad even special-ordered this getup for me. But at least I can wear it at our haunted house—*with* the hood and ears."

Everyone had laughed, before Bennie had added, "I wanted to wear the *whole* suit to school today, because life here at Arbor High isn't, as Ralphie says in the movie, 'a veritable nightmare.' Not yet, anyway."

* * *

The nightmare—for Bennie Pressler and the rest of the Barf Table crew— didn't begin until around seven o'clock on Saturday evening. In fact, Friday night's homecoming game against the Pinecrest Christian Patriots, a middling non-conference opponent, had been the type of dream that everyone would have wished for, one in which everything went right and nothing went wrong. Off his crutches but still limping on his sprained ankle, Artie Bauer hadn't played that night; however, his backup hadn't caused any big problems at center, partly because he had relinquished long-snapping duties to Tommy White.

In practice on Monday, Leah had suggested that Artie, still on crutches, work with Tommy on long snaps for punts and placekicks. Tommy had learned how to play center on special teams, while Leah had held the ball for Ricky Duran's field-goal and extra-point attempts in their practice by themselves. Toward the end of each day's team practice session, Leah had headed back to the bleachers; Tommy and Ricky had rejoined the offense for special-teams practice; and Ty had held the ball on kicks, as usual.

On the sidelines in his wheelchair, Bennie had dared Leah to pull the ball at the last second, at least once, as Lucy does Charlie Brown, but Leah had played it straight in order to give her trusting young friends all the practice they both needed.

And their practice had paid off on Friday night, as Ricky had extended his streak of successful PATs to eight straight without a miss, and he had kicked three field goals out of four attempted. His only miss had been from 40 yards out, when Coach Johnson had decided to test Ricky's leg in a game situation. In practice, he had kicked field goals of 40 and 45 yards, but those kicks had been against the Bruins' second-string defenders. Friday night's final score had been Arbor 30, Pinecrest 24, with Ricky's kicks making the difference for the win.

There had been no surprises at halftime of the homecoming game. Josh Stark's gold-digging girlfriend, escorted by Brett Woods, had been crowned as homecoming queen. Nicie Evans had looked ravishing in her long, red-sequined dress and black stiletto heels, standing with Ty as his representative on the court. Brett and Ty had appeared on-field in their soiled uniforms.

For the first time, Leah had appeared in public not wearing either her usual gray hoodie or her brother's old football jersey, both over-sized on her. She had chosen a dark-green pantsuit that had matched the color of the coaching staff's team jackets and the home jersey that Artie had worn that night with dress slacks and shoes. Little Leah had looked feminine standing next to big Artie on the field at halftime without drawing attention to her slight frame.

Earlier that evening, during a short pregame ceremony just before the National Anthem, Leah had walked out onto the field with her parents, Principal Church and Coach Johnson. The three Russos had stood arm in arm, their heads down, as Mr. Church and Jug had taken turns regaling the homecoming crowd with highlights of the late Reuben Russo's career on that very gridiron. The men had held up a green-and-gold No. 3 jersey that later would be framed and hung in the gymnasium.

And from the press box, Bennie Pressler had announced for the first time, "Welcome, ladies, gentlemen, alumni, parents and students … to Reuben Russo

Memorial Stadium."

* * *

The doors to the school gymnasium opened for the dance at seven o'clock that Saturday evening. Earlier in the afternoon, Thelma Hopper's cheerleaders and Spirit Squad members had decorated the gym with green-and-gold streamers, balloons and crepe-paper covers for the tables from the cafeteria.

With Tommy White's help, Bennie Pressler—who had agreed to deejay the dance—had set up his sound system and speakers on a table in one corner at the far end of the gym. From the other far corner, a long, rectangular table for the homecoming court and their escorts extended to the baseline of the basketball floor. Between that seating area and Bennie's setup was a large round table meant for any teachers who came to chaperone the event. It was the actual Barf Table, though its laminated top was covered with gold paper that hid all the stains and blemishes from its daily abuse in the lunchroom.

Neither Principal Jerry Church nor Coach Jug Johnson was in the gym when the dance started. They both arrived much later, too late to keep the inevitable from happening. In fact, the only faculty members present all night were pretty Miss Hopper, who was too busy to sit still, and crusty old Mr. Carson, who went outside every five minutes to smoke.

Teachers had been encouraged but not ordered to chaperone the dance, due to complaints from one prudish teacher whose preacher taught that dancing was sinful. Harry and Pearl Bauer had once attended that little country church, but had stopped going after Artie's mother ran off and left the baby boy to be raised by them. Both Grandma and Grandpa had grown tired of all the pointed sermons and whispered gossip about Artie and his mother, and had sworn never to return to that little church, even though many of their kin people lay buried in the cemetery there. That was why Grandma had been so easily offended years later when they attended huge Solid Rock Christian Church with that one uppity church lady and her sensitive nose.

No one on hand in the Arbor High gym that Saturday night had a problem with the Macarena, the Running Man, the Tootsie Roll or the Electric Slide leading to any other kind of behavior. Dancing wasn't the problem, not even slow dancing and swaying to Bennie's music.

The Oleander County Sheriff's Department had sent a lone deputy to watch both the front door and the punch bowl on the refreshment table just inside, but the young fellow was distracted by Miss Hopper's perkiness and often left his post to run errands for her. Most of the teenagers there that night had come just to have fun, and—as the big banner hanging over the homecoming court's table stated—to "Make Magical Memories."

As it turned out, no one would forget what happened late that night, a fiasco that ranked above even the worst Barf Table incidents in school history. Unfortunately, the eight unlucky souls seated around the Barf Table that Saturday night once again experienced firsthand a mess of epic proportions.

* * *

After working together much of the day on the Bauer farm, the regular Barf Table gang had freshened up and changed clothes late Saturday afternoon in the old homeplace that was being renovated. The old frame structure had become something of a clubhouse for the friends as it was being fixed up, first to be a haunted house at Halloween, then to be the Duran family's new rental home.

Abe Pressler had picked up Bennie and Tommy shortly after lunch so that they could set up Bennie's deejay equipment in the gym. Artie, Ty and little Ricky had changed into their best Sunday suits and had relinquished the old house's bathroom to the girls. Leah and Nicie had dressed in their homecoming court attire from the night before. Nicie had looked as ravishing as ever in her long dress and heels.

"Girl," Nicie had said to Leah, "we need to do something about your hair."

Leah had looked at herself in the bathroom mirror and had shrugged. "Could you?" she had replied. "At least I don't dye it black now. I usually wear a hoodie or a ball cap. But that isn't gonna cut it tonight, huh?"

Nicie had shaken her head. "Nope. It ain't a ball cap kind of night, hon. And we need to look extra good for our dates. I even saw Artie shining his shoes out there in the living room."

Thirty minutes later when the two girls had emerged from the bathroom, Ricky had seen Leah first and had whistled. *"Que bonita!"* Ricky had exclaimed. "Artie, I am jealous. Are you *sure* that your grandmother does not want to go to the dance?"

Artie had been frozen in silence as he stared at the visions of beauty standing before him. Ty, however, had stepped forward, gone down on one knee, and bowed his head to both girls. "My ladies," he had said, crossing both hands over his heart like a knight errant, "please grant us the kindest of favors by accompanying us to the ball this evening. Our carriage awaits outside."

Extending her hand to him, Nicie had replied, "Rise, knave—I mean, *knight*. Just don't let that old car of yours turn into a pumpkin before midnight."

The five friends had piled into the White Whale, so that Ty could drive them up the lane past the barn to the Bauer farmhouse, where Grandma and Gabby Duran had prepared a pre-dance meal. The teens had also wanted to visit Grandpa to let Nicie and Leah fuss over him, and to let him see how nice they and the rest of the Barf Table "farmily" looked.

The group had headed off to Arbor High for what they had all hoped would be a memorable evening of dancing and socializing with their friends. They all had felt that way even without seeing the huge banner hanging over-top the homecoming court's table in the gym.

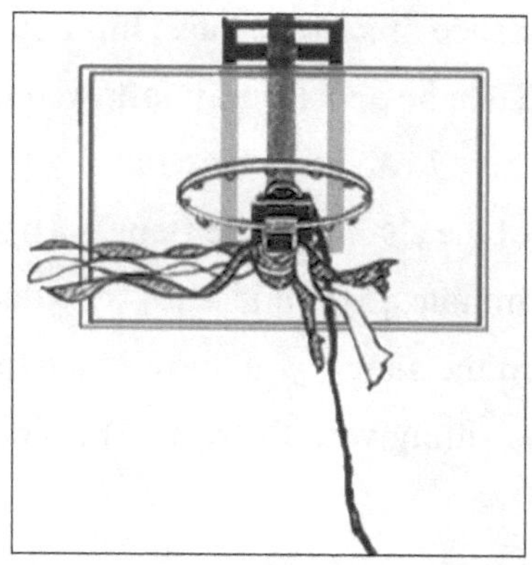

CHAPTER 24 – The Return of 'Prince Charming'

THE WHITE WHALE didn't turn into a pumpkin, but it managed to blow a front tire and run off the road into a pumpkin patch on the gang's drive into Monk's Landing. Ty and Artie took off their suit coats and white shirts, and changed the tire as quickly as they could. Still, the delay put them thirty minutes later than they'd planned, and there were no unclaimed chairs left at the long table for members of the homecoming court. There were *empty* chairs, but—like in the cafeteria—they had been saved for other, more popular girls and their guys.

Josh Stark's old girlfriend sat like queen of the castle, not just of homecoming itself, at the head of the table in the darkest corner of the gym so that she could survey her entire court and the whole room without having to turn her pretty head. Brett sat in the chair to her left, with his back to the gym floor. He didn't have to turn his head, either, because his full attention was on his date. The chair on her right was empty.

With Bennie's music blaring and couples already dancing, Nicie turned to Leah and said, "Looks like we all have to sit by ourselves at a round table again— just like lunchtime."

"Good," said Leah. "I don't want those snobs to even *think* I like them. We'll have more fun at our own table, anyway."

Artie, Ty and Ricky had jogged over to Bennie's deejay booth to check out his sound system, the same one he'd be using in three weeks at their haunted house. Bennie started the dance mix of the latest hip-hop hit to give himself some time off the microphone. Then he and Tommy followed their three buddies to the dressed-up, round table where Leah and Nicie sat.

Tommy removed one of the chairs to give Bennie a parking spot for his wheelchair. "I've got about ten minutes," Bennie said. "My disc player is on autopilot, but I like to intro and outro the songs, you know?" He turned to Nicie and Leah. "Hey, why aren't you guys sitting with the rest of the court? Are you too good to sit with cheerleaders?"

"Your *mouth's* on autopilot," said Nicie. "Be quiet, fool."

"Yeah," Leah said. "This *is* the Barf Table, isn't it? I'll bet if we took up the gold paper, we could still see the gravy stains from Krakatoa Tuesday. They'd never move the faculty table in here. Besides, there's no faculty here to sit at it, just Miss Hopper and Mr. Carson."

Bennie nodded. "I know. We've been here for three hours, and Miss Hopper hasn't sat still yet, not even for a minute."

"And Mr. Carson hasn't gone without a smoke for a minute," added Tommy. "During school, he usually stands out there on the breezeway with Coach Johnson, but I don't think the coach is here yet. I haven't seen him, anyway."

Ricky piped up. "The coach smokes?" he said, surprised.

"No," said Artie, joining in the conversation. "Coach dips snuff. You know what that is, right? Dipping snuff? Having to spit? His spitting gets kinda out of hand in baseball season."

"That's nasty," Leah said, screwing up her face in disgust.

"No joke," said Ty. "We've got to keep track of where Coach sets down his spit cup in the dugout. That thing is gross. When I was a 10th grader, my cousin came off the field and grabbed the wrong cup once, and, well, the rest is Arbor High baseball history."

"Did he drink it?" Ricky asked.

Artie puffed out his cheeks and almost gagged at the memory. "Yeah, he did," said Artie. "Well, one swig, but that was all it took."

"All it took?" asked Leah. "To do what?"

Ty laughed. "Let's put it this way, guys. We don't call my cousin 'Ralph' for nothing. Right, Artie?"

"Yeah," Artie said, "I'm glad I didn't have to wash all the uniforms after *that* game. *Pee-yew*, what a mess. And it was *hot* that day. The bus ride home from Mimosa Beach was terrible."

Now it was Nicie's turn to laugh. "I remember that," she said. "I was on the softball team at Mimosa Beach that year. The coaches had to hose out the visitors' dugout after you guys left. They said they shouldn't have let your team go to the concession stand for hot dogs and sodas before the game. It *was* a mess."

"I have another question," said Ricky. He paused until he had everyone's attention. "Did we lose the game that day? Or were we the *weeners*."

Preparing to wheel himself back to his sound booth, Bennie held up his hand and said, "I got this one, guys." To his little Guatemalan friend, he added, "There were no losers that day, Ricky. *Everyone* was a wiener—or wiped one off his shirt, right?" He spun the wheelchair around and rolled back toward his station.

The whole group laughed out loud. A long table away, Brett twisted his head to see where the laughter was coming from. Recognizing his four teammates, Brett smiled for an instant at the fun they were having and turned back to refocus on his evil queen and her latest command.

With a nod, Brett rose and hurried off toward the refreshment table just inside the gym entrance. He picked up two red plastic cups of punch and tried to glide back like a tightrope walker so as not to spill the contents of the red chalices. He knew that Her Majesty would view her cup of nectar as half empty, though he would still see it as being half full.

When Brett neared the royal table, however, he encountered a troupe of line dancers and had to detour behind the round table where Artie, Ty and Ricky sat with Leah and Nicie. He could have completed his assignment if Ricky hadn't bounced out of his chair and tugged Nicie up to join the dancers. The sticky, purplish liquid that sloshed from what would have been Brett's own cup hit the floor at Nicie's stiletto-heeled feet.

"Smooth move, bowels," said Nicie, stepping back from the wet mess. "Your little beach bunny over there—Queen Digger—I'm surprised she'd date a guy who can't move and hold his red plastic cup steady at the same time. Isn't that how you dance on the beach—when you shag?"

Embarrassed, Brett looked for something to wipe up the spill, but Ricky beat him to it by grabbing some paper napkins from the tabletop. Ricky knelt to sop up the pool of purple punch on the lacquered gym floor. "I got it for you, Brett," said Ricky. "Just don't spill anymore of that punch while I'm kneeling here, especially not on my back, okay?" With a hint of a smile, Ricky looked up and winked at his teammate.

Brett smiled in return. "I'm sorry that happened, Ricky," he said. "I really am—the thing in the lunchroom the other day. If I had it to do over, I'd just keep my mouth shut and mind my own business." Brett nodded toward the dark corner of the gym where the queen awaited her drink. "I'd better get over there," he added. "I know you and Nicie want to dance."

"You got that right," said Nicie. "Ricky is the only one of these three who will line dance with me. Artie says he's still too crippled to dance, and Mr. Ty Green here—my so-called date—is too bashful to do the Macarena with me." She looked at Ty and turned up her nose.

"Hey now," Ty said. "I'll dance with you before the night's over. But it needs to be the Jelly Roll or the Running Man or something to *real* music. I need to have a little talk with Bennie about his playlist—too much country music." Ty grinned and took the wet napkins from Ricky, and added, "I'll throw these away and go talk to Bennie right now."

Brett set the half-full cup down at an empty chair and headed toward the adjoining table, steadying the full red plastic cup with both hands to keep from spilling it. Artie looked at Leah in the chair next to him, tapped her on the arm, and said, "I'm sorry, too, Leah—about not dancing with you tonight. You look really nice. I'd *like* to dance with you."

She patted his hand. "Don't worry, Artie," she said. "I haven't been in a dancing mood for a long time." She smiled. "But thanks for the compliment. You look really nice, too—even after changing that flat tire on our way into town. I hope the

White Whale gets us all back home tonight without any more flat—"

Leah was interrupted by Nicie, who had started dancing with Ricky in the last line of dancers, but had hurried back to the dressed-up Barf Table. "*Oooo*," Nicie began, leaning down to be heard above the music. "Would you look and see who just came to the dance. He must not have liked Digger going out with his best friend after all."

It was Josh Stark, and he was seated in what had been the empty chair to the queen's right. Brett, still clutching the one red cup, stood behind his own chair to her left. Brett's brow was furrowed, but he wasn't saying anything.

Wearing a designer jacket, unbuttoned, a crisp white shirt, and a tie and suspenders that perfectly matched the queen's emerald-green dress, Josh rocked in his chair, laughed and pointed at his old girlfriend, then at Brett. The girl did nothing to calm Josh down. Instead, she appeared to be amused by the situation—two boys ready to fight over her. The music was too loud to make out any of Josh's words, but Artie had no trouble reading his former teammate's body language, if not his lips, and recognizing the dilemma that Brett, his current teammate, faced. Should Brett empty his remaining cup of punch on the couple? Or just punch Josh in the nose?

Brett did neither. To Artie and Leah's surprise, Brett handed the queen her drink and walked away with a forlorn look as he approached Artie and Leah. Artie reached out and beckoned to the dejected young man. "You can sit with us, buddy," Artie said. "We got an extra seat. And if Josh tries anything else, we got your back. He doesn't look sober."

"He isn't," said Brett, taking a seat across the round table from Artie and Leah. "That's why I didn't do anything. I've seen him that way before, and he gets crazy when he's drunk." Brett nodded toward the dark corner where Josh and the queen sat. "See? It's already started."

Still laughing about stealing Brett's date, Josh had taken off his necktie and tied it like a headband around his frosted, slicked-back hair. He jumped onto the seat of his chair and pretended to surf, holding his arms out and swaying to the music's beat until the end of the song.

Segueing into the next tune, Bennie announced over the rising music, "Here's an oldie but a goodie, gang. 'Strike a pose!' Let's Vogue!"

Josh Stark didn't miss a beat. Still swaying, he removed his jacket and tossed it aside, and cocked his arms this way and that, at all the angles he could think of to frame his face for an imaginary camera. The queen grinned at his antics and pretended to click photos of him. But she also stole looks at Brett, to see how he was reacting to the show.

"Now," Bennie said over the fading bars of the last song and into the opening drumbeats and recorded howls of the next, "it's time for some Jungle Love! O-ee-o-ee-o!"

That was all Josh needed to hear, to jump off his chair and scramble toward the closed-up set of bleachers nearest him. Like King Kong scaling the Empire State Building, he climbed the wall of long, wooden bleachers to the top. There he stood with his arms extended above his head as he screamed like an enraged ape. In his drunken mind, he was Josh Stark, king of Oleander County, and he was showing off for his queen.

By then, Principal Jerry Church and Coach Jug Johnson had arrived to help chaperone the dance, but they had stayed outside with old Mr. Carson and chatted in the gym lobby until this latest disturbance. Alerted by Miss Hopper, Mr. Church peeped through a square window in one gym door, to see Josh's gyrating silhouette atop the farthest set of bleachers. Afraid that the inebriated boy might fall, the principal hurried across the gym floor, threading his way through couples that interrupted their dancing only to point and laugh at drunken Josh.

Jug Johnson, a red plastic cup in hand, followed his boss at a respectable distance. Jug wasn't anxious to confront Josh again, not with the boy quarterbacking their cross-county rivals. The old coach was still smarting from the insults and threats that Josh's father, Joel Stark, had leveled against him. Jug wanted nothing more to do with the Stark family—at least, not until the Bruins faced Solid Rock in the last game of the regular season in four weeks.

Mr. Church waved for the deputy to come help him talk Josh down from the top of the bleachers. As the principal marched into the gym's darkest corner past the queen still seated at the head of her table, he peered up at Josh but said nothing, thinking better of barking orders before his reinforcements—or, rather, his adult witnesses—arrived on the scene.

Mr. Church thought Coach Johnson was right behind him, but turned and saw Jug pulling up a chair with his star players at the round table. Ty was headed back to the table after talking to Bennie in the deejay booth and stopping to chat and dance along the way. Nicie and Ricky were finishing up their last dance, ready to rejoin their friends.

With a sigh, Jug lifted his red plastic cup and spat discreetly, then set the cup down on the table and laid his other hand on Artie's shoulder. "Yogi, between you and me, I'm getting too old for this mess," said Jug, picking up his cup and spitting again. "That boy just about tore our team apart this season, didn't he? It was all I could do to handle him and his daddy. And now it looks like he's fixing to mess up our homecoming."

"Yeah, Coach," said Artie, "that kid is a real loser, even though he has everything going for him. Somebody needs to put him in his place—and his father, too."

"From your lips to God's ears, young man," Jug said, lowering his spit cup.

Artie nodded at his coach, and welcomed Ty, Nicie and Ricky back to the table. "Well, hello, strangers," said Artie. "I'm glad you could give us a little of your time tonight. So, Nicie, how well can Ricky dance? You guys were out there for, what, three dances, weren't you? Leah and I were getting lonely over here."

"Yeah," Ty said. "What's up with that? I mean, I was over there trying to get Bennie to play some funk, and you guys were dancing to whatever he put on." Ty acted hurt but was just having fun with his friends.

"You hush up, Ty Green," said Nicie. "I'll have you know that Ricky can really move on the dance floor. As a matter of fact, we didn't even get one whole dance with each other. Every time I turned around, he was off dancing with a cheerleader."

"Which one?" Brett asked, knowing that the queen hadn't left her seat, but that most of the other cheerleaders on the court had excused themselves before

Josh's outburst, even if their dates had remained seated. Brett wondered which girl had been attracted to Ricky.

"Which *one*?" Nicie said. "*All* of them. I think he danced with every last one of them, some of them twice."

Jug laughed and almost swallowed his dip. Artie and Ty broke into grins at little Ricky, and Ty said, "My man!" Brett wasn't quite ready to ask Ricky for dating advice, but the look of surprise on the jilted boy's face was unmistakable.

"What can I say?" said Ricky. "Girls like to dance, but many boys are too shy to go out on the dance floor. They do not want anyone to laugh at them—unless they have been drinking, like Josh Stark." He pointed up at Josh, still atop the last section of bleachers.

On the floor below, Principal Church and the deputy motioned for the boy to come down, but Josh grew more agitated and started pacing on the top bleacher, almost tripping over the cable that anchored one end of the long "Make Magical Memories" banner. With its opposite end attached to the retracted backboard supports, Josh looked down at the cable, lifted his head and squinted halfway across the gym at the basketball goal, then back down at the thin but strong wire tied into a thick, metal eye-bolt at his feet.

"Come down here, Mr. Stark," said the principal. "If you can't climb down on your own, we can pull out this section of bleachers and you can walk down. Or we can come up there and help you down, if that's what it takes."

The deputy took out his big, black flashlight and shined its beam up at Josh, blinding him for a few seconds. "Turn off that stupid light," Josh shouted. "I'm not hurting anybody. I'm just having fun. Leave me alone." To keep from losing his balance as he waited for the spots in his eyes to clear, he crouched on the top bleacher. He started fiddling with the cable and eye-bolt.

"What are you doing, Josh?" asked Mr. Church, before noticing that the banner over his head had started to bounce, like a full clothesline in a stiff breeze. "Don't mess with that cord. The whole thing will come down on us."

Josh was way ahead of him. Removing his end of the cable, the drunken boy was still strong enough to lift the banner so that he could wind a bit of line around his fist. He looked down at the queen first, next at the point on the backboard support where the cable's other end was attached, then on across the gym to Bennie Pressler's deejay booth in the other corner.

Annoyed, the queen finally stood and moved out from under the banner, not really wanting to step down from her throne and relinquish the spotlight to her boyfriend. "Josh Stark," she called out, as she moved toward the round table where Brett was now standing, "if you don't come down here, I'm gonna let Brett take me home."

"Alrighty then!" Josh shouted back. "Me Tarzan, you Jane!" And with that, he gripped the cable tighter and hopped off the top bleacher.

It was Josh's drunken luck that the backboard support midway across the gym was higher off the floor than the cable's overall length. In other words, he didn't slam onto the hardwood court mid-swing. Instead, he grazed the far end of the queen's long table and barely missed hitting the round Barf Table head-on, where the queen was standing with Brett and the others.

Like a pendulum, Josh started his upward arc toward the flashing lights of the deejay booth. At the farthest end of his swing, at its highest point, Josh released the line and tumbled feet-first into Bennie's largest speaker, knocking down the whole setup like bowling pins. The sweet song that Bennie was playing so that couples could slow dance ended with a second of shrill feedback, then silence.

The deputy ran across the floor to help Josh up and to escort him outside. Mr. Church took the queen by the arm and began to question her about the alcohol that Josh had been drinking and why he was even there to begin with. She'd had the forethought to carry her own drink from where she had sat all evening and to set it on the Barf Table when the principal started his interrogation. Her cup was the same one that Brett had gotten for her, but that Josh had spiked with odorless vodka from a flask he had smuggled into the gym and left on the floor beside his chair. Now her tainted cup was sitting on the round table with other identical cups. It could have been anyone else's red plastic cup.

"I want to ask a favor of you, young lady," Mr. Church said to the queen. "If you honestly haven't been drinking, as you say, I may need you to drive young

Mr. Stark home in his car. But if you *have* been drinking, I'll need to call his parents to come get him."

The queen stiffened. "I haven't had a single sip out of that flask," she said, balancing on the thin edge of truth. "That was all Josh. I came with Brett tonight." She didn't bother to explain why Josh's clothing matched hers so well, or why she had saved him a seat next to her. And since Mr. Church hadn't arrived on time that evening, he didn't know enough to ask.

Brett Woods, however, did know. Drawing closer, Brett said to the queen, "Yeah? Well, when I came back from the refreshment table, why did you laugh when Josh told me to 'run along, sonny boy'? He said you two have been looking forward to tonight for a long time, and that I wasn't going to mess it up. And you just laughed at me." When all the queen did was roll her eyes, Brett said, "I need to go make sure Bennie's okay," and he stalked off.

Having remained seated through it all, Jug Johnson had been taking everything in—his former player's antics, the principal's response, the queen's sly moves to avoid her own incrimination, and all the discussion going on around the old coach. Despite his proclivity to give pep talks laced with malapropisms, Jug was a good listener and observer of others. That was perhaps his greatest strength as a high school coach. He could recognize the athletic potential of youngsters in different sports, as he had done with Artie Bauer and before him Reuben Russo, and now with Ricky Duran and Tommy White.

Jug Johnson had also noticed Josh Stark's girlfriend deposit her cup of spiked punch on the Barf Table, closer to his own cup than she herself might have been aware. He stood, picked up her cup and sniffed it, put it back down on the table, smiled to himself, and walked away empty-handed.

Stung by Brett's accusations, the queen watched her escort walk away, then turned back to the principal and said, "He's making all that up, Mr. Church. Josh didn't tell him to 'run along,' and I didn't laugh at him. That would be mean." She batted her big, brown eyes at the man, as if she were hurt enough to cry. "I guess I can drive Josh home—that is, if you're done with him."

The principal was quiet for a few seconds as he considered his alternatives.

He nodded and said, "I appreciate that. I'll go have a word with Josh, and then you two can leave." Mr. Church turned away to walk back across the gym. With no music now, the dance was over, and students also were exiting the building.

The queen held her breath for a moment as she watched the principal step away. She smiled and turned to say goodbye to the other cheerleaders who had returned to the long table to gather up their things before leaving. Several smiled and waved to Ricky and told him how much they'd enjoyed dancing with him. The queen glanced back at her cup sitting on the round table and purposely left it there, feeling as if she were now out of danger.

Like Coach Johnson, Leah Russo was a skilled observer—a talent that served the budding reporter well. When she saw the queen leave the cup of spiked punch behind, Leah called out to her, "Hey, don't forget your drink. Mr. Church may come back here and find it, and *somebody* might tell him whose it was."

Leah leaned toward one particular cup, but the queen hurried over and snatched it away. Lifting it to her lips, she sneered and said, "Not if I get rid of the evidence," before downing the dark liquid that half filled the red plastic container. It was the one that Coach Johnson had used as his spit cup.

Artie, Ty, Ricky and Brett had just returned from checking on Bennie and Tommy. When the two older boys had seen the queen pick up that cup to chug its contents, they both had howled, "Noooo!" But it had been too late.

The queen's eyelids slammed shut, her pert mouth closed tight momentarily, and her smooth cheeks turned a sickly shade of green before they ballooned out like a puffer fish. Dizzy all of a sudden, the girl spun around to seek aid from her cheerleader friends, members of her attending court, but most of them saw what was about to happen and took cover wherever they could. Back at the Barf Table, even Leah and Nicie rose and moved out of the queen's range.

Her output was prodigious in both volume and distance. The homecoming queen heaved and wretched in a multi-colored yawn, expelling what seemed like gallons of chunky brown, purple and red vomit whose colors revealed all that she had consumed within the past six hours. She threw up on her own dress, on her friends' dresses, on the pantsuit of Miss Hopper, who made the mistake of trying to help her, and all over the long table where she had reigned supreme for that one night, at least.

But not one drop of the queen's effluent hit the dressed-up Barf Table, where the castoff crew of Arbor High stood and watched in jaw-dropping amazement. Even Bennie wheeled over with Tommy in tow to see the spectacle that the queen and her male consort had wrought.

"*Hmm*," said Bennie. "Dinner *and* a show."

Nicie leaned forward for a closer look. "*Ewww*," she said. "That girl needs to chew her food. That's nasty."

"And they say *I* have an eating disorder," said Leah. "Well, I've seen enough. Let's head home, guys—unless we need to help you, Bennie."

He shook his head. "No, Tommy and I can handle it, and Dad is on his way over with the van. I called him a few minutes ago."

Despite the dance's abrupt end, everyone was in a thankful mood. Bennie thanked Tommy for helping him with so much every day, not just with the sound equipment that night. Ricky thanked Bennie for being such a funny guy and for playing such great dance tunes, if only for half the evening. Brett thanked the whole gang for making a place for him at their table. Nicie and Leah thanked Ty and Artie for being their knights in shining armor with the flat tire on their way to the dance. Ty and Artie thanked everyone for being good friends on what had been a challenging night, all things considered.

Their difficulties weren't over, though. When they left the building and walked across the parking lot to the White Whale, they saw that another tire was flat, this one purposely harpooned. Just who was to blame—whether it was Josh or the queen or both—couldn't be proven that night or ever, probably. Having already used the big white car's spare tire, Ty asked Nicie to go back into the gym and call her father for help.

A bit aggravated, Artie suggested to Ty that "Likely To Die" might be a more appropriate name for his car after all, at least on this night. But as they waited, Artie had to admit that none of this misfortune was of their own doing—certainly not what had happened at the dance—and that they had actually enjoyed each other's company despite the evening's challenges.

Mr. Evans soon arrived in his tow truck and got the Whale afloat again. By midnight, they were all home safe in their beds, dreaming of dazzling lights, catchy beats and magical memories not soon to be forgotten.

CHAPTER 25 – Taking Out the Trash

THE FALLOUT FROM Saturday's homecoming dance didn't settle until the following Monday morning, when all the parties involved in the fracas gathered in Principal Church's office. That meeting accomplished a greater purpose than to resolve a simple school matter. For the first time since the Presslers' surfing-related lawsuit had been filed against Woody's Surf Shop months earlier, Abe Pressler and Woody Woods came together for more than a few minutes and finally talked, as they waited their turns to speak with Jerry Church about the dance debacle in the gym. What the two businessmen realized was that the person responsible for all the trouble at the dance—drunken swinger Josh Stark—was the same person to blame for the surfing accident that had injured Bennie Pressler.

The men's lawyers were nowhere in sight, but the pair decided to find an equitable settlement that would compensate Bennie for his injury, free the Woods family from the stigma of having had a part in hurting Brett's former friend, and punish Josh Stark and his father for pushing Woody to carry a defective surfboard leash in the first place. The surf shop would no longer sell that particular leash; however, Josh still counted its manufacturer as one of his surfing sponsors. Woody assured Abe that he would make some calls to the surfing equipment company. Abe said he was sure that Bennie and Brett could be good friends again.

At the end of the day, Principal Church decided not to pursue a petition in juvenile court against Josh Stark in exchange for his father's promise to reimburse the school and the Presslers for all the property damage that Josh had done at the dance. That did not include the damages to the queen's and her court's homecoming gowns, nor to their pride, because other attendees had been involved in that muddled mess—Jug, Leah and potentially anyone else who had passed the Barf Table after the coach had set down his spit cup.

The principal also didn't punish Josh for crashing the Arbor High dance, with Mr. Church reasoning that as a former student, Josh could arguably be called an Arbor alumnus, a status that might have convinced him that he had the privilege to attend the homecoming event. After all, wasn't that what homecoming was all about—former students coming home to their old school? At least that was Joel Stark's—and his attorney's—reading of the situation.

Josh wasn't even required to miss any classes that Monday in E-ville in order to deal with his Saturday night transgressions in Monk's Landing. His parents—and Stark Realty's lawyer—had represented him. The Arbor High students, however, had been pulled out of their classes and forced to wait until the principal sorted their involvement out.

When Artie's turn in Mr. Church's office had come, Artie had spoken up—as the principal himself had encouraged the senior leader to begin doing—and he had insisted that the school administration press charges against Josh.

"If you don't punish Josh," Artie had told Mr. Church, "you'll be telling him—and every other kid like him—that they can get away with anything here. And then Josh—not to mention his friends—will do worse and worse stuff. With all due respect, sir, you need to report what he did here Saturday night to juvenile court."

Mr. Church had disagreed, saying, "No, we need to be forgiving, Artie. Everyone makes mistakes. We all deserve a second chance to make things right. Besides, Josh has promised to be on his best behavior from here on out, and to come on campus only with his Solid Rock athletic teams—well, that's what Mr. and Mrs. Stark promised, and I believe them. I don't think we need to worry about Josh or to punish him for his, well, youthful indiscretions."

"Youthful indiscretions?" Artie had said. "I'm sorry, Mr. Church, but isn't everything bad that happens here a youthful indiscretion? Isn't it a principal's job—isn't it *your* job—to do something about youthful indiscretions on school grounds?"

"I'm sorry you feel that way, Artie," Mr. Church had said, "but that's how it's going to be. And, young man, you aren't going to speak to me that way. Maybe if you give up your senior privileges, at least for a week, you'll know your place. You can return to class now, and when the senior lunch bell rings, you can spend that time taking out trash for Frankie. Please send in Miss Russo on your way out."

The principal's change in attitude had surprised Artie, though it hadn't been that much of a shock, considering the Stark family's prominence in Oleander County. The Starks had always thrown their weight around, often resorting to threats or bribes. Artie suspected that Joel Stark had found Jerry Church's price and had either paid it or promised to pay it.

As he had left Mr. Church's office, Artie had wondered what would happen if, instead of summoning Leah for her meeting and reporting to the lunchroom to work, the two of them just took off for an afternoon at the beach. Artie had Grandpa's pickup truck. He and Leah could leave campus, drive to nearby Sandpiper Beach, get some sun, listen to the surf, and drive back to campus for football practice. He had wondered if those decisions would be seen as youthful indiscretions deserving forgiveness and second chances, or if Mr. Church would throw the book at them. He hadn't "forgiven" Artie's question about his judgment.

"What did he ask you about Coach's spit cup?" Leah had asked when Artie had emerged from the principal's office. "I didn't hand it to her, or tell her to drink it."

"She told him you did," Artie had said, "but I told him what really happened—that she picked up that cup all by herself, and that she killed it because she thought it was her cup with liquor in it. I saw all that with my own eyes. You didn't do anything."

Leah had nodded and said, "Yeah, that's right. But I did remind her to get her drink before she left, and I did imply that I was going to tell on her for drinking.

She chugged that cup of spit without even looking at it. Who does that? Man, I've never seen so many colors of puke."

With that vivid image in mind, Artie himself had turned green as he had remembered his childhood friend named Ralph and how the imaginary playmate had gotten his name. Looking at his wristwatch, Artie had said to Leah, "Yeah, thanks for that. It's almost lunchtime. I'm gonna head on over to the cafeteria— even though I've lost my appetite. I have to help Frankie, anyway, so I'm just gonna go now. See you over there."

"Save my seat, okay?" she had said, with a wry smile. "Don't let anybody else get it—as if anybody else wants to sit at the Barf Table."

Artie had nodded and wished her luck with the principal. The two friends had gone their separate ways—Artie to the lunchroom, Leah into Mr. Church's office. They had been the last two students waiting to see him, even though he later interrogated one more prime suspect in The Case of the Guzzled Spit Cup—Coach Jug Johnson.

* * *

When the lunch bell rang, Artie was already seated at the Barf Table, having spent the previous twenty minutes emptying trash bins from that morning's breakfast crowd and wiping down the tray-return counter. Artie didn't mind relieving Frankie of those duties, because the young cashier—despite his mean appearance and death-metal T-shirts—had always been kind to the kids who, for whatever reasons, had been forced to sit at that round table. Even though Artie knew he needed to eat something before practice, his mind was still fixed on the queen's colorful behavior of two days earlier and on the anger he felt toward Principal Church, and so he didn't get himself a lunch tray for the time being. He trusted that Frankie would save him some food, if he asked him to.

Ty Green and Nicie Evans slid into their seats, both of them with sodas from the lobby in hand. Nicie gave Ty a plastic-wrapped sandwich from the brown paper bag she carried and took out another one for herself.

"Nicie, your dad was a lifesaver Saturday night," Artie told her. "We would have been stuck here another hour or two if you hadn't called him."

Nicie smiled. "He was glad to help," she replied. "Oh, before I forget again, he said to tell you that he's almost finished fixing your grandpa's tractor. He said this morning that he might be able to haul it out to your farm tomorrow or the next day, depending on how busy he is."

"That's great," said Artie. "See? He really is a lifesaver. Ricardo had to borrow an old tractor from our neighbors, and he's about to lose his religion with it overheating all the time."

Ty chuckled. "So you're learning some new Spanish words, huh?" Ty said, adding, "I wanted to cuss, too, when I saw that slashed tire on the White Whale the other night. Ol' Lurch Church said he isn't gonna make Josh pay for the tire, because we can't prove he did it—even though we all know he did. Now, doesn't that suck? Mr. Evans will get stiffed, too, for fixing it."

"No, I'll pay him," said Artie. "I'll add that to his bill for fixing our tractor."

"No, you won't," Nicie said. "Daddy told me this morning that he isn't gonna charge you anything for the tractor. He said that'll be his contribution to our Halloween project. He also said he and Mama are gonna tell everybody they know to come to our haunted house and get lost in our corn maze and then go for a hayride. He's proud of fixing up that tractor, and if you ask him, he may even drive it on the hayrides for us."

Leah entered the cafeteria and walked straight to the Barf Table, pulling out her chair and plopping into it without a word. Frowning, she flipped up her hood, crossed both arms, and stared down at the bare tabletop.

"Uh-oh," said Nicie. "I know *that* look. This girl is not happy, not one bit. So what did Lurch tell you, girl?"

Leah shook her head sullenly and looked up at Nicie across the table. "That jerk Josh Stark crashes our dance, brings liquor in, gets drunk and acts like a monkey, and *then* he tears the place apart, just to show off in front of his gold-digging, spit-guzzling girlfriend. And nothing happens to him—or to her! Well, not really." She fell silent again.

"That's what I thought," Artie said. Turning to see Ricky, Tommy and Bennie waiting in the lunch line, Artie started to rise and walk over to join them for some food himself. But he noticed Coach Johnson and old Mr. Carson come into the lunchroom. Carson headed for the teacher table; Jug was headed straight for the Barf Table, with much the same look on his face as Leah had shown minutes earlier.

When Jug reached them, Leah spoke first. "So, Coach, did you and Mr. Carson get lunch detention, too?" she asked. "By the way, I might be late for practice. Starting today I have to go outside and pick up trash in the parking lots—like I was the one who did something wrong at the dance the other night. It isn't fair."

Jug turned a chair around and straddled it backwards. Scooting it up to the table, he said, "From your mouth to God's ears, little lady." He shook his head. "I ain't never seen a mess like this one. But, sweetie, don't feel like the Lone Ranger or nothing. Carson and me are on notice, too, with Jerry—no more smoking, dipping, no spit cups, no skipping lunch duty, no nothing at school that gives life meaning." He grinned. "Of course, I been thinking about switching to sunflower seeds, anyway—or bottles instead of cups. Easier to hide. Know what I mean?"

The old coach struggled to stand. He turned the chair back around and slid it under the table. "I'll see you boys later," he said to Artie and Ty. "You, too, ladies—that is, whenever you get done with your chores out in the parking lot, Miss Russo. If any of you need me, I'll be over at the teacher table with Carson— the whole dang lunch period, for the rest of the durn year. I tell you what. This may do me in, what with everything else going on."

Jug trudged off, nodding to Ricky, Tommy and Bennie as he passed them at the cashier's stand. With surprised looks on their own faces, the three boys hurried over to their table to see what Coach Johnson had said.

"Good news and bad news," Artie began. "Which do you want first?"

"Well," said Bennie, "if your bad news is that Josh Stark isn't getting punished for all the stuff he did Saturday night, you can just skip right to the good news. I could use some. My dad is pretty steamed, too. Lurch told us that the only piece of equipment the Starks have to pay for is that one speaker Josh crashed into, not all the other stuff he knocked over and broke."

Tommy, who normally was quiet, spoke up. "Their lawyer even had the nerve to say I didn't set up the sound system right," he said, "and that I should've put it on a bigger table—and that the disco lights I set up blinded that stupid jerk when he was swinging across the gym. They said it was *my* fault. Do you believe that?"

Artie nodded. "Yeah, I do."

But Tommy wasn't finished. "Mr. Church isn't being fair. He doesn't care about us, just about the popular kids and their pushy parents. You know what? The other night he didn't even come over and see if Bennie was okay. You guys did—and Brett Woods did, too."

Like a genie summoned from its bottle, Brett appeared at the doors to the cafeteria. He couldn't have possibly heard them talking, but he was looking straight at the Barf Table gang. He headed toward them, carrying two white bags from Woody's Grill. He had one large, grease-stained bag in each hand.

"Hey, guys," said Brett, as he stopped at their table and smiled. "Dad was a little late getting back over here after our meeting with Mr. Church. He wanted you guys to have this." He opened one of the large bags and showed them its contents. "You all like Dad's fries, right?" he said. "Two bags of the best fries on the beach—and plenty of ketchup packets, too."

"*Oooo*," said Nicie, reaching for the unopened bag. "You do know the way to a hungry girl's heart, even if she is going steady with somebody else."

Ty pretended to be confused. "Wait. We're going steady? You do mean *me*, right?" He laughed and took the long, crispy French fry that she offered him.

Even Leah sampled a small handful of fries and smiled for the first time that day. "Thank you, Brett," she said. "You remembered that I don't eat meat."

"And that I don't eat pork," added Bennie. "Yeah, thanks, Brett. Your dad's a good guy. I sure have missed his cooking—and your mom's."

Brett nodded. "They miss you, too, Bennie. Dad told me so this morning. Maybe you can start coming over to our house again now that things are settled. You know about that, right?"

It was Bennie's turn to nod. "Yes," he said, "and once I get out of this wheelchair, we'll go surfing again."

Everyone around the table sensed what was happening. Brett and Bennie's reconciliation had been a long time coming. No one dared say anything that might change this positive turn, not even the two girls, who ordinarily would jump right in with sarcastic remarks. Still, Brett was hesitant to join the group without being invited. He just stood there, not really knowing what to do with himself now that he'd delivered his father's gift of fries to the table.

More so than anyone else, Bennie felt the emotion of the moment, because he had been suffering for so long and had harbored so many dreams yet to be fulfilled. His greatest wish was to walk again, but he also wanted his old life on the beach back, of which Brett and Woody had been a big part.

Looking up at his old friend for a moment, Bennie reached over and tapped the back of the empty chair beside him. "Have a seat, buddy," said Bennie, "I mean, if you want to." His voice cracked on the word "want," and he felt his eyes begin to fill. So he turned to Artie and said, after clearing his throat, "We all knew the bad news, big guy. What's the *good* news?"

Artie smiled, as Brett moved around the table to take a seat and grab some fries for himself. "You know what I think, Bennie?" Artie said. "The good news that I was talking about has *nothing* on this—us getting a new friend and team-mate here at our table. Brett really is part of our *farmily* now. But my good news is related."

"What?" Ty said, through a mouthful of fries. Nicie slapped him and pushed the greasy white bag toward Tommy and Ricky.

"It's bad news that we're all being punished for nothing," said Artie, "and that Josh Stark is getting off with just a slap on the wrist. Some of us have to serve lunch detentions, including Coach. And one of us has to pick up trash before practice, but—"

"Hold on," Brett said. "How did you know I'm supposed to pick up trash every day? Did Lurch tell you?"

"No," said Artie. He glanced at Leah, and his heart skipped a beat. "Okay, correction—*two* of us have to pick up trash. But I don't understand, Brett. Why punish you?"

Brett huffed and said, "Well, that stupid girl I was with said—"

"Digger?" said Nicie. "That's short for *gold-digger*. She is one, you know."

"Yeah, that gold-digger I was with changed her story," said Brett. "She told Church that I was the one with the liquor, and that Josh wouldn't have been drinking if I hadn't brought it. Dad stood up for me this morning, so Church backed down—well, kind of."

"Jeez," Artie said. "That *is* bad."

"Then what's the *good* news, Artie?" asked Ty again. "I didn't say so before, but Church told Nicie and me that we can't keep sneaking out at lunch—or any other time. Ol' Lurch said he's gonna be watching us. I need to hear something positive."

With a serious look, Artie delivered the good news. "Let's put it this way, Ty," he said to his friend. "With Coach and Mr. Carson sitting over there at the teacher table every day, and with five varsity football players—you, me, Tommy, Ricky and now Brett—sitting here at *this* table, I'm *positive* that we aren't gonna see another Krakatoa Tuesday or Waisin Wednesday or any other day like that for a long time."

Artie continued, "I'm tired of being nice, and I'm tired of watching helpless kids get harassed by stupid jerks. So we're gonna do like Nicie said before. If people decide to pick on anyone at this table, this table is gonna fight back—all of us together." He looked around the table and added, "And do you know why?"

Bennie held up one hand to Artie and his other hand to little Ricky, who was itching to answer. "I got this, guys," said the boy in the wheelchair. "We're gonna fight back. And I'll tell you why. Because we aren't the losers they say we are. We … are … a team."

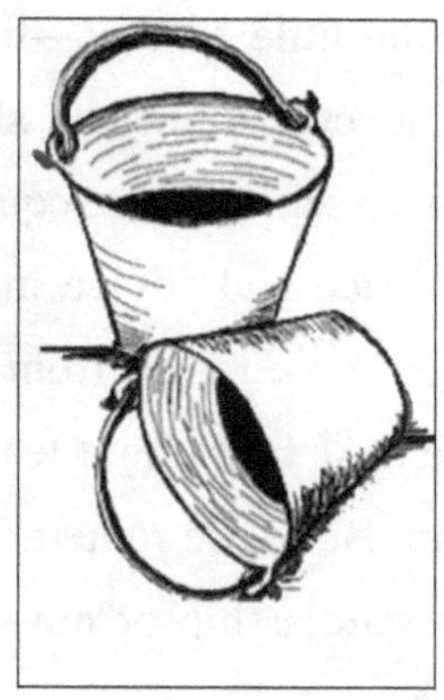

CHAPTER 26 – Standing Out in Their Fields

RICARDO AND GABBY DURAN—and Ricky, too, for that matter—were perfect additions to the Bauer farm family. After only a few days of meeting Ricardo, Grandpa came to trust this young husband and father who knew how to do a little bit of everything that a farmer might face. When the hard-working man poked his head into Harry Bauer's bedroom every morning and evening, Ricardo would give him an update on finishing the harvest, caring for the livestock, boarding the new horses, renovating the old homeplace, or preparing for the upcoming Halloween activities. Ricardo was on top of everything—a fact that took much pressure off Artie. The two older men also discussed marketing the farm's winter crops and the next spring planting. Grandpa agreed to add beans, peppers, tomatoes and herbs for Gabby Duran to use in her cooking.

It took a bit longer for Pearl Bauer to relinquish control of the farmhouse's kitchen to Gabby, but after a couple of weeks the younger woman didn't have to keep asking permission to plan their meals or buy food when it ran out. By their third week living together, Grandma freely admitted that she liked the tostadas, tamales, mole sauce and pepian that Gabby fixed—as long as it wasn't too spicy—and that Gabby's baked goods were comparable to Pearl's own. Gabby also was a kind and gentle caregiver to both Grandpa and Grandma when she wasn't working her outside jobs to keep money coming into the household.

Little Ricky soon became more than Artie's teammate, Barf Table buddy and fellow farmhand. He was like the little brother—the real, not imaginary, friend and companion that Artie had never had but had always wanted. Ty Green was still Artie's best friend, but the two seniors were equals. Ricky, a lowly freshman, looked up to Artie for his guidance and advice in all endeavors, as a younger sibling would. Sometimes when Artie rested from his farm chores, he worried that his going off to college the next year might leave Ricky feeling as lonely as Artie had felt for so many years. But Artie remembered that he might be able to attend Iron Harbor A&M—on scholarship or not—and basically stay at home. That would be ideal, he thought.

At Arbor High, things were also going well for the Bruins football team. They embarked on a two-game road trip, first traveling to Mimosa Beach, then to Port Oleander. With Artie back in the lineup, Arbor avenged its earlier loss to Mimosa Beach with a 34-28 upset win. The Bruins trounced the winless Port Oleander Pilots 42-6, making up for the early-season squeaker that Arbor had won at home. Even substitute lineman Tommy White got into the Port Oleander game for Arbor's last offensive series. He subbed in for Artie, whose ankle was still tender.

With only two games left in the regular season, the Bruins were 5-3 overall and 3-3 in Suncoast Conference play. Both season-ending games would be at home. First, Arbor would host the undefeated Iron Harbor Gray Dukes, then face the Solid Rock Harvesters—with all-everything linebacker Jimmy Gore and new quarterback Josh Stark—in a long overdue rematch. The conference standings showed Iron Harbor in first place, Solid Rock and Mimosa Beach tied for second, and Arbor a game behind them in fourth place, with Port Oleander in the basement.

* * *

The evening before Arbor's home game with Iron Harbor, Artie came in from the barn and was greeted by his grandfather who was still confined to the new downstairs bedroom off the kitchen. "Artie, you got a telephone call a minute ago," Grandpa said. "You didn't answer the squawk box those boys hooked up, and I couldn't run to the back door and holler for you."

"That's okay, Grandpa," said Artie. "I know what you mean; I was outside.

Who called? Did they leave a number so I can call them back?"

Grandpa nodded and reached for a slip of paper on his nightstand next to the desk phone and intercom that Bennie Pressler and Tommy White had installed for him. "Yep," Grandpa said. "He said his name was Jimmy—that he was a ballplayer friend of yours."

"Jimmy?" said Artie, taking the number from Grandpa. "There's nobody named Jimmy on our team. And this is an Ebenezerville phone number. Was it Jimmy *Gore*? I wouldn't exactly call him my friend." Artie chuckled and wondered aloud how hard Jimmy Gore hit his enemies.

"Well, whatever he is to you," began Grandpa, "he said you need to call him back tonight and that he'd wait up for your call. It must be important."

Artie agreed and went back into the kitchen to use the old telephone on the wall, though he knew that Grandpa might eavesdrop on his bedside extension. He dialed the phone number and waited through only two rings before hearing a deep voice answer, "H'lo? Gore residence."

"Uh, yeah, this is Artie Bauer. May I speak to Jimmy?"

"Speaking," said the Solid Rock linebacker. "Artie, I'm sorry to bother you at home—I know about your granddad and all—but there's something you need to know about. I just heard about it. It's supposed to happen this Saturday night—a Halloween prank—I guess you could call it that. But I don't think it's very funny."

"What?" Artie asked. "What's going on?"

"Well, first," said Jimmy Gore, "I wanna thank you for sending Josh Stark to Solid Rock. We haven't had a moment of peace since he got here—but we're winning, and that's what Coach cares about. This is about him—Josh Stark, not the coach."

Artie just shook his head. "I'm listening," he said. "I can just imagine what he's up to now. Did you hear about our homecoming dance?"

"I did," said Jimmy Gore. "This is worse. He's been mouthing off about you and Brett Woods and that little Russo girl getting him in trouble. He claims it was Brett's fault—that he got Josh drunk and got the Russo girl to poison Josh's girlfriend. He says he's gonna 'even the score' with Brett—that's what he said, 'even the score'—and he's gonna get even with all of you this coming Saturday night. He's coming to that Halloween thing you're throwing on your farm."

"What's he gonna do?" asked Artie. "Is it just him—or is he bringing somebody?"

"He's trying to get some players to go with him," Jimmy said. "That's how I heard about it. But it only takes one or two jerks like him to cause a lot of trouble." The teenager hesitated, then added, "Josh said he's gonna burn you guys out once it gets dark. I don't know if he was talking about the corn maze or haunted house or what. But he said the fire is gonna light up the sky for miles around, and that your granddad will *beg* Josh's dad to buy your place when it's all over. He was talking crazy. That boy *is* crazy."

Artie took a moment to let Jimmy's words sink in. "You got that right," Artie said finally. "I appreciate you calling me, Jimmy, but … if I call the sheriff's department, they're gonna want to know where I got my information. Can I tell them that *you* told me?"

"I wish you wouldn't," said Jimmy. "My folks have a farm, too, and I'm afraid the Starks would go after us if they found out it was me who told on Josh. His dad could even mess up my scholarship offers. That guy bad-mouths *you* all the time to Coach, and I don't want him turning on me, too, not before I sign with somebody."

"Okay, well," Artie said, "I'll do what I can to keep you out of it. Like I said, I appreciate you warning me."

The line was silent for a long second. "One other thing," said Jimmy Gore. "I know we're not exactly friends—even though I told your granddad we are—but you're a good player, you're tough, and you play hard. I've always respected you on the field. But when we play each other next week at your place, this phone call never happened. I'm gonna go after you and Ty Green and Brett Woods as hard as I ever would. But I don't play dirty. I keep it clean and mean."

Artie started to laugh at the linebacker's rhyming but caught himself. "I understand, Jimmy," he said. "I wouldn't expect you to play any other way. And thanks again."

Hanging up the phone, Artie leaned to one side to see if Grandpa had been listening in, but he appeared to be asleep already, his gray head resting on his pillow and his hands by his sides. That image gave Artie a slight jolt—seeing Grandpa lying so still and so peacefully, even with the hint of a smile on his lips.

But the scene also gave Artie an idea about how Grandpa could help out at the Halloween festival on Saturday night and not be stuck home alone while everyone else was having fun at the haunted house, corn maze and hayride. But before talking to Grandpa, Artie would have to check with Ricardo, because the busy farmhand's carpentry skills would be needed right away—to build Harry Bauer a crude, wooden coffin.

* * *

Jimmy Gore's warning about Josh Stark's threats convinced Artie that there was no time to lose—that he needed to line up help that night while he still could. The Iron Harbor game on Friday would keep him and the rest of the Barf Table gang busy all day, even though it would be played in Monk's Landing at Reuben Russo Memorial Stadium. Artie knew he would see people on game night who could help him—like Abe Pressler, Woody Woods and Rachel Green, all members of his extended farmily—but he feared that they would all be preoccupied with their own problems, and be less likely to focus on his latest worry if he waited until the last minute to seek their advice and assistance.

Artie figured a person might say, "Well, good luck with that; I wish I could help," but do nothing. It was a rare individual who would put someone else's needs first. Just as classmates at Arbor High had shown Artie their respect and sympathy in their concern over his grandfather's injury, Artie knew that they had only sacrificed their money, not their time nor their reputations. It was different with his Barf Table buddies, but they'd also have their hands full on Friday and all day Saturday. Besides, they, too, were being threatened and needed protection.

Artie knew he couldn't keep Josh's threat to himself and simply hope that he and his best friends could fend for themselves on Saturday night. He didn't want to worry his grandparents—not yet, anyway. And the Duran family wasn't home, having driven into Ebenezerville for groceries and other supplies. Artie would talk to them later that night. But he knew he should call the three adults—Abe, Woody and Rachel—who had helped him so much over the past two months since Grandpa's accident. Artie trusted them and valued their advice. If they told him to do so, he could call the sheriff's department and report what Jimmy Gore had told him, even at the risk of having to name Jimmy as his source of information.

Later that evening, after Grandma had gone upstairs to bed and Grandpa was definitely asleep, Artie placed his first call to Ty Green's mother, Rachel. He explained the situation and sought her advice on how to proceed. He also asked her to inform Ty of the threat.

"I'll certainly tell him," said Rachel Green, "and then you two can talk it over tomorrow at school. I'm glad you called, though, because I was planning on bringing my first-aid kit to the Halloween festival Saturday, anyway—you know, for any cuts and scrapes that the little children might have. But I can handle more than just cuts and scrapes, if I have to."

As soon as Artie thanked her, she added, "You know, I can see if another nurse from the hospital—he lives near us—if he might want to come to the festival with me. He's a big guy, and he's a volunteer fireman, too. He handles all sorts of bad calls at work in the ER and also as a first responder. Maybe he can even get his fire station to park their old fire engine at the festival—you know, for kids to sit in. They have a spotted dog, too. The kids would love that."

Likewise, Abe Pressler was helpful. The businessman listened patiently to Artie's news and offered the paid services of two security officers from the Pressler's Department Store in E-ville. He assured Artie that both men were licensed to handle serious problems on the job.

"Something else occurred to me the other day," Pressler added. "Well, actually it was Bennie's idea. How about if we bring some walkie-talkies for all you guys to use on Saturday? You'll be able to spread out on the farm but stay in touch with each other, in case anyone needs help real quick."

Artie accepted, but asked if the two officers could come in Halloween costumes—just not pink bunny outfits like the one that Abe had bought for Bennie. Pressler chuckled and promised that his men would wear something appropriate, maybe zombie or clown outfits.

The call to the Woods household was the most difficult one for Artie to make, because, according to Jimmy Gore, Josh Stark oddly blamed Brett Woods for the homecoming dance fiasco and had specifically threatened his former best friend.

Woody Woods was understandably concerned about the danger to Brett. He thanked Artie for the heads-up and offered his insight on the situation. "We need to have a record—a video or something—that's proof of what actually happens at your festival," said Woody. "If the boy gets drunk and does something stupid again—like he did the other night at the dance—we need evidence, undeniable proof of what he did and the damage he caused."

The surf shop owner said he would bring his video camcorder to the farm on Saturday, so that either he or one of the teenagers could videotape the event from start to finish. "We tape all the surfing competitions that we sponsor," Woody said. "Brett is a good cameraman, too, not just a good surfer. He and I can trade off taping things Saturday."

"That's a really good idea," said Artie. "I'll check with Coach Johnson tomorrow and see if he'll loan me the team's video camera, too. Bennie Pressler has used it at practice, and I'm pretty sure Leah Russo also knows how to work it. That'll give us two cameras."

None of the three adults advised Artie to call the sheriff's department just yet. All three recommended that he wait to see if Josh even showed up on Saturday night. If Artie were to call the authorities *before* Josh had the opportunity to commit a crime, the big-mouthed boy's threats could be downplayed as mere bragging, and, once again, Josh would get off the hook for his abusive talk and misbehavior. Artie didn't want all that to happen again.

Artie was glad that Jimmy Gore, a tough opponent, had thought enough of him to call earlier that evening. And Artie was relieved that he had taken the time and effort to seek counsel from his three adult friends. They had given him solid advice on how to prepare for potential trouble. Also, Artie had tried to ask one of his mentors for help in another matter, one that had troubled Artie all of his young life. That friend was Woody Woods, and the topic was Artie's abandonment by his mother, whom Woody had known.

Before retiring to his bedroom, Artie waited for the Durans to get home from shopping to tell them what he'd learned. Ricardo and Gabby reacted in the same manner that the other three parents had. Even though Ricky hadn't been singled out by Josh, the Durans had a vested interest in protecting the Bauer family, their farm, and its visitors. This was their new home.

"You and your grandparents have welcomed us," said Ricardo. "We cannot stand by and let anyone hurt our friends and destroy all of our hopes—neither yours, nor ours. You are our family, Artie. We will always stand by you no matter what happens."

That night when Artie laid his head on his pillow, he breathed more easily than if he had kept his worries to himself. In the top bunk, Ricky was quieter than usual. Both boys' brains were buzzing as they thought about what lay ahead in the days to come.

"Ricky? You awake?" asked Artie from below.

"Yes. I am awake. What do you want?"

Artie paused. "Your parents are great."

"So are yours, Artie—your *abuelos*, I mean."

Artie fell silent for a moment, then confided, "I talked to Woody Woods, you know. He knew my mother—my real mother and maybe my father, too."

"What did he tell you about them?" asked Ricky.

Artie hesitated. "He said it would be really hard to figure out who my father is. He said not to ask why. But I can guess what he meant."

This time Ricky was quiet. "I am sorry, Artie."

"Me, too. I guess that's why nobody ever told me anything. But I wanted to know why she left me—why she didn't take me with her."

"Did Mr. Woods tell you?" said Ricky. "Does he even know why?"

"Yes. He knows. Everybody has known all along—everybody but me." Artie considered Woody's explanation again before sharing it with his roommate and friend. "He said my mother was in such bad shape and in so much trouble that she couldn't take care of *herself*, much less a little baby, and she wouldn't let anybody help her. He said the smartest thing she did was leave me with my grandparents and disappear."

"I'm sorry," Ricky said again. "Are you glad you know the truth now?"

"That isn't the whole truth," Artie said, "but it's enough. Look, I'm sorry I kept us up. I have a feeling we're gonna need all the rest we can get over the next couple days."

Ricky agreed. "Yes. We are going to be busy this weekend, but the festival should be great fun. It is like our *Dia de los Muertos*. It is my favorite holiday."

When trouble did arrive on that special day, Ricky and the rest of the Barf Table family were as ready as they could be for what Josh Stark threw at them. What they couldn't count on was how Josh's greedy, land-grabbing father would defend his spoiled son to the bitter end.

CHAPTER 27 – Gray Dukes and E-ville Clowns

WITH ARTIE BAUER PLAYING the entire game and his team firing on all cylinders, Arbor gave Iron Harbor more fight this time around than the undefeated team had encountered in conference play all season. The Iron Dukes had far and away the best defense in the state, giving up fewer than eight points per game on average. Playing at almost full strength, Arbor was much improved from when they had met Iron Harbor early in the season. The Bruins' helmets—mainly those of the starters—were covered with little green-and-gold football stickers bearing Reuben Russo's No. 3. Ricky Duran's helmet bore nine of the decals. Even Tommy White, a substitute, had three stickers, which he wore with pride.

To Artie, this game was special, not because the Bruins, on a three-game winning streak, faced the conference leader or because two college coaches were spotted in the stands that night, there to scout Iron Harbor's top players. Before the game, Artie was beaming on the sideline as he looked up into the home stands and waved to his two biggest supporters, his grandparents. It was the first time either grandparent had seen Artie play football since his freshman year when Coach Jug Johnson had put him into the lineup for just the last, meaningless play of the game. That had embarrassed both Artie and Grandpa—that Jug had thought enough of Artie to bring him up to the varsity for the last game of the season, but hadn't recognized how much the boy had wanted to contribute to the team effort, not just wear the jersey on the sideline. Grandpa felt that Jug had wasted his and

Grandma's time when they had so much else to do on the farm.

But this night at Reuben Russo Memorial Stadium was different. It represented a goal that Grandpa had set for himself and had met, with much help from others who loved him and his grandson. Bundled up against the cool night air in her warmest coat, Grandma fussed over Grandpa, who sported a freshly ironed pair of dark-blue overalls and a crisp, white shirt under Artie's green letterman jacket. Harry Bauer sat in his wheelchair, with his wife on one side and Rachel Green on the other. Gabby Duran, who had borrowed one of her church's handicapped vans in which to transport Grandpa, sat next to Grandma to support both Artie and Ricky. Nicie Evans sat next to Rachel, partly out of habit but mainly because the two had come to enjoy each other's company.

At halftime, the score was Iron Harbor 21, Arbor 10. The Bruins' first-half touchdown came at the end of a 12-play drive that ended with a 28-yard screen pass from Ty Green to Brett Woods. Ricky Duran kicked the extra point and later a 33-yard field goal. He missed a longer field-goal attempt late in the half, when Ty bobbled Artie's snap and then didn't have time to spin the ball's laces out of the way.

Despite the miscue, the Bruins on the field and the fans in the home stands were proud when the halftime horn sounded, giving both teams fifteen minutes to rest and regroup. Coach Johnson saw that his boys were playing above their heads, especially on offense, but Jug also knew that the pigskin could take some strange bounces on the gridiron and that "winning" in high school football could be defined in different ways.

* * *

In the stands, the Bauers greeted well-wishers of all ages who stopped by to shout their support above the marching band's halftime show, and to shake Grandpa's hand or give Grandma a hug. They mentioned how highly they thought of Artie and what "a fine young man" he had become.

One of the two college coaches in attendance—this one a young guy from State College—waited a minute with a soda in hand to ask Grandpa if Artie might be interested in a campus visit, but walked on back to his own seat when he saw how long the line to the Bauers had grown. He knew he could contact Jug Johnson anytime and that no high school player in the state would turn down his offer.

The other college coach—from nearby Iron Harbor A&M—had seen all he needed to see and had already left the stadium. He could watch the second-half highlights on Iron Harbor's local TV station, as they had sent a camera crew. Besides, he planned to return to Monk's Landing the next week to see Arbor's season-ending game against Solid Rock, mainly in hopes of signing Harvester linebacker Jimmy Gore.

Nicie Evans leaned toward Rachel Green and spoke into her ear. "We need to make sure all these people know about our Halloween fair," said Nicie. "Tell Mr. Bauer to invite everybody who talks to him—and have him tell Mrs. Bauer to do the same thing."

"She'll catch on," Rachel said. "When Pearl hears Harry inviting everyone, she'll follow suit. She wants this festival to be a success, too, maybe more so than the rest of us."

After Rachel passed the word to Grandpa, she turned back to Nicie and said, "It's gonna be a lot of work tomorrow, but it'll be fun—don't you think?"

Gabby Duran had risen from her seat on the other side of Grandma and was excusing her way past the Bauers' visitors to join Rachel and Nicie. "I'm so proud of our boys," said Gabby. "Ty and Ricky and Artie have played well tonight. I hope they score many more points and beat these Gray Ducks."

Nicie laughed. "That's *Dukes*," she said. "Gray *Dukes*. And we'll be lucky to stay this close to them for the rest of the game. They're *that* good."

"I just hope no one gets hurt again," said Rachel. "Artie's ankle isn't quite a hundred percent yet. And Ty and Brett are taking some pretty big hits out there. Maybe if Iron Harbor puts the game out of reach, Coach Johnson will sent in our subs again, like he did against Port Oleander last week when we were so far ahead. We need everybody healthy next week against Solid Rock."

"Well," said Gabby, "I'm going to do *my* best tomorrow to fatten all of our boys up so that they are healthy and strong next Friday." She smiled as she took a folded sheet of paper from her purse. "These are the things I will be selling tomorrow at our festival." She read off a long list of baked goods and Guatemalan foods that she would offer at a stand that her husband was building that night.

"Where will you be set up?" asked Rachel, with a smile. "You need to be far enough away from the boys—and I'm including Ty, too—so that they don't eat up all your profits."

Gabby nodded. "Yes, I know," she said. "My little Ricky eats as much at the dinner table as big, strong Artie does. But they are growing boys, and I will do my best to feed them and their good friends, not just tomorrow but for as long as I cook for them."

She added, "Ricardo said he'll put the food stand between the old house and the corn maze. He said there will be plenty of traffic there. I'm not sure what he meant by *traffic*."

"Foot traffic," said Rachel. "He meant that a lot of people will walk past your stand on their way to and from the corn maze—and from the hayride, too, I imagine."

Nicie piped up. "My daddy will have so much fun driving Mr. Bauer's tractor and pulling the hay wagon," she said. "He's been looking forward to our festival all week. He even bought himself a pair of bib overhauls and a straw hat!"

"Oh, my," said Rachel. There was a break in the Bauers' line of well-wishers, so Rachel turned to Grandpa and laid her hand on his shoulder. "Did you hear that, Harry?" she said, loudly enough for Grandma also to hear. "You're gonna have some competition tomorrow night."

"What kind of competition?" asked Grandpa. "You told me all I gotta do is lay there in the parlor and look dead. Who's gonna be competing with that? You gonna kill Pearl off, too?"

"What?" Grandma said, now paying attention. "Kill me off? I thought I was supposed to dress up like an old hag and welcome people into the house—even though I ain't found nothing to wear yet." She frowned at her husband and shook a bony index finger at him. "And don't you tell me again, Harry Bauer, that my Sunday dress would make a good witch's frock."

"Oh, old gal," said Grandpa, "that's just the devil in me talking." He winked at his wife, and turned back to Rachel, Nicie and Gabby. "So, has Ricardo ever built a pine coffin before? He said he'd have it done tonight by the time we get back home, and I could try it on for size."

Still listening, Grandma leaned forward. "Just don't you get too comfortable in that pine box, old man," she said. "I don't plan on you seeing another one—or using that one for real—for a long, long time." She added, "That is, unless you keep poking fun at my pretty dresses." They all laughed as they watched the band march off the field.

Bennie Pressler's voice boomed over the stadium speakers to remind fans about that night's 50-50 drawing. Sitting in the press box with Leah Russo, Bennie was coming into his own as a PA announcer. He enjoyed spinning the dials and pushing the buttons on the mixing board, and speaking into the big desk microphone. He also liked sitting throughout the game next to Leah, who fed him some of the official stats that she was keeping for the team and for her own use in writing her newspaper stories.

In addition to writing for the school paper, Leah had agreed to phone in Friday night reports from Monk's Landing to the daily newspapers in Iron Harbor and Mimosa Beach. She also called in scores and highlights to the sportscasters at the television stations in both cities. And outside of their official capacities, Bennie and Leah had become good friends and enjoyed each other's company.

"That Bennie Pressler sounds better every week," said Rachel, "and I'll bet he's gonna do a good job with the sound system that he set up at the haunted house."

Nicie added, "He hid some speakers in the corn maze, too. I was walking through it the other night, and he just about scared the pee out of me."

With a smile, Gabby rose to go back to her seat. "Oh, before I go," she began, "Ricardo said there will be two clowns at the festival. Mr. Pressler told him that the security guards he is sending from his store in Ebenezerville will be dressed as clowns—evil-looking ones like in the movies, for Halloween. They will be there to help us if we need it. They will be ready, but—"

"Hold on," said Rachel. In a lower voice, she continued, "Does *everyone* know—about the clowns and all?" She tilted her head and cut her eyes toward Grandpa to indicate that she was actually asking if the Bauers knew about Josh Stark's threat.

Nicie held up her hand to stop Rachel. "No, not yet," Nicie said, glancing up at Gabby. "That's right, isn't it? Artie called Daddy around lunchtime and told him. Artie had just found out they'd be clowns, not zombies or something."

Gabby nodded. "Ricardo told us about the clowns this morning after Mr. Pressler called him," she explained. "Ricardo said the clowns will help with traffic and make sure no one gets lost and wanders to the farmhouse or barn." She added in a softer voice, "He did not say out loud that they might try to go there on purpose. Do you know what I mean?" Both Rachel and Nicie nodded.

As he'd been advised, Artie had insisted upon keeping his grandparents from learning about Josh's wild talk until an actual threat was more certain. Artie had talked Grandpa and Grandma into playing their parts at the haunted house so that everyone could watch over them better than if the couple were staying home alone. Also, Ricardo would be hitching up Tom and Dick, the team of workhorses, to give carriage rides from the haunted house and corn maze down the lane to the farmhouse and back. That would give him an opportunity to check on the farmhouse and barn every few minutes. The clowns would also be patrolling the entire area. The two-way radios that Abe Pressler was supplying would keep everyone in close touch, in the event of an emergency.

* * *

Leading their offensive unit back onto the field for the second half of the Iron Harbor game that Friday night, Artie and Ty felt more at ease there on the gridiron than they would feel the next afternoon and evening on the farm. The Gray Dukes' "Iron Curtain" defense could shut down even the most high-powered offense on any given day, but the Arbor Bruins kept playing inspired football into the fourth quarter and matched Iron Harbor score for score until Ty took a vicious hit from two rushers at once and fumbled the ball away on the Arbor 15.

A play later, the Iron Harbor quarterback hit his tight end in the end zone to put the Gray Dukes up by 17 points. After Arbor's next punt—what Bennie in the press box called a "three-and-out"—Iron Harbor scored again, this time on another pass to the tight end, followed by a breakaway run by their star halfback, who until then had been quiet.

With six minutes left in the game, Iron Harbor led 49-24. Jug Johnson called for his boys to huddle up on the sideline before they returned to the playing field for what could be their last offensive series of the night.

"You young men have played one heckuva game tonight," said Jug, "but it ain't over, not by a long shot. We've got six more minutes to finish this thing right. We need one more score. I don't care if those boys out there are their first stringers or their dang scrubs. We're gonna score on them again before we go home tonight."

Artie glanced across the huddle at his best friend Ty, who still looked some-what shaken from the jarring sack that had caused him to fumble. Artie himself was weary from all the hits that he, too, had taken on the line, but he knew that his coach was right. If the Bruins just rolled over and died on their last series, what they had done for three quarters would have been in vain. However, if they managed to score again—a touchdown or even a field goal—they could truly hold their heads high, with the knowledge that they had put more points on the scoreboard than any other Iron Harbor opponent so far that season.

Only the Capital City Red Caps had scored more points against the Gray Dukes' Iron Curtain. In that early-season, non-conference match-up, the Red Caps had tallied 26 points in a losing effort. The Bruins offense was stuck on 24.

In what did turn out to be Arbor's last offensive series against Iron Harbor, the Bruins took Jug Johnson's pep talk to heart and drove the ball up the field, grinding out yards on short passes and strong-side runs. But Jug's conservative play-calling also chewed up valuable time.

At the Iron Harbor 29-yard line with :04 on the game clock, Arbor called its last timeout. It was fourth down. This would be the last play of the game unless there was a defensive penalty. Jug's dilemma was choosing between a long pass to the goal line or a longer field-goal attempt than his little kicker had ever made—a 46-yard attempt. Ricky Duran had drop-kicked a 35-yarder for a win earlier in the season; his longest kick from Ty Green's hold was 36 yards. In practice, Ricky had kicked one 45 yards, but that wasn't against the best defense in the state.

"We need a big play here, boys," said Jug Johnson, breathing hard after having chugged onto the field to huddle with the offense. "We need to make a statement. What do you say? The Reuben. That would do it. They won't see it coming."

This time it was Ty Green who straightened up and shot a look across the huddle at Artie. Ty shook his head. Artie understood and agreed.

"Coach?" said Artie. "The Reuben *might* work. But if we use it tonight—when we can't really win the game—we won't be able to use it next week. And we might *need* it then. We can kick a field goal and get that score you want. Ricky can do it."

Of course, the situation was more complicated than that. Arbor had used the Reuben early in the season, and it had worked with Ty at quarterback. They had even faked the Reuben and scored a passing touchdown in a game. But as far as using it the next week against Solid Rock was concerned, Josh Stark—now a Harvester—knew about the trick play, because he had been a Bruin when it was conceived and because he had tried to run it himself. Not only was Josh the Solid Rock quarterback, he played safety on defense and would know how to defend against the Reuben if Arbor attempted it the next week. But this week's opponent, the Iron Harbor Gray Dukes, just wanted those last four seconds to expire so that they could pack up their duffel bags and head home with another win under their belts. This last play was nothing to them.

Not used to being overruled in the huddle, Jug started to snap at his co-captain, but took a second to consider Artie's point. Sure, Josh Stark knew about the Reuben, and the new Solid Rock coach had certainly seen film of the early-season game in which the Bruins had used the play. But Jug agreed that his team didn't need to refresh everyone's memory, especially with an Iron Harbor TV crew on the sideline videotaping highlights for their station's late sportscast. If they ran the Reuben and it worked, the video clip of it would be played all weekend long and would become the talk of the county.

"Well, boys, you know we only play one game at a time," said Jug, rising from one knee to look around the huddle at each of his players. The old coach's eyes came to rest on the player he knew the best, Artie Bauer. "That's the way it is, but Yogi here has a good point, and I trust his judgment. We're kicking." Jug turned and motioned for Ricky to come onto the field.

Before lining up to kick, Artie patted Ty on the shoulder pad. "Remember, bud," said Artie, "it's one – two – three, one – two – three. Simple as that. Like ballet."

Despite being tired, Ty's eyes flashed in recognition. "You just worry about the 'one,' Artie. I'll take care of the 'two,' and Ricky will handle the 'three.' We can do it."

This time Artie was the one who botched the field goal attempt. The big nose tackle across from Artie jumped when Ty started his snap count. Flinching like a baseball fan reacting to a foul ball into the screen behind home plate, Artie jumped, too, but hiked the ball at the same time, taking Ty and Ricky by surprise. No whistles blew and no yellow flags flew, as the game officials also wanted to go home without further delay.

Again, Ty bobbled the snap, as he had done on the failed field goal attempt to end the first half. But now he didn't even give Ricky a chance to kick from a bad hold. Ty picked up the ball and tried to run, but there was nowhere to go.

With a wave of rushers bearing down on him, Ty ducked his head, hugged the ball and prepared to become the turkey sub that his friend Artie had ordered up for him. This wasn't the Reuben by any means. Then he heard a small voice up close behind him. "Ty, give me the ball!" And he felt Ricky pulling the pigskin from his grasp.

The tiny boy was off in a flash, reversing course and heading left through the backfield. Artie reacted quickly enough to push two rushers on past the little ball carrier, and Ty held off another defender. As Ricky approached the line of scrimmage, only two men were between him and an open field. Brett Woods launched himself into one Gray Dukes safety, but the other defensive back blocked Ricky's path to a touchdown. Two other Iron Harbor players had picked themselves up off the turf and were also headed toward him. These guys didn't give up.

But neither did little Ricky. Seeing his chances of scoring a touchdown fade, Ricky fell back on what had earned him a place on the team—his kicking ability. Again, as he had done to win the Port Oleander game, he drop-kicked the pigskin through the uprights, taking care to stay behind the line of scrimmage when he connected with the ball. This was a more difficult kick to make than the earlier one had been. It was from a wider angle and from 40 yards out, longer than any field goal he had made in a game.

The final score was Iron Harbor 49, Arbor 27. Even though Jug Johnson's boys now held the season scoring record against the Iron Curtain defense, the weary Bruins and their tired coach were too worn out to celebrate their moral victory that night. Once the officials had signaled that Ricky's kick was good, Artie's mind had switched back to his grandparents in the stands and his need to shower and change quickly so that he could help take them home to their farm. The same church van was waiting, but Artie wanted to help load Grandpa into it—and to see how much he had enjoyed the game. Artie hoped Grandpa didn't feel as if he had wasted his time again simply because the Bruins hadn't beaten the Gray Dukes.

As kicker Ricky Duran told the Iron Harbor TV crew in his post-game interview, "Yes, we did play well tonight, but our team still lost the football game." And then little Ricky added, "The Gray Ducks were the real weeners tonight."

Later that night when Jug Johnson finally settled down in his den and flipped on the TV for the late sports, he heard the diminutive kicker's comments for the first time. Jug just shook his head. "From your lips to God's ears, little man," he muttered to himself. "I'm glad we don't play them again this season."

CHAPTER 28 – Was It a Trick or a Treat?

ON SATURDAY EVENING at the Halloween festival, the first clue that the day wasn't going to end well on the Bauer farm was the Roman candle that lit up the dusky sky beyond the cornfield. The column of fireballs, smoke and sparks streamed from a distant neighbor's property in a high arc onto the brown stalks standing on the other side of the barbed-wire fence and drainage ditch that divided the two farms. Someone had waited for nightfall to begin this fireworks display, and had aimed their pyrotechnics away from their own fields and toward the acres of corn that Harry Bauer had tilled, planted and cultivated before his tractor accident.

Until nightfall, everything had gone well on the farm. Throughout the afternoon, children of all ages had arrived in cars, vans and buses to show off their Halloween costumes, to collect candy and gumballs in brown paper bags at various stations on the grounds—at the haunted house, the corn maze, the hayride, and the carriage ride—and to sit on the old fire truck, pet the volunteer firemen's spotted dog, and crank the pumper's old-fashioned hand siren. Everyone seemed to be having a great time—the children, their parents and the volunteers putting on the festival. The Bauer farm was the place to be on this Saturday at the end of October.

Leah Russo helped care for the workhorses, Tom and Dick, between carriage rides given by Ricardo Duran. She also showed the bravest youngsters how to brush the horses and feed them carrots and sugar cubes. Nicie Evans kept kids from falling off the hay wagon as her father pulled it with Grandpa's tractor.

Tommy White again served as legman for Bennie "Bunny" Pressler, who wanted an occasional sound check of the shrieks and groans going over the hidden loudspeakers. Tommy wandered the grounds with his eyes and ears open so that he could report on the children's reactions, especially in the corn maze. He also carried a video camcorder to document the fun. Ricky Duran helped his mother at her food stand. Brett Woods and Ty Green handled the corn maze, venturing into its farthest reaches every so often to rescue a lost child or adult.

Rachel Green and Artie Bauer stayed at the haunted house to be near Grandma and Grandpa, and to be ready in case anyone—not just the Bauers—had a medical situation, no matter how slight. Rachel's nursing expertise was needed only once before dark, when Grandma claimed that her blood pressure was up because "Harry Bauer is getting on my very last nerve." Checking Grandma's BP twice, once on each arm, Rachel found it to be only a bit elevated and was about to recommend that Pearl take a break when they both heard a distinct *blurp* come from Harry's coffin.

A few seconds later, Grandpa, resting in peace for the time being, opened his eyes and giggled. "Excuse me," he said to no one in particular, then added, "Miss Rachel? Would you happen to have some Beano in that bag of yours?" She gave him a dose of Gas-X instead that within minutes relieved both his and Grandma's complaints.

Woody Woods sat at a table on the front porch of the haunted house. There he collected admission from teenagers and adults as they walked inside. Children got in for free. Using his own camcorder, Woody also videotaped scenes in and around the house and yard, to make sure that anything big happening near him on the grounds was recorded. Abe Pressler stayed close to Bennie, whose mixing board was set up under a canopy tent in the side yard between the house and the corn maze entrance.

In addition to managing the sound system, Bennie also operated a projector that allowed him to show horror movies like *Frankenstein, Dracula,* and *I Was a*

Teenage Werewolf onto a white sheet attached to the side of the house. This was not an old-fashioned film projector like in a movie theater or school room; it was one that was attached to a videocassette player so that Bennie could show scenes that Tommy and Woody had shot that very day. Everyone liked to see themselves on the big screen, even if they were shown screaming in terror or jumping out of their skins at something scary.

From his post with Bennie, Abe also coordinated the two-way radio traffic on the farm that day. Everyone carried a walkie-talkie, everyone except Grandma and Grandpa Bauer. Abe checked in with each mobile unit every twenty minutes to make sure that nothing was amiss and that the radios still worked in different locations. The two security officers that Abe had hired—both, in fact, dressed as scary clowns—divided the Bauer farm in half so that they could patrol the whole property as quickly and efficiently as possible.

When the Roman candle went off on the neighboring farm at sundown, the clown closer to it headed in that direction. The other clown repositioned himself closer to festival activity but farther from the Bauers' farmhouse and barn. That was where the next incident occurred—at the barn, in the hayloft.

From a point on the shoulder of the road up the main highway, a skyrocket shot through the brisk night air and landed with a hiss just inside the open door of the loft, now filled with the hay that the Durans' church friends had baled and that Artie and Ty had restacked weeks earlier. The rocket's target might have been the barn; however, it wasn't aimed with much precision, and it landed in the hayloft by chance—or so Joel Stark later claimed. His son, Josh Stark, pulled into the parking area at the Halloween festival only minutes after the skyrocket was fired.

Josh looked like a juvenile delinquent—a greaser—from the 1950s, wearing a brown leather jacket, white T-shirt, blue jeans, white socks and black sneakers. His hair was dyed pure white and gelled so that it stood straight up as if he had just seen something that had scared him half to death. But he was the one whose actions now scared everyone else.

The volunteer firemen, who had come thinking they would only be showing off the old fire truck that day, jumped into action when they saw the hayloft ablaze. They shooed away the kids who were waiting their turns to climb into the cab, and fired up the pumper's motor. Once the way was clear, the driver pulled out of the yard, crossed the highway, and roared up the farm lane to the barn. There the two men unrolled a hose and doused the flames high above them with a long stream of water. When the small blaze appeared to be out, the volunteers climbed into the loft with fire extinguishers and hit remaining hot spots to keep any embers from reigniting.

Artie and Ricardo had also rushed to the barn and released milk cows Bessie and Bossy into the pasture, along with the two horses being boarded. Having gained temporary stays of execution thanks to Artie's soft heart, hogs Frick and Frack remained in their smelly lot and later enjoyed the extra mud provided by the runoff from putting out the barn fire. The Bauers' chicken coop was far enough from the barn that it wasn't in danger.

Meanwhile, back at the haunted house, children cheered the firemen's heroics, many of them thinking that the small blaze had been part of the Halloween entertainment and not real. To the kids, most everything that day was a wonder to behold, though frightful—the spooky sounds, old hag and corpse in the haunted house; the horror movies about monsters and other evil beings on the outdoor screen; and the fear of being lost forever in the corn maze. But the festival provided its share of goodness, too, with the sweet treats given to the children, the opportunity to pet and feed the horses, and the fun of riding behind them like royalty in a white carriage or atop a load of hay pulled by a real farm tractor. Both tricks and treats abounded on the Bauer farm that day.

The sweetest treats came from Gabby Duran's baked food stand, which sat between the haunted house and corn maze. The plywood structure was situated near the main highway, close to the mown field where festival goers parked their vehicles. As Ricardo Duran had said, traffic there was good, with the intent being that the festival goers would buy something to eat while on the grounds and buy something else to take home at the end of the day.

Gabby had baked the usual Halloween cookies and cupcakes, along with Guatemalan foods, sweet breads and pastries. She sold more loaves and rolls of *pan de muerto* than anything else, once helper Ricky explained to the children and their parents how this special "bread of the dead" fit into his family's traditions. The rolls represented the tears shed for departed loved ones, he explained, and their round shapes stood for the so-called circle of life.

"Like you, we have fun during our version of Halloween," said Ricky. "On this night, we enjoy frightening each other—our friends as well as ourselves. But we make time to remember and honor all the people we loved and lost in the past. We do this in many ways—by displaying photographs of them and showing things they enjoyed doing while they were alive; by flying colorful kites to touch their spirits in the wind; and by eating our traditional foods, like *pan de muerto* and *molletes*."

Before the excitement caused by the fireworks, Leah Russo had heard Ricky's spiel about his mother's Halloween sweet bread and had been surprised by it. Leah had never thought about *eating* to honor a deceased loved one; she had always *not eaten* as her way of mourning the loss of her beloved big brother, Reuben Russo.

After his death in the car crash the previous year, Leah had decided that one who mourns must be miserable, and that her misery must be visible to all, instead of embracing what the dead person had loved. In Reuben's case, that would have been sports—football, in particular—and, as much as she hated to admit it, pulled pork and ribs like what Woody Woods served the team at his grill.

Still, Leah was glad that Artie had granted Frick and Frack reprieves, because she valued life most of all. She had to admit that her involvement with the football team—as statistician and sports reporter—had made her feel closer to Reuben and had helped her deal with her grief more so than any of the physical suffering that she had inflicted upon herself.

The sweet roll that Gabby gave Leah to sample that night and the cup of well water that she drank with the roll were the first meal that the girl allowed herself to enjoy, as she considered how much Reuben Russo would have loved helping his teammates, friends and little sister put on this festival for their community. Reuben had loved the Arbor High Bruins and Monk's Landing, and the townspeople had loved him. After her first taste of *pan de muerto* that day, Leah had felt her brother's presence, whether his spirit were in the air or in her heart.

Josh Stark's appearance at the festival right after the fireworks went off that evening sent a chill down Leah's spine, as she was the first volunteer to recognize him. He wasn't alone, having arrived in a shiny red pickup truck with two other Solid Rock football players, both of them offensive linemen and both larger than Josh. The more hulking of the two Harvesters wide-bodies was the pickup's driver. The lesser-sized lineman was the meanest-looking boy in the group. All three wore greaser outfits. The two linemen had simply slicked back their hair and hadn't dyed it white as Josh had.

As soon as she saw them, Leah stepped behind the horse carriage and radioed Abe Pressler to alert the other volunteers.

"Base to all mobile units," Abe's voice crackled over the radios. *"Base to all mobile units, be on the alert for three male subjects in leather jackets and with slicked-back hair—one boy with white hair. They were in a red, late-model pickup, but are now on foot, moving toward the haunted house. Do not—I repeat, do not—confront these subjects without backup. Security officers, advise your locations as you move toward the house. Clown One?"*

The first clown officer said he was headed back through the corn maze and that he had left Ty and Brett there to extinguish stray sparks from the Roman candle. Clown Two reported that he was running back from the barn where he had backed up the firemen, Ricardo, and Artie.

In fact, Artie had left the hayloft fire right behind the clown and was sprinting back to the haunted house as fast as his healing ankle would allow. He was afraid that Josh might hurt Grandma, standing at the front door, or Grandpa, laid out in the parlor. It was too late to warn either of them that Josh Stark had threatened to "burn [them] out" so that Grandpa would have to sell the farm to Stark Realty. To protect them, Artie had to get to his grandparents first—or to Josh Stark before he reached the haunted house.

Even though Leah thought she was hidden from the three bullies' sight, Josh spotted her behind the carriage and shouted, "There's the anorexic little witch that poisoned my girlfriend. Let's make her pay, boys."

Leah moved back into the open, first telling the children nearby to run and find their parents. She reached for the workhorses' bridle reins to try and steady Tom and Dick, just as the mean-looking boy slapped Tom's flank and threw a handful of bang poppers on the ground. The horses reared—Tom first, then Dick because the pair were harnessed together. Leah fell and tried to roll away from the horses' hooves.

From across the highway, Artie saw Leah fall and changed course to help her. By the time he could calm the horses so that Leah could get back on her feet, Josh and his goons had moved on.

As the trio of greasers passed Gabby Duran's food stand, the biggest boy tossed a string of firecrackers onto the hay bales that people had sat on to eat their snacks. Ricky shielded his mother from the sparks and smoke, jumped out of the stand and dove into the big teen's legs to take him down. The second greaser grabbed Ricky and jerked him up, holding him so that the first boy could rise and slug Ricky in the belly until he crumpled to the ground.

"Go home, you little wetback," Josh Stark said, looking down at Ricky. "C'mon, guys." He spat on Ricky and headed on toward the haunted house. Before following, Josh's two friends squatted and hefted one side of the plywood stand, then flipped it over with Gabby still standing within the structure.

On the sidewalk out front of the haunted house, Rachel Green tried to stop the three bad boys' advance but was shoved aside by Josh and thrown by another greaser into the trunk of a shade tree. Disoriented, she fell to the ground. She could not stop them by herself.

Seeing the overturned food stand, Artie left Leah with the horses and ran first to Gabby. Tommy White, who had been shooting video outside, also rushed to the woman's aid and helped Artie lift the wooden structure off her. While Artie made sure that Gabby wasn't injured badly, Tommy hurried over to little Ricky and helped him up onto a bale of hay.

Woody Woods, who had been taking up money on the front porch, was nowhere to be seen. He had ducked into the house to check on the Bauers as soon as the skyrocket had hit the hayloft and burst into flames minutes earlier. Like Artie, Woody had been worried that mere word of the fire would be enough to distress the old couple. He wanted to make sure that they knew what was actually happening before they got too upset. It was a "need to know" situation. But that was about to change.

Woody had set down his camcorder and was talking to Grandma when the big front door opened and Josh Stark stepped into the foyer, leaving his gang outside on the porch as lookouts. He locked the front door behind himself.

With an evil grin—made more fiendish by his shocking white hair—Josh looked first at Grandma, then at Woody Woods. "Where's that butthead son of yours?" Josh said to Woody. "I have a score to settle with him."

"Get out of here, Josh," said Woody. "You need to go home before somebody gets hurt."

Josh smirked. "Gets hurt?" he said. "Too late for that."

"What do you mean?" said Woody. "Who's injured?"

"Where's Brett?" Josh asked again, this time spitting the name out. "I'm gonna make him wish he was never born—the traitor, after all I've done for him." Scowling past Woody at Grandma, Josh added, "And then I'm gonna take care of that fatso grandson of yours."

At that moment, Brett Woods was hacking his way straight through the corn maze with a group of festival goers who were there when the fireworks had started. Ty Green was still busy wetting down burnt stalks that had caught fire at the back of the field. Nicie Evans and her father were helping people get off the hay wagon and were sending them to their vehicles in the parking area, while Abe and Bennie Pressler were assisting the throng of movie goers in the side yard. Seeing the two Solid Rock players on the front porch, Artie ran around the house to enter through the back door, if he could. Everyone was accounted for, except for the two clowns and Grandpa Harry Bauer.

When the security officers had reached the haunted house and had assessed the situation, they had radioed for backup from the Oleander County Sheriff's Department and had split up again—one covering the front porch, the other heading to the back porch so that neither Josh nor his accomplices could escape before deputies arrived on the scene. They didn't know if the three boys were armed, and they didn't want to risk getting anyone hurt in what could become a hostage situation. As professionals, they knew that a swift response was needed, but that they shouldn't storm the house without knowing what they were up against. So far, no actual shots had been fired, just fireworks and firecrackers. The clowns needed more evidence than that in order to risk using deadly force.

Artie Bauer, however, wasn't thinking beyond the present moment. He knew that his grandparents were in danger and that he had to do whatever he could to save them. On the screened-in back porch, he tested the main door into the kitchen and found that someone—maybe even Grandma—had locked it. Looking around, he saw leaning against the wall beside the screen door behind him an old hoe, shovel and rake that Grandpa stored there for yardwork on that side of the highway. Artie would have used one of the long-handled implements to break through a back window, but then he remembered the key that Grandpa kept on a nail above the door frame.

Artie had retrieved the key and was turning it in the door lock when he heard the screen door creak behind him and felt the porch floorboards shake under heavy footsteps. He turned to see the big greaser—the larger Solid Rock lineman—swinging the hoe handle like a baseball bat, with Artie's head being the ball. The greaser connected and stepped back as Artie fell to the floor.

The big boy laughed, tossed the hoe aside and pushed the door the rest of the way open. But Josh's last words to him and his buddy had been to stay outside, so the bruiser turned away and left the back porch through the same screen door. He was back around the house before the backyard clown could take his position in the oleander bushes.

Back inside the house, Josh Stark glared at Grandma again. "So where's Artie hiding, you old hag?" said Josh, with a sneer. "Either you tell me or I'll beat it out of you." Josh started to reach inside his leather jacket.

Woody assumed that the crazed boy was going for a gun or knife, and stepped in front of Grandma, holding his hands up to shield her from any attack. "No,

Josh!" said Woody. "Don't do it, whatever you're thinking!"

Josh laughed again. "Why do you give a crap about these stupid dirt farmers, anyway?" he asked. "Dad says all these shacks out here in this part of the county need to be torn down—or burned down."

Instead of a weapon, Josh took from his shirt pocket a shiny butane lighter—the old-fashioned kind—and he flicked it open. "I'm just helping Dad out, one shack at a time," he added, spinning the lighter's spark-wheel with his thumb and extending the orange flame toward the front window's curtains.

The unmistakable click of a double-barrel shotgun snapping shut made Josh freeze. The wild-eyed teen turned and stared into the candlelit parlor and saw the haunted house's late, great patriarch—proud dirt farmer Harry Bauer, very much alive—sitting up in his coffin and pointing his twelve-gauge shotgun directly at Josh's chest.

"That isn't loaded," said Josh, but he snapped shut the lighter on its flame. "That's just something to scare little kids with."

Grandpa's eyes flashed. "Wanna bet?" Harry Bauer said, dead serious. "I don't think you're that lucky—you little punk."

Josh edged away from the window and sidled toward the front door, having decided not to call Harry's bluff. Grandpa continued, "And if I *ever* hear you disrespect my sweet wife or my grandson again, I'll make *you* wish you'd nev—"

Harry stopped and lowered his shotgun when he saw Josh bolt up the hallway past the stairs and head toward the back door. The boy's footfalls pounded through the kitchen and out the open door onto the back porch, where they paused for a second. At the front of the house, Harry, Pearl and Woody heard the screen door to the back porch stretch open and slam shut on its spring, followed by a short yelp and a heavy thud, like a body falling down the back steps.

The backyard clown jumped from behind his oleander bush, grabbed Josh Stark and hustled him around to the front yard. Likewise, Josh's two henchmen were subdued out front, not by the other clown alone, but also by the two sheriff's deputies who had just reported on scene in separate cars with blue lights flashing.

As Josh and the other two bullies were being loaded into the cruisers, a dark sedan veered off the highway and into the yard, skidding to a stop behind the vehicle that held the Solid Rock quarterback. The sedan's driver was Joel Stark, and he was boiling mad. "You'd better get my boy out of that car right now," Stark said, "or I'll have both your badges. I can do it, too. That's Stark reality, because you know who I am. And get those handcuffs off him. He's barely sixteen years old. I'll handle him at home."

The young deputy that Stark was addressing happened to be the same officer who had worked Arbor's homecoming dance three Saturdays earlier and had witnessed Josh's outburst there. "I'm sorry, Mr. Stark," the deputy said. "You can have my badge if you want, but this isn't the first time your boy has caused trouble. I saw what he did at the high school the other week, and I saw him get away with it, too. The principal talked me into standing down because he was afraid of you. Well, this time I can't look the other way, not with what your boy just did to all of these good folks here tonight."

The deputy pointed at the haunted house in whose front yard most of the adult and teen volunteers had gathered to see the three bullies off to jail. Only Grandpa and Grandma, and Artie and Rachel Green were still inside the house.

"I don't care what you saw or when you saw it," Joel Stark growled at the deputy. "You don't have any evidence against my son—nothing that would stand up in court, anyway. You're all a bunch of hayseeds who don't have the sense that God gave a mule. The old man who owns this farm is a stubborn fool. I've made him good offers, and if he knows what's good for him, he'll sell his land to me. If he doesn't, I'll put him and his old wife and that stupid grandson of his in the poorhouse and just take the farm away from them. I don't care if the old man *is* in a wheelchair. And I'll do the same thing to any of his ignorant neighbors who get in my way. Joel Stark doesn't take *no* for an answer."

When his last statement drew whispers and nervous laughs from several people standing in the yard, Stark blew up. "What?!" he bellowed at them. "Do you think I'm kidding?!"

In response, Woody Woods held up the videocassette that he had just taken from his camcorder. It had been running throughout the entire confrontation with

Josh inside the house. Woody had set the camera down but had forgotten to turn it off. "We do have evidence, Joel," said Woody, waving the tape. "I'm sure the district attorney will send a copy of this tape to that high-priced lawyer of yours before the trial. How's that for Stark reality?"

Joel Stark stared for a long second at Woody Woods and might have asked for further explanation if, in fact, his lawyer had been present. Instead, he shook his head and gave his son Josh a look of disgust before getting back into the dark sedan and speeding off. He was headed toward the sheriff's office in Iron Harbor, where his and Josh's legal counsel would be waiting.

Abe Pressler, who had been silent throughout Josh's arrest and the angry father's threats, looked around and asked, "Tommy? Tommy White? Did you get all that?"

Tommy stepped out from behind the tree trunk where he had been videotaping Stark's rant. "Yes, sir," said Tommy. "And I got some shots of the barn fire and of the other stuff Josh and his friends did tonight. You wanna see it?"

"Yes, I do," Abe said. "Let's go right now and take a look at both tapes and see what we have. If I know Joel Stark, he'll use anything he can to get his son off the hook, so we need to be ready for whatever he and his lawyer hatch up."

With a graver look, Abe saw Ty moving toward the front door of the old house, and he said, "Artie will be okay, Ty. I called E-ville for an ambulance, like your mother asked. Tell her they should be here in a couple of minutes, okay?"

Ty looked back and nodded, then disappeared into the house to check on his mother and on his best friend before the paramedics arrived.

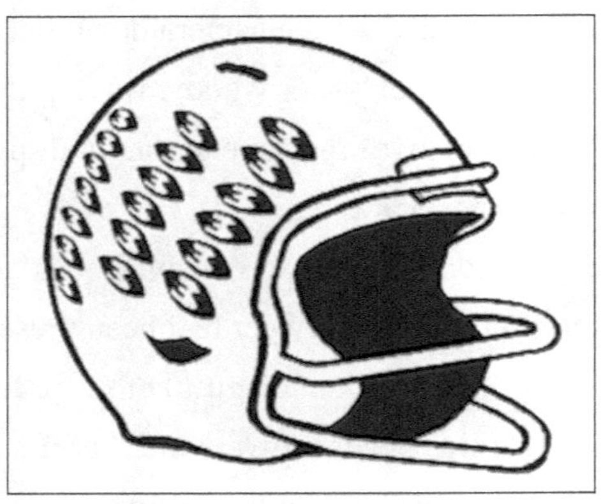

CHAPTER 29 – The Barn Burner at Arbor High

IN THE LOCKER ROOM before Friday night's home game against the Solid Rock Harvesters, Coach Jug Johnson told his Arbor Bruins not to worry about winning and losing. It was the last game of the season—for Arbor, anyway—as they were in fourth place in Suncoast Conference play, one game behind Solid Rock and Mimosa Beach, the two teams tied for second place. Iron Harbor was still undefeated and, win or lose, would again claim the league championship and top state playoff spot.

In turn, Solid Rock and Mimosa Beach vied for the conference's remaining playoff spot and the unofficial "county championship"—in other words, the county's best team that *wasn't* Iron Harbor. So Solid Rock still had a good chance for post-season play. If they beat Arbor tonight and if Mimosa Beach lost to Iron Harbor as expected, the Harvesters of E-ville would finish the regular season in sole possession of second place to claim the second state playoff spot and win the so-called county championship.

Neither Arbor nor Solid Rock was playing at full strength in this final meeting at Reuben Russo Memorial Stadium, as key players on both teams had been sidelined for different reasons. In the Bruins' case, kicker Ricky Duran had suffered bruised ribs at the Halloween festival when he had fought to protect his mother. Ricky could still play, but the pain he felt when twisting his torso to kick soccer-style cost him at least ten yards in distance and made him less accurate.

Artie Bauer was the other injured Bruin. Because it was Senior Night—the final home game of Artie's high school football career—the big farm boy dressed out in his green-and-gold uniform, but did not expect to play much, if at all. During the week Artie had worked through what was called "concussion protocol." The small gash along the side of his head had been stitched but still required bandaging and extra padding so that he could wear his Bruin helmet, adorned as it was with more No. 3 stickers than any other Arbor player.

As for the Harvesters, the big lineman who had beaten Ricky Duran with his fists and had bashed Artie Bauer with the hoe handle was still in jail. So was the big bruiser's accomplice, the other greaser who had helped destroy Gabby Duran's food stand and had assaulted Rachel Green. However, their partner in crime and their de facto leader—Solid Rock quarterback Josh Stark—had been released into the custody of his influential father.

The Stark family's attorney had assured the new Harvester head coach that Josh wouldn't go to trial for a long, long time, and that he would be exonerated by any Oleander County jury who might hear the case. By order of the court, father Joel Stark had attended team practices all week and now stood on the visiting sideline next to his son.

Before the Arbor marching band played the National Anthem, Artie Bauer, Ty Green and the four other Bruins seniors walked to midfield with one or both of their parents, and were introduced to the home crowd. Bennie Pressler's best radio voice boomed over the PA speakers as he read off each player's name and position, the parents' names, and what the player's future plans were at that time. Three of the young men were headed into some branch of the military; another senior planned to attend state college and study pre-med.

Standing with his mom and dad, Ty Green put on his game face and held it as Bennie announced that Ty would further his education and play collegiate sports. Neither the college nor the sport was specified.

Artie was introduced last. He had smiled when his grandparents—Artie pushing Grandpa's wheelchair with Grandma walking by their sides—had gotten a standing ovation minutes earlier just by taking the field.

Bennie Pressler announced, "*Last but not least, please put your hands together for Arthur 'Artie' Bauer, team co-captain and starting center for the third year, and his grandparents, Pearl and Harry Bauer of Rural Route 3, Monk's Landing. Artie plans to major in either agriculture or business in college, and he intends to come back here to Oleander County where his family has farmed for five genera-tions.*" The crowd cheered again, louder than they had for anyone else.

Grandpa tried to stand for the National Anthem, but Artie assured him that no one would mind if he remained seated. "Is it okay if I take off my hat?" Grandpa groused, removing his cap and holding it over his heart. With Artie's head bowed as the band played, he studied Grandpa's bandaged hand and the old railroad cap that Harry had worn when the tractor rolled over him and almost killed him. Pearl had taken care to retrieve and clean the cap simply because her husband had insisted that she do so. He hadn't wanted a new hat; he wanted his old cap. Lying in the E-ville ICU for days, Grandpa had focused on something that he and the love of his life could control—saving that cap—and Pearl Bauer had not let him down. Here was the evidence.

Standing together there on the football field that night, Artie put his arm around Grandma and hugged her tight, then bent down and whispered in Harry Bauer's ear, "I love you, Grandpa. Thank you for being my hero," as the final strains of the anthem played.

* * *

Minutes later, after the team had huddled with Coach Jug Johnson on the sideline, Artie Bauer walked back to midfield with Bruins co-captain Ty Green to meet the Harvesters' senior captain Jimmy Gore for the coin toss. Artie knew that he might not play more than one offensive series, maybe even just one play if he started feeling dizzy. But he was determined to finish his duties as co-captain with his best friend, and he was proud to shake the hand of an opponent that he respected both on and off the field.

"Good to see you, Artie," said Jimmy Gore. "Your granddad, too. So he's doing okay?"

"He is," Artie said. "Thanks for asking."

Ty's turn now, the senior quarterback stepped forward and shook Jimmy's hand. "Go easy on us tonight, Jimbo," Ty said with a sly grin. "That little dust-up we had last weekend with your boys was kinda rough, you know?"

Jimmy nodded. "Not *my* boys. But, yeah, I heard about that. That's why two of them are still guests of the county. From what I hear, it should be *three*—but you know how that goes."

"We do," said Artie. "No hard feelings—toward you, I mean."

"I understand," Jimmy said. "But you know I'm gonna play as clean and mean tonight as I ever would. You guys should, too—if you can. A couple of college coaches are here to see—"

"Okay, ladies," the referee said, stepping in and holding up a coin. "Let's cut the chit-chat and get this party started. Solid Rock, you're the visitor, so you call it—heads or tails. Call it in the air." Jimmy Gore took heads and won the toss. He elected to defer, meaning the Bruins would receive the opening kickoff and the Harvesters would get the ball first in the second half.

Artie wasn't sure if being tested on offense right off the bat was good or bad—for his team or for himself personally—but he was about to find out. At linebacker, Jimmy Gore would be the Bruins' immediate concern. But one of the Harvesters' safeties—Josh Stark—would have something to prove tonight on defense, not just as starting quarterback on offense.

Artie figured that Josh would be "head hunting" in the Harvester defensive secondary. That meant he would try to injure Bruins receivers with clothesline tackles and other blindside hits to their upper bodies. Whereas Jimmy Gore had always played defense "clean and mean," Josh Stark had learned how to punish vulnerable receivers, whether the new Solid Rock coach approved of Josh playing dirty or not. If he didn't approve, the young coach never disciplined Josh for cheating and wouldn't be doing so tonight, not with the boy's father standing on the Harvesters sideline.

On the Bruins' first play of the game after a modest kickoff return, Josh Stark made his presence known. Coach Johnson had wanted to give the Solid Rock defense and star linebacker Jimmy Gore immediate notice that the Arbor offense would not hesitate to throw the ball. Jug had called for a pass play that sent the Bruins receivers on crossing patterns behind the Harvesters linebackers. Ty Green needed to hold the ball an extra second to give his receivers time to run their pass routes, but when he saw his tight end get free in the left flat—away from Jimmy Gore on the right—Ty zipped the ball toward his young teammate.

The Bruins tight end, who had taken Ty Green's spot early in the season upon Josh Stark's defection to Solid Rock, leapt high to snag the pass, leaving himself unprotected from defenders' hits. As he gathered the ball to his chest, the tight end did not see that both Harvesters safeties had converged upon him from behind, one on each side. The two defensive backs hit the exposed boy at the same time— Josh high, his partner low.

Josh had also learned to use his helmet as a weapon and to target his opponent's head without being penalized under high school rules. The tight end went down under the twin attack and held onto the ball. But he didn't get up on his own. No flag flew. No penalty was called. The boy was carted off the field and didn't return to the game.

That brutal opening play set the tone for the entire contest, not just from the Solid Rock players' perspectives, but also from the home team's standpoint. True to his word, Jimmy Gore gave no quarter when he had the opportunity to take out a blocker or tackle the ball carrier. He blitzed often, sacking Ty Green twice in the first half and downing Brett Woods three times for losses.

Likewise, Jimmy Gore did not hesitate to give Artie Bauer his best shots when the big center tried to block him. In fact, a clean hit from Jimmy midway through the second quarter was the blow that made Artie's head spin and sent him to the sidelines for the remainder of the half.

But the game wasn't one-sided by any means. Playing without two of their own starting offensive linemen—the two bruisers who were cooling their heels in jail—the Harvesters attack proved to be as ineffective as the Bruins offense was. Though he didn't set another conference record for sacks, QB Josh Stark was caught in his own backfield twice and also tackled for little or no gain four times before the half.

Josh hadn't learned through the course of the season that passing the ball or handing off to a running back was the best way to keep his own jersey clean. He was still determined to be the center of attention, even if that meant denying his teammates their own chances for glory on the field. On offense, he wanted to hold the football for as long as he could, because he knew that fans and cameras followed the pigskin.

As a defender, Josh also had a nose for the ball, hunting down and punishing receivers and ball carriers with impunity. He was rarely flagged, whether because of his own defensive wiles or because of his father Joel Stark's vindictive reputation. Josh also knew when it was better to be penalized—for example, to incur a 15-yard penalty for defensive pass interference—than to give up a passing touchdown when the open receiver had gotten past him.

Josh Stark had an uncanny sense of how long he could take to hit a defenseless receiver or runner that his teammates had tackled moments earlier, without being called for piling on. That infraction happened on almost every tackle that was made anywhere near Josh, but was never called for whatever reason.

At the half, the score was knotted at zero. In the press box, Bennie Pressler didn't need to check Leah Russo's statistics to declare over the PA that the contest was a defensive struggle. He and any fan who had sat through the first two quarters sensed that this grudge match might come down not to a great offensive play, but to maybe a single offensive miscue. The winner could be decided by a fumble, an interception or a blocked kick at any point in the second half, maybe on the last play of the game or in overtime.

What Bennie announced to the crowd when the halftime horn sounded was appropriate, if not downright prophetic: *"So that's the end of the first half, folks, and, boy oh boy, do we have a real barn burner on our hands tonight—no pun intended. Enjoy the halftime show, Bruins fans, but get your popcorn and get back to your seats before the second half starts. I have a feeling that our boys in green and gold are gonna come out of this defensive struggle on top—without piling on, of course. And while you're up, don't forget to buy a 50-50 ticket. Winner of the drawing will be announced at the quarter break. Every ticket's a winner, whether you win the pot or not, 'cause it goes to a good cause. So don't be a greedy loser. Buy a ticket—or you'll go stark-raving mad."*

Leah punched Bennie in the side for that last remark, but he had already shut off the mic. Only a few fans on either side of the stadium caught Bennie's jokes. But on the visiting sideline, Joel and Josh Stark both heard and understood the punning references to a "barn burner" and to someone going "stark-raving mad," whether Bennie's banter alluded to Josh's drunken outburst at the homecoming dance or to Joel's arrogant rant outside the haunted house. But what Bennie Pressler couldn't have known was exactly how on the nose his comments would prove to be later that night.

CHAPTER 30 – We Are Winners

WITH THE GAME'S FINAL MINUTE ticking off the clock, QB Ty Green moved back into the shotgun and surveyed the defensive secondary. It was fourth down. The Bruins had this one play to keep their hopes alive. But ten yards wasn't enough. They needed at least fifteen yards to put the ball inside bruised place-kicker Ricky Duran's field-goal range.

If the Reuben worked this time, if Arbor's trick play surprised the Harvesters defense for a big-enough gain, the Bruins could stop the clock with maybe a second left and send Ricky onto the field for the most important kick of his young career.

But just going into the shotgun formation had told Solid Rock safety Josh Stark what play was coming, because Josh had run the Reuben himself as Bruins quarterback earlier in the season. Also, linebacker Jimmy Gore started shouting instructions to reposition the other linebackers and defensive secondary when he saw Ty backpedal two steps during the snap count.

Seeing the defense adjust, Ty shook his head and called his team's last time-out. The score was still 0-0. The ball sat on the Solid Rock 35, with :31 on the fourth-quarter clock.

* * *

Each team had managed a sustained drive in the third quarter, but had failed to put points on the scoreboard. Solid Rock had returned the second-half kickoff into

Bruins territory, then had moved the ball to the Arbor 13-yard line before being stymied. There, Josh Stark had attempted his shortest field goal of the night and had shanked it off the right-side goalpost.

On the Harvesters sideline, father Joel Stark had screamed in anger at his son's miss, what turned out to be Solid Rock's best chance to score all game. Joel Stark's expletive-laced tirade was so hateful and loud that even some Arbor fans felt sorry for the boy. Solid Rock would have had the lead on its final defensive stand if Josh had nailed that field goal attempt.

Until the last series of the game, the Bruins' only scoring opportunity of the second half had come right before the quarter break. Coach Jug Johnson had called for a quick pass to Josh Stark's side of the field, along the sideline where the Harvesters bench players, coaches and still-steaming Joel Stark stood. The Bruins receiver had run a stop-and-go route right in front of Mr. Stark, who hadn't quit fussing at his son about the missed field goal.

The man also hadn't lost sight of the game's importance to Solid Rock's play-off hopes and had spent most of the third quarter with his cell phone pressed to his ear. He had checked every couple of minutes on the Iron Harbor-Mimosa Beach score, to make sure that Mimosa Beach didn't get an upset win and put even more pressure on Solid Rock to do likewise.

Realizing that he'd been beaten on the pass play, Josh had shoved the Arbor receiver after the ball had left Ty Green's hand. A yellow flag for interference had been thrown, but the action hadn't ended there.

Distracted by news he'd just gotten on his cell phone, Joel Stark had looked up just as the ball had caromed off the receiver's fingertips and smacked Stark squarely in the face. In seconds, blood had started gushing from his nose and all over the front of his athletic jacket. EMTs from the ambulance near the stadium entrance had rushed to him; however, Stark had refused their aid, choosing instead to keep yelling at his son through a white towel that the Solid Rock trainer had given him to stem the blood flow.

The elder Stark had continued to berate his boy at the quarter break, even though the Bruins had squandered the 15-yard penalty that Josh had handed them.

Arbor had been forced to punt on a three-and-out after the interference call that had put them in Solid Rock territory. But Joel Stark had turned his fury away from Josh and toward the game officials, who had made the mistake of gathering on the same side of the field as the Harvesters bench.

Stark had shaken his head—bloody towel and all—and had screamed at the whole crew that they hadn't been calling the game fairly, that they had called more penalties on Solid Rock than on Arbor, and that Josh, at quarterback, had not received the same protection from the officials that Ty Green had been afforded throughout the game. When the referee—the man in the white cap—had shaken his head *no* to disagree, Stark had stomped his foot and shaken his fist at him.

It was then that Bennie Pressler, watching the spectacle from the press box, had cued up and played the first of two audio clips that he had copied from the videotape of Joel Stark's rant at the Halloween festival. Pressing *PLAY*, Bennie had made Stark's voice echo throughout the stadium: "*Joel Stark doesn't take* no *for an answer.*" The home crowd had taken the cue and started to jeer at Stark in unison, "No! No! No! No!"

Hearing his name and recognizing his own voice, Joel Stark had first looked up at the nearest loudspeaker, then had whirled around to stare across the field into the press box. Not understanding the context of the sound clip or the crowd's chant, the officials had begun to question Stark, as if he might have somehow been responsible for the taunts they were hearing from the stands. That had enraged him even further, and he had launched into another tirade.

"*You're all a bunch of hayseeds who don't have the sense that God gave a mule,*" Stark's metallic voice had boomed over the PA, sending the flesh-and-blood man into another fit of fury. The whole crowd had laughed, but their mirth had turned to disbelief upon Bennie's next announcement during the quarter break.

"*Here's a shocker from Mimosa Beach Athletic Park,*" Bennie said. "*The top-ranked Iron Harbor Gray Dukes now trail the Mimosa Beach Waverunners by seven points, going into the fourth quarter of play. C'mon, let's hear it for the underdogs from Mimosa Beach, the team we beat two weeks ago on the road. This must be the night for upsets in Oleander County!"*

At the end of the quarter break, Bennie's announcement of the winning number in the 50-50 drawing hadn't caused much of a stir. No one had jumped to their feet to celebrate winning the jackpot and no one had come to the press box to claim it, and so Principal Jerry Church had decided to let the pot roll over until basketball season if no one stepped forward by game's end. He hadn't wanted any more problems with disgruntled fans than he already had with Joel Stark, who had caused more trouble that fall than any principal needed to deal with for a lifetime.

As incriminating as the sound clips that Bennie had played were for Joel Stark, the real estate developer could do little or nothing to retaliate against the Presslers without making *all* of his Halloween festival comments even more public than they were when he made them. He knew that the videotapes showing Josh and his gang of greasers shooting fireworks, setting blazes and committing mayhem would be used in court soon enough, and he silently confessed there on the Solid Rock sideline that continuing to show his own true self to a stadium full of people was bad for Stark Realty, as simple as that.

That was his new Stark reality. Joel decided to back off for the moment and pretend to be the supportive father who lets his son live with his own choice to win or lose, between the thrill of victory and the agony of defeat. He would be Daedalus to his son's Icarus. This fourth quarter under the lights of Reuben Russo Memorial Stadium would tell the tale.

* * *

During the timeout near the end of the game, Bennie Pressler's voice again came over the loudspeakers: *"Here's the final score from Mimosa Beach, folks, the one you've been waiting for. It's in the books—Iron Harbor 28, Mimosa Beach ..."* He stopped and took another look at the paper he'd been handed. *"Hold on, folks,"* he said. *"That's Mimosa Beach 31, Iron Harbor 28. Mimosa Beach defeats once undefeated Iron Harbor 31-to-28! Now, let's go, Bruins!"*

The home crowd cheered. Fans in the visiting stands were strangely silent. What Mimosa Beach's unlikely win meant for Solid Rock was that the best they could hope for now was a win over Arbor and a tie for second place in the conference with Mimosa Beach. A loss to the Bruins would knock Solid Rock out of contention for post-season play and for all bragging rights as the Suncoast Conference runner-up. With a loss, the Harvesters and their rookie coach would reap a third-place tie with Arbor High in the final conference standings.

When Ty Green called that final timeout at :31, Coach Jug Johnson looked up at his other co-captain, Artie Bauer, standing next to him on the home sideline. "What d'ya say, Yogi?" said Jug. "Do we still run it? The Reuben? I just don't know. They saw us set it up, and they're ready for it now."

Artie looked down at the old coach and smiled. "That was the *old* Reuben," Artie said, "the one that Josh learned when he was with us. You know, we could spice up that old play a little bit and give them a surprise."

Jug cocked his head to one side in thought, just as Ty Green arrived on the sideline. "You mean, put a little mustard on that old play?" Jug asked, with a grin.

"More like salsa," Artie replied, then addressed Ty, too. "How about if we go ahead and put little Ricky into the game, and then, Ty, you drop the ball backwards to *him*. That gives us an extra option. Ricky could try a long dropkick if he can't lateral the ball back to you in time to hit Brett downfield—or Ricky could run the ball himself."

Both Ty Green and Coach Johnson winced at the thought of little Ricky Duran getting hit by Jimmy Gore. But Ty nodded. "That'll work," he said. "It has to. I'll tell Ricky and Brett when we get back in the huddle." He waited for a second, as Jug subbed Ricky into the game for one of the slot receivers. The two teammates jogged back onto the playing field together.

After the Bruins broke their huddle, the two teams lined up for the game's deciding play. "Green 34," shouted Ty from the shotgun. "Green 34 ... hut ... hut ... hut."

Tommy White, who had played most of the game at center for Artie, snapped the ball to Ty Green and rose to help block one of the three down linemen who tried to penetrate the Bruins offensive line. Jimmy Gore, the other Harvesters linebackers and the secondary stayed back in zone protection to allow a short pass that might gain a few yards, but to defend against a longer throw close to the goal line.

Jimmy had seen Ricky go into motion from his slotback position and had shadowed and followed him back across the field upon the ball's snap to Ty. Crossing behind the tall quarterback, little Ricky snatched the dropped ball from Ty and took off like a shot, as if he had no intention of tossing the ball back.

On the other side of the field, Brett Woods flew down the sideline and ran a post route through the defensive secondary. At safety, Josh Stark stayed behind his former friend but within an arm's reach, ready to break up a pass or be called for interference, if necessary. A penalty could give Arbor an automatic first down and another chance to score, even if no time were left on the clock. Everyone knew that the game could not end on a defensive penalty.

But it didn't come to that. When Jimmy Gore saw Ricky Duran take off with the ball, the big linebacker closed in fast, in an attempt to stop the little runner near the line of scrimmage. If Ricky had been tackled, Arbor would have turned the ball over on downs, and Solid Rock would have had a play or two of their own to score. Stranger things had happened on last plays—desperation "Hail Mary" passes or hook-and-ladder runs for touchdowns.

If the Harvesters could get the ball back, the worst they would probably do was run out the clock and send the game into overtime. But that didn't happen, either.

Seeing Jimmy Gore closing in on him, the little placekicker stopped dead in his tracks, glanced back at Ty and saw him being blocked, then looked downfield and flung a perfect spiral pass toward the goalposts an instant before the linebacker hit him. It wasn't roughing the passer, but that didn't matter.

Without breaking stride, Brett Woods caught the pass head-high, tucked the ball under both arms, and took the blows that Josh delivered—the first one meant to punch out the ball; the second one, a forearm aimed at the Bruins receiver's helmet. Brett wheeled away from Josh and stumbled toward the goal line, dragging the safety the last five yards before falling into the end zone for the winning touchdown.

The two officials on the goal line extended their arms straight up to signal the score, and stopped the clock with :01 remaining. That meant Solid Rock had a fleeting chance—on the kickoff or maybe on one last play from scrimmage—to tie the score. The outcome hinged on whether Arbor added an extra-point kick or a two-point conversion. The clock would not run on PAT plays. It would start on the ensuing kickoff as soon as the ball was touched by a member of the return team.

With a helping hand from Ty Green and a pat on the back from Jimmy Gore, little Ricky Duran picked himself up from the big hit that the star linebacker had delivered and trotted down the field with Ty for the point-after attempt.

"We didn't know you could throw the ball like that," said Ty. "We thought all you soccer guys used your feet to do everything."

Ricky grinned. "You did not ask me if I could throw," he said. "I can do many things, and do you know why?"

"Yeah, I do," said Ty. "It's because you're a winner. Now let's go kick the extra point and get this game over with, once and for all."

On the sideline, Coach Johnson checked with Artie to see if he wanted to end his high school career on the field instead of there on the sideline. "It don't matter if we get this point-after or not, Yogi," said Jug. "We're gonna win. I know it, you know it, and they do, too. Just look over there at ol' Stark screaming his head off."

Jug was referring to Joel Stark, not to sullen Josh, who stood waiting at the goal line for the teams to line up for the point-after kick. The father had tossed aside his bloody towel and had forgotten his earlier resolution not to rage at his boy. What he yelled was embarrassing, not just for Josh, but for every Harvester on the field. He called them all losers.

Finally, the officials approached the young Solid Rock coach and said that if he didn't do something about Stark's verbal abuse, they certainly would. The coach went to Stark and pushed him toward the bench. Two big assistant coaches stepped in to help restrain the irate man during the extra point.

"Yes! Yes! Yes! Yes!" the home crowd chanted as they watched Joel Stark being put in his place for a change.

"No," Artie told Jug about entering the game for the PAT. "Tommy has played a heckuva game tonight. He needs to be in there, not me."

Like a dance routine, Tommy White snapped the ball, Ty Green placed it on the turf, and Ricky Duran kicked it through the uprights, putting the Bruins ahead 7-0 with one tick left on the game clock.

In the press box, Bennie Pressler and Leah Russo gave each other high fives. In the home stands, Nicie Evans, as well as the Greens, Presslers, Woodses, Durans, and, of course, Pearl and Harry Bauer—the entire farm family—all cheered as if the Arbor High Bruins had won the state championship.

Joel Stark continued to rage on the Harvesters bench. He broke away from the assistant coaches and charged onto the field to confront young Josh, whose back was turned as he moved toward his position to receive the ensuing kickoff. It looked like the father wasn't going to stop—that he would hit his own son there in the open field.

But as Joel Stark crossed the 10-yard line, Jimmy Gore blindsided the man with a bone-jarring tackle that drove him into the turf. Not knowing what exactly had happened, Josh turned, saw his father on the ground, and went for Jimmy. Josh removed his own helmet and swung it at his teammate. The all-star linebacker fended off Josh's attack, slammed the boy to the ground and held him down until the men in striped shirts arrived.

Both Joel and Josh Stark were removed from the stadium, taken into custody by the young sheriff's deputy who had worked the homecoming dance and handled the Halloween festival arrests.

"Bye! Bye! Bye! Bye!" chanted the crowd, as the Starks were escorted down the hill toward the parking lot and the awaiting sheriff's department cruiser.

On the home sideline, Coach Jug Johnson put one big arm on the shoulder of the young athlete he had come to respect and trust more than any other in his long coaching tenure. Jug loved Artie as if the big farm boy were a member of his own family, one of his own sons. Their eyes met for an instant, before Artie turned his head and looked up into the stands behind them.

"Don't worry about them college coaches sitting up there," Jug told Artie.

"There's more important things than just playing football, and you, young man, are gonna do a lot more in your life than this."

Artie smiled as he watched Ricky's line-drive kickoff skid past the front line of the Solid Rock return team, hit a Harvesters player squarely in the chest, and spin to a stop on the 30-yard line, where the horn sounded and a Bruins player touched the ball to down it.

The game was over. Arbor High had beaten Solid Rock Academy. For both teams, football season had come to a definite end.

"You're right, Coach," said Artie, about his future. "There's wrestling this winter—starts in about a week, right?—and baseball next spring. I'll be awful busy on the farm, but with a little help from you and my friends, I can do it all."

Jug laughed. "From your lips to God's ears, Yogi," the old coach said. He patted Artie on the back again and headed onto the field with him to celebrate, because that night the Barf Table gang and their family were anything but losers. They were the finest kind of winners.

THE END

About the Authors

RAHN ADAMS and TIMBERLEY GILLIAM ADAMS are retired school teachers and former award-winning journalists who have spent their careers living and working from the mountains to the coast of their native North Carolina. They are co-authors of another young adult novel, *Night Lights; or, Golf, the Blues and the Brown Mountain Light* (2004). Timberley is author and illustrator of a children's picture book, *Turtle Beach* (2019), and a young reader's chapter book, *Henry Heron Finds His Home* (2021). The couple are publishers of their own imprint, Gaillardia Press, and proprietors of Little House on the Hill, their studio and private art gallery in the North Carolina foothills.

Also by Rahn & Timberley Adams

Night Lights; or, Golf, the Blues, and the Brown Mountain Light

Also by Timberley Gilliam Adams

Turtle Beach

Henry Heron Finds His Home